Ride Away

This Large Print Book carries the
Seal of Approval of N.A.V.H.

A CORRIGAN BROTHERS WESTERN

RIDE AWAY

COTTON SMITH

THORNDIKE PRESS
A part of Gale, Cengage Learning

GALE
CENGAGE Learning·

Farmington Hills, Mich • San Francisco • New York • Waterville, Maine
Meriden, Conn • Mason, Ohio • Chicago

GALE
CENGAGE Learning®

LIBRARY OF CONGRESS CATALOGING-IN-PUBLICATION DATA

Names: Smith, Cotton, author.
Title: Ride away : a Corrigan brothers western / Cotton Smith.
Description: Waterville, Maine : Thorndike Press, 2016. | © 2016 | Series: A
  Corrigan brothers western | Series: Thorndike Press large print western
Identifiers: LCCN 2015046970| ISBN 9781410487292 (hardback) | ISBN 1410487296
  (hardcover)
Subjects: LCSH: Large type books. | BISAC: FICTION / Westerns. | GSAFD: Western
  stories.
Classification: LCC PS3569.M5167 R53 2016 | DDC 813/.54—dc23
LC record available at http://lccn.loc.gov/2015046970

Published in 2016 by arrangement with Pinnacle Books, an imprint of
Kensington Publishing Corp.

C084 2670
4/16

Printed in Mexico
1 2 3 4 5 6 7 20 19 18 17 16

To Katie, Bobby, Gus, Maggie, and Jesse

CHAPTER ONE

The Texas midmorning sky looked like God hadn't decided what to make of the day as Tade Balkins drove the stagecoach toward the Wilkon relay station. No driver got more out of his horses, taking great pride in always being on time. He was well respected on the Southern Overland Mail line that ran from Hays City to El Paso, then on to Santa Fe, Tucson, San Diego, and finally Los Angeles. Even with railroad construction heating up again after the war, it was still an important route.

As far as the eye could see was empty desert plain, marked with rock, catclaw, dry brush, mesquite, and a creek bed with only the memory of water. To the north were dark crests promising better land and water. Tade was holding the six-horse team to a steady trot, talking to them as usual. He would bring them into a controlled run when the stage got closer to the station. A full gallop was really for appearance. It looked impressive to pull the charging horses to a hard stop in front of a destination. Sitting beside him, Hank Johnson rode shotgun and was having difficulty staying awake. Last night had been a drunken one.

"Doin' good, boys. Doin' good. Ah, that's just a tumbleweed. Nothin' to worry about," Tade assured the horses, then glanced over at the dozing guard and nudged him awake. "Better stay alert, Hank. Bad country along here."

"Yeah, I know. Jes' got a nasty headache."

"Atlee Forsyth, she'll have some good hot coffee. That'll help."

"Wish she had some whiskey."

Tade frowned and returned to talking to his horses.

Inside the coach, seven passengers were dulled by the never-ending bouncing and the ever-swirling dust.

"Is your ranch near here, Mr. Corrigan?"

The question to Deed Corrigan came from Rebecca Tuttle, the younger of the two women sitting across from him. Clearly she wanted to talk and had been doing so almost nonstop since the stage rolled out in the morning.

Dressed like a woman ready to stroll down the main street of El Paso, her green dress shimmered with its overskirts caught up and accented with black ribbons. Her flat-crowned straw hat held one large bow in the center of her forehead, matching the smaller ones on her dress. A jacket bodice, with a neckline close to her neck and black cuffs, completed the outfit. Brown ringlets framed her round face; light rouge highlighted her ample cheeks. To those in the coach, she looked like a woman of high social standing. Nothing could have been further from the truth. Her last cent had been spent on this stagecoach ticket.

Without waiting for Deed to answer, Rebecca explained that she was on the way to El Paso to meet her intended, a farmer she had met two years before in Ohio. Indeed, it was her only hope. That wasn't expressed — just a sweet smile when she stated her intention.

Politely, Deed Corrigan touched the brim of his ill-shaped hat and explained that his ranch was about three hours' ride from the station and he was returning home from a cattle drive to Kansas. It was more than he had said on the trip so far. His face, accented by a thick mustache, was deeply tanned from countless days on horseback. Long brown hair brushed against his shoulders. The bullet belt around Deed's waist held a heavy Remington .44 revolver with its long barrel extending past the holster's open end. Tan leather cuffs covered the frayed ends of his faded red shirt. A once-blue neckerchief hung loosely around his neck. Spurs were Mexican in styling and his worn Levi's were shoved into knee-high boots.

Around Deed's neck hung a small, Oriental-looking brass circle on a rawhide thong. Engraved on the circle was the Japanese word, *Bushido.* No one asked what it meant. Hanging unseen down the back of his shirt was a sheathed throwing knife, attached to the thong.

Next to him sat a fat drummer, Persam Torce, representing several companies making fine linens and other cloth goods. He had declared often of their quality, whether anyone asked or not. Stuffed into a store-bought suit that didn't fit, he said he, too, was headed to El Paso and wondered if it was much farther, or if a railroad went there.

"It's a ways, mister. No railroad yet either," Deed said, grinning. "Better get used to this."

Frowning, Persam Torce looked at Deed. "Is it really necessary to be armed as you are, sir?"

"Only if you want to stay alive . . . *sir.*"

10

Deed's answer carried an edge.

Torce pulled on his collar. "Surely, there are law officers with the responsibility to protect us."

On the far side of the same bench, sitting next to the drummer, a well-dressed passenger with long sideburns, thick spectacles, and black bowler leaned forward, laughed, and said, "Tell that to the next bunch of highwaymen, or war party, we see."

Returning to his reading, the gentleman's Victorian black suitcoat flared open to reveal the butt of a silver-plated revolver in a shoulder holster. He also carried a sleeve gun, probably a derringer, Deed figured by the way he favored his right wrist. On the man's lap was an opened book of Tennyson he had been enjoying since the coach left Hays. This was the first time he had said anything to anyone, except to introduce himself earlier to Deed as James Hannah. A name known to many in the region; the name of a man of the gun — a gun for hire. The singular introduction was an indication Hannah was aware of Deed Corrigan's reputation as a fighting man as well.

In the middle bench sat another drummer who sold Swedish furniture and held tightly to one of the straps hanging from the coach roof for use by middle-bench passengers to balance themselves. Wearing a dust-covered top hat, he acted as if he hadn't heard the conversation or cared about it. He hadn't said where he was headed.

The far bench seat held Rebecca Tuttle and a German couple. Neither Hermann Beinrigt, a skinny farmer in worn overalls, nor his wife, Olivia, had talked to anyone so far, only whispered to each other in German. Tade Balkins told Deed earlier the couple hoped to lease land for farming near El Paso, where relatives lived. Their farm in Kansas had been lost to drought and grasshoppers.

As the coach rattled and banged across the uneven prairie, Rebecca glanced at James Hannah, eager for a new target for her thoughts, and asked, "Are you going on to El Paso?" Her smile was warm, very warm.

Hannah looked up from his book.

But the question went unanswered as Torce glanced out the window and yelled, "Oh my God, it's Indians!"

Rebecca turned to the window and screamed.

Eighteen painted Comanches on horseback had appeared over a shallow ridge and were swarming toward the coach, like bees near a disturbed nest. All carried painted war shields. Half were waving rifles or revolvers and the rest, bows and arrows or short lances. Without a word, Deed and Hannah yanked free their revolvers and turned to their respective windows.

"Giddyap, boys! Earn your pay. Come on!" Tade yelled and snapped his nine-foot bullwhip over the horses' heads to get their full attention. They were running full out in five strides and surprised the war party with their sudden swiftness.

CHAPTER TWO

Quickly, the menacing war party reacted to the now-racing coach. Riding as if they were part of their horses, the warriors had long black hair decorated with feathers, glass beads, silver conchos, and pieces of fur. A streak of color lined the central part of each warrior's head, from forehead back along the crown. Eagle feathers were attached to their side locks. A beaver-fur-wrapped braid on each side of their heads was highlighted with bright cloth, and a special braided scalp lock, accented with a smaller feather, bounced on top of their heads.

Several wore antelope skins as breech clouts or war shirts, a sign they were of the Antelope band, the fiercest of Comanches and the terror of the entire region. Deed, Hannah, and the stagecoach guard began firing at them, but without success. The bouncing of the heavy vehicle made accuracy nearly impossible.

Hurdling across the land, the stage slammed across a shallow creek that fed into the bigger stream near the station, spraying water and launching its passengers against each other, then cut through a crusted band of dried alkali, sending up a snow of white powder.

Four warriors outraced the rest of the war party and closed in on the hard-running stage. Two went on one side of the coach; two, on the other. The guard fired at the closest warrior and managed to kill his horse, sending its rider stumbling onto the prairie. Hank Johnson scrambled to find the sack of shotgun slugs at his feet. Hannah leveled his Smith & Wesson .44 Russian revolver, holding it with both hands, and fired at the second warrior, whose face, chest, and leggings were striped in black. Hannah's bullets cut across the Comanche's stomach and slammed into his right arm. Yelping in pain, the Indian swung away from the coach.

On the left side of the coach, the other two warriors were spread out; one was nearing the hard-running team and the other, just out of Deed's line of sight, was near the back of the coach. The front warrior, with his lower face painted red, drew an arrow from the handful he held next to his bow.

15

Stretching out behind Tade Balkins to shoot, the guard fired too quickly and missed, barely catching the Comanche with a few stray buckshot. Deed leaned out of the coach window and fired, missing twice. His third and fourth shots slammed into the warrior's back just as he unleashed an arrow. The shaft struck the front edge of the driver's box. Deed emptied his Remington into the Indian's flailing body. Tade yelled his thanks as Deed ducked back inside.

The fourth warrior swooped near the same window. He swung low on his pony to thrust his lance inside, but Deed saw him coming. As the Comanche shoved it through the opened coach window, Deed Corrigan dropped his empty gun, grabbed and yanked hard on the spear. He pulled the surprised warrior, still holding the lance, from his horse and slammed him against the coach. For an instant, the warrior's face was pinned against the coach window. Deed's open left hand drove into the Comanche's exposed Adam's apple as if his hand were an axe.

The blow was so swift and fierce that only James Hannah and the farming couple realized what had happened.

A soft gurgle followed the Indian as his limp body slid down the outside of the coach. Deed Corrigan let go of the lance and retrieved his Remington revolver, pushed his hat brim against its crown, and began reloading. The lance bounced off the top-hatted drummer's knees and fell harmlessly on the coach floor.

"Will they go away now?" Rebecca blurted.

Deed finished reloading and looked up. "Doubt it."

The coach banged over a small ridge and slammed through a cluster of stunted cedar trees. Their stout branches scraped along the coach and forced Deed to duck back inside, but the trees gave the stagecoach a moment of reprieve from the war party as they were forced to ride around the trees or slow down to ride through them.

Leaning out the window, Deed yelled at the driver to hand down a rifle, then fired his revolver twice at the rest of the Indians racing to catch them and missed both times.

"Ain't got one, mister," Tade Balkins yelled back. "Unless you can get yurn in your gear. In the back boot." He licked his lips and added, "Pull down them leather curtains. It'll keep some of them arrows out." He cracked his whip again and yelled at the horses. "Won't do much about them bullets though."

Hannah looked over at Deed and said, "Don't even think about going up there to get your rifle, Corrigan. You'd be a pincushion in seconds."

"If I could get to my Spencer, it'd make them think twice."

"Yeah, well, the only word that counts there is *if,*" Hannah growled and fired again. "We're doing all right. Could use another shooter though."

"I've got to go now. Once they get around the coach, we won't be able to handle them." Deed said, "An old Japanese warrior friend says to always find a way to attack."

"Wonder if he ever fought red devils like these?"

"Count on it."

Both men pulled down the leather curtains at the same time. Quickly, Deed replaced the two spent cartridges in his handgun and unbuckled his heavy gunbelt. Beside him, Persam Torce was whimpering and praying loudly.

In the middle bench, the top-hatted drummer looked like he couldn't believe what was happening as he heard the war party's yells become louder again. He held a handkerchief close to his mouth to avoid any unexpected vomiting. His eyes went from Deed Corrigan to James Hannah to the

18

lance at his feet.

Rebecca Tuttle sobbed and slid to the floor, as if it would keep her safe. She held her hands over her head and squeezed her eyes shut. An arrow burst through the closed curtains and slammed into where she had been. She glanced at it and shrieked.

"God could use a little help here, partner. Can you shoot?" Deed said to the praying Persam Torce, holding out his holstered revolver and gunbelt. "N-No, sir. I am a m-man of G-God."

"You can pray *and* shoot, you know. Lots of folks do. My big brother does. Real good at it, too."

For a moment, Deed considered giving his gun to Torce anyway, but decided against it. He swung back to the coach window, aimed at an Indian's exposed leg over the back of his running horse, fired and missed. The coach itself flew in the air, then banged back to the ground, jarring everyone inside. The drummer on the middle bench grunted and grabbed his chest. A crimson circle appeared on his boiled shirt. He looked down and collapsed in front of the praying Persam Torce.

"Get down there and see if you can help him. Stop the bleeding. Do something. Anything," Deed said and returned to the coach window, touching the brass circle at his neck and mumbling some ritual-sounding phrase to himself.

The stage station was in sight, barely, but the young rancher didn't expect much help there. It was a relay station, not a fort. He must go now, before the entire war party encircled the coach. He must. He jammed a new cartridge into the Remington and was ready to go.

James Hannah looked at the terrified Torce and growled, "At least you can pray for him, dumb ass." He pushed aside the leather curtain and fired at a warrior galloping past, barely visible by swinging to the outside of his horse.

Persam Torce's hands trembled as he fumbled for a handkerchief.

"*Guten tag, Herr Corrigan.* If *du* vould, *Ich* vould . . . borrow *der* gun," the thin-faced German farmer said. "I vould . . . do *der* covering *für du.*"

Deed stared at him, nodded, and handed over the gun and gunbelt.

"This has a hair trigger. Better point it out the window before you cock. There's six beans in the wheel. Uh, six bullets. Usually I leave the chamber under the hammer empty. Not now though."

Taking the handgun as if it were hot, the

farmer pushed aside the curtain, pointed the weapon out the coach window, aimed, and fired. Missing.

"*Ja.* God bless *du, Herr Corrigan,*" the farmer's wife, Olivia Beinrigt, whispered.

Opening the door, he swung out on it. The hinges creaked with his weight. He shoved his boot into the window where he had been shooting and tried to balance himself as the coach rocked and bounced. A misstep here would be fatal. A blue-faced warrior swung his lathered horse closer to the coach. As the warrior shrieked his war cry and swung his tomahawk, Deed let go of the coach rail with his right hand and grabbed the warrior's forearm as it came at him. His powerful move stopped the downward motion, but the Comanche grinned at him and reached for the knife carried at his waist.

Deed thought about gambling and letting go of the Indian's forearm and reaching for his own knife. The chances of doing that and staying on the coach weren't likely. As he shifted his boots, he heard the German farmer fire three times and the warrior groaned and fell away.

"Thanks, you saved my bacon," Deed yelled and released the limp Indian's arm.

"*Ja. Bitte sehr.*"

Guessing that meant "you're welcome,"

Deed Corrigan pushed the body away and clambered onto the coach roof. Scurrying across the roof to the back boot, he found his gear and yanked free the Spencer carbine and a box with reloading tubes. Each tube held seven cartridges for quick reloading. The 52-caliber breechloader held one bullet in the chamber and seven in the magazine. After loading the big gun, he yanked two suitcases free of the boot and arranged them on either side of him. The thick luggage would provide some protection from bullets and arrows. Stretching out, he balanced the carbine against the railing, cocked and aimed the big gun. Bullets sang past his head and an arrow thudded into the coach roof inches from his thigh.

One warrior with his mouth painted with a yellow handprint got close enough to the coach to grab the canvas covering the back boot. A shot from Deed drove the warrior from his horse, but his grip tore open the canvas. Three suitcases and a mailbag flew into the air and banged on the ground. Three warriors jumped from their horses and ripped open the luggage and waved colorful pieces of clothing as each treasure was uncovered. A thick-waisted Comanche, with his face and body painted half white and half blue, yanked a tweed suitcoat over his breastplate and painted arms; another tried putting on a dress; a hand mirror became a prized find for the third. Their stay was short as Deed's Spencer tore into the warrior staring at himself in the mirror. He staggered and fell. The other two quickly returned to their mounts, wearing their new garments.

Steadily, the war party gained on the weary coach horses. The coach banged along the well-defined road with Comanches on both sides, but wary due to the shooting of Hannah, Beinrigt, Johnson, and especially Deed. In the driver's box, the shotgun guard straightened and tumbled over the driver's box with two arrows protruding from his throat and chest. Tade Balkins tried to grab the dead guard's shotgun, but couldn't reach it as the weapon fell against the corner of the driver's box. He returned his attention to the horses, snapping his nine-foot-long whip over the lathered horses and urging them on as they bounded closer to the line of cottonwoods that edged the open yard of the relay station.

The fat Persam Torce sat cross-legged on the coach floor, praying beside the dead man in the top hat. He looked at the others as if this couldn't be happening and began to laugh weirdly and then to sob. Olivia Beinrigt patted the hysterical Rebecca's shoulder and told her it would all soon pass.

Deed's accuracy took down a warrior in a white-woman's dress. James Hannah yelled that he was hit and dropped his fancy gun. It thudded on the coach floor. Rebecca Tuttle wailed hysterically. The German woman told her to be quiet. The stagecoach thumped over some rocks and everyone was jolted again; Deed thought he was going to be thrown and grabbed the railing.

"I'm all right. I'm all right. It just burned my damn elbow," Hannah said gruffly and picked up the weapon and straightened his eyeglasses. His right coat sleeve showed a trace of blood, but he continued to focus on the war party outside.

"Sehr gut," Olivia Beinrigt said, watching her husband carefully aim and fire. From his silence, she assumed he hadn't hit a Comanche. She hid her concern from the distraught younger woman; expressing her fear would do nothing. Above, she heard the loud roar of Deed Corrigan's Spencer and said a silent prayer for his safety. Her husband looked down at the gun to reload it and an arrow slammed through his shoulder with the bloody point extruding from his back. Hermann Beinrigt looked at his

wife and collapsed. The gun thudded onto the coach floor. His wife sobbed, bit her lip, then leaned forward to stroke her wounded husband's pale face.

CHAPTER THREE

Unaware of the incoming stage's peril, Wilkon Station Manager Caleb Forsyth led a fresh team of horses out of the corral in preparation for the expected coach to the relay post. Morning sounds were strangely missing and he thought it was too quiet, but shoved the concern out of his mind. Not even the leaves of the cottonwoods, guarding the northwest edge of the stage station area, were fluttering.

A lone dirt devil spun its way across the open ground and disappeared over the hill as if hurrying to the nearby town of Wilkon. The well pump groaned about the day and the two lead horses were nervous, their ears on full alert. Off to the side of the yard was the separate adobe home where his family lived and a small cooling house for meat, milk, and butter. A barn, corral, blacksmith shed, the relay station building itself, and its accompanying outhouses, were the only other structures.

The coach wasn't in sight, but would be soon; Tade Balkins was never late.

"Easy, boys. It's all just fine an' dandy. Tade'll treat you right," he said and patted the closest bay's neck.

As always, Caleb's twelve-year-old son, Benjamin, was at his father's side. He was a good helper with a knack for handling horses. The boy patted the nose of the other lead horse and called him by a name no one else used. Beside the boy was a black-and-white dog named Cooper. The happy animal was rarely away from Benjamin and today was no exception.

Behind them, the one-eyed Mexican, Billy Lee Montez, was closing the corral gate next to the weathered barn with one hand and swatting at a horsefly who wanted to make his acquaintance with his other. He had been with the Forsyths since they took over the station two years ago. Billy Lee was good with horses and a better-than-average blacksmith. The Forsyths had developed the swing relay station into one of the best-run operations on the route, a station with a reputation for excellent food, fast service, and cleanliness. All of those attributes were due to Caleb's wife, Atlee.

All three heard the gunfire before the

coach was in sight. It was Billy Lee who first realized what the sounds meant.

"Oh Lord me God! It ees Comanche!" the Mexican yelled.

"Go to the station, Benjamin! Stay there. Take Cooper with you," Caleb commanded, pushing his son toward the main building where his wife was preparing a meal for the passengers. The frightened boy hesitated, then ran to the building with Cooper at his heels.

His face taut with the knowledge of what was coming, Caleb turned the team toward the corral. "Billy Lee, let's get these horses back in the corral."

"*Sí. Pronto.*" The Mexican had already reopened the gate "Gonna get *mi* shotgun. It is in de barn," he yelled over his shoulder.

Caleb Forsyth hurried the anxious horses into the corral and closed the gate. He stepped away, saw his son and dog disappear into the relay station, and returned his focus to the as yet empty horizon. Turning, he ran to the house and grabbed the offered Henry from his son, ignored his wife's plea to come inside, knelt on the planked porch, and waited. It was his duty to protect the stage.

Without further discussion, Atlee Forsyth grabbed the seven-shot Spencer carbine from the rack of rifles on the wall and went to a gun port in the wall. A heavy weapon, she had mastered its kick. Frowning, Benjamin aimed a Burnside carbine from another gun port. His father had taught him how to shoot with the weapon. The rack still held an English Whitworth musket, another Burnside carbine, and a double-barreled shotgun. Several pistols lay at the base of the rack.

A few minutes later, the coach roared into view with warriors snapping at it like mad dogs. Inside the coach, only Hannah was shooting now. Deed's firing had kept them farther away than they wanted. From a safe distance, the war leader studied Deed Corrigan. To quit now would mean his disgrace; no warrior would follow him again into battle. Across the leader's shoulders was draped an antelope skin decorated with silver conchos and bits of colored cloth. In the leader's scalp lock was a black feather with a red circle near the top.

His striking appearance was reinforced by the glistening sorrel horse he rode, painted for war and wearing feathers streaming in the powerful mount's mane and tail. Seeing Deed reload, he commanded two warriors to kill the lead coach horses. He raised his shield to the sky, then leaned over and touched the ground with his shield, both movements made to reinforce his war medicine. A hundred yards from the relay station's barn, two warriors raced forward to comply with his command; one on each side of the coach.

Deed whirled from his position on top and missed twice. Inside the coach, Hannah cursed and also missed. The Comanches fired their rifles at close range and the two lead Morgan horses grunted and tumbled forward, sending the coach in a furious, sideways skid. Deed brought down one of the Comanches. But it was too late; the damage was done. The other warrior spun away, yelling his war medicine. The coach was uncontrollable as Tade fought to stop the other horses and keep the wobbling vehicle upright. Inside, Hannah cursed and was unable to fire. Both women cried. Deed grabbed for the railing and hung on.

"Whoa, boys! Whoa! Stay up. Stay up, damn you, stay up!"

As the one-ton Concord stage lurched and skidded to a stop, Tade Balkins dropped the reins and jumped down from the driver's box. Whinnying, the remaining horses stumbled against each other. The two carriage-suspension thoroughbraces, three-inch-thick strips of leather, groaned but held. The middle horses went down in a snarl of harness and flailing legs. The two rear horses stutter-stepped fearfully, but remained upright, coming to a complete halt. Tade staggered toward the barn and was helped inside by Billy Lee Montez.

"I'm getting out. God will protect me," Persam Torce yelled, then pushed open the door and tumbled out of the coach before Hannah could stop him. A few feet from the coach, Torce knelt and began to pray, holding a cross in his hands.

A warrior, wearing a sleeveless military jacket reined up next to him and raised his tomahawk. Hannah fired twice and the savage shuddered, slid off his horse backward, and thudded on the prairie, facedown. Torce stood and began walking to the station as if it were a nice day in the park, but two other warriors rode past the coach yipping, and the first clubbed him to the ground and leaped off his snorting horse to scalp him. A third warrior was close behind. Caleb Forsyth's shots from the station's porch snapped into the warrior as he grabbed the dead man's hair. The Comanche jerked, tried to step away and collapsed, dropping his knife.

"Get inside, Caleb! You can't help him," Atlee declared from the window and returned to the gun port a few feet away.

Caleb Forsyth swung around to go inside as two bullets tore into his body. He stumbled and reached for the door. An arrow drove through his back and the bloody steel point came out his stomach. He took a step and fell. Opening the door, Atlee threw his gun inside, then grabbed her prone husband and, with Benjamin helping, dragged him inside, leaving a trail of blood. Cooper barked and ran around the mortally wounded man. With Caleb inside, she slammed shut the door and shoved the heavy support beam in place as bullets and another arrow hammered against it.

"God, hold him here with us . . . please," she gasped.

Cooper laid down next to Caleb, resting his head on the man's unmoving shoulder.

With only a momentary glance at her husband, Atlee returned to her post and aimed the Spencer through the gun port — this time at two warriors, now dismounted and coming toward the porch.

"Reload Pa's gun," Atlee commanded, not taking her eyes from the Indians.

One of her shots ripped through the right leg of the tallest and he staggered. A second bullet hit him in the chest and he fell against the porch. The other brandished his bow, but ran for his horse. Her shots missed him. Benjamin fired the reloaded Henry, but also missed. The second warrior grabbed his horse's mane, swung onto its back, and galloped away, yelling.

"Ma, I've only got eight bullets after this." Benjamin finished reloading the Henry. His voice was drained of emotion and he dared not look at the unmoving face of his father.

"All right, son. The Burnside is loaded. So is the Whitworth. The shotgun's ready, too."

"They only shoot once."

"We can reload. Get them down. There's ball and powder in the cabinet. Shotgun shells, too."

"Ma? Are we going to die? Is Pa . . . dead?"

Atlee glared in her son's direction and declared, "No, we are not. We are going to fight. Your father would want that. He's in God's hands now." She turned back to her shooting post. "Benjamin, two men in the coach. One's on top. They're shooting at the Comanches! I can see them. They're good, Benjamin."

"As good as Pa . . . was?"

"Nobody's that good, son."

Her face was flushed and her brown hair was halfway out of its regular tight bun. Even under stress, she was an attractive woman. Her light blue dress was torn at the right sleeve and her bosom was heaving, but she had never wavered or whimpered, only grabbed a gun when she saw the war party. It wasn't the first time Comanches had attempted to stop a stagecoach coming to their station and they had managed to successfully drive them off without any loss. But this was different. She knew her husband was dead.

The other Forsyth child, Elizabeth, was six and sat near the fireplace, ablaze with flame. She was playing with a cloth doll; her round cheeks were flushed from the heat, but seemingly, she had no sense of what was happening.

"Our horses! They're after our horses!" she muttered, took careful aim, and fired through the rifle hole, winging a yellow-painted warrior.

Leaving the wounded brave, three other warriors headed for the corral and the agitated coach horses there. Deed resumed shooting from the top of the coach, making them retreat. One staggered and fell a few feet from the corral gate. The two remaining Indians headed for the barn that held two additional teams of coach horses and the family's three personal mounts and a milk cow. Billy Lee Montez emptied both barrels of his shotgun at them. One warrior fell in the doorway. The last warrior hurried to his horse as Deed's big gun slammed against a spent shell. A new cartridge tube was shoved in place and he looked for other targets as the warrior galloped away.

From the other side of the coach, James Hannah fired at a fleeing warrior and missed. He yelled, "Deed, I thought they'd come at us hard now that we've stopped, but they're gathering behind us. Near those trees. Are they quitting?"

"We've stung 'em. Maybe we can help them with that thought."

Meanwhile, the remaining war party had pulled back fifty yards with the war leader waving toward the coach. Deed figured they were puzzled by their lack of success. Half the warriors were down. Dead or wounded. They hadn't expected to lose men in battle, not like this anyway. Some of the warriors were openly questioning their leader's war medicine. They were used to hitting outlying farmers or ranches, or attacking a lone stage coach, all easy prey for red raiders who struck like lightning. Not so today. It must mean their war leader's *puhahante,* his war medicine, was broken.

Stretching out, Deed balanced his carbine against the railing, cocked and aimed the big gun. The war leader's war cry jerked to a stop and he folded from his horse; his head a bloody mess with a huge bullet hole between his eyes. His fellow warriors stared at their dead leader in disbelief. They must flee or be destroyed by the angry spirits now turning on them. Deed fired again and another warrior's chest became a crimson ball as he fell from his horse. The remaining warriors kicked their ponies into a frightened retreat. He emptied the Spencer at their retreat, taking another Comanche from his horse.

Triumphant cheers exploded from the coach. The German woman said something to her husband that no one understood. Leaving his book in the coach, Hannah popped open the coach door and stepped out, holding his revolver. He told Rebecca it was safe to come out. She glanced at Deed as she left and hurried to the station. The gunman looked up at Deed.

"Looks like we got it done, Corrigan."

"Yeah. How's it inside?"

"Ah, the German took an arrow. In his shoulder. He's hurt bad, I think."

"Damn."

"Yeah."

With that, Hannah began walking among the closest downed Comanches, shooting each one again. Deed swung down and saw the wounded farmer in his wife's lap. He was conscious, but in considerable pain.

Opening the coach door, Deed said, "That arrow needs to come out. The sooner, the better."

Olivia Beinrigt blinked and told him what had happened.

"Let me get the arrow out, then we can get him to the station. All right?"

"Ja, danke."

Acrid gunsmoke laid heavily inside the coach as Deed entered and grabbed his sheathed throwing knife from behind his collar. He knelt beside the struggling farmer and cut off the arrowhead with his blade. A fly found the oozing wound and he swiped at it with his open hand.

"I'm going to pull this out now. It's going to hurt. You ready?" he said to the white-faced Beinrigt.

"J-Ja."

Putting his left hand against the man's bloody shoulder, Deed Corrigan took hold of the arrow shaft with his right and pulled it free. The farmer grimaced and fainted. Removing his neckerchief, Deed wadded and pressed the cloth against the bleeding.

"We can clean that wound when we get to the station." He looked up at the German woman. "You take care of your man till then. Keep this pressed tight. Let up in a few minutes, then do it again. Need to stop the bleeding. I'll get Mr. Hannah to help carry him."

Spiderwebs of crow's feet jumped around Olivia's pale blue eyes. Her plain gray dress was splattered with her husband's blood.

"Danke," she said and patted his arm. *"Du* are most brave."

He smiled and buckled on his gunbelt and yelled to James Hannah.

The bespectacled gunman returned to the coach to help Deed carry the wounded farmer, leaving the dead top-hatted man in the coach. Olivia walked proudly beside them, holding her husband's hand.

"How bad they get you?" Deed asked, glancing at the gunman's bloody coat sleeve as they walked.

"It's nothing. Just a scratch," Hannah said. "How's the German?"

Deed glanced at Olivia. "Going to be all right, I think. Lost a lot of blood. He'll need some time." He adjusted his hold on the wounded man's shoulders. "He saved my life, you know. Cut down one of those bastards when I was in a bad spot getting on top."

"Yeah, you're a lucky man, Corrigan. I'll

have to remember that." Hannah's laugh was warm.

"You'd better." Deed chuckled.

CHAPTER FOUR

At the relay station, young Benjamin Forsyth opened the door for the incoming passengers. Cooper barked for attention. Rebecca Tuttle was talking loudly to no one in
particular.

"Thanks, son," Deed Corrigan started to
say something else, but saw the unmoving
man stretched out on the planked floor.

The look in the boy's eyes was the only
answer he needed. At the fireplace, Benjamin's younger sister continued to play with
her doll, unaware of what had happened to
her father or the violence that had occurred
outside.

"I'm mighty sorry," he said and looked at
James Hannah. "Let's put Mr. Beinrigt over
there. On that bunk." Bunks were set up in
the back of the station for drivers and
guards, but not for passengers. If necessary
to stop overnight, passengers would have to
sleep on the floor.

The boy turned away so no one could see him crying as the two gunfighters laid the wounded German on the bunk. Olivia Beinrigt asked for water to clean the wound and a tearstained Atlee Forsyth brought her a bucket filled from their inside water barrel. Cooper moved to be next to Benjamin and the boy scratched his floppy ears as unstoppable tears ran down his freckled face.

With her straw hat in her hand, the agitated Rebecca Tuttle hurried over to Deed and Hannah and asked, between sobs, "Are they gone? Will they come back?"

"Guess nobody knows about Indians for sure," Deed said. "But I reckon we're safe. For now. They'll head back to their camp. Take a vote on a new leader. That won't come fast. Or they might just head south. Look for an easier target. We cut them up pretty bad. They aren't used to that."

She smiled and said, "Thank you. You were so brave. So were you, Mr. Hannah."

"Just trying to stay alive, Miss Tuttle," Hannah said, adjusting his glasses.

"Mr. Beinrigt did his part and more," Deed added.

Atlee stepped beside them. "I'm Mrs. Forsyth. My husband and I run this station. I want to thank you for stopping the Comanches. That's the worst it's ever been."

Her youngest, Elizabeth, wandered over and hugged her mother's leg, receiving a warm pat on the head. Atlee glanced at her husband's body. "T-They k-killed my Caleb."

The younger woman frowned at Atlee's interruption, slammed her hat back on her head, and walked away with its ribbons flopping in her face.

"I'm so sorry we couldn't save your husband." Deed took off his hat. "Ma'am? Would you like us to . . . carry Mr. Forsyth . . . somewhere? Till we can bury him proper?" His voice was gentle and his eyes met hers.

"Thank you, Mr. —"

"It's Deed Corrigan, ma'am. Deed, if you please."

"Thank you, Deed. Please call me Atlee."

"Yes, ma . . . Atlee."

"My son and I will be serving supper soon. I'm sure all of you would find some food and coffee refreshing, after this awful time." Her face looked like it was going to crack.

"Atlee . . . let us take care of that. You and your son, why don't you go to your home. Be by yourselves," Deed said.

"No. This is our station. Our job. Caleb would want us here."

Deed Corrigan shook his head, stepped away, and asked James Hannah to help him move the body. The bespectacled gunman nodded and the two of them left carrying the body. After whispering some instructions to Deed, Atlee Forsyth watched them leave, swallowed hard, and went to the station's kitchen. Benjamin and Cooper followed.

Elizabeth studied the men carrying her father out of the house, turned toward her mother, and asked, "What's the matter with Pa? Is he sick? He's so quiet."

Atlee swallowed. "Your father is with God. Please come and help me."

Elizabeth's next question went unheard.

As they carried the dead man to his house, Hannah observed, "Never liked looking at a dead man. Even one I killed. One minute, he's full of life. The next, he's dirt."

"Yeah. Especially when he's a good man." Deed eased around a large clump of grass, holding Caleb Forsyth's shoulders. "Watch that bunch of grass."

"Got it. The man's heavy, isn't he? Think those red bastards'll be back?"

"Don't think so, but we'll have to keep an eye out."

Not far away was a small stream that also provided a spring-fed well, assisted by an energetic windmill. Just over the hill was the small town of Wilkon, named after the man who built the first general store to assist travelers. They passed a chicken coop surrounded by a fence, housing a dozen chickens and a rooster. Next to it was a well-tilled garden, yielding potatoes, carrots, onions, cabbage, and corn. Deed was certain the two far trees were apple trees. Ten feet from the house was the stone cooling shed.

"Looks like they're pretty near self-sufficient here," Hannah observed as he shifted the dead man's weight in his arms.

"Yeah. Bet we'd find a milk cow in the barn," Deed answered.

Deed balanced the body with one hand and opened the door to the house with the other. "We were lucky those Comanches didn't get the horses earlier."

"Yeah. Interesting way to live," Hannah said, keeping the door open with his elbow as they stepped inside. "You know, all they do is fight." He grinned. "The two of us would've fit right in."

"Could be. Wouldn't care much about slapping paint all over me though."

Hannah chuckled.

"That's quite a good-looking pistol you're carrying, James," Deed said, nodding in the direction of Hannah's opened coat.

"Oh, yeah. Really like this gun. Smith & Wesson made them for the Russian army. Most accurate handgun I've ever found," Hannah said. "Got this one, well, let's just say I found it."

"That's good enough for me."

The Forsyth's adobe-and-timber home was clean, tidy, and felt of a woman's presence. Following Atlee's directions, they laid Caleb Forsyth on the bed in the front bedroom; Hannah straightened his coat, now smeared with dried blood. Deed covered the dead man's still face and body with a blanket that had been folded in the corner of the room. A second bedroom, built on for Benjamin and Elizabeth, stuck out from the core of the house.

A stone fireplace with an open hearth held a gray bank of coals in need of stirring to keep them producing warmth. In the main room, a large brown sofa was pushed against the south wall. A torn spot on the side of the sofa had been sewn together. A large table with four unmatched wooden chairs held a small vase of prairie flowers, now days past their prime. In another corner of the main room was an ornate desk, accented with Spanish-style carving. Above the desk was a framed photograph of Caleb and

Atlee on their wedding day. A small kitchen held a cast-iron stove and a row of cabinets.

"That's one tough lady," Hannah said as they walked back to the front door. "Didn't fall apart when her man went down."

"Got a feeling she will . . . when everybody's gone," Deed said.

"Going to be rough on these folks. Wonder what she and the kids'll do?"

Deed didn't want to think of their options and merely shook his head.

Hannah studied him a moment and said, "Holt Corrigan is your brother, I take it."

"Yeah. Haven't seen him for a long time."

"Heard he was in a gunfight in Amarillo. Got himself killed."

"Heard that, too. Possible, but I doubt it. Not Holt."

Hannah grinned. "Me too. No offense, but there's another story. About you. Two years ago in Austin the way I heard it. Three fellas were leaving the bank after robbing it and ran into you." He cocked his head and pushed back his glasses. "You took down the first gunman with only your hands — while he was pointing a six-gun at your belly. In a split second, you grabbed the gun, killed the second outlaw, and wounded the third. Heard that story all over Texas." He paused and added, "Thought it was

46

crazy talk . . . until I saw you in action today. Now I've got a hunch it was true."

"Didn't have much choice."

"Sure. It's good to be lucky, too."

As they left the small house, two shadowed figures rode up to the far edge of the station area, beside the cottonwoods, leading a third saddled horse. The closest rider swung his Winchester to his shoulder from its position across his saddle and studied the now-quiet attack scene. The second rider, an older Japanese man, carried a long, curved sword on a sheath across his back and a long knife was belted at his waist. From the station, Cooper barked but made no attempt to leave the safety of the station.

Shielding his eyes with his hand, Hannah declared, "Two men are out there. Just rode up. Don't think I know them. One's an Oriental. The other's white. I think he's only got one arm."

Deed smiled. "Sounds like my brother. And my best friend, Silka."

"What?"

"My brother. Blue Corrigan. Lost his left arm in the war. I'm the youngest of the three of us." Deed shook his long hair, brushing against his shoulders. "We planned to meet here. I'm on the way back from our cattle drive to Abilene. Looks like they've

47

got a horse for me.

"And that's Silka with Blue. Silka's our partner. Nakashima Silka is his full name. Silka's easier to say and he doesn't mind. He used to be a samurai warrior back in Japan. Kinda think of him as our uncle. Long story." Deed smiled "Come on, I'll introduce you."

"You go on. I'll head back to the station and see how things are going there," Hannah said, waving his hand in dismissal. "I'll meet 'em later."

"Sure."

CHAPTER FIVE

Blue Corrigan watched the bespectacled man head for the station while his younger brother strode across the open yard.

Without warning, a wounded warrior Hannah had overlooked, jumped up and ran at Deed waving a tomahawk and yelling. In one smooth motion, Deed pivoted to his left, grabbed the Indian's right wrist with his left hand, and smashed his right elbow into the charging Comanche's face. Deed yanked away the tomahawk, then drove his fist into the attacker's chest. The Comanche gasped and fell.

A shot from one of the riders ended any further attempt. Smoke trailed from the barrel of Blue's rifle. He had fired it like a pistol, one-handed, pushing the stock against his leg. Licking his lower lip, he returned it to his saddle scabbard and swung down. The Oriental nodded and dismounted, too.

As if nothing had happened, Deed strolled over to the two riders. Of medium height and build, the two brothers looked a lot alike, resembling their late father, even down to their once-broken noses, courtesy of their brother, Holt. Deed was eight years younger than Blue, an inch taller, fifteen pounds heavier, and definitely wilder. Blue was as intense as Deed, but directed it toward building a great ranch.

Deed's reputation for fighting grew as well; Holt's reputation was more like that of a ghost. Neither Blue nor Deed had seen him since the war ended. Two years younger than Blue, Holt had been riding the outlaw trail, still fighting the war that had ended so long ago. Distinctly, the three brothers had elements of their mother's approach to life within them. Deed cared about all things of nature, from snakes to birds to deer, much like that of an Indian; his fighting instincts, however, came from their father.

Holt had picked up their mother's fascination with superstition and reincarnation, believing he had once been a Roman soldier, a knight in King Arthur's Round Table, even a jaguar in South America, in different lifetimes. He carried a panther's claw in his pocket and had since he was twelve. His first experience in believing he had lived before had occurred during the war. An enlightening experience, he said. His superstitious ways increased then as well. No one laughed when he told the stories, not even Deed. Like his younger brother, Holt's fierce fighting abilities had come from their father.

Blue's beliefs, however, were more traditional. In fact, he served the Wilkon church as a part-time minister, along with a townsman, whenever the circuit rider wasn't available. Their mother had loved reading, especially the Bible, and so did Blue; their father believed in the need for righteous behavior, but also in never backing down.

Blue's coat and chaps showed signs of trail dust. The sleeve of his left arm was pinned against his coat. Yankee artillery fire had blown it off; he was lucky to have survived. One of his pockets was jammed with extra cartridges. In the other was a small Bible his mother had given him. He always carried it, even during the war, and credited the scripture with saving his life. At his hip was a holstered Walch Navy 12-shot revolver with two triggers and two hammers. Weighing two pounds, it was twelve inches long. Rarely seen in this part of Texas, Blue had taken the gun from a dead Union officer during the war and decided he liked it, especially since reloading a standard six-shooter wasn't easy one-handed.

"Glad you could make it." Deed gave his brother a warm hug, then turned to Silka and hugged him, saying, *"Nana korobi, ya oki."*

The old samurai smiled, recognizing the Japanese saying: fall down seven times, get up eight. "Velly good. A warrior must do so."

The short, stocky Japanese man was many years older than the Corrigan brothers, had a graying mustache, and wore his hair pulled back tight to a tail in back. Carried in a sheath across his back was a classic samurai sword. Nakashima Silka's clothes were nondescript, but definitely those of a cowboy; a broad-brimmed hat was weathered and flopping. Around his neck was a small engraved brass circle just like Deed wore. It, too, carried a hidden knife behind the Oriental's back.

He had left Japan when the samurai were forced out and made his way to Texas, learning English as he traveled. In many ways, he was like a stepfather to all three Corrigan brothers and had taught Deed, in particular, how to fight — and fight well — with any weapon and with one's hands and feet. Silka taught the classic samurai way of the warrior, *Bushido,* the importance of inner strength and determination, with moments of concentrated energy. At its core were honor and freedom from the fear of death. His swords were the only physical remains of his previous way of life. Under his careful training, Deed had become a fierce warrior even though he didn't want the reputation.

Deed, Holt, and Blue, with Silka's considerable help, had built up their family's ranch southeast of the stage station and a few miles outside of Wilkon. Theirs was one of five ranches doing well in the region; two were quite large, the Bar 3 and the Lazy S. Their mother and sister had died of pneumonia when Blue was eighteen; Holt, sixteen; and Deed, ten. Their father had died six months before their mother from a broken neck after a horse threw him. Three years later, Blue and Holt left to fight for the Confederacy while the much-younger brother, Deed, stayed with Silka to keep the ranch afloat. While the older brothers were gone, Silka had honed Deed's fighting skills.

"It'll be good to get home," Deed said, patting the nose of the extra horse, a steady buckskin that he favored. "Seems like I've been gone a long time."

"Well, you have, Deed," Blue said and glanced at the station, "but one of us needs

to go on to El Paso. Just bought a fine stallion . . . from August Magnuson. Figured
we'd breed him with some of our best
mustang mares."

"Magnuson? He's got some mighty good
horseflesh. Usually wants a lot for 'em, too."

Blue smiled. "He's in a bind for cash.
Made us a mighty good offer. Couldn't pass
it up. Silka agreed." His smile got wider and
he glanced at the former samurai who nodded agreement. "At least, I hope you've got
money from the trail drive."

"In my gear." Deed motioned toward the
coach. "I can go on. I'll take what we need
to pay Magnuson and give the rest to you
two. We did well."

Blue looked around and said, "Good.
Sorry we didn't get here sooner. That
must've been a bad bunch." He closed his
eyes briefly and said a silent prayer for the
dead souls.

"Came out of the earth, it seemed like,"
Deed said.

The Oriental asked, "How many hurt?"

"Two passengers as well as the shotgun
guard are dead. So is the station manager.
Another passenger, a German farmer, got
hit hard in the shoulder," Deed said. "He's
inside being cared for by his wife." He
shook his head.

"What happened to your driver?" Blue asked.

"Last time I saw him, he was running for that barn. I think the stock tender's in there, too. Haven't had time to look. Or cared to." Deed motioned toward the barn, then turned toward three painted Indian horses standing with their heads down, adorned with paint and feathers tied to their manes and tails. He gathered their simple reins and led the ponies to the water trough, then let them loose in the corral. Blue and Silka tied their own horses to the trees and headed for the coach's downed horses.

As they walked, Deed asked, "Ever hear of a gunman named James Hannah?"

Blue nodded. "Most have, I reckon."

"Yeah. Doesn't look like a gunman though."

"*Hai,* what does gunman look like?" Silka asked, a slight smile working its way onto his flat face.

"Some would say Holt, I guess. Or me." Deed bit his lower lip.

Silka waved his arms in disagreement. "No. You are *fighter.* Warrior. Big difference."

Deed rubbed his mouth with his thumb. "Anyway, Hannah was a big part of our making it. He and I just took the station

55

manager's body to his house. We'll bury him later. Wherever Mrs. Forsyth wants."

"Where's he headed? James Hannah," Blue said, glancing at the station again.

"Going to El Paso, I think. Why?"

Blue said, "Well, it's one more gun."

"Yeah, a good one."

Finally Tade Balkins and Billy Lee Montez emerged from the barn; the one-eyed Mexican holding his shotgun and looking both ways with each step. Tade's face was taut and his rapid-fire speech made it obvious he was coiled and nervous. Silka's presence seemed to make him even more on edge.

"Any more of those red devils left?" He glanced at Silka without meaning to do so, then looked away.

"They're gone — or dead. We killed their leader and that sent the rest running," Deed said, motioning to the bodies lying across the yard.

"Thank God for that," Tade shook his head.

"Yes, thank God," Blue repeated.

"Never had 'em come at me like that before. Holy damn!" Tade shook his head again. "They got Hank early on. My guard, ya know. Was. Then the bastards cut down my two lead horses. Damn them to blazes.

56

They were great Morgans. Two of the line's best."

"O soroshi," Silka said solemnly.

Tade stared at him as if the old samurai had just given a war cry. Both Corrigan brothers recognized the Japanese word for "awful," but added no comments of their own. It seemed to Deed that the driver was more upset about his two horses dying than losing his guard. He introduced Tade to Blue and Silka, and asked to be introduced to Billy Lee. After mumbling an introduction, Tade walked over to the coach while the others exchanged greetings.

"Hard to believe. Those red bastards didn't even try for the gold." The stagecoach driver shook his head and motioned toward the heavy box under his seat. It was filled with gold coins, certificates, and bars for the El Paso Bank.

Deed glanced at Blue, then Silka, then back to the high-strung driver. "They got the station manager, too, while you were hiding out in the barn."

"Caleb Forsyth? They killed Caleb? My God, that's awful!" For an instant, it looked like Tade was going to kick the closest Indian's body. Either he didn't get the bite of Deed's remark or chose to ignore it.

"Yeah. You lost two passengers, too. Another, Mr. Beinrigt, is hurt bad. We carried him into the station."

Silka walked over to the coach and muttered something in Japanese. Tade licked his lips and stared at the dead drummer still wearing his top hat, as if seeing the body for the first time, then gazed at the expressionless Silka. "Where are the womenfolk?"

"They're inside. They're all right."

"Oh. Well, that's good." Tade walked over to the two dead horses. "I've got to get going again. Mail's gotta get through, ya know."

It was Blue who spoke first and his words were practical. "Well, we can't leave these dead horses here to rot. Maybe we can pull them out of the way. We're going to need to hook up some of the team in the barn to haul the dead ones away."

"Sure. Sure." Tade was already gathering strewn-about clothing from the broken-open luggage and laying the garments and suitcases in the coach. One mail bag was ripped apart so he gathered the loose envelopes and boxes and placed them inside the coach as well.

"We're going to need your help *here,*" Deed said.

Tade looked up. "Oh, sure. I wasn't thinking. Wasn't thinking."

Billy Lee Montez laid the shotgun against the coach and helped untangle the harness. The two rear horses were eager to get away from the nightmare of snarled leather. The left rear horse reared and snorted. Billy calmed the frightened horse into standing again. Unharnessing the animals was slow work, but gradually they freed one of the downed middle Morgans and the animal stood, shook itself, and was ready to be led away with the other two. The remaining middle horse had a badly broken leg and couldn't stand. Mercifully, Deed shot the animal, then knelt, touched the dead animal's head, and said a silent prayer. Blue and Silka watched without comment.

Billy said, "I bring grease for de axles."

"Let's get these horses out of here first," Blue affirmed. "We'll need some horses to pull them."

"*Sí.* I bring two hosses. Enough?"

Silka nodded. "Velly good. Bring rope also."

Billy hurried away and Blue and Silka walked the three unhurt coach horses to the holding corral. Returning to their own horses, they led them to the water trough and then retied them to the outside of the corral gate. Billy brought a set of harnessed horses and they finally got the three dead horses dragged away into a long ravine, surrounded by brush. Tade urged them on while leaning against the coach and watching the old samurai walk among the downed Comanches, using his long sword to assure himself that they were all dead since James Hannah had obviously missed one.

"What do you want to do about these dead Indians? The ones close in here?" Deed asked. "They'll bring coyotes and buzzards — and smell like hell."

Tade shook his head. "Well, I've got to get this coach going. Hate to leave you with that mess, but I gotta."

Blue shook his head. "You're full of all kinds of good news. We need to drag these Indians off someplace out of sight and smell."

"I guess I'll help," Deed said.

"Well, those Comanches will come back to get them. Count on it." Blue motioned toward the horizon with his good hand.

Silka agreed. "Hai. They will come. It is their way."

"Sí," Billy added.

Blue recommended they wait until the coach left, then haul the dead Indians beyond the stage yard and out of sight. The stage could be moved up closer to the station so the passengers wouldn't have to walk among the dead to get on. The dead passengers and the shotgun guard would require separate graves. How and where the dead station manager would be laid to rest would be Atlee Forsyth's decision. Deed reminded Tade that two suitcases on top would need reloading and the removal of some arrows. There were a few bullet holes too; but not much could be done about them.

The anxious driver said he would take care of the suitcases. After greasing the axles, Billy Lee helped Tade lead out the fresh team and harness them to the coach. Tade was obviously eager to get moving again. He headed to the station to get something to eat and tell the passengers that the coach was ready. The Mexican disappeared into the barn again.

After lifting the dead drummer from the stage and laying him on the ground, Deed, Silka, and Blue headed for the house, talking to each other.

CHAPTER SIX

"So the drive went well? Your wire said so," Blue asked his brother, patting him on the back, as they walked toward the station.

"Real good, big brother. Got top price. Those boys were eager to get beef headed east."

"Hontou?" Silka asked.

"Yeah, really."

All three laughed. Deed said again that the cattle-drive money was hidden away in his gear. He added, "Lost three steers crossing a river. Another five were trampled during a stampede. But we picked up twenty stray head along the way. Willy found most of them. Unbranded stuff."

"What started the stampede? A storm?"

"Yes and no. One night the herd was tense, wouldn't settle because a storm was coming. You know how Willy can start burping when he's nervous," Deed explained. "Well, he belched so damn loud after eating, it took us half the night getting the herd back together," Deed said, chuckling. "Some of the men took to calling him Boom."

"Is he worth keeping? That could've been bad."

"Willy works harder than three men," Deed said. "Belches louder than three men, too."

"Sure. Your call."

"He'll stand."

Blue glanced at his younger brother and started walking again. "While you were gone, we had some terrible tragedies around here." He paused and frowned. "The Regan family was murdered in their home. Looked like Comanches hit the Bar 3."

"My God! Jason and Martha . . . their kids? That's awful, Blue."

"Yeah, it was; Isaiah Tuscott came to our ranch just after dawn to tell us," Blue said. "He was going there to help Jason with an addition to their main house. We rode there as fast as we could. Little Jeremy had hidden. We found him and brought him home to stay with us. But he was the only one that made it."

"How'd you know it was Comanches?"

Shifting his shoulders as if to remove an unseen burden, Blue explained about finding arrows, a tomahawk, unshod horse tracks, and that the adults had been scalped.

Deed grimaced. "I'm surprised the war party attacked at night. Thought they were afraid a warrior killed would never find his way to heaven. Did they burn the ranch house?"

"No."

"That's strange too."

"Yeah. You know, usually a ranch is pretty empty during roundup and trail-drive time, but Jason doesn't go on the drives anymore. That busted leg of his won't hold up. So it was he and his family except for their six-year-old son, Jeremy. All dead. And scalped." Blue looked away. "You remember Ol' Joel, don't you? They got him, too. Bless his soul. Looked like he fought them for a long time."

"Damn. How long did he work for the Regans?"

"Must've been thirty years, at least."

Blue straightened his back. "It gets worse. The Wilkon Bank foreclosed on the Bar 3. Had a big loan, according to the bank president."

"So who owns the Bar 3 now?"

"Same fellow who bought the bank. Lives in El Paso. It all happened not long after you left for Abilene," Blue said. "He bought the H-5 and the Roof-M, too."

"That's convenient," Deed snorted. "So only three ranches around here now. His combined spread, the Lazy S, and us."

"Hai. It is so," Silka agreed. The former samurai studied the brothers without saying more, then examined the station area, and looked at the Corrigan boys again.

"I take it you don't think it was Comanches," Deed said, cocking his head.

"Not sure. Once I got him to talk about it, Jeremy said some things about white men attacking the place," Blue said, a little above a whisper. "And the whole thing with the bank loan. Don't know why they would have borrowed money. Not them anyway. Must have been a cash-flow problem." He rubbed his chin. "I can understand the H-5 and Roof-M selling out. They're both small. Probably tired of it all. You know, they've been putting their trail herds with the Bar 3 the last couple of years."

"Well, I saw the Bar 3 herd on the trail when I was coming back. A big one. At least three thousand head," Deed said. "Didn't recognize any of their hands on the trail. Or their trail boss. Thought it was strange. Now it makes sense. So, what happened to the money from their drive?"

"Bank has no record of any deposit like that."

Silka's face hardened. "Hai. Blue, you know it was not Comanche. You know it was this Agon Bordner."

"Who's Agon Bordner?" Deed asked.

"The guy who bought the bank — and the Bar 3 and the other two."

Deed glanced at Silka. "That's a mighty big spread. Biggest around here. Even bigger when you add in the H-5 and the Roof-M."

"It is so," Silka declared and studied Deed's face.

Blue explained he hadn't met Agon Bordner, only heard that he lived in a big house in El Paso, adding that he thought a man had a right to take advantage of a situation if he could. It was like him to view everyone in a positive light. Almost as much as their late mother had.

Silka looked at him and grinned. "He is velly fat, they say."

Blue quickly added Bordner had a fine reputation in El Paso — that he was active in the Baptist church there, even sang in the choir.

"What happened to the Merefords and the Hansons? Are they still around?"

"No. Both families left right away, right after they sold," Blue said. "And that's even worse. Comanches hit their wagons somewhere north of here. Killed them all."

"That's awful. Awful."

"Yeah, they were good folks," Blue said.

All three men were quiet.

Deed was the first to speak, "Well, who's running the Bar 3 now?"

"A fellow named Dixie Murphy's the new foreman. Met him once in town. A hard man to like. But I'm sure he's a good cow-man." Blue licked his lips and changed the subject. "How many of our boys are coming back?"

"Just the regulars. Willy, Harmon, Chico, Little Jake and Too Tall are bringing back the chuck wagon and the remuda — and Judas."

Judas was the name they called a large, black longhorn steer that led their herds to market. The rest of the drovers had hooked on to a drive headed for Wyoming. Too Tall was what everyone called their cook, a short, stocky man with a temper to match. Deed said Taol Sanchez hit town with a big herd of over two thousand, two days after they got in. Oldest son of Felix Sanchez, the owner of the huge Lazy S, he was also happy with the prices received for his beef.

Blue stopped walking and turned to Deed. "How are those folks doing, the ones in-side?"

"About like you'd expect, I guess. Mrs. Forsyth's trying to go on," Deed said, glancing at the station as they resumed walking. "The Forsyths had turned this into a damn good relay operation, you know."

Looking around at the readied coach, Deed added, "Guess Mrs. Forsyth and her kids will need to go in the stage. To somewhere safe. El Paso's the next big town. Unless they want to go into Wilkon. Don't think they have much money. Won't be easy for her."

A black snake slid across their path. Blue reached for his holstered gun as it stopped and hissed.

"Let it go. He's not disturbing us," Deed said and knelt beside the snake. Behind him, Silka drew his long sword.

"It's all right. No one will hurt you," Deed spoke to the agitated reptile.

Neither Blue nor Silka moved, but watched the snake. Slowly, it uncoiled and resumed its journey. Silka said something in Japanese. Deed stood and the three men began walking again with no further mention of the reptile. Blue knew his younger brother had a sense for nature that few could match. It reminded him of their mother.

Silka thought he should remain outside

and let them bring him something to eat, instead of going into the station. Not everyone liked to have Orientals near, he indicated. Both Corrigan brothers rejected the idea.

"If they don't want you, they don't want us," Deed said and slapped Silka on the back.

The old samurai faked being hurt by the affectionate display and smiled.

Stepping inside, Cooper growled as they entered, then hurried to greet them with his tail wagging. Deed bent over to return the greeting. They were surprised to see Atlee Forsyth serving Hannah, Rebecca, and Tade around the long table as if nothing had occurred. Large bowls of beef stew, baskets of biscuits, and fresh coffee were being enjoyed. Hermann Beinrigt was lying down on the couch, and Olivia was putting a wet rag on his forehead. Little Elizabeth stood next to her, holding a bowl of water. Deed walked over to them and put his hand on the farmer's good shoulder.

"How's he doing, Mrs. Beinrigt?"

"He *ist* fair, I think. Much *blut ist* lost. *Du* save his life." Olivia held out a slightly shaking hand.

Taking hers with both hands, Deed leaned toward her and smiled. "He saved mine."

Releasing the handshake, he stood and introduced his brother and Silka who removed their hats.

Olivia looked up and greeted both.

Stepping next to Deed, Elizabeth declared, "My papa is dead, you know. He is in heaven."

Deed blurted, "I'm so sorry."

The little girl lifted the bowl so it could be fully seen. "I'm helping Mrs. Beinrigt."

"I'm sure you are. I'm sure you are." Deed realized the little girl had no concept of death. Why should she?

Her next statement made him wince. "Papa is with Washington now. He was our cat, till he died last year."

Deed knelt beside her and brushed away the long strands of hair that had stuck to her warm cheek. "Uh, I'm sure they will be very happy together."

She turned to him and declared, "I think Papa will be back in a week or so. Like when he went to El Paso."

Deed swallowed and couldn't think of anything to say.

From behind them came Atlee Forsyth's, with what seemed to be an overly bright salutation. "Deed, I'm glad you're here. Mr. Hannah said you'd be coming inside. There's plenty of stew and biscuits. Coffee's hot and fresh." She wiped her right hand on her apron. "Who are your friends?"

Deed turned toward her. "This is my brother, Blue Corrigan. We own a ranch not far from Wilkon." He pointed at Blue, then at Silka. "And this is our best friend and partner. Most folks call him Silka."

Silka bowed formally.

"How nice to meet you," she said. "Please have a seat. You are most welcome."

Blue touched the brim of his hat with his hand. "Glad to meet you, ma'am. Awful sorry about your husband."

Her eyes took in his sewn-up sleeve, then went to his face. "Thank you. He was a very good man. But we'll make do. We have to." Her eyes brightened. "Caleb would have wanted that."

Tade rose from his chair and waved his arm. "Told her she should go with us to El Paso. She won't go. Maybe you can talk her into going into Wilkon."

Still holding the bowl of water, Elizabeth walked over to her mother. "Is that like going to Heaven?"

"I'll tell you later, sweetheart. Please be quiet now."

Folding her arms, Atlee stared at the three men. "Please sit down. Mr. Balkins informs us the stage will be leaving soon."

Mrs. Beinrigt came over and guided Elizabeth back to the couch, asking for her help. Deed sat down at the table with Silka and Blue on either side of him. With separate trips, Atlee placed bowls of stew in front of them, along with ironware, cups, and a basket of biscuits. Blue murmured a prayer of grace before beginning to eat. Hannah watched him without saying anything.

"Ma'am, I know Willard Epson, your district agent. A good man," Blue said, looking up and watching her move along the table, refreshing coffee cups.

"Yes, I have met Mr. Epson several times." Her voice was rigid.

"Of course" — Blue licked his lips — "he will need to know —"

Atlee Forsyth stiffened, holding the coffeepot near her bosom. "Because he will want a *man* running this station?"

Blue looked at Deed, then Silka, and said, "Most likely . . . ma'am."

"So don't tell him. I just told you that we will do just fine."

Blue stared at her, wishing he hadn't started this line of conversation.

"I can run this station. I'll hire someone to help Mr. Montez — and we'll keep serving passengers well as we have always done." Her eyelids blinked back tears that were trying to get attention.

"Yes, ma'am. I'm sure you can."

The room was silent while Atlee resumed pouring coffee for everyone. The others were finishing their dessert, fat slices of gooseberry pie. Pushing away from the table, Tade Balkins headed for the door and announced the stage would be leaving in five minutes.

Wiping his mouth with his sleeve, Tade said, "I have to report what happened, Mrs. Forsyth. Part of my job." His eyes didn't meet hers as he opened the door.

It was Deed who spoke first, "Tade, if you have to say anything, tell your boss the station is operating well, and that Mrs. Forsyth has hired additional help." He looked at Atlee. "If you'll let me, I'll stay on and help Billy till you can find somebody regular."

Blue tried not to look surprised, but this was so like his younger brother to step into a fight. Any fight.

Deed glared at the stunned driver. "You don't have to report that last part."

For a moment, Deed thought she was going to rush over and hug him. Instead, she swallowed, bit her lip, and said, "That would be most helpful. W-We appreciate your generosity."

Rebecca Tuttle put down her coffee cup

hard, almost spilling the remaining contents. "You mean you're not going on with us? What will we do for protection? Mr. Hannah can't do it all." Her eyes were wild and her hands trembled.

Deed glanced at Blue. "My brother will be riding guard, Miss Tuttle. You will be quite protected. We've got business in El Paso."

A hint of a smile tugged at Blue's mouth. He should have known Deed would pull him into the situation. He always did.

"But he's, he's . . . injured."

"Blue can shoot better with one arm than most with two," Deed said. "He'll keep you safe."

With a deep sigh, Rebecca nodded and stared into her coffee cup as if just realizing it was there.

Blue glanced at his brother. "Yes, I intend to ride as the guard to El Paso."

Blue recalled Deed carrying a hurt fawn two miles to their home when he was ten. He had found it when out hunting. The little deer had healed under his care and been returned to the wild, but it always stayed close to the Corrigan house. Blue and Holt teased Deed that the animal thought he was its mother. One day the deer didn't come back. Deed and his brothers searched for the deer all day before deciding it had found a deer family of its own. Much of the rest of their childhood was deeply marred by their parents' deaths.

Tade rubbed his hands and feigned more satisfaction than he felt that a one-armed man would be riding guard. "Mighty good. Finish up folks. We need to get going." He turned and left the station, slamming the door behind him.

The Corrigan brothers talked quietly for a few moments, with Deed thanking Blue for understanding his sudden change of heart. Silka said he would return to the ranch, taking Blue's horse with him. The extra mount brought for Deed would remain at the station for their later return. Blue would throw his saddle, saddle bags, and bridle onto the coach for the ride back from El Paso on the new stallion or he would buy an extra mount there. Silka was to tell his wife what had happened. Bina wouldn't like it, but she would understand. The former samurai would take the trail-drive money with him, too, after Blue took what he needed for the new stallion and expenses in El Paso.

Her shoulders rising and falling with relief, Atlee came forward and said, "I should be able to hire someone in a few days."

"Sure."

Benjamin burst in from the kitchen, his eyes reddened and his face flushed. "We don't need anybody's help, mister. I'm the head of the family now. It's my job to take over for Pa. Nobody else." Cooper was at his side.

Setting his fork on his plate, Deed hesitating before answering, "I know how you feel, son. Blue and I lost both of our parents when we were about your age. It's rough. Nobody's taking the place of your pa. I'm just helping Billy with the horses. You and your ma will run the place."

"That's enough, Benjamin. Mr. Corrigan is being most generous." Atlee's face was hard and her eyes sought her son's.

The boy started to say something else, then spun around and went back into the kitchen. Cooper trotted alongside. Elizabeth noticed his performance and headed toward the kitchen, almost spilling the bowl with its remaining water.

Blue, Deed, and Silka returned to eating without more comment. Atlee left the table and went over to the Beinrigts at the couch.

"If you want to stay here until your husband is better able to travel, you are most welcome," she said, putting her hand on Olivia's shoulder. "There are two beds here.

For drivers and guards when they need them. Nobody will be needing them."

Olivia patted her hand and said, "*Danke.* Dat vould be most *gut. Mein* Hermann *ist* . . . veak. I could also vork for *du.* To help."

At the table, Blue introduced himself to the bespectacled gunfighter, "James Hannah, I believe." He stood and leaned across the table, extending his hand.

Pushing his glasses back with his left hand, Hannah rose to shake Blue's hand. "Glad to meet you."

"My brother tells me you made the difference today."

"Glad I could help." Hannah returned to his seat. "Say, do any of you know anything about a fella named Agon Bordner?"

"Well, he just bought the bank in Wilkon . . . and a big ranch near here, the Bar 3, and two others. Biggest rancher in this neck of the woods now," Blue said. "Likes to sing in his church choir, I hear." A frown gathered above his eyes. "Why do you ask?"

"He wants to hire me. Sent gold for my expenses. I'm supposed to meet him in El Paso. To discuss a job."

CHAPTER SEVEN

In El Paso's finest restaurant, the Lone Star, Agon Bordner was enjoying a noon meal of an enormous rare steak, six fried eggs, three baked potatoes, sliced beets, a basket of fresh biscuits, and a bottle of red wine. As usual, he ate alone in a back room reserved for parties and meetings. A waiter stood quietly next to the closed door to accommodate any need he might have.

Bordner was a huge man with bulging eyes that rarely seemed to blink; his hair was thinning and long over his ears, curling around his white paper collar. He wore a custom-tailored, navy blue suit, accented by a huge, gold watch chain stretched across his mountainous stomach and vest. Like his voracious appetite, his business desire was to join the handful of great ranchers — Charles Goodnight, Richard King, John Chisum, and Henry Miller — with, like them, hundreds of thousands of acres under his control. They had overcome drought, fluctuating cattle prices, and Eastern financial panics. All he had to do was take control of the five ranches around Wilkon, and he already had three — one of them, the largest in the region. He smiled at the thought, took another bite of steak, and washed it down with half of his wineglass. The waiter rushed over to refill it.

His strategy to achieve this goal was simple, brutal — and, so far, effective. First, he had purchased the Wilkon Bank. Well, the price was basically a steal with several of his gunmen convincing the president-owner that it was time for him to leave. His men had gotten a big laugh out of actually stealing a bank, not robbing it. One of his men, Willard Hixon, had taken over as president. From there, Bordner would take control of one ranch at a time. The initial ranch acquisition was the Bar 3, the largest ranch in the region. The former owner and his family were murdered in the night. Comanches were blamed. He took over after a large Bar 3 loan from the Wilkon Bank surfaced.

The two small ranches abutting the Bar 3 were then coerced into selling. When the two families left for a more peaceful life, Bordner's men followed and killed them, taking back the money used in the purchases. Again, Comanches were blamed. Keeping his operation flush with actual cash was a secondary, but essential, strategy.

Taking another mouthful of potato and gravy, he let his mind wander over the details of the Bar 3 massacre, as his right hand man Rhey Selmon had related. His fascination with such gory details had no bounds. Of course, he wasn't personally involved in the night's savagery. Such endeavors had ended years ago when he murdered his stepfather, cut up the body, and fed the pieces to the family's hogs. Since then, he had mostly hired his killings done. But not always.

Smiling, he hummed part of a hymn that his church choir was practicing, then began singing,

"Rock of ages, cleft for me,
Let me hide myself in thee;
Let the water and the blood,
From thy wounded side which flowed,
Be of sin the double cure,
Save from wrath and make me pure."

He stopped singing and gulped a drink of wine. Singing made him thirsty. He loved singing and had bought robes for the choir so there would be one big enough for him. It didn't hurt his image either, he knew. On several occasions, he had even sung a solo, but only when requested. People would have a difficult time believing such an upstanding churchgoing man could be behind the largest land grab in Texas history. That was the idea.

He hummed more of the hymn and motioned to the waiter, told him to bring more gravy and another bottle of wine. The anxious man hurried away to handle the request. Agon Bordner had come from New Mexico Territory with his gang under Rhey's direction. Together they had built a gang of thieves, gunmen, bank robbers, and rustlers, as well as specialists. Specialists like Willard Hixon, a wizard with numbers and an artist at forging signatures. They could have stayed in New Mexico, enjoying the fruits of their well-planned stagecoach and bank robberies. But Bordner wanted more; he wanted a cattle empire. And Texas was the place to take it. His men were happy to follow him — especially now that they were settled into the Bar 3, glad to leave their camp in the hills. The money earned from the Bar 3 trail drive gave him the kind of cash he needed to keep them happy.

Snorting and laughing, Bordner yelled,

"Texas! Look out, here comes Agon Bordner!"

The fourth ranch on his list of acquisitions was the Lazy S, almost as big as the Bar 3 and owned by a Mexican family with deep roots in the region. The attack would take place within the month with the same strategy and Comanches would be blamed again. That would leave only the Corrigan spread with its excellent, year-round water.

However, the first step in that acquisition, a crucial one, would be to eliminate Deed Corrigan. Even Rhey Selmon, his right-hand man and excellent with a gun, wanted no part of him. Neither did Macy Shields, his next best gunman. Nor did Sear Georgian, the brute with a lust for beating up men and women, who had especially enjoyed the Bar 3 massacre.

After Deed was killed, that would leave Blue Corrigan and the crazy Japanese fighter who rode with them. The two would still be a significant force, but without Deed, Rhey was certain he and his men could handle them. Once they were dead, a bill of sale would surface. Bordner had sent for the well-known gunman, James Hannah, to join in this phase of elimination and expected his arrival any day now. Rhey Selmon had mentioned the possibility that the third brother, Holt Corrigan, might get involved, but just in passing. Holt was a known outlaw and not part of the LC ranch operation. Rhey wasn't certain if he was even alive. There had been talk of a gunfight in an Amarillo saloon that had ended his life, though Sear Georgian told them it wasn't true. Just a saloon tale that actually involved another man named Holt.

Bordner grinned and steak juice ran down his chin. The waiter returned with a bowl of hot gravy and a bottle of wine. The large man accepted them without comment and the waiter returned to his post by the door. After pouring gravy over his remaining potatoes, beets, and eggs, he started eating again.

Since coming to Texas, his wealth had grown greater by a series of stagecoach and bank robberies all done with care. Owning the Wilkon Bank gave him access to the timing of shipments of gold and gold certificates. Rhey Selmon took it from there, sending teams of gunmen wherever they were needed. Whenever possible, they made sure Holt Corrigan was blamed. It kept the Texas Rangers and Pinkertons looking for him.

Utterly without scruples, Rhey was the driving force in Bordner's scheme to become the dominant rancher in the region.

Another member of the gang, Dixie Murphy, took care of the cattle operations; he was a mean man, well suited to Bordner's task. Two days ago, Dixie wired Bordner about catching up with the Bar 3 cattle herd en route to Kansas, successfully selling the beef in Abilene, and now returning. Left unstated in the wire was what had happened to the original Bar 3 drovers.

A knock on the door startled both Bordner and the waiter.

"Boss, I need to talk with you." The voice was Rhey Selmon's.

Bordner motioned for the waiter to let in his associate. How unlike Rhey to interrupt his lunch. Surely this had to be more than a report of moving the gang to the Bar 3 as planned. Bordner planned to move there himself in the next week or two.

Tall and skinny, Rhey Selmon entered. He was loyal to one man, Agon Bordner, and one cause, helping Bordner become a cattle baron. The two were alike in their love of greed and power. Physically, they were as different as night and day. Although hollow cheeked and thin, Rhey was quite strong and never seemed to sleep much. Regardless of the weather or the season, he wore a long bearskin coat. His clothes were of the range and nondescript. His eyes were ice blue and slightly crossed. Black hair strung from a narrow-brimmed hat. At his waist were two crossed gunbelts holding twin silver-plated revolvers with pearl handles, the only things of distinction that he wore or owned.

"What is it, Rhey? Can't you see I'm dining?" Bordner said angrily. "Surely your news could have waited."

"One of the Regan kids is alive," the tall gunman blurted.

Bordner stared at his lieutenant without speaking, then motioned for the waiter to leave the room. Gulping his words, Rhey told him one of his men had overheard Blue Corrigan's wife buying canned milk and candy at the general store and telling why the purchase was necessary. For a moment, the fat man thought he was going to vomit. How could this be?

"I thought you were better than that, Rhey," he growled and slammed a fat fist against the top of the table. The filled glass jumped and spilled red wine down the side. "You've got to find that little brat — and kill him before he starts telling the world what really happened."

"Right," Rhey took a deep breath.

Bordner crossed his fat arms. "Wait. Nothing's been damaged. Not really. Nobody's going to believe that kid. What is he, five or six? Give me some time by myself and I'll figure out our next move."

"Do you still want us to get the kid?"

"No. If you shoot him now, it'll only look suspicious. We'll wait until James Hannah gets here. I'll give him that job." Bordner speared another slice of steak with his fork. "Say, three of Rose's best doves are coming to my place tonight. Want to join in?"

Both men laughed.

"Are the boys outside?"

"Yeah, except the men I sent to hold up the stage."

"Send 'em in. I need to talk to Sear. Tell the waiter, we're going to need more food. Lots of it."

CHAPTER EIGHT

Although nervous at first, Rebecca Tuttle began to relax as the stagecoach rumbled across the Chihuahuan Desert. James Hannah had been nice enough, but he was inclined toward reading and sleeping and she was left to her thoughts most of the time. She found herself thinking about Deed Corrigan. She wished he had continued with them and felt a little jealous that he had stayed to help Atlee Forsyth.

She told herself Deed had stayed because the new widow was frightened about being attacked again, but Rebecca wasn't certain that was the reason. She tried to concentrate on the farmer waiting for her, the man she was going to marry. His face wouldn't come to her mind. Only the face of Deed Corrigan. Her unstoppable conversation focused on Hannah, even though he wasn't particularly responsive.

At last the Franklin Mountains came into

view, indicating the coach was nearing El Paso. Tade Balkins was visibly weary and Blue Corrigan was having trouble staying alert as well. The edgy driver had mentioned missing his regular guard at least six times and each time Blue had acknowledged how hard it must be. Tade had followed each statement with a concern about a one-armed man being tough enough if they had any more trouble. The rest of their conversation had been strained. Tade was upset about losing time in delivery of the mail and Blue's words of comfort did little to help his stress. Nor did Blue tell him that he had been a sharpshooter for the Confederacy during the war.

Ahead, the road took a jog to the left, disappearing behind a cluster of huge yellow and gray boulders that looked like God had placed them there for no other reason than that he could. As the tiring team of Morgans neared the large rocks, four masked horsemen swung into view, firing their revolvers in the air and demanding that the stage stop.

"Halt! This is Holt Corrigan," one masked holdup man yelled.

"No. You're not." Blue's reaction was an instant assault. Sliding forward to kneel in the driver's box, he placed his Winchester against the front edge and fired the gun six times — as fast as he could aim, pull the trigger, and lever a new cartridge with his one hand. Two outlaws spun from their saddles and hit the ground, groaning. Their pistols spun by themselves, as if frozen in the moment, before thudding near the wounded men.

"Keep 'em going, Tade!" Blue yelled.

Smoking shells popped around Blue as he focused on the remaining two outlaws who were firing at them. The jerking coach made it difficult to aim, but Blue kept leveling the rifle to maintain a steady field of fire, now shooting with the gun against his hip for balance. One of the outlaw's bullets clipped Blue's hat; two others drove into the front of the driver's box and sent a wood sliver into Blue's right hand and the sudden pain forced him to stop firing for a moment, then he resumed as if nothing had happened. The coach thundered toward the outlaws with Tade yelling and snapping his whip to keep the horses in an outright run. The outlaws' mounts became difficult to control. Stutter-stepping. Rearing. Shaking their heads wildly.

An outlaw in a tan vest and dark blue shirt backed his horse off the road, far enough to settle the mount. He wrapped the reins around the saddle horn, drew a second handgun and began firing again with both weapons. The other outlaw, blond hair streaming from his hat, spurred his horse wide of the road and into a hard lope with the intention of getting Blue in a crossfire.

"I've got this one, Blue!" Hannah yelled and fired three times from the coach's window.

The blond outlaw grunted and slumped against his horse's neck. Hannah aimed his Smith & Wesson with both hands and fired again, popping a black hole in the man's exposed check, in spite of the coach's uneven movement. The gunfighter smoothly shoved new cartridges into his gun and told the once-again screaming Rebecca that it would soon be over.

In front, the remaining outlaw held up his hands with his guns still in them.

"Keep going, Tade. He's had enough."

As the coach rumbled past the stunned stagecoach robber, Hannah fired three times and the remaining outlaw crumpled from his saddle.

"Hey! He was finished," Blue yelled back at the bespectacled gunman.

"Any man holding two guns isn't finished in my book," Hannah answered. "But you're welcome." He reloaded his gun and shoved it back into his shoulder holster. "Miss Tuttle, it is over. There is nothing more to be afraid of."

"Oh thank you, sir. Thank you."

"A hug would be nice."

She stared at him for a moment, then leaned over and gave him a warm embrace.

Above, Tade Balkins looked over at Blue reloading his rifle, shoving new cartridges into the gun with it laying on his lap. "Be all right if I ease 'em down a mite? They've been pushed hard. Too hard, maybe."

"You bet. Bring them to a walk. They did well."

Wiping his brow with his hand, Tade pulled on the horse team to bring them out of their run. "Well, I sure had you figured wrong. Never thought you'd come out shootin' like that. Lordy!" He grinned. "That was somethin' to see."

"I understand," Blue said, laying the reloaded rifle on his lap. "The good Lord expects us to defend ourselves against evil, whether we've got one arm or two." He smiled. "Besides, there wasn't much time to turn the other cheek."

"Easy now, boys. Easy." Tade pulled on the reins and watched the tired animals slowly slip into a trot and finally, a walk. "I can sure see how you and Deed are brothers. That's for sure. No offense."

"None taken. We *are* alike in many ways. But Deed is a far better fighter." Blue could hear Rebecca jabbering inside the couch. Hannah would have his hands full calming her down, he thought.

"Man said he were Holt Corrigan. Any kin?" Tade asked.

"Holt's our brother and that wasn't him. Haven't seen him much since the war. He would've been involved in every bank and stage holdup in three states, if you believed everything you hear."

"Prob'ly best," Tade said and decided to mention a story he'd recently heard about Holt Corrigan. "Speaking o' that, heard your brother . . . Holt . . . was in a gunfight over near the border. Last year, it was. Said he died."

"Yeah, heard that, too. Like I said, I don't put much stock in gossip."

Tade waited for more, but none was coming and he said, "Heard he was one of the heroes who stopped all those Yankees at Sabine Pass. Just forty-three Confederates with rifles and six small cannon stopped a Federal fleet of fifteen thousand men tryin' to land."

"That's true. Holt was there and part of that victory," Blue said. "Lieutenant Richard Dowling led them. Sank a gunboat, captured a couple more, and turned away the rest of that whole fleet. Took four hundred prisoners. Best of all, they didn't lose a man."

Tade nodded. "Yeah, that must've been something. Heard every one of them boys got a silver medal from Jeff Davis, only command that got that. Really something."

Tade wanted to ask why Holt was an outlaw, but decided he shouldn't and the talking ended for a while. "Ya see that mountain? That's Franklin. Got a red clay shape in it. Real odd-like. Indians think it's a thunderbird." Tade was actually smiling. "Supposed to be a holy place for 'em."

"I'm sure it is," Blue said. "Doesn't have to be a cathedral to talk to God. Or listen. My dear mother, bless her soul, used to say a man's own church is within his heart."

Tade looked over at Blue. "Hey, you're bleeding. They hit ya?"

"Naw, just a piece of wood caught me." Blue studied his bloody hand.

"Better have a look at that," Tade said, talking warmly now.

"No. I'm all right. Just a nick. The bleeding will stop soon enough."

"Want me to stop an' he'p ya?"

"No thanks. I'm all right, really."

Tade nodded and returned to studying the passing arid land.

Blue had never been to El Paso before, or for that matter, seen the Rio Grande defining the border between El Paso and Mexico. The business with Magnuson's horse had been done by telegraph. So he enjoyed the scenery and the driver's change in attitude. Tade pointed out a volcanic peak to the west, rising from within the Rio Grande Rift and actually on the New Mexico side of the big river. He said there were a number of ancient volcanic craters a couple of days' ride west. The town itself had responded well after the war and was a distinctive mixture of domed Spanish mansions, adobe tenements, and new structures of wood and brick, more northern in style and texture. Blue listened without comment, enjoying the driver's sudden interest in talking.

Ahead of the coach, on the outskirts of town stood a three-story, Victorian-styled home, surrounded by a white picket fence. Elaborately trimmed in shades of brown and light blue paint, the wooden building featured a wraparound porch with a matching deck on the second floor. It would have been a distinctive house in any Eastern city, but in El Paso it was absolutely dominant.

"That's Agon Bordner's place. He's kinda

new to town," Tade drawled and motioned with his head. "Bought the Bar 3 north o' here, you know. An' a couple o' small places, too." He waved his hand toward the house.

"Heard that. Bought the Wilkon Bank, too."

Tade continued talking as if Blue hadn't spoken. He said Bordner had come from New Mexico and liked to live elegantly.

"Yeah, there's all kinds of stories about his one-man banquets," Tade laughed and massaged the sets of reins in his right hand. "Biggest man I ever seed."

"Interesting he lives here and hasn't moved to his new ranch," Blue said, studying the advancing signs of town.

"Hear tell he leaves all that to a hard-assed cowman name of Murphy. Dixie Murphy. Got a finger missing from his left hand," Tade held up his left hand. "Roping problem." He shook his head. "Also heard he's got a reputation for having some cows with an awful lot of calves. Too many calves."

"I don't put much stock in gossip."

As they passed the big Victorian mansion, Blue couldn't help wondering what kind of man this Agon Bordner was.

"Over there's the ol' Peterson place," Tade interrupted Blue's thoughts, pointing toward the gray skeleton of a house. "Nobody knows what happened to him. One day he was gone. Just gone. Nobody lives there now."

They passed a small adobe cottage where a middle-aged woman was outside, separating cream from milk, pouring the white liquid through a hand-crank separator. Six chickens clucked across the sandy earth in front of her. Tade waved and she waved back.

At Blue's suggestion, Tade didn't make his tired horses run again to have a showy entrance at the stage station and reined them easily to a stop. A major point in the route, from here the stagecoach headed toward Santa Fe with a new driver as well as a new team of horses.

Commercial activity in town was strong with four-story hotels, general stores, saloons, grocery stores offering East Coast delicacies, and theaters crowded against distinctive Roman Catholic cathedrals and old missions. Newcomers included businessmen, priests, prostitutes, and gunfighters. After the Civil War's conclusion, the town's population began to grow and talk of the railroad coming to El Paso fueled even more interest in the town.

Everywhere Blue looked, there seemed to

be aristocratic ranchers and rich merchants mixed with cotton farmers and copper-mine workers. In the distance, he saw a church and two Catholic cathedrals. The town was full and loud. He felt very tired and glad to have arrived. His mind darted to his wife, Bina. He missed her and their son and daughter very much. He always did when away. And now there was Jeremy. He couldn't wait to get home.

A tall man in a rumpled suit and an ill-fitting bowler bolted from the station. His long-jawed face was red and his right hand kept making and unmaking fists at his side. In his left hand was a heavy bag of new mail and express.

"Balkins, you're late!" Willard Epson, the stage-line district agent, snapped.

"Well, you oughta be damn glad we made it at all. Had serious Comanche trouble outside of Forsyth's station," Tade blurted, waving his arms. "An' four masked owl-hoots tried to hold us up just outside of town. Blue, here, cut 'em down hard. He an' Mr. Hannah, one of my passengers."

"What? Comanches? Holdup men?" Epson stopped and put his hand over his mouth in surprise. He was all set to give his driver a dressing-down for being late and realized they had been lucky to get through at all.

"Was the gold — ?"

"Safe as a baby's behind." Tade Balkins swung down and explained what had happened, complimenting Deed and Hannah — and Blue — for their help in getting the mail and gold through safely.

Tade took the mail bag from Epson and handed him the El Paso–bound mail bag. Meanwhile, Blue grabbed his saddlebags and bedroll from the rear boot and threw them down. He would wait to get his saddle until the driver unloaded the boot itself. Cradling his Winchester between what remained of his left arm and his good right arm, he climbed down, grasping the coach rails with his lone hand. He made a fist to drive away the lingering pain from the slight wound.

Epson listened intently as Tade began unloading the luggage that belonged to Rebecca and Hannah. He told his boss about the two passengers being killed and wondered what to do about their luggage, about losing Hank Johnson, his guard, about the German couple staying at the Forsyth station, and finally, that Caleb Forsyth had been killed. For the first time, Epson noticed Blue only had one arm. His eyes asked the question.

"Lost it in the war, Mr. Epson," Blue responded to the unstated concern. "Been shooting one-handed since then. Pretty good at it. The Lord decided I needed to show others that two hands aren't necessary to be successful."

"Guess so."

Forcing himself into a state of control, Epson thanked Hannah and Blue, and asked Rebecca if she needed assistance to the hotel. She glanced at Hannah and said that she did not. From across the street came a strutting bank president puffing on a large cigar and eager to retrieve the gold box.

Blue studied the oncoming man for a moment, a tall man in a tailored suit with a trim mustache and receding hairline. Two men carrying shotguns and wearing side-arms were a few steps behind him.

"Say, aren't you Dave Copate? Fought with my brother at Sabine Pass?" Blue asked.

"Well, howdy, Blue. You bet I am. It's good to see you again," Copate held out his hand and Blue laid down his rifle and shook it. "What brings you to our fair town?"

Blue told him and Copate asked, "How's Holt doing? Really doing, I mean. I hear all these awful stories and I don't believe them.

He saved my life, you know."

"Wish I knew. Haven't seen Holt for years, I'm sorry to say. I don't believe the stories either, but I'm his brother."

"Well, when you do, tell him Dave Copate asked about him and sent good wishes."

"Sure will."

"Excuse me, Blue, but I'd better get this to the bank," Copate said.

"Of course. Need some help?"

"No. That's what these two are for." He chuckled, waved, and motioned to the two armed men. Shifting their shotguns to their left hands, each man took one of the straps on the heavy box and followed him away.

Epson paled and started to shake. "Holt Corrigan your brother?"

"Yes. Why?"

"N-No reason, I guess. Just —"

"You were wondering if I was going to rob your stage, is that it, Mr. Epson?" Blue growled. "I'm here to buy a stallion from Mr. Magnuson for our ranch. My brother Deed and I own a spread near Wilkon." He cocked his head. "Haven't seen Holt in years. Not since the war. You'd know more about him than I would." He paused and added, "If I were you, I wouldn't believe every story that came along about my brother. As far as I know, he hasn't broken any laws. He didn't like losing the war, but a lot other men felt the same way. He also didn't think he had to beg for amnesty. I'm proud of him for that."

"Oh, of course. Of course. Well, welcome to El Paso," Epson smiled. "If I can do anything to make your stay better, please ask."

With his saddlebags and bedroll draped over his shoulder and his Winchester in his right hand, Blue explained that he had ridden the coach to assure the red-faced district agent that the station was in good hands. Tade added his support, saying Mrs. Forsyth had already hired Deed Corrigan to help her; the driver glanced at Blue, who shook his head, and Tade said nothing more. Behind them four new passengers waited for their luggage to be taken and to board.

"Deed Corrigan? Didn't you just say he was your brother?" Epson asked.

"Yes. I met up with him at Forsyth's station," Blue said, leaning his Winchester against his leg. "He was returning from a trail drive to Abilene." He called it the *Forsyth's station* deliberately.

Folding his arms, Epson said, "He's mighty good with a gun and his fists, I hear."

Blue's smile didn't reach his eyes. "He's a very good man — and this coach wouldn't be here if it weren't for him and Mr. Han-nah."

Epson rubbed his mouth and looked away. "Yes. Yes. But I still have to replace Mrs. Forsyth. We can't have a *woman* running our relay station. Surely you understand."

Blue put his lone hand on the other man's shoulder. "I surely don't, Mr. Epson. And if I were you, I'd rethink that idea. From what I hear, that's one of your best stations. And it isn't because the horses are harnessed correctly or your barn is always clean. Or hadn't you noticed the way your passengers talk about Mrs. Forsyth's food." He took his hand away and picked up his rifle. "Now I'm going to get something to eat, a little sleep, and go buy a horse tomorrow. All right if I put my gear in your station until then?"

Apologetically, Epson said it was fine to leave his things there, added that he owed Blue for riding guard, and offered him a regular guard job. Blue thanked him and declined without an explanation, adjusting the saddlebags and bedroll on his shoulder. He walked over to the boardwalk and laid them down.

Epson turned away and told Tade to take the luggage of the deceased into the station and he would attempt to find any relatives to inform them of the sad loss. Behind them, the tired team of horses was led away by a black man and a new team brought out. A passenger asked Tade a question and he said a new driver would be taking them west. Blue returned to the stagecoach, gathered his saddle and placed it on the boardwalk next to his saddlebags and bedroll, keeping his rifle. Tade insisted that he take Blue's gear inside for him.

After retrieving his handsome valise and talking quietly with Rebecca, Hannah joined the two men.

"Blue, I'm headed to the Lone Star across the street for a steak and some whiskey before I meet with that Bordner fella. Care to join me?"

"Sounds good." Blue grinned.

"How's your hand? Should we have a doc take a look at it? You need to take care of that one, you know," Hannah said, motioning toward Blue's bloodstained hand.

"Oh, no thanks. It's nothing. You probably got hit worse at the station." Blue pointed at the dried bloodstains on Hannah's coat sleeve.

"Guess we're both lucky. Like your brother."

"Yeah."

"Gentlemen, let me buy your dinners,"

Epson said eagerly. "Our stage-line owes you a debt of gratitude."

Hannah pushed on his glasses. "That's true. Instead of two dinners, let's make it two hundred apiece. We saved your ass outside of town — and his brother and I did it earlier against those red bastards. In fact, make it another two hundred for Deed. And we'll call it even. I don't care much for debts of gratitude."

Epson swallowed and looked like he had been slapped, but managed to find his voice. "Well, of course. Of course. Let me just do that. I'll go get the money. I'll bring it to the Lone Star." He spun and left.

"Think we'll see him again?" Hannah chuckled.

"Good question. He looked scared enough."

CHAPTER NINE

James Hannah and Blue Corrigan walked into the crowded Lone Star restaurant and looked for an empty table. Blue noticed that several men saw them and whispered something. He guessed they recognized the infamous gunman. It made him smile.

The smoky room was filled with tables of ranchers, copper-mine workers, and a few hungry cowboys. The walls themselves flickered with the presence of oil lamps attempting to drive away the grayness. Blue's gaze didn't latch on to any person he recognized, but he didn't expect to see anyone. Hannah said he planned to meet Agon Bordner here. Someone like the fat businessman would be easy to spot anywhere, Blue thought. There was a back room. Maybe Agon Bordner was already there.

They found an empty table in the middle of the restaurant. After laying his valise on the floor next to his chair, Hannah drew his handgun as they sat and laid the weapon in his lap. An old habit. Blue laid his rifle on the floor under his feet. The table wobbled on an uneven leg. Frowning, Hannah took one of the forks on the table and pushed it under the short leg.

"There. That's better," he said and tried the table's steadiness with both hands and was satisfied.

"Nice work. You remind me of Deed."

"I take that as a high compliment."

"It was so intended."

A round-faced waiter with a patchy beard took their order and quickly retreated to the kitchen. A few minutes later, a well-made-up woman of uncertain age brought a tray holding a bottle of whiskey and two glasses. Her fringed crimson dress swayed rhythmically as she approached their table, enjoying the attention she created.

She glanced at Blue and turned to Hannah. "Your steaks will be coming real soon. If there is anything else I can do for you, gentlemen. Anything at all. I'm Cheyenne."

"Thank you, Cheyenne. Maybe later." Hannah winked.

She smiled and the corners of her mouth crinkled. After pouring whiskey into both glasses, she flitted her eyelashes and looked again at Blue. "I've never taken care of a one-armed man before." She curtsied and left, swishing her red dress as she left.

Hannah chuckled and reached for the drinks, handing one to Blue. "Must be nice to be liked."

"She wanted some spiritual guidance."

"Well, I'm sure she'd be happy to be on her knees. In front of you."

"Bless her." Blue smiled.

They toasted each other and downed the fiery liquid. Hannah poured both another drink. "Not to be nosey, Blue, but when are you headed back?"

"Tomorrow, I hope. Plan on a good night's sleep at the hotel, then get a horse at the livery tomorrow morning and head out to Magnuson's ranch. We're buying one of his stallions for breeding. Then I'll start back. Take both horses with me. Might buy a third for a packhorse."

"Not taking the stage?"

"Had enough of those for a while."

Hannah sipped his drink. "Yeah. Me too."

Blue nursed his as well. He didn't drink much. Never had. Not because of any religious dedication; Silka had warned them years ago of whiskey's power to rob a man of the ability to react smartly. All three brothers had taken his advice to heart, even

Holt. At least, he wasn't drinking the last time Blue saw him.

Their conversation slid easily over a range of topics: Comanches and their ways; the holdup and whether the posse would be successful in finding any of the bandits; guns; El Paso; cattle; books; railroads; and women. Blue shared that his brother Holt was superstitious, but didn't say anything about his belief in reincarnation. That led to a discussion about religion. Finally they talked of horses and Blue repeated about the Magnuson horses and how good they were, and that the Corrigan brothers planned to do some breeding with some strong mustangs they owned. Blue told him about his wife, Bina, and their daughter, Mary Jo. He mentioned a young boy was staying with them because of a recent tragedy to the boy's family and indicated it was a Comanche raid.

Before Hannah could ask more, the waiter brought their steaks, sizzling and steaming on white plates, along with large helpings of chili beans, sliced beets, and warm tortillas. The one-armed cattleman asked for coffee and the waiter hurried to bring it; his responses had increased considerably since someone told him that he was serving the infamous gunman, James Hannah.

Hannah watched Blue bow his head and move his lips.

"You do that at every meal, Blue?" Hannah asked.

"Yes, but I didn't mean to embarrass you. Forgive me."

Hannah shook his head. "I think that's what religion's all about isn't it? Forgiveness."

"Good point."

Hannah asked if he needed help with cutting the steak. Blue declined, saying that he had learned to cut meat with one hand. Without more talking, both men began to eat with gusto. After they were finished, Blue enjoyed a second cup of coffee and Hannah savored another whiskey.

"Do you like to read, Blue?"

"Yes, I do. Our sweet mother got me hooked," Blue said. "Other than the Bible, I favor Tennyson. Anything Tennyson."

" 'My strength is as the strength of ten.' "

" 'Because my heart is pure.' "

Hannah grinned. "And you thought I was going to say 'All in the valley of death rode the six hundred.' "

It was Blue's turn to smile. "Read anything besides Tennyson?"

"Well, not the Bible. But I've got a book in my gear that's about a clergyman who's accused of stealing, *The Last Chronicle of Barset,*" Hannah said. "It's the second part of *The Small House of Allington.*"

"A preacher accused of stealing, huh? *The Last Chronicle of Barset.* I'll have to check that out."

"You'd like it."

Hannah rolled his head to relieve some stiffness and asked about Silka. Blue told him that Silka had come riding up a few months after the loss of their family. All three boys were exhausted and depressed; cash money was nonexistent. The Oriental became sort of a second father to the boys, guiding their development of the ranch itself.

Blue smiled. "The first time we met him, he said, 'I am Nakashima Silka. I am Samurai.' Put his right fist against his heart and added, 'Warrior. In Japan. I lived Bushido . . . way of the warrior. None dare to challenge me. Silka always win. Kill all enemy.' " Blue took a sip of the hot coffee, lost in yesterday.

Looking away for a moment, he continued the story. Silka had brought his wife and two children to California to protect them from the revolution that was tearing at his homeland, but they had died.

"Silka kept telling us 'Soon, samurai will

be no more.' The old man is a fascinating fellow. Told us stories that were wild and hard to believe, but I'm sure to this day they were all true." He cocked his head to the side and grinned.

"Seems like he spoke pretty good American. How'd that happen?" Hannah twirled his forefinger in his drink.

Blue explained Silka had learned English while traveling across the country, worked hard at it, and was proud of the way he now talked. His accent was only visible on certain words, usually ones with an *r*. Or an occasional Japanese phrase when he was excited.

"He didn't want to work on the railroad like so many from his land. So he rode to Texas . . . found us. Glad he did. Don't think we would've made it without him." Blue took another sip of coffee and studied the room again as he did.

He said Deed, in particular, followed the old man's instructions eagerly. Most of the training was in the evenings after chores were finished for the day. Each night turned into a lesson on fighting strategy, or defending oneself with "empty hands" — without weapons — and handling a sword and a knife.

"I can see his training in both of you,"

Hannah said and told about Deed's take-charge actions during the Comanche attack.

"Sounds like Deed. Over and over, Silka would say, you must train your muscles to do what you want. Without thinking about it. You cannot expect any move to be right, if you do not practice it."

"Makes good sense. Wish I'd had somebody to teach me like that."

Blue nodded. "He's one special man, that's for sure. Always positive. Always stressed the importance of quick moves. 'When you are attacked, time is vital. Practice each move a hundred times. A thousand times. Until you are comfortable with a move. Every move. Speed comes with such practice. The trick is to unbalance the opponent. You must be calm. Confident,' he would say and, if we did it right, 'Ah so . . . good.' "

Blue continued, "Right after the war, Deed, Silka, and I kept Northern carpetbaggers from taking over our ranch. The Union-controlled government left us alone as well. We had no back taxes or bank debt, thanks to Silka's careful management during the war."

Both men smiled. Hannah finished his drink and poured himself another; Blue declined any more whiskey, but waved at the waiter for more coffee. The waiter hurried over to fill Blue's cup and paused to ask Hannah if he needed anything. The gunman waved him away.

"What did you do in the war?" Hannah asked without looking up.

"Sharpshooter. Part of Ewell's outfit. Holt was with Dowling at Sabine Pass. Lucky we both made it."

"Heard about Sabine Pass. Holt's a hero in a lot of Texans' eyes." Straightening his tie, Hannah volunteered, "I was a sharpshooter, too. Only, for the boys in blue. With Sherman when he cut Georgia apart."

"Terrible time, that war."

"Yeah. Terrible."

After another drink, Hannah said he grew up in Indiana; his father was a minister, but his mother was the churchy one. He was the middle of three sons; the oldest died in the Civil War. The youngest was a farmer in Ohio. Early on, Hannah had taught school. He came home early one day and found his wife in bed with their neighbor, killed both, and rode away. The only thing he was good at was killing people and he found out there was money in it. He didn't say more and Blue nodded his head.

Sipping his coffee, Blue asked if he expected Agon Bordner to come to the restaurant. Smiling, Hannah said he was certain the man was in the back room already. Blue started to ask if he was going to take the job when a distraught Rebecca Tuttle burst into the restaurant and stood in the doorway, looking around the room.

"Something must be wrong with Rebecca . . . ah, Miss Tuttle," Hannah said and stood.

Blue turned in his seat to watch her advance and got out of his chair to greet her. He was annoyed that her sudden presence had kept him from asking about Hannah taking a job with Bordner.

"Afternoon, ma'am," Hannah said warmly. "Would you care to join us?"

"Yes, we'd be honored," Blue added.

"Oh, James, I don't know what to do," she desperately wanted to hug the gunman but didn't. "Elmer Risner isn't in town . . . and no one seems to have even heard of him."

Hannah stepped close to her. "There, there. Sit down. Tell us about it."

The distraught young woman almost fell into the offered chair. Hannah waved at the waiter.

"Have you eaten, Miss Tuttle?"

She tried to say no, but couldn't and began to cry. Hannah poured whiskey into

Blue's empty glass and handed it to her.

"Sip on this. It'll make you feel better."

After tasting the offered drink, wincing, and eventually swallowing the hot liquid, Rebecca explained her situation. She had used all her money to pay for the trip to El Paso and didn't know what she was going to do. Both Hannah and Blue listened silently. Finally, she stopped talking and a lone tear dribbled down her right cheek.

Hannah leaned forward, laying his arms on the table. "Life deals bad hands. To all of us." He paused and motioned toward Blue. "Blue, here, lost both his parents when he was a kid. His arm in the war." He licked his lips and swallowed. "I lost my wife, the only woman I ever loved."

He straightened and a cold appearance returned to his face. "So, you can wait to see if this Elmer Risner fellow shows up — or make new plans."

Rebecca put her hand over her mouth to curb her rising emotions. Hannah reached into his coat pocket, retrieved a small sack of gold coins and laid it on the table in front of her.

"Here," he said. "This'll take care of you for a while. Till you figure out what's next."

Her eyes took in the sack in disbelief, then she gushed, "Oh! Oh! Thank you. Thank you. How can I repay you?" She looked at Blue, then back at the amused gunman. "You can have me any time you want, I promise."

"That's not necessary, my dear. We all need a little help from time to time." Hannah glanced at Blue and grinned.

Her hands rose to cup her breasts to demonstrate her sincerity when Willard Epson made a surprise appearance and with a dramatic presentation gave both men an envelope, then another one for Blue to give to Deed. Blue thanked him; Hannah began checking the contents of his envelope. Epson said he needed to get back to the station and left.

"How about that, Blue. I thought we'd have to go over there and scare him to get this," Hannah said and chuckled. "Mine's right. How about yours . . . and Deed's?"

"Haven't looked."

As Blue reviewed the gold certificates in the envelope, a stocky man in a bowler hat and an ill-fitting suit strolled over to the table. His sneer looked permanent and thick eyebrows mingled in the middle of his forehead.

"You James Hannah?" he asked.

"Who wants to know?" Hannah said, looking at Rebecca.

"I do."

The response came with a slight jerk at the corner of his sneer. The man wore a Mexican-tooled cartridge belt holding a holstered Colt. Blue noticed a slight bulge under his coat, indicating a second gun in a shoulder holster.

"Funny name. *I do,*" Hannah growled without looking at the man.

Blue smiled. "Wonder if he has a brother named *I don't.*"

Hannah laughed and pushed his eyeglasses into place with his left hand. His right dropped to his lap and curled around his gun. Unaware of the growing tension, the waiter stepped around the standing gunman and placed a filled plate in front of Rebecca. Blue was fascinated to see her begin eating as if she hadn't had food in days. How quickly a few coins changes one's perspective on life, he thought.

The stocky man's eyes darted from Hannah to Blue to Rebecca and back again to Hannah. Through gritted teeth, he said, "Mr. Bordner wants to see you. In the back room."

"He knows where I am . . . Mr. *I-do.*"

The man moved both hands to his gunbelt and locked his thumbs into place. It was a slow, deliberate move, so he wouldn't be mistaken, but still an attempt to threaten. Blue's hand eased off the table toward his own holstered Walch revolver and flipped off the thong holding its hammers. This wasn't his fight, but he had no intention of staying out of it. Hannah downed the rest of his whiskey, holding the glass in his left hand. He put it down on the table and winked at Blue.

Cocking his head toward the waiting Bordner henchman, he growled, "You still here? You're starting to bother me. Go away."

"I'm supposed to bring you to his room. In back. Now. Those are my orders," the henchman said. "Oh, Mr. Bordner said this meal was on him. All of it."

"Nice to have a generous boss," Hannah growled.

Blue thought there was a softening in the man's voice as if wishing someone else had been given this task.

Blue spoke first, "James, I need to check out the livery. I'll see that Miss Tuttle gets to the hotel. You go ahead and visit with Bordner. From what I hear, he's a fine Christian gentleman. No reason to get this poor fella into trouble."

"Will I see you later?" Hannah asked, ignoring the waiting henchman, whose face showed signs of relief.

"Probably not. I'll be headed out early."

Hannah turned toward the flushed henchman. "Tell your boss I'll be over in a few minutes. Wouldn't want to get you into trouble."

The man's face blinked with relief and he spun and left. After saying good-bye, Hannah stood, reholstered his gun, and walked to the back room and slowly opened the door.

Around the table sat five men. It was easy to tell which one was Agon Bordner. He looked like a huge bullfrog in expensive clothes. As far as Hannah could tell, the fat man wasn't armed. Bordner was finishing a second meal of fried chicken and mashed potatoes with a large glass of dark red wine. Already seated at the table with him was the henchman from a few minutes ago and two other hard-looking men, all armed. Another skinny man with greasy hair and a worn suit looked out of place. Their plates were empty and their glasses held whiskey, not wine.

Only a handful of minutes before, Bordner had just learned that three of his men were dead after the ill-fated stage holdup. Only Curly Matthews got away. From the excited outlaw's description, it was that one-armed cowboy — and James Hannah — doing the shooting. Bordner had told Curly to stay out of sight, ride for the Bar 3, and stay there until he was called.

"Mr. Bordner, how are you?" Hannah said, easing into the room.

"Fine, sir. Absolutely fine." Bordner raised his hand in a warm gesture. "I understand you've been a little busy, getting rid of vermin on the road."

"News travels fast in El Paso. Yeah, we did have a little activity coming in. Four amateurs. One got away."

"Too bad. We need law and order around here. It wasn't Holt Corrigan and his bunch, I take it."

"No. it wasn't."

As if on cue, three of the four men rose and left, headed for the bar. The remaining gunman wore a bearskin coat like Hannah had never seen before. At his waist were two crossed gunbelts holding twin revolvers. One gun lay in his lap. Nothing in his eyes indicated he liked Hannah. Rhey Selmon was known for three things: being fast with a gun, being loyal to Bordner, and owning big horses. Currently he was riding a bay over sixteen hands high and weighing well over eleven hundred pounds. The animal was far and away the fastest horse in the region. Selmon had been in two cattle wars, served a prison term, and killed three men in standup fights before he met up with Bordner.

"James Hannah, meet Rhey Selmon. You two will have a lot in common."

CHAPTER TEN

Blue Corrigan walked with Rebecca Tuttle to the hotel; his rifle was at his side. She wanted to talk about James Hannah, or rather ask questions about him. He was eager to be rid of her, but tried to hide his impatience.

"Is James, uh, Mr. Hannah, married?" she asked, straightening her collar, and tried to act casual as they navigated the rutted street.

"His wife died a few years ago," Blue said, watching a freighter rumble past.

"Oh, that's too bad." She couldn't hide a smile. "Is he coming . . . to the hotel?"

"Don't know about that, Miss Tuttle," he answered. "He was talking business, I believe."

A fancy carriage, pulled by two handsome bays, bounced in front of them. An older gentleman with curly white hair drove; a trim lady, wearing a tilted blue hat with matching feathers, sat at his side. She glanced at Blue and smiled. He nodded.

Blue was glad Rebecca was silent as they completed crossing the street. Stepping onto the boardwalk, he opened the hotel door for her. She bobbed her head and entered. The lobby was lined with big leather chairs and a matching sofa. In the far corner, a large Regulator wall clock proudly told the time. Adjacent to it was an elk's head with antlers. Musty-smelling, full-length curtains flanked the main window. A drummer sat in the corner, smoking a cigar and reading a newspaper. In an adjoining room, the hotel restaurant was quiet.

Rebecca had checked in earlier and Blue wondered how she had intended to pay, but said nothing. She thanked him and asked if he would tell Hannah that she was in room 211. He reminded her that he wasn't likely to see him. With barely a pause, she turned to the desk clerk and told him that a Mr. Hannah should be informed of her room number. The round-faced, bald man with wispy brown hair edging around large ears said he would do so and smiled slightly.

Blue almost felt sorry for Hannah.

As she hurried upstairs, Blue told the manager that he, too, wanted a room. The chubby clerk asked if he wanted one next to

Miss Tuttle's. The one-armed Corrigan brother grunted negatively.

The manager turned toward the maze of cubbyholes for keys and mail behind him. "One-fourteen's open."

"Fine."

"Two bits. In advance."

Blue shoved coins across the desktop, wondered if Rebecca had been required to pay in advance, then took the key and left, heading for the stage station. Epson was sitting behind a desk and nodded as he entered. Blue tied his saddlebags and bedroll to the saddle, then shoved his rifle in its saddle sleeve. Putting everything together made it easier to handle it with his lone hand. He swung the saddle over his shoulder and headed for the livery. Epson muttered a half-hearted good-bye.

As Blue Corrigan stepped off the boardwalk to cross the alley, a familiar voice called out, "Blue."

Even before he turned, he knew it was his brother Holt. Grinning, Blue turned into the shadowed alley. His pinned-up shirtsleeve fluttered as he spun.

"How are you, Holt?"

"Sixes and sevens. No fires turning hollow. Haven't come across any knives on the ground either."

"Better than aces and eights." Blue laid down his saddle and held out his hand. Holt took off his right-hand glove and grabbed Blue's hand. They shook hands and then hugged each other. He knew Holt's references to fires turning hollow and finding knives were superstitions that indicated bad things were coming.

In a low-crowned black hat and full beard, Holt was two inches shorter than Blue. In his hatband was a red cardinal's feather, something he considered especially lucky. Under his coat, he wore two shoulder-holstered Russian Smith & Wesson .44 revolvers. An ivory panther silhouette was inlaid in each black grip. He looked older, much older, than the last time Blue had seen him two years ago. His face was drawn and his eyes, dark and tired. Over the past several years, Holt Corrigan and other ex-Confederates were charged with plundering their way across the region, robbing banks, military payrolls, and stages.

North of them, the James-Younger gang had discovered trains were easier to rob than banks. Sympathetic Southerners had taken to calling Holt Corrigan "el Jaguar." Blue wondered if they had heard about Holt's belief in having been the animal once, or if it was simply a tribute to his cunning and bravery.

"Saw you in the Lone Star, having dinner with James Hannah," Holt said, holding his one glove in his gloved left hand. "I was there. In the corner. Most folks don't know me by sight. Just reputation."

Blue told him what had happened and asked why Holt hadn't come over to join them. Holt smiled, but didn't answer.

"Deed in town, too?" Holt asked, taking a cigar from his coat pocket.

"No, he's helping at the Wilkon coach station."

"Doing what?"

Blue explained the situation.

"She pretty? This widow?" Holt cocked his head to the side and snapped a match into flame off his pants.

"Yeah, but —"

"Never mind. Say, I heard a wild tale about him taking down some bank robbers. In Austin, I think it was. One had a gun on him and Deed took him with his bare hands. That right?"

"Well, that's what happened."

"Is he nuts?" Holt held the flame to the cigar.

"No. Just good. Very good."

"Silka worked his magic I guess, while we were fightin' Yankees."

Blue smiled. "Well, I heard you were in a gunfight in Amarillo . . . and were killed. Anything to that?"

Holt chuckled. "Guess not. Don't think I'm dead. Yet. An' I haven't been in Amarillo in a long time." He turned his head slightly again and exhaled the smoke. A stray string of sunlight caught the long scar on his right cheek, a reminder of a cavalry battle. "You still preachin'?"

"I help with services in town from time to time. Me an' another man fill in when the circuit rider can't be there."

"Good for you. How's Bina and the kids?"

"Doing well. Thanks for asking." Blue said, "Didn't know you were in El Paso."

"Yeah, got an apartment not far from here. Nice an' quiet." Holt pulled on the cigar again.

"Nobody looking for you?" Blue was aware that, at the mention of the apartment, his brother hadn't invited him to stay, but also realized it was Holt's way of keeping Blue from appearing to be involved if something should happen and his cover was blown.

"Nobody's looking for Samuel Holton." Holt watched a circle of smoke wander away. "That's what I go by in town."

"Oh, okay. Samuel Holton. I'll have to

remember that," Blue said.

A quick look at the alley entrance was followed by Holt changing the subject and telling Blue that the attempted stage holdup men were part of Agon Bordner's gang. Blue was surprised and told him about the Bar 3 ranch now being in Bordner's hands.

A pulsing vein dancing down his forehead, Holt said, "That fat sonuvabitch wants to own everything around there. Those were his men that hit the Bar 3, you know. And killed the folks who owned the H-5 and Roof-M, after they sold out. Got Bordner's money back that way."

"I didn't know. You sure of that?"

"Yeah. He'll be coming after you boys soon. That boy's got plans as big as he is."

"Well, there's only the Lazy S and us left."

A couple passed along the alley entrance, talking loudly. Holt retreated into the shadows until they were gone.

Blue started to say his brother was too jumpy, but decided against it. Instead, he put his hand on Holt's shoulder. "Come home, Holt. We've got a place for you. We need you. The ranch is growing. War's been over a long time."

"That's all you need," Holt said, removing Blue's hand from his shoulder. "There'd be lawmen all over your place. It'd give that fat bastard just the opportunity he wants. Believe me, Blue, he's going to come after the ranch hard, like a raccoon after bread crumbs."

Blue rubbed his unshaved chin. "Holt, you're our brother, pure and simple. We stand together. Always have. Always will." He paused and said, "Give yourself up. All of us got amnesty. No Texas jury is going to convict you. You can start over with us. We could sure use the help and your bedroom is waiting for you."

Smiling, the third Corrigan brother shifted his weight from his right to his left side. "That's mighty nice talk, Blue. Like something from one of your pretty sermons. But the time is long past for that . . . and you know it as well as I do. Every bank robbery and stagecoach holdup in Texas is supposed to have been done by me."

Blue glanced back at the alley opening, but no one was crossing. He looked again at his brother. Holt had changed, no longer the cocky kid who loved to fight and loved to win even more. More than the war had changed him though. Holt's longtime sweetheart had married another man while Holt and Blue were at war. That heartbreak had sent Holt riding, looking for a war that was no more, except in the minds of some bitter

Southerners. He had never returned.

"Did you know Allison Johnson's a widow?" Blue said, mentioning Holt's former sweetheart. "Her husband died of pneumonia last year."

"Who?"

"Come on, Holt."

Taking a long pull of his cigar, Holt exhaled and watched the smoke ring dance in front of his face again. "Deed needs to be careful," he finally said. "Going to be some crazy young guns wanting to try him. Get a reputation quick." The statement was an indication Holt didn't want to hear any more about coming home or his former sweetheart.

"He knows. You didn't answer my question about how you knew it was Bordner's men who attacked the Bar 3."

Holt frowned. "I wasn't with them, if that's what you're wondering. A couple of Bordner's men told me. They were drinking heavy and happy to be moving to the Bar 3. Their hideout was none too comfortable, I reckon. You know Bordner's got that no-good Rhey Selmon with him."

"Rhey Selmon? Heard of him. Thought he was in New Mexico."

"He was. They all were. Rhey is Bordner's right-hand man. Likes to kill."

"Sorry to hear that."

"Yeah. Sear Georgian's with him, too. A nasty bull of a man. Huge. Likes beating up men and women, I hear. Awful good with a gun though," Holt said, "Macy Shields, too. He rode with Bloody Bill Anderson. Remember?"

"I remember."

They talked a few more minutes about cattle and horses before Holt asked him if the family had any money in the El Paso Bank. Blue said they didn't and asked why.

"Well, it's a Yankee bank. Figured we might relieve it of some those Yankee dollars."

"No, Holt, it isn't a Yankee bank," Blue said. "That bank is owned by three ex-Confederates. One of them is Dave Copate. You rode with him, remember? At Sabine Pass." He licked his lips. "I ran into Dave at the stage station. He asked about you and said to greet you. Said he didn't believe the stories he'd heard . . . about you robbing banks."

Holt looked surprised, then caught himself and drew the revolver from his left shoulder holster with his right hand, opened the loading clip, half-cocked the gun, and spun its cylinder to check the loads. His right-hand glove remained in his left hand. "We'll see.

You know my spirit demands that I fight. That's what I am, what I've always been."

Blue shook his head negatively. "Building a ranch is a fight. A tough one. So's raising a family or helping a town grow. Lots of ways to fight. Lots of ways better than robbing banks. Or pretending to fight a war that was lost a long time ago."

Holt's only response was to toss the cigar on the ground and crush it with his boot. He named the four former Rebels riding with him. Blue knew two of them; they had been childhood friends. They were camped north of El Paso in an old cabin while Holt stayed at the apartment as Samuel Holton.

Behind them came the swish of a dress, then a sweet call to Blue. He turned to see Rebecca Tuttle standing between the two boardwalks. Her hat was slanted a bit sideways but her smile was warm. Holt stepped back quickly; his right-hand glove dropped to the ground.

"I thought that was you, Mr. Corrigan. Are you talking to Mr. Hannah? It's hard to see in that alley," Rebecca proclaimed.

Blue stepped in front of Holt and heard his revolver cock. "No, Miss Tuttle, I'm not. Just met an old friend from the war."

"You haven't seen him, have you?"

"No, ma'am, not since you and I left the

Lone Star."

She tossed her long curls and they danced along her shoulders. "Oh. Of course. I think I'll walk over there and see if he's still there."

"Sure. You do that. Be careful crossing the street."

She turned with a flirty bounce and was gone.

"What the hell was that all about?" Holt said, easing the hammer down on the weapon and returning it to his shoulder holster.

Blue chuckled. "She was on the stage with us. Supposed to be meeting some Ohio farmer to get married. Only he hasn't showed." He motioned in the direction of the restaurant. "Afraid that means Hannah was elected. Only he doesn't know it yet."

"Poor bastard."

"I can introduce you. She's real pretty."

Holt laughed, then looked down at his dropped glove. "No thanks, but would you mind picking that up for me, big brother?"

"Sure, Holt." Blue bent over and retrieved the glove. He recalled Holt saying it was bad luck for a man to pick up his dropped glove, or any dropped glove. He smiled and handed the glove to his brother. "Does this mean I'll have bad luck?"

"Oh no, Blue. Returning a glove brings

good luck. I'm sure of it."

"Good."

They shook hands again and Holt went out the back of the alley, reminding his brother that Agon Bordner would be coming with a lot of gunmen and every intention of taking control of Wilkon and everything around it. Blue stood, watching him disappear, wishing he could do something to bring his brother home — wondering if he should go after him and try again. Maybe Holt was right; maybe it was too late. He retrieved his saddle and headed for the livery. A prayer for Holt's safety came from his lips.

The livery smelled of grain, manure, hay, and leather as Blue walked through the opened doors. A bear of a man with crossed eyes and an old derby perched on his head approached from a back stall, holding a pitchfork.

"Good day to ya. Stranger in town, I reckon," he said, leaning on the fork handle.

"Yeah. The name's Blue Corrigan. From up around Wilkon."

The livery operator glanced at Blue's pinned-up sleeve and said, "Reckon ya bin in the war, mister. That ri't?"

"Yes. I fought for the Confederacy. We lost."

"Yeah, I know'd. Fought fer the Stars 'n Bars myself. Rode with Pickett till we got all cut up at Gettysburg." The man's face saddened.

"I was with Ewell."

The liveryman started to hold out his hand to shake Blue's, realized his mistake, and hurriedly put his hand to his side. Blue grinned, swung the saddle to the ground, and held out his own. The man shook Blue's hand warmly. The man's name was Abe Jennings and he had worked at the livery for two years.

"Always glad to meet a fella Rebel," Jennings said, pulling on the straps of his overalls.

"Me too," Blue said. "I came to buy a horse. If you've got a good one for sale. Riding back to Wilkon. A gelding."

"You betcha. Got a couple ya'd like. That buckskin ri't back thar. Fourth stall. You kin have 'im fer . . . say twenty." He pointed toward the stall. "Or I've got this bay. Ov'r hyar. I let ya have 'im fer the same price. I'll throw in the head leather. Unless ya got some elsewhar. Got a few more out in the corral out back. These are my bestest though."

"Got a bridle. I'll take a sackful of oats instead."

"Sure nuff. Say, ya ain't related to that outlaw fella, Holt Corrigan, are ya?"

"He's my brother."

Abe's face tightened and he bit his lower lip. "Whaddya say I let ya have either one o' them . . . fer ten dollars?"

"Abe, that's kind of you, but twenty each is fair."

"No sah. We gonna make it ten . . . an' two sacks o' grain. Iffen I were ten years younger I'd join 'em. By Gawd, I would."

Blue said, "Mind if I look them over."

Abe smiled and his face glowed with relief. "Ya go ri't ahead, Mistah Corrigan. Take all the time ya need, yes sah."

Blue went to the bay first and talked with the horse, running his hands along the animal's legs. The gelding stood quietly, but its ears were on alert. Thick chested, the bay looked like it could run all day. He decided on the horse without looking at the buckskin. He paused and decided to take both horses; the buckskin would carry his supplies.

"That buckskin work as a packhorse?" he asked, patting the bay on the neck.

"Sure nuff. Broke to most anythin'."

"I'll take both, Abe."

"Fine choice, Mistah Corrigan. Fine choice." The huge man licked his chapped lips and added, "Iffen ya sees yer brother, tell him Abe Jennings tolt him to ride well."

"Sure."

CHAPTER ELEVEN

As soon as he left his brother, Holt Corrigan rode to the most southern part of town, keeping mainly to the back streets, more out of habit than necessity. Few really knew what he looked like. He reined in outside a small cantina bursting with music. He'd been here several times before, but not lately. They knew he was Holt Corrigan and went by the name Sam Holton, but left him alone. Friendly, but not too friendly. He wrestled with his thoughts; Blue's words wouldn't leave him no matter how hard he tried to laugh them away.

Pulling his coat over his holstered guns, he pushed through the door. It took a moment for his eyes to adjust. The room was small and a fire in the fireplace brought warmth to the entire saloon. Holt noticed the fire was even, then saw flames dart up and disappear. That meant strangers were coming. That was logical, in a saloon. Dart-ing shadows played with each other along the walls as gas lamps did their best to chase them away. In the far corner, an old Mexican was singing and playing the guitar. His voice was smooth and clear.

A bar dominated the room. Behind it was another Mexican named Emilio who owned the cantina. He wore a multicolored shirt, was broad-shouldered, and looked tough, but his smile was warm as he recognized Holt. The rest of the cantina was filled with tables and chairs. At the bar, four vaqueros glanced Holt's way, nodded, and returned to their conversation. Holt moved to an empty table and sat down, making sure the doorway was in his direct sight.

He slid one of his revolvers from a shoulder holster onto his lap, along with the glove from his right hand. He wouldn't drop it again. A young woman with long black hair came to the table. He wanted tequila.

With a toothy smile, she returned with a bottle and a glass. He thanked her, poured himself a drink from the bottle, and dipped the glass against his coat sleeve, letting some of the tequila spread onto the cloth. Only then did he savor the smoky taste of the liquor. Having a drink poured on someone was good luck. His mind was racing. Blue's words stung even more. Was he kidding himself to think he was fighting the war? Blue had moved on and the ranch was prospering. Had he been fooling himself with his belief that he only robbed Yankee banks? Blue had jerked him hard with the news that the town bank was owned by former Confederates — one of them, a soldier he had been with at Sabine Pass.

He sipped the tequila slowly. Was Blue right? Could he give himself up and get a fair trial? What if he did and they whisked him away to some military tribunal? They'd hang him quickly, he knew.

Holt forced himself to look around the cantina. The music was lively now and smiling men at the table closest to the old man were clapping in rhythm. He started to pour himself another drink, but decided against it. What had the old samurai told him and his brothers? He chuckled to himself; Deed had listened well and learned much from Silka. More than he and Blue had.

Could he really become a rancher as Blue had said? Was his brother right about no Texas jury convicting him? He was aware that many robberies had been attributed to him, and many gunfights, when he had never been close. What if he gave himself up to the lawman in Wilkon? Blue and Deed would be close by to help him with his defense. He had never killed anyone robbing a Union bank, but had wounded Union soldiers who pursued him and had definitely robbed stages and banks that held Yankee money.

Who was he fooling? He was an outlaw, a wanted man. He missed his chance when the war was over. Why hadn't he been smart enough to rejoin his brothers and the others when he could have done it. That answer he already knew; he couldn't come to grips with the idea that the Confederacy had been beaten.

Beaten!

He had never been beaten before. Oh, he'd lost fist fights growing up, but not many, and not for long. If an older boy or boys had whipped him, he thought of nothing else until he could return the favor. He told himself, even then, that they were from a previous life and that he had been victorious over them in that earlier time. He recalled several campfires turning hollow before the news of Lee's surrender to Grant. A fire turning hollow in its middle was a sure omen of death, death to the Confederacy.

He shook his head to clear it. The young girl who had waited on him was dancing beside the old man and every man in the cantina was clapping and yelling. Everyone was happy. His mind jumped to a happy time when he was walking with Allison Johnson, holding her hand.

Three men burst through the door and Holt's hand dropped to the gun in his lap. The music continued, but the woman quit dancing. At a nod from the bartender, she hurried toward the bar. Holt knew the man in the bearskin coat. Rhey Selmon. A known gunman who worked for Agon Bordner. He guessed the other two were Bordner henchmen as well. They were looking for someone, that was obvious. The three gunmen sauntered toward the bar. The second gunman, a blond-haired man with strange eyes and a weak chin, shoved the waitress out of the way as they moved. She stumbled against the closest table and fell down. Selmon was talking quietly to the bartender.

Holt drew his second gun as he grabbed his first. "Help the little lady up. And apologize."

The music stopped and the room was silent.

Turning toward Holt, the strange-eyed gunman said, "What did you say?"

"You heard me. You were rude to that woman. Help her up. Say you're sorry."

"Or what?"

Holt smiled. "Guess. It involves lead."

The woman stood, brushed herself off, and said something in Spanish. The bartender said, "It is all right. She no hurt." He started to add "Señor Corrigan," but quickly changed it to "Holton."

Selmon turned slowly toward Holt as did the other two gunmen. "There are three of us, mister. That doesn't add up well for you."

Holt held his right-hand gun on the strange-eyed gunman and his second on Selmon. "You don't count real well, friend. Look around."

Angry, Selmon and the others glanced around the room. Every Mexican in the cantina was holding a gun on them, even the old man with the guitar.

"There'll be another time, *Mr. Holton,*" Selmon said.

"Any time you want to die."

Selmon's mouth was a snarl and he motioned for the others to follow him out. Holt watched them go, then kept his attention on the door in case they burst in again. The thought hit him that they could be looking for Blue. He decided to go after them. Grabbing the glove on his lap, he stood and tossed coins on the table. Before he could shove the chair out of the way, the bartender came over.

"Señor, they look for a James Hannah. I do not know him," the bartender said. "Do you?"

Holt remembered Blue telling him about Hannah and the attempted stage robbery.

"No, can't say that I do. Heard he's good with a gun," Holt said, returning his guns to his shoulder holsters. "But I know that fellow in the bearskin coat. Rhey Selmon. He's one mean bastard. Works for that fat man, you know, Agon Bordner."

"*Sí*. He is *mucho* bad *hombre*."

"Yeah, he's that. An' more."

Looking around to make sure no one was listening, the bartender said in a hoarse whisper, "My friend, Pedro . . . he tell me the fat one hires more guns."

"Scary."

"*Sí*."

"Thanks, amigo, I'll be back one of these days." Holt took the tequila bottle in his left hand.

"Thank you for helping Regina. That was good. You are always welcome here, Señor Holton. *Vaya con Dios*."

They shook hands and Holt left, carrying the bottle and his one glove. He didn't see Selmon or his men anywhere. He slipped the bottle into his saddlebags and mounted.

144

Riding back through town, he thought about stopping at the bank to see if Blue was right about Dave Copate being there. Just to say hi. Chuckling, he pulled up in front of the adobe building with the big BANK sign. A week ago, he was thinking about robbing it with some other ex-Confederates and returning to his apartment to hide. No one thought Samuel Holton was the notorious Holt Corrigan. He even gave some consideration to finding Blue and riding with him.

For the first time in years, Holt felt good, as if a huge weight had been lifted. Was this sensation related to a previous life? He believed that many such incidents had their birth in another time. He shook his head to eliminate the thought. What did it matter? He was here and this was now. He was a wanted man, but his face wasn't well known. Somewhere he had read that the authorities in Missouri didn't know what Jesse and Frank James looked like either.

He swung down, flipped the reins around the hitchrail, shoved the tequila bottle into his saddlebags, then removed both gloves and put them in as well. He pulled his coat to fully cover his guns. Maybe he should leave them with his horse. Finally, he decided to leave one gun in his saddlebags beside the bottle, but he hesitated about being unarmed. Sliding the second gun into his back waistband, Holt adjusted his hat, touched the cardinal feather for luck, and went into the bank.

The lobby was busy with lines in front of three tellers. A young man in a too-large business suit greeted him, asking how he could be helped. His manner was condescending and Holt figured it wasn't personal, that he was so with all customers. Holt smiled and figured the arrogant young man would pee in his pants at the first sign of a holdup, or if he knew he was talking to Holt Corrigan.

"I'd like to see Mr. Copate, if he's in."

"I see. Do you have an appointment?"

Holt tried to keep smiling. "No. I'm just an old friend from the war. If he's too busy, I'll come back."

"Your name, sir?" The young man licked his lips. "I'll check with Mr. Copate. He is a very busy man, you know."

"I'm sure he is. Tell him . . . Samuel Holton is here. We fought together at Sabine Pass."

The young man's eyes widened at hearing Sabine Pass and he spun and disappeared into an office just off the lobby.

Holt touched his hat brim as an older

couple passed him on the way out. He was uneasy; he couldn't recall being in a bank for any reason other than to rob it. He rubbed his chin. This was silly. Why would a successful businessman come out to see a man whose name he didn't know?

He turned toward the door and a familiar voice called out, "Mr. Holton, how good to see you! It's been too long."

Spinning around, Holt saw a tall man in a tailored suit smiling. They shook hands and the banker's voice dropped to a whisper, "I was sure it was you, Holt. Please don't tell me you're going to hold up my bank. I've heard all the stories." Copate said, "Never believed them for a minute."

Holt tried to smile. "You're good to see me, Dave. Don't have any reason to be here. Headed for my brothers' ranch. Up near Wilkon." He was amazed the words came out of his mouth. He glanced at a stocky businessman passing. "Going to start . . . over. Going to try anyway." Now he was really surprising himself. "Yeah, the newspapers have me in every holdup in the Southwest. I must have some damn fast horses."

Copate chuckled. "Glad to hear you're headed for your ranch, Holt. Let me know if I can help," he said, putting a hand on

Holt's shoulder. "You saved my life, you know."

"You'd have done the same for me."

Copate bit his lip. "I don't know, man. You cut down six Yankees with your rifle and handguns and took out four more with the butt of your empty rifle." He smiled. "Come into my office. We need to catch up. Got some good whiskey there." He winked.

"Uh, sure. Never been in the office of a bank president before."

Copate laughed.

A half hour later, Holt left the bank and rode north toward his apartment.

Across town, Agon Bordner was perplexed; he had expected James Hannah to accept the job to get rid of Deed Corrigan for three hundred dollars, another two hundred for eliminating the Japanese warrior, and two hundred more for the remaining Regan boy. A bonus of another two hundred would be paid when Bordner took actual control of their spread. That was an attractive offer. Anywhere.

The delay was especially puzzling since the gunman had made the trip all the way from Kansas just to talk with him about the job.

"Wonder if I should've offered more

money?"

Only a few hours ago, Hannah told him that he would consider the offer and get back to him, then left the Lone Star. None of Bordner's men had seen him around town since then. He wasn't used to having a hired gun ask for more time to consider his offer. He decided that he would go as high as four hundred for Deed, three hundred for the Oriental — and leave the killing of the boy to Rhey Selmon.

Coatless with his vest unbuttoned, he stormed about his mansion's second-story library, swearing and waving his massive arms. A cold cigar lay forgotten on the edge of the walnut desk. Next to it was an untouched cup of coffee and a plate of donuts. His coat and hat lay on the desk chair. He thought better with them off — and by himself.

"Maybe he's afraid of Deed Corrigan," Bordner said to himself. "Or maybe he's made friends with his brother. Willard said that was Blue Corrigan with him . . . and a young woman." He didn't believe the statement, but it was always smart to state the worst possible scenario and work from there. It kept him from being surprised.

On a hunch, he had sent Rhey Selmon to check on the possibility of friendship be-

tween James Hannah and Blue Corrigan
with the stage-line district agent; his top
gunman had returned saying a friendship
was likely, that it was Hannah and Blue who
stopped the holdup — and it was Hannah
and Deed Corrigan who earlier stopped a
real Comanche attack on the coach. Un-
asked, the district agent had also told him
proudly that the stage-line had paid them
bonuses for their efforts. Rhey said he
would look for Hannah around town.

With Rhey's report whirling through his
mind, the fat businessman walked over to
the elongated window overlooking the
street. He glanced back at the crumpled
telegram on his desk from Willard Hixon,
president of the Wilkon Bank and one of his
New Mexico gang. The message informed
him that two Texas Rangers were in town to
investigate the Regan murders and the Bar
3 takeover. Hixon would handle the situation without any problem, Bordner was
convinced of that. Neither the county sheriff
nor the Wilkon marshal would be a factor.
After all, the only witness was a six-year-old
boy. But it reminded him that he needed to
meet with the county sheriff and see if an
understanding could be struck. His thoughts
wandered to the idea of Macy Shields taking over as the town's marshal. Sear Geor-

gian would assist him, but not wear a badge. That would be too great a stretch. He chuckled at the thought.

"What could that boy say?" Bordner rubbed his double chin. "The worst, that it was white men. Not Comanches. So what? That could describe Comancheros." He licked his rubbery lips. "There's absolutely nothing tied to me. I'm just a businessman who happened to be in position to profit from someone else's misfortune. Happens all the time." He chuckled, remembered his cigar, and returned to it, relighting the black cheroot with a match from his vest pocket.

Clenching his fists, he stepped away from the desk, puffing vigorously on the cigar, and acknowledged that he was worried that he hadn't heard from Hannah. A fleeting thought passed through his mind: what if Hannah had decided to go to work for the Corrigans?

"Couldn't be. Couldn't be. They don't have that kind of money in the first place." His heavy jowls jiggled as he paced. Sweat gathered on his shirt in places where it touched his skin. The only reason they were eating together was the coincidence of their traveling together. That's all. His mind wandered to the other Corrigan brother, the outlaw. Was there some way he was involved and Hannah didn't want to deal with him as well? The boys said Holt Corrigan was an outcast from the others and didn't have anything to do with them or the ranch. Still —

A knock on the closed library door brought a hard response from Bordner.

"Whaddya want?"

"I's be . . . sorry, suh," a gray-haired black butler stammered, bowing slightly. "Mistah Hannah, he be hyar. He say ya tolt him to come. Yessuh, that's what he say."

Bordner's eyes flashed, and for a moment, he looked like an attacking wolverine; then his face lightened. "Uh, sure. Sure, Adam. Send him in" — he looked over at the desk — "bring some fresh coffee. For both of us." He waved his arms. "No. Bring whiskey. My best. And two glasses."

"Yessuh."

Buttoning his vest, Bordner refocused his mind.

After leaving his buckskin horse at the livery, Holt walked to his apartment, unsure of what he should do next. His statement about returning to his brothers' ranch had come without any conscious decision. It sounded good at the time. But now it seemed like a silly idea. He was an outlaw.

152

His simple room seemed even smaller and lonelier than before. A bed and a scratched dresser with a washbasin and pitcher were the only items in the room, except for a tiny closest where he kept his extra clothes, ammunition, and several guns. In one pair of pants was a handkerchief that had belonged to their mother. And in another pocket was a piece of a Confederate flag. Usually he carried them. Probably the reason he saw Blue was the fact he hadn't been carrying either.

Holding the bottle of tequila in both hands, he stood in the center of the room and shook his head. What a crummy way to live. He knew most outlaws spent their lives in similar or worse conditions. Always running. Always hiding. After taking a long drink from the bottle, he sat down on the edge of the bed and began his daily exercise of cleaning his two handguns and the rifle from his saddle sleeve. The ritual was precise, ending with him touching each gun with the cardinal feather from his hat. The tequila bottle sat on the floor near his boots. His conversation with David Copate bubbled in his mind; Copate was enthusiastic and positive. Why couldn't he be that way? Holt returned the feather to his hat, reached down, retrieved the bottle, and drank.

Thoughts of all kinds spun through his head as he oiled the weapons. Images of the war . . . earlier times with his brothers and Silka. Sweet moments with Allison Johnson, once when they peeled an apple and threw the peelings over her head. The peelings were to land in the shape of the first letter of the name of their first child. It was sort of an *S*. The awful moment when he got her letter of good-bye and the madness afterward when he tried to get killed by rushing an entrenched Yankee patrol and ended up killing them all. The rush of reality afterward that he had lived before, perhaps many times. Then the completeness of defeat and the recollection of spiritual signs he had missed that the Confederacy was doomed. The one-man attacks he made on Union camps. How could anyone accept the fact that the South had lost? He drank some more and laid down on the bed with his clothes on. He rarely slept any other way, and he rarely slept well. To sleep well was to die.

Sleep came slowly and brought fierce nightmares of pumas, Roman gladiators and knights, fires and apple peelings . . . and Allison.

CHAPTER TWELVE

Time passed quickly for Deed Corrigan. Caleb Corrigan's body was buried under a small cherry tree at the north edge of the station area; the family had planted the slender tree three years earlier. The dead Comanches were dragged away, and that night warriors returned to take away the bodies. There had been no Indian problems since. Nor was there any sign of them.

The two dead passengers were buried on the north side of the cottonwoods and identified with simple wooden head markers. Before driving away, Tade Balkins had promised to have the district agent wire their relatives about the sad event, if any could be located. Atlee planned on preserving selected fruits and vegetables in jars for the winter. A nearby farmer was happy to sell them fresh corn, beans, cucumbers, and tomatoes.

Stages came and went regularly. Passengers of all sorts stopped at the station and enjoyed Atlee's food. Cattlemen and farmers, miners and hunters, drummers and peddlers, newspapermen and actors, gamblers and gunmen, prostitutes and soldiers, men and women from everywhere. The routine of the stagecoach operation was harder and more demanding than Deed had realized. Monday, Wednesday, and Friday departures from each end of the Hays City–Santa Fe run were operated with the same running time of four and a half days. The stage-line ran twenty-four hours a day, every day, regardless of weather. The Barlow and Sanderson Company was the line's owner, but they sublet contracts running from Santa Fe to El Paso and Tucson to Sand and Cook's Stage-Line, headquartered in El Paso.

All in all, the entire line covered 2,000 miles, using 1,200 animals and more than 300 regular employees. About every fifteen miles or so was a relay station waiting with fresh horses. Home stations were those with food and overnight lodging for the passengers. The Forsyths had hoped to become such a location. Of course, Wells Fargo controlled everything involving the mail, west and north. And mail delivery was always the primary objective; passengers were an afterthought.

No railroad existed west of Fort Worth, which is why the relay stations continued to be important, especially the Forsyth station since it had such a good name. Elsewhere in Texas, independent railroad companies were stretching their wings. The days of the stagecoach and relay stations as the king of transportation were ending, but feeder lines like this one continued to profit.

Billy Montez and Caleb Forsyth had done an excellent job of managing the horses, keeping them well fed and healthy, and maintaining the harnesses in top shape. Little things eventually made big differences. Deed's mentor, Silka, the former samurai, had taught him that, and the stage operation was clear testimony to that fact. Harnesses were checked each night and whatever horses were at the station were examined for leg problems, sore backs, or broken horseshoes. From the beginning, Caleb had insisted on having an extra team of horses on hand at all times, in addition to the team being readied for the next stage. Billy had gone to a neighbor and secured horses to replace the ones killed in the raid, with the promise that the neighbor would be paid as soon as the next stage came with the money.

Work with the horses was constant. Since a horse's stomach was small, it needed to eat a lot of small meals during each day, usually four. This was complicated by the daily arrival and departure of a team of horses. The order for feeding was important: water first, then hay, and lastly, grain. Always in small rations. And never any water after grain. Water expanded the grain and brought on colic. Billy was a stickler when it came to the quality of hay, using only good green, clean and bright. Usually timothy. Nothing dirty or dusty — and definitely not moldy. Mold was poisonous and could kill a horse. Mucking out the stalls was a daily task.

Feeding was just part of the work. All of the animals had their hooves picked daily — to remove packed manure, dirt, and small rocks — and checked for loose or cracked horseshoes, as well as stone bruises. Billy liked to say, "No foot. No mistah." All of the horses were brushed and combed. Deed told himself they would start implementing the same kind of procedures at the ranch.

Deed and Billy had become a good team handling the horses, and Atlee worked long hours, making certain incoming passengers were well fed and the setting was bright and cheery. Olivia Beinrigt had become an excellent help inside as well; she and her husband slept in the bunks set up for employees, but rarely used. They had moved the beds into a corner and put up a bedsheet to provide privacy. Hermann Beinrigt was slowly recovering. Benjamin spent most of his time helping his mother and Olivia; Deed saw him only during meals and figured that was best. The boy was grieving and rarely spoke to him or anyone, except his mother.

Atlee never talked of losing her husband, but Deed heard her sobbing late one night when he was unable to sleep and was walking past the cabin to make certain she and her kids were okay. The next day, he asked if she needed to talk and her response was negative, swift, and brittle. He never asked again. Blue would be returning from El Paso soon with their new stallion, and they would ride to their ranch together. He wasn't sure how he felt about that.

Midday brought two hard-looking riders headed from the direction of Wilkon. Deed told Billy to get his shotgun and stay out of sight, but close by. The one-eyed Mexican laid the hammer beside his anvil and hurried the horse he was shoeing into the barn. Deed was positive he didn't know the men.

Something about their easy lope in the open made him think these weren't outlaws, but he couldn't be certain in this wild land. A survey of the surrounding land convinced him they were alone.

He walked over to the corral and picked up the Spencer carbine resting there along with a box of reloading tubes. He had kept both handy since the Comanche attack. Cocking the big gun, he slid into the shadows. No sense in making a target of himself until he knew who they were.

"There are only two, Billy. No others behind," Deed whispered.

"*Sí.* That is 'nuff."

"Yeah."

Even at this distance, Deed was impressed with the appearance of their horses. Powerfully built and long legged, they were animals made for speed and endurance. Definitely not ranch horses; the kind outlaws rode — or lawmen. The advancing riders' hands were empty, except for the reins they held. He was now sure they were alone and not looking for trouble.

At the outskirts of the station area, the two men reined up near the cottonwoods. One of them reached into his coat pocket, produced a badge, and pinned it on his vest. The stouter of the two did the same. Rangers, Deed thought. Texas Rangers.

Deed stepped out of the shadows and hailed their arrival.

"Afternoon, men. How can we help you?"

His movement into the sunlight surprised them. Their first reactions were movements toward their holstered guns. Seeing the cocked Spencer in Deed's hands stopped that idea before it was too late. They walked their horses closer and stopped a few yards away.

"Howdy. We're Rangers," the lawman in front announced, moving his hands slowly to his saddle horn.

"I can see that by your badges. Welcome. Climb down and water your horses."

"Many thanks," he said, swinging easily from the saddle.

Both lawmen wore knee-length boots, heavy Mexican-roweled spurs, buttoned vests, and long black trail coats. Double-rowed cartridge belts carried a six-gun and a Bowie knife, holstered on the left side with the gun butt forward. Even their thick mustaches looked alike. The only differences between them were their heights and their hats. The man who had spoken was taller and wore a flat-brimmed hat that the wind had permanently pushed up in front. The shorter, stockier lawman wore a weathered hat with a tripointed crown and wide brims curled up on the sides and gathered in the front.

The taller Ranger took off his hat and swatted at the trail dust clinging to his coat and clothes.

"Just came from Wilkon." He squinted and crow's feet rushed into the corners of his gray eyes. "You look familiar, mister. Do we know you?"

Uncocking his carbine, Deed chuckled. "Now that's a question a fellow doesn't want to hear from a lawman. I'm Deed Corrigan."

The second Ranger, now dismounted as well, stomped his heavy boots making the spurs sing and said, "Thought so. Holt's your brother, right?"

"He is."

"Easy now, I wasn't pushing. My own brother rode owlhoot for three years."

"Sorry to hear it. Haven't seen Holt since the war."

"We talked with your wife. Bina, right?" He pulled the glove off his right hand and held it out.

"No, that's my brother's wife, Bina. Blue's in El Paso on business."

"Oh sure. She told us you were helping here till things got settled from the Indian attack." He nodded toward the station. "I'm Hendel Rice. And this here long-legged galoot is Revel Williams. We're part of Captain Waters's company."

"Glad to meet both of you." Deed shook hands with the two Rangers and called out for Billy. The Mexican eased from the barn door, laid his shotgun against its weathered side, and walked over. Deed introduced him to the Rangers.

"You boys look like you were expecting trouble," Revel Williams said and motioned toward Billy's shotgun and Deed's Spencer.

"Better safe than sorry, the saying goes." Deed patted Billy on his shoulder. "Had a bad time with Comanches a week back. Killed the station manager and two passengers."

"You didn't think we were Indians, did you?" Revel asked with a hint of humor in his eyes.

"No, but men riding horses like these aren't cowhands or farmers." Deed rubbed the nose of the closest bay.

The Rangers explained they had come to the region because of the Bar 3 massacre, Agon Bordner taking control of the ranch because of the overdue loan, and the killings of the two other ranch families.

"All the killings Comanches?" Deed

glanced at Billy.

"Appears so."

"You're sure?" Deed rubbed his chin with his left hand; his right held his carbine at his side.

"Now look. We don't like this either, but there's nothing illegal we can see. Nothing we can prove anyway. Agon Bordner wasn't even close by. Lives in El Paso, you know, living grand. We've seen his place." Rice looked Deed in the eyes. "Has a good reputation there. Strong churchgoing fella. Hear he's generous to the church an' all."

Deed studied both men. They were typical Rangers. Hard but fair. Naturally inclined to be suspicious.

From the station doorway, Atlee appeared. "Deed? Do we have visitors?"

He turned toward her, smiling. "Yes, Mrs. Forsyth. Rangers. They were investigating trouble nearby." He hadn't told her about the Bar 3.

A frown slid across her face, but was followed by a warm smile. "Please tell them to come in for coffee and something to eat. You and Billy, too."

Cooper came to the door, wagging his tail.

"Yes, boss." He had deliberately not used her first name — and called her boss — wanting to reinforce the fact she was in charge. Turning back to the Rangers, he said, "I'd suggest you take her up on that. Best food anywhere around."

"Heard that. You don't have to ask me twice." Rice chuckled. "Neither one o' us are much for trail cookin'. We get by, but it's nothin' to crow about."

Deed pushed his hat back on his forehead. "We had heard that the bank was holding a big loan. How about their trail-drive money? That was a big herd they brought in. At least three thousand head. Saw it myself when we were headed back. I was a week or so ahead with our herd but was still in town."

"The bank has no record of any deposit," Williams responded. "No one's found any money at the ranch either."

"What about the money Bordner paid for those two small ranches?"

"Don't know if anybody's said anything about it," Williams said. "Guess they had it with them when the Indians hit 'em."

"Comanches don't take money."

"No, I reckon they don't."

Without speaking, Billy Montez took the reins of their horses and led them away while Deed walked with the Rangers towards the station door. Atlee and Cooper had already disappeared inside.

"Sometimes bad things happen to good

folks," Rice observed, watching Billy take the horses to the big watering trough. "It's going to take a few years to get rid of the Comanches, but we'll get it done."

"I wasn't talking about Comanches."

Changing the subject, Williams asked Deed what had happened here a week ago. Deed told them about the Comanche attack, about Caleb Forsyth and two passengers being killed, and that Mrs. Forsyth had assumed the responsibilities of running the station. The Rangers were surprised to hear a woman was in charge, but Deed assured them that she was managing quite well and he was only helping out until she could hire someone permanent.

"You mentioned meeting my brother's wife," Deed said and pulled his hat back down on his forehead as he went ahead up the steps and opened the door. Cooper came out and waited in the doorway to greet everyone.

"Yeah, and the Regan kid," Williams added. "A hard-lookin' Chinese fella was there, too. She said he was a longtime family friend."

"Japanese. He is. The best. Nakashima Silka. He's also our partner." Deed leaned over to pet Cooper.

"We had heard about the kid's survival. In

Wilkon, folks are pretty upset about what's happened," Williams said, studying the station as they approached. "The boy told us it wasn't Indians. It was white men." He bit his upper lip beneath his mustache. "But he was real scared and didn't see much. Hid in a cooling shack. Gosh, he's only six, you know."

"Yeah, I know. My brother and some friends found him."

"As far as we can tell, this Bordner fella just happened to be in the right place at the right time to pick up the ranch. It adds to the other two he just bought," Rice added as stepped onto the front porch of the station.

"Again, there's nothing wrong with the deal. Just good business. Best we can tell he was only taking advantage of a bad situation, one that wasn't his doing." Williams waved his arms as they reached the porch. "County sheriff agrees. So did the Wilkon marshal."

Deed didn't respond, but watched Cooper waiting at the door.

Removing his second glove, Williams paused over a large bowl of water resting on the porch railing, and laid both gloves beside it. "Could've been Comancheros riding with the redskins, you know." He washed his hands and doused his face, then dried himself with the clean towel resting nearby.

After tying the Rangers' horses to the corral rail, Billy hurried and caught up with them as Rice took his turn washing up. Elizabeth came rushing through the door and held up her arms for Deed to hold her, which he was happy to do. Cooper changed his mind about going inside and spun around to be next to the two of them.

"I got flowers from our garden," she said, smiling into his face. "You'll see them when you come in."

"Well, I can hardly wait."

He introduced her to the Rangers and Elizabeth greeted them enthusiastically and asked if they had met Cooper. Both Rangers smiled and said they hadn't had the pleasure.

"This is Cooper. Cooper Forsyth," she said and motioned toward the dog.

"Glad to know you, Cooper," Rice responded and doffed his hat in an exaggerated motion.

Elizabeth giggled.

Williams also tipped his hat and knelt to scratch Cooper's head.

Inside Atlee greeted the Rangers warmly and directed them to the table, covered with a red-and-white checkered tablecloth. What remained of the flowers Elizabeth picked from the Forsyth garden had been gathered into a bright bouquet in the center. Behind the sheet, Hermann Beinrigt was sleeping soundly on the farthest cot. Even Deed was impressed with the appearance of the entire room. Cooper took a position near the fireplace, stretched out comfortably to watch everything. The planked floor had been swept clean and the station looked cheery.

To himself, Deed thought the coach line would be foolish not to let her run the station; Atlee Forsyth was the consummate host. He put Elizabeth in the chair beside him and sat down. She smiled at him and asked if all the horses were well. He assured her they were.

Smiling, Atlee brought in a plate piled high with thick beef sandwiches; Olivia brought bowls of pickles, baked beans, and scalloped corn. Both women quickly filled the men's coffee cups and returned to the kitchen. Minutes later, Atlee and Olivia joined them with plates of their own. Atlee was eager for conversation of happenings outside of her world. So was Olivia. Rangers Williams and Rice were happy to oblige with stories from their travels throughout Texas.

Benjamin wandered into the room, looking sad, but determined to find out if the Rangers were here to take them away from the station. Atlee introduced him and he became defensive.

"If you had been here a week ago, my pa wouldn't have been killed," he declared.

"That's enough, Benjamin. These men have many responsibilities. Not just this corner of Texas," Atlee snapped.

Benjamin folded his arms. Elizabeth began to cry, and Deed leaned over to whisper to her. She wiped her eyes and sat up straight. Williams responded that he was sorry about what had happened and added that a ranch west of the station had been raided two months ago and everyone on it had been killed; two other families had been killed leaving the area; and that they were sorry not to have been able to get to the station in time to save Benjamin's father.

"Sounds like you messed up some more," Benjamin said and marched out the door, slamming it hard.

Flushed with embarrassment, Atlee said, "I'm so sorry, gentlemen. My son has taken the loss of his father very hard. But that is no excuse for such rudeness."

Williams finished his coffee. "Think nothing of it, Mrs. Forsyth. We wish we'd been here, too. Now we need to get riding. Our captain is expecting us in Waco."

"Certainly, gentlemen. It was my honor to serve you."

CHAPTER THIRTEEN

Nightfall found Atlee Forsyth alone in her bedroom. Everything was readied for the stage tomorrow morning. Having Olivia was proving a special advantage. Every bone in the young woman's body ached from the hard days of work, labor that never seemed to end, only to begin again the next morning.

She whimpered and then chastised herself for feeling sorry for herself, but this was actually the hardest part of the day. Being alone at night. Alone with her memories. She and Caleb had planned to eventually start a hotel of their own, probably in Wilkon. Now that was gone, along with his warmth and love.

Beside her bed was a narrow walnut table Caleb had made. An opened Bible lay across its top. Next to the good book was a flickering gas lamp and a pad of paper and pencil. Every day since his death she had made a list of the things that needed to be done the next day. Tomorrow. That was what had kept her going. Tomorrow. She could hear her children sleeping in the other room. Just barely, but she could hear them.

Benjamin was struggling with the loss of his father; Elizabeth, however, seemed content, especially when Deed was around her. After the Rangers left, she asked Deed what he had said to Elizabeth to stop her crying and he said he told the little girl that her mother needed her to be strong and not cry. Atlee smiled. Elizabeth would miss Deed greatly when he returned to his ranch. At her questioning, he had also told her about the Bar 3 massacre, the curious ownership that followed, the purchase of two other small ranches, and the killing of the two families involved. She hadn't asked any follow-up questions and he hadn't elaborated.

Raindrops popped along the roof, the vanguard of the expected rain. Good, she thought, that will help knock down the dust. Atlee stared into the darkness toward her dresser and imagined a film of dust on its top, just as there was dust seemingly everywhere no matter how hard, and often, she and Olivia cleaned.

She needed to go into Wilkon for supplies

and to hire a man to replace Deed. What would she have done without him? Her mind raced, thinking about his steadfastness, his courage — and his caring. His warm smile came to her mind and she shook her head to rid its appearance. She had heard the stories of his fighting skill. In the West, such tales traveled fast. There were stories about the third Corrigan brother, Holt, but they were darker and it didn't seem, to her, like the man could be related to Deed at all. Seeing him, hearing him, being around him had made her feel secure. She didn't want to admit that, even to herself.

"Forgive me, Caleb. I am so lonely. So lonely," she muttered and a single tear dribbled down her cheek.

Billy had told her about Deed — and James Hannah — fighting and destroying the will of the war party attacking the stage, as well as killing several warriors while she was also fighting and watching her husband die. That awful day was a dull ache to her. Billy said both were quick with a gun — dangerous men. He smiled when he said it.

Atlee and Caleb had come here from eastern Texas after two years of drought had forced them from their farm. Just as drought had brought the Beinrigts to the stage station. She had been mulling over the idea of asking them to stay; Hermann might be a good fit to work with Billy. Then she wouldn't need to hire someone she didn't know. Olivia had become an excellent help in the kitchen and with serving the passengers. It wouldn't be long before Hermann would be up and around. She decided to talk with them about it tomorrow. They could build a room onto the cottage or section off the station for them to live in.

Tomorrow.

There was no choice but to make the station the best on the route, to make it impossible to replace her. Elizabeth and Benjamin depended on her success, even though they didn't realize it.

"Caleb, I miss you so much." Her eyes crinkled and more tears came. She was powerless to stop them. For minutes, the sobbing consumed her, taking all of her energy, all of her will.

Finally, with a cough, she stopped crying. It was time to plan, not to feel sorry for herself. Her father had always told her that thinking was what separated man from animals. The ability to evaluate situations before acting. To look for the best option before one chose. She gathered her small pad of paper and pencil. Her list of needed supplies took only a few minutes to prepare. When in town, she would also explore a possible replacement for Deed. Surely there were good men looking for steady work, if her idea about the Beinrigts didn't pan out.

Deed Corrigan. What a mysterious man. In Western parlance, he would be considered a "bad man" she was certain. Not an outlaw, rather a bad man to mess with. But he had his own concerns; the Corrigan ranch needed him as much as she did. His face came again into her mind. Smiling. Always smiling. She shook her head to make the image leave. She had no business thinking of him in that way. Her husband was barely cold in the ground. She shook her head even more strongly and took a deep breath.

In thinking about the other killings, it was clear he didn't think Comanches were to blame for the ranch being attacked or the families wiped out. From his way of talking, it seemed he believed a rich man in El Paso was behind the atrocities. She shuddered at the thought. Surely Deed had to be wrong. How could anyone be so cold to want wealth that way?

Rain was coming harder now, bringing thunder and lightning. She heard footsteps and knew the noise had awakened her children and Cooper. Benjamin wouldn't want to admit it, but he would like to sleep in her bed as much as Elizabeth.

Slipping from the covers, she grabbed the gas lamp and met them in the doorway. "What do you say we all sleep together tonight? It's a good rainy night for that," she offered warmly.

Cooper barked joyfully and both children laughed.

Across the open yard, Deed listened to the pounding rain in the comfort of his blankets in the tack room. Billy Sanchez was asleep in the tiny room built for him at the south end of the barn. All of the horses were in the barn and safe. His mind wandered from the horses, to the Corrigan ranch, to Atlee. He had no business thinking of her; she was a grieving widow. Yet he couldn't get her face out of his thoughts. At least, not for long. Thoughts of her would sneak into his consciousness when he least expected it. Foolish, he told himself. And wrong.

As soon as Blue returned from El Paso, they would leave for their ranch. He wasn't worried about Agon Bordner coming for their land — not yet anyway — even with its fine valleys and excellent water. But it was wise to plan for that attempt. Acquiring the region's biggest ranch would take time to fully control. And another ranch attacked right now would draw serious attention from the Rangers. They were already suspicious. Besides, their ranch was small compared to either the Bar 3 or the Lazy S, although much bigger than the two small ranches Bordner had also acquired.

Caleb Forsyth, or someone, had built the relay station and the barn well; there were a few leaks here and there in the barn but they were tiny. The tack room held all of the harnesses on wooden pegs, better than nails because they didn't rust. Each horse's stall had a manger for feed and a rack built underneath for hay. The rack was built low to keep dust out of the horse's eyes. Smart, he thought.

As he settled into sleep again, a different sound caught his ears. Slight. Muffled. Then a soft whinny. It was probably nothing. Just one of the horse's acting up.

No. His mind locked on to the issue.

Someone was trying to steal the horses!

He spun from his bed with his revolver in hand, ignoring his boots. Barefooted, he eased from the tack room with his cartridge belt slung over his shoulder and shoved the second Remington usually holstered there into his waistband. His eyes adapted quickly to the darkness and he saw definite movement at the stables. Four Comanches had returned to steal the stagecoach horses. It would be the ultimate show of bravery and daring to prove the strength of their war medicine by coming back to the station where so many of their war party had died. A rainy night was perfect they had decided; no white people would be awake or listening.

Like tanned ghosts, the warriors moved silently to open the stalls and lead out the horses. Capturing such fine animals would, indeed, bring worthy praise from their fellow tribesmen. A big bay was agitated by the Indians and reared.

Shooting now was too risky. Deed couldn't be certain where a horse's head ended and a Comanche began. He must get closer. One warrior swung bareback onto a big sorrel and directed the animal toward the opened barn door. Heavy rain glistened from the opening. If Deed waited any longer, the warrior would vanish into the wet night with the treasured horse. He guessed the remaining warriors intended to make the horses run from the barn and that this mounted warrior was the leader of the horse-stealing party.

In one motion, he cocked the Remington and fired. Three times. The continuous roar was a bomb in the barn. The warrior tumbled from the horse and the animal reared, but someone slid in front of the frightened animal, blocking the door, then slamming it shut again. Deed heard whispered Spanish and the horse settled where it stood, stomping its hooves and snorting. From that silhouette came the unforgiving boom-boom of a shotgun and a second warrior collapsed as he ran toward the barn door. In the brief flash, Deed saw what he already knew; Billy was there, blocking the way.

From the closest stall, a painted warrior hurled himself at Deed, swinging his tomahawk. Deed fired and missed. The war club slammed against the top of his hand and drove the gun from him. Deed's right hand was numbed and bleeding from the glancing blow. Instead of reaching for the second revolver in his waistband, Deed jammed his open hand against the warrior's chin. A follow-up left-leg power kick drove into the Comanche's stomach and a third blow, again with his left hand, was a vicious open-handed chop against the Comanche's neck that stopped the warrior completely. Deed shook his right hand, trying to regain feeling.

Leaving the horse he was leading from a middle stall, a fourth warrior came at Deed, screaming a fierce war cry that filled the barn. Deed blocked the downward thrust of his tomahawk with his left hand raised against the warrior's arm. In one fluid motion, Deed delivered an open-handed smack into the Indian's throat with his injured right hand. As the warrior gasped for breath, Deed drew his second revolver from his waistband with his left hand. He rammed his gun into the warrior's stomach and fired.

In minutes, it was over.

Deed was drenched in nervous sweat and his right hand had no feeling and a cut along the back of his hand brought fingers of blood across it.

"Billy? You all right? That's the last of them, I think, but we'd better check."

"*Sí*. And you, amigo?"

"Yeah. Let's check the stalls and get these horses settled down. We were lucky."

"*Sí*. That is so."

Lights were on in the Forsyth cottage and the station itself. From the door way of the cottage, Atlee peered into the rain and yelled, "Deed . . . Billy? Are you all right? What's happening?"

Olivia was at the doorway of the station, holding a lamp in her left hand and a pistol in the other. In a handful of yelled sentences, Deed explained the attempted raid and that all was well. Olivia invited everyone to come to the station while she put on coffee and warmed up some biscuits. Even in the rain, it sounded good to all of them.

"Put your hand in de water. Leave it there, amigo," Billy said. "I will get the hosses back into their places."

"Thanks. Good idea." Deed went to a water bucket near the tack room and put his right hand into the cooling liquid. The wound had stopped bleeding, but the numbness remained.

Soon a celebration of sorts took over the night, although nearly everyone was soaked. Deed and Billy, Atlee and her two children and Cooper gathered around the reenergized fireplace. Hermann was up and had stoked the fire into compliance. Atlee was shocked to see Deed was wounded as Billy recounted with some awe in his voice how the young gunfighter had bested three of the attackers. Olivia put on a pan of water to boil for cleaning the wound.

Deed insisted that the wound was not serious, but neither woman paid any attention to his protestations.

CHAPTER FOURTEEN

"Señor Deed, it is time to get de horses ready," Billy Montez announced, coming out of the barn. Last night's attempted horse stealing was forgotten for the moment. The four dead Comanches had been dragged out of sight, left for their fellow tribesmen to retrieve, if they dared.

Deed chuckled to himself. He didn't need reminding by the Mexican who felt it was his duty to tell him every time a stage was coming. This coach would be arriving from the north. They gathered a fresh team with Billy coaxing them in Spanish. Since the raid that killed his father, Benjamin hadn't helped with the horses, but Cooper had and was bouncing alongside Deed.

"Billy, that back bay's got something wrong with his leg." Deed pointed with his left hand; his right was painfully sore and badly bruised. "Back right." He had taken to carrying a revolver in his waistband for left-hand use.

"*Sí*. We must check it."

An examination showed the animal was nursing a strained leg muscle. It wasn't serious, but running with the team now could lead to something permanent. The limping horse was removed from the team and replaced with another. The injury might have occurred during the failed Comanche raid on the barn, but it was impossible to know for certain.

"Waco will not like being away from his friends. Bingo will not either. But it must be so," Billy said. Waco was the name he called the limping horse and Bingo was the name of the replacement. He had a pet name for every horse that came through the station. Deed did his best to remember them; although he was certain the names changed occasionally.

"Kinda like people, I guess," Deed said, leading the injured horse away.

"*Sí*. Liniment is inside."

"Good."

Soon, a bearded driver with a cocky attitude brought the coach into the station with a hard gallop as all drivers liked to do. A huge wad of tobacco in his mouth made it difficult for him to speak without shifting it to the side of his mouth.

"Whoa, you fleabags! Whoa!"

As if on cue, the glistening horses stutter-stepped to a stop. The coach's wheels groaned as he slammed on the brake and reined hard. Unlike Tade Balkins, Pip Mateau was a scruffy-looking teamster in a soiled leather jacket with long, matted fringe and a bowler hat.

Pip spat a thick, brown stream and hollered, "Ever'body out. Good chow. Hot coffee waitin'. Outhouses in the back. Will be a' goin' again in thirty minutes. Not thirty-five. Thirty."

He wrapped the reins around the brake and eased down, greeting Billy warmly. "Hey, Billy, you ol' Mex, this new team any good?" He waved his arms at the new horses and spat again. "I'm givin' ya a ri't smart, good bunch. You betcha. Don't let Balkins have em, ya hear."

Billy grinned and hollered back something in Spanish. Deed picked up several choice swearwords, all delivered in good-natured fun.

"Hey, who's this hombre packin' the six-gun — an' the busted-up hand?" Pip Mateau stopped his advance as passengers filed out, stretching their arms, behind him.

"*Sí*. This is Señor Deed Corrigan. He's helping. For a short time. *Bueno,*" Billy said.

185

Yanking off his dirty gloves, Pip held out his right hand. Deed smiled and extended his left. "My right's a bit sore." The driver switched hands and shook Deed's left heartily.

"Ain't you the fella who took down a gunman with your hands — and him pointing a six-gun at your belly? Heard that last year, I'm thinkin'. Down in Austin, it was."

"Didn't have any choice." Deed leaned down to pat Cooper.

Pip eyed him carefully and changed the subject. "Got a load of express this trip. No gold. Big load o' mail," Pip declared. "And eleven passengers." He motioned toward the two men climbing down from the coach's roof and spat, admiring the thickness of it.

Deed didn't think either man was armed.

"Can ya believe it, I've even got one o' them spirit guys on board."

Deed watched the passengers head for the station. "A spiritualist?"

"Yeah. You know, hears ghosts and makes them write stuff on magic slates . . . ring bells an' sech," Pip spat again and nearly hit his own boot. "Scary pecker, if ya ask me."

"That him?" Deed nodded toward a well-dressed man in a black broadcloth suit with a scarlet scarf around his neck.

The man's handsome face was accented

with a black goatee. His dark eyes seemed to take in everything and his smile looked like he had a secret worth laughing about. Beside the man was a woman of undeterminable age, wearing a veil attached to a triangular black hat. Her dress was also black and flowing and she carried a large purse as if it contained something sacred. The man glanced at Deed, Billy, and Pip as he strode toward the station. The woman only looked ahead.

"Yeah, that's him. Longstreet, I think. Like the Rebel general. No relation. I asked him," Pip said and rolled his neck to relieve the stiffness. "Heard him asking about Mrs. Forsyth here." He rolled the wad around in his mouth. "The word's out 'bout her dead husband, ya know. He wanted to know all 'bout it."

"Excuse me, Pip," Deed said. "Billy, can you handle the team? I'm going to make sure he doesn't bother her."

"*Sí.*"

Scratching his beard, Pip watched Deed hurry to the station. He turned to Billy. "Hear tell he's a heller with a gun — or his fists."

"*Sí.* He save many life when Comanche attack stage. He and a man name of Hannah. James Hannah." The one-eyed Mexican glanced at the fast-walking Deed. "Last night, Deed kill three Comanche who try to steal our hosses. I kill one."

Pip shook his head in admiration. "What happened to his right hand? Looks all black and blue."

"A Comanche hit him with tomahawk." Billy swallowed. "Señor Deed kill him with bare hands."

"Lordy." Pip watched Deed. "Did you say James Hannah? Everybody knows that name. He's supposed to be meaner than Hardin."

"*Sí*, it is so."

"Is this Deed feller that good, too?"

"*Sí.*"

"Damn." Pip spat a long, brown stream, admiring its strength. "Say is he any relation to that Rebel outlaw, Holt Corrigan? A bad one, I hear."

"Maybe so. He no talk of it. I no ask."

"Sure."

Deed hurried to the station, adjusting the gun in his waistband. Cooper bounded ahead of him. He wasn't particularly good with a gun left handed, but he couldn't even grip one with his right. He stepped inside, allowing the dog to enter first, and saw Longstreet talking to Atlee and Olivia as they served the other passengers. Hermann

Beinrigt had moved to the sofa and was sitting up. The spiritualist's assistant stood near Longstreet as if she were attached.

"Mrs. Forsyth, your late husband, Caleb, has been trying to reach you," Longstreet declared in a silky voice. "Have you heard any strange sounds at night? Or felt a soft breeze that shouldn't be there? That was your beloved . . . Caleb," he oozed. "I know because he has come to me . . . for help. I am Eugene Longstreet, noted spiritualist and mesmerist. Many have found spiritualism to be quite comforting in such an awful time of grief." He paused and motioned toward his assistant. "And this is Amenmeit, my assistant. She comes from Egypt and is schooled in the science of the otherworld."

Olivia appeared annoyed. Atlee's face was unreadable.

Deed stepped between the women and Longstreet. "Mister, please take a seat. Mrs. Forsyth is busy."

The look from the mesmerist was one of pure hatred. "I am sharing something personal and very important to Mrs. Forsyth. Please leave us alone."

"I can handle this, Mr. Corrigan. Is the new team ready?" Atlee's voice was stern.

Deed nodded and left, hearing Longstreet say, "Not everyone understands what it's like to lose a loved one. Or to learn that one can actually communicate with him again. I can arrange to stay over and conduct a special séance for you. My work in El Paso won't begin until next week."

Angry, Deed went outside where Pip and Billy were finishing with the harnessing of the new team. Cooper was inspecting something in the kitchen and didn't make the retreat in time to follow.

"Did that ghost hombre go at her?" Pip asked and spat.

"Said she could handle it."

Pip spat again. "Wanna bet that bastard stays over?"

"Mucho bad," Billy said.

"None of my business." Deed patted the lead horse's neck with his left hand. "You ready to go?"

"Whenever. I'd like to grab some of Mrs. Forsyth's good stew real quick," Pip said.

"Go on. I'll help Billy."

Pip nodded, spat, and headed for the station.

Inside, Longstreet continued, "Your husband wants me to tell you how proud he is of you — and of Benjamin. He misses you and —"

"Excuse me. Mr. Longstreet, isn't it? But we must take care of our guests," Atlee declared, moving past the mesmerist. "Olivia, will you begin pouring coffee please? Thank you." She turned toward Longstreet. "If you want to eat before the stage leaves, I would suggest you sit down."

Amenmeit's only response was a disgusted snort. She turned and walked out, leaving Longstreet alone with the two women.

"If it pleases you, Mrs. Forsyth, my assistant and I could sleep there." Longstreet's smile was waxen and his eyes sought hers as he pointed to the cots set aside for coach employees, now used by the Beinrigts.

Atlee stopped, holding a large bowl of biscuits. "Mr. Longstreet, I guess I need to be more clear. I have no interest whatsoever in your nonsense. You are a guest here as all passengers are. If you want to eat something, please sit down. If not, please leave."

Longstreet appeared stunned for a moment. Atlee thought he was going to burst into a rage, but he forced himself to calm.

"As you wish, I will tell your husband that you have no interest in talking to him." He made a dramatic turn toward the door, hesitating and expecting to be stopped.

"Do make sure *die Tür ist* shut ven you leave," Olivia Beinrigt growled.

Outside, Amenmeit walked up to the coach, looking for Deed. She walked over to him, standing close. "There are spirits around you. They speak of danger. You are a dangerous man, they say. Your own spirit carries something of the Orient."

"Well, good day to you, too, ma'am," Deed responded and continued checking the harness.

"I will tell the Great Longstreet that you are not one to be bothered. There is much death around you."

"Tell *Great* anything you want" — Deed leaned his outstretched hand against the coach — "but if he messes anymore with Mrs. Forsyth and her children, he's going to have to answer to me." He glared at her. "He won't like that outcome."

She blinked and stepped closer, letting her bosom brush against his extended right arm. "I was hoping we could be together tonight." She batted her thick eyelashes. "Amenmeit will make you very happy."

"You aren't worried about all those ghosts around me?" Deed grinned.

"You mock Amenmeit."

"You catch on fast," he said and stepped past her. "Excuse me, but the ghosts and I have work to do."

Her eyes flashed hatred as he brushed past.

"Billy, have you double-checked the back

boot?" Deed spun around and strode toward the rear of the coach.

"No. I have not, Señor Deed. I will."

With her hands on her hips, the dark-skinned woman snarled, "Deed Corrigan, you will die a horrible death. I can see it." A savage statement of foreign words followed.

Deed didn't respond as he double-checked the harness.

From the station, a disgruntled Longstreet appeared, walking toward the coach. Amen-meit went to him and spoke angrily, pointing and waving. The spiritualist glanced up at Deed several times. Finished with the new team and checking the coach, Deed and Billy walked toward the corral, paying no attention to either of them.

Puffing out his chest, Longstreet said something to her and headed toward Deed, now leaning against the corral. Deed watched him advance and decided he wasn't going to wait for the spiritualist to perform. He stood straight, waiting. A look of surprise popped into Longstreet's eyes as he realized this strange man was definitely not going to avoid him. He had counted on his fiery advance to make Deed go elsewhere to avoid contact.

Fifteen feet from Longstreet, Deed stepped closer and growled, "Ghost-man, this isn't one of your night shenanigans. If you want to face me, you're going to join your ghosts. Here and now. Your choice. Make it."

Longstreet shivered visibly, then turned around, shouting more loudly than necessary, "Let's get in the coach, Amenmeit. We need to get to El Paso as soon as possible."

"Good idea. More ghosts there. And gullible folks," Deed snapped, watching the mesmerist retreat.

Longstreet's strange assistant started to respond; her eyes blinked rapidly but she decided to enter the coach instead. Longstreet followed, mumbling under his breath. Behind them came the other passengers, talking among themselves about the good food.

As Deed stepped away from the corral, Blue rode into the open area on a tall bay and trailing a handsome sorrel stallion and a buckskin packhorse on lead-ropes. He was weary from his long ride from El Paso, but happy to see his brother.

"Hey, Blue, you're back," Deed yelled. "How'd it go?"

Reining up, Blue told him about the attempted holdup; Rebecca Tuttle being stood up; James Hannah's meeting with Agon Bordner; meeting briefly with Holt; and their outlaw brother's assessment of the fat man's intentions.

Deed glanced around, "So James Hannah is now working for Bordner. How about that."

"Probably, but I don't know that for a fact," Blue said, swinging slowly from his horse. His legs felt like they wouldn't support him. He stood beside the tired horse he'd been riding, leaning slightly against the animal. Beside it, the sorrel and buckskin were sweating lightly and the stallion looked ready to run. "Last time I saw Hannah, he was strolling across the restaurant to see Bordner — in a back room."

Blue patted the bay horse he had been riding and changed the subject. "How're things going here? What happened to your hand, Deed?"

In a few short sentences, Deed told his older brother how things were going at the relay station, complimenting Atlee on her attitude and determination. He briefly mentioned the raid on the horses and dismissed his hurt hand as not much.

Blue guided his three horses to the water trough with the reins and the lead-ropes in his right hand. Their conversation was interrupted by Pip Mateau, who came out of the relay station and yelled the stage was leaving. With only a nod to the two brothers, he climbed onto the driver's box, unwrapped the reins, and yelled again.

"Everyone's in, Pip," Deed assured him. "Including the ghost man . . . and his whatever."

Pip Mateau laughed, waved, and shouted a good-bye. With a vigorous spit toward his horses, the bearded driver snapped the reins and the horses began to gallop.

After the stage left, Deed walked over to the drinking sorrel and patted its back. "How is this big rascal? Did you ride him?"

"Oh yeah. Handles good. A little head-strong. Probably could run all day," Blue said, from the other side of the sorrel, "He'll be a hit with our mares."

"Reckon so. What's his name?"

"Magnuson called him Captain."

"Captain. I like it."

Blue told Deed that he had gold certificates for two hundred dollars for him from the stage-line, a reward for fighting off the Comanches. He told about Hannah's demands and his surprise that the manager had complied.

"Good, we can put that to good use at the ranch," Deed said, slapping his brother on the back. "You can buy something nice for Bina, too."

"Already did."

"All right, big brother." Deed smiled, took off his hat, and wiped his forehead with his single forearm, then returned the hat.

He suggested they take the horses to the barn for rubdowns and some oats while they talked. Billy passed them, holding a broken piece of harness and talking furiously in Spanish. Inside, Blue took off the heavy saddle and saddle blanket and began to rub the livery horse's back with his fist full of straw. The horses chewed on hay while the brothers groomed them. Deed loosened the pack on the buckskin's back and placed the canvas arrangement on the ground, using mostly his left hand, with his right only for balance. The weight was still painful. With a currycomb and brush, he started brushing the quiet horse.

"Man, that is one fine looking animal," Deed praised.

"Yeah, thought so, too. Magnuson said he's pretty gentle for a stallion," Blue said, turning away from rubbing the livery horse.

"Did you talk to the district manager . . . about here?" Deed asked as he worked.

"Yeah. Willard Epson didn't sound like a man who was comfortable with the idea of a woman station manager," Blue said, shaking his head. "I told him to keep his mind open. That this was his best station. And it wasn't because the horses were harnessed correctly. Or given good rubdowns."

"Couldn't have said it better, big brother."

"I'd expect him to make a surprise visit soon. To see for himself."

"Tell her that."

They finished cleaning the horses and left them enjoying buckets of oats. At the doorway to the station, Atlee Forsyth stepped onto the porch, hailed Blue's arrival, and invited him in.

"Had anything to eat today?" Deed asked. "This is when we usually do. After the coach leaves."

"Coffee and jerky this morning on the trail. You saw my pack, getting thin."

"Then you're ready for some good chow. Atlee's one fine cook."

"Atlee?" Blue cocked his head.

"Uh, Mrs. Forsyth. She asked to be called by her first name."

"Sure."

They took a few steps toward the house and Blue asked, "Are you going to be able to leave here now?"

Deed stared at the house for a moment before responding. "Got no choice. You and Silka are going to need help."

"Yeah. You're right," Blue said. "Does . . .

Atlee know?"

"I'm sure she's guessed. It was just supposed to be until you got back from El Paso."

As they entered the station, Billy went directly to sit down. Deed and Blue went to the smiling young woman. "Atlee, you remember my older brother, Blue."

"Of course, I do," she said and smiled. "How did the trip to El Paso go? Well, I trust."

Blue was surprised to see how fresh and happy Atlee appeared. Olivia Beinrigt was in the kitchen, humming a tune only she and her husband knew. Even Hermann Beinrigt was looking definitely improved and stood, stoking the fireplace. Cooper watched the German farmer for a few moments, then trotted over to greet the Corrigan brothers. Blue noticed that Benjamin was not around and decided not to tell her about the attempted holdup. There was no need to burden her with such news.

"It went fine, ma'am. Thanks for asking." Blue removed his hat. "I did talk with Mr. Epson for a few minutes." He added, "After Tade Balkins told him about the Indian trouble here."

"I see." Her response was cool, but not quizzical.

Folding his arms, Blue told her about the exchange, making no attempt to whitewash the district manager's remarks, but added that he thought Epson would make a surprise visit soon — and before making any judgment.

She smiled. "We're ready. Anytime."

Motioning toward the table, she changed the subject. "Please sit down, Mr. Corrigan. I'm certain you're hungry."

"It does smell mighty good. And please call me Blue. I get real tense when I hear *Mister.*" He looked over at Deed sitting down next to Billy. "Reckon I'm going to have a hard time getting my brother back to the ranch after all this good food."

"My name is Atlee. And Deed shot a deer several days ago. He and Billy skinned and dressed it. We're so lucky to have his help."

Blue glanced at Deed and winked.

Elizabeth hurried to get a chair next to Deed. As they gathered around the table, Atlee asked Deed if he would favor them by saying grace.

"Or course." He folded his hands and closed his eyes. "Dear Lord, thank you for this bountiful food set before us. Thank you for giving us one of your precious animals that we might be strengthened to serve you better. And bring your gentle hand upon all

200

of us that we might have peace. In your name we ask this . . . Amen."

Blue glanced at his younger brother and smiled. It was the first time he could remember Deed saying grace since they were youngsters. Deed smiled back.

Dishes were quickly passed and the group began to eat. Little conversation passed among them. From the kitchen, the young boy appeared. Both Blue and Deed watched him from the corner of their eyes. It was Deed who spoke first.

"Benjamin, after we eat, I'd sure like to get your opinion on one of the coach horses if you've got the time. Leg problem." He paused and added, "And I'd like you to see the new stallion my brother just bought in El Paso. He's a fine one."

Without waiting for a response, Deed turned to his brother beside him. "This young man has a real eye for horses, Blue. Learned from his pa, I reckon."

Licking his lips, Benjamin responded, "I have chores." There was no emotion in his eyes or his words.

Atlee brought a cup of coffee to her mouth and paused. "Olivia and I will do just fine, Benjamin. You go on ahead and help . . . Deed." She sipped her coffee and returned the cup to the table.

Benjamin said nothing, but sat down at the empty chair next to his mother. Atlee filled his plate without asking what he wanted.

"I'm not hungry," Benjamin declared. "You know my pa used to shoot deer for us all the time."

"I'm sure he did," Blue said.

"It's no big deal like my ma is trying to make it."

Atlee's eyes flashed. "That's enough, son. Deed has been gracious enough to help us for a few days. Till we get everything settled again."

"We don't need no help."

Deed's eyes met Blue's, then he turned toward the boy. "I'm sure you don't. Anyway, I'll be leaving with my brother in the next day or so. We've got work to do on our ranch."

The look on Atlee's face was a mixture of sadness and anger. She wiped her mouth with a napkin to hide her emotions. She intended to ask the Beinrigts to stay, but hadn't done so yet, telling herself that Hermann needed to recover more. And, therefore, she needed Deed to continue helping she had told herself.

It was Olivia who spoke first, "Herr Corrigan, you vill be missed. Much, I think. You are needed here a little longer. *Ja*."

Atlee coughed and regained her composure. "We all knew he couldn't stay long. We have been most fortunate to have . . . his help this long."

Elizabeth looked at Deed with a face that was close to tears. "Y-You c-can't go."

Placing his coffee cup back on the table, Blue studied Atlee's tortured face and knew what had to happen.

"Deed, I think you need to stay here another week or so. At least until Epson makes his inspection." He rubbed his chin. "I'll go on to the ranch."

Chapter Fifteen

Blue Corrigan rode away from the stage station, happy he had convinced his younger brother to stay. It hadn't been hard, but Deed needed a reason. A reason other than spending more time near Atlee Forsyth.

He swung the big bay past the line of cottonwoods, down a brush-guarded wash, past a whitened buffalo skull and headed toward their ranch. On a long lead-rope tied to his saddle horn, trotted the sorrel stallion and packhorse behind him. It would be good to get home to Bina and their children, five-year-old Mary Jo and three-year-old Matthew. He missed them sorely and wondered how Jeremy was adjusting.

Obviously, his brother had feelings for the young widow. And she for him. There was energy between them that they couldn't express. It was too soon, way too soon. He just hoped Deed wouldn't be hurt emotionally. Sometimes, though, that couldn't be helped with things of the heart. Maybe he should have told Deed that she needed time. A lot of it. No, Deed would have just gotten angry at the idea that he cared about her. Blue eased his horses out of the wash, across a long grassy draw, and past an undercut bank that protected the remains of an old campfire. A startled antelope bounded away, disappearing over the rolling hill.

The sky was cloudless with the beginnings of fall's crispness in the air. On patrol, an eagle flew crossing patterns high above. As Blue rode, his mind wandered to his small church and being glad to return to the pulpit. It felt right there. Not that he thought he was a gifted speaker, rather that he could offer words that would sometimes help and comfort. Words that came from God, he thought. He had been working on a return sermon based on the idea about how a person responds to receiving a few coins he or she didn't expect, as was the case with Rebecca Tuttle. How this simple blessing could be seen in many other forms of living. His mother had talked often about the need for happiness in a person's life and the ability to find it in everyday things. She thought the power of self-control was the way to true happiness. She believed that little miracles happened all the time but, for the most part, people didn't see or appreciate them. Of course, she also saw good and bad luck omens in all manner of occurrences. Holt reminded him of their mother in that respect.

Turning sharply out of the draw, he picked up the trail that led to Wilkon and, after a half mile, turned to the right, across flat grasslands toward their ranch. Passing a gentle slope that ended in a shelf of rock, his thoughts also took in the attack on the Bar 3 ranch and the murders of the Merefords and Hansons after they left. People would be on edge, worried about Comanches attacking again. From the pulpit, he should speak reassuringly about being prepared, about praying, about working together and that this awfulness would also pass. Yes, he must do that. Maybe he should tell his parishioners about the attack on the stagecoach so they would understand that he knew what he was talking about. It might sound like bragging, but Deed — and James Hannah — had saved lives.

He wasn't ready yet to pronounce that Agon Bordner was behind the tragedy. He struggled with that thought; Holt wasn't one to overstate issues, but he was the brother who saw evil everywhere, especially

Yankee evil.

Craggy sandstone hills lay ahead and to his right, a lonely caprock that had marked this trail for centuries, he guessed. The slopes didn't look high enough to hide anything, but Blue knew they could keep an entire war party out of sight until they wanted to be seen. He eased his horses down a draw flanked by brush and mesquite on both sides. Not far was a muddy stream flanked by pecan, live oak, and cottonwood trees.

Blue's mind drifted back to Agon Bordner and what he had done. It was still hard to believe the man had made the killings and takeovers occur. Both Holt and Deed were positive he had, but they were always inclined to question and challenge. Holt had been quite firm about what he heard from some of Bordner's men. It didn't sound like one of Holt's pronouncements about Yankee maliciousness.

Riding out of the draw, he forced himself to pay attention to his surroundings. He had been riding for over two hours without actually being aware of where he was going. That was a good way to ride into serious trouble, especially with the possibility of Comanches around. Ahead, the muddy creek had gotten deeper and ran smoother, parallel to the trail. He pulled his horse toward the relief and the big sorrel and buckskin followed, balking initially at the tug of the lead-ropes. The stallion didn't like being led; it wanted to lead. A small hollow had once been a buffalo wallow.

Swinging down, he led the horses to the trickling water and let the animals nuzzle its coolness. After tying the reins to a low-hanging branch and the lead-ropes to another, he squatted against a large rock to rest for a few minutes. The ride from El Paso had been long and hard.

A twinge came to the stub of Blue's left arm, as if his limb was yet there and his arm was simply aching from overuse. His mind spun away to that awful day when his Confederate cavalry successfully attacked a larger, entrenched Union force. As he had swung his sweating horse toward retreating Federal troopers, a howitzer shell exploded near him, killing his horse and tearing up his arm.

He rarely allowed himself to think of that time. It served no purpose. Even in his shell-shocked memories, he recalled Holt coming to him and yelling for a medic. He recalled Holt cursing at himself for not picking up a black feather laying on the ground and sticking it upright. Not doing so was what had caused Blue's injury. His outlaw brother had remained with him at a field hospital, returning to duty only after the threat of court-martial. A month later, General Robert E. Lee surrendered. Blue saw Holt only briefly, trying to get him to return to their ranch with him. Soon stories of Holt Corrigan were popping up in Texas, about bank and stagecoach robberies, even Union paymaster wagons.

He shuddered and returned to the present, but only momentarily as his thoughts spun to his younger brother. Silka had taught Deed how to deal with an enemy who puts a gun to his ribs, a different situation than when a gun is presented to one's back. In one split-second motion, Deed learned to pivot to his left, wrapping the enemy's right wrist with his left arm, and smashing his elbow into the man's face. Keeping control of the man's wrist, Deed would then grab the top of the gun barrel and push the gun away from his own body. Silka liked to end this movement with a grab of the man's throat or by driving one's fist into the attacker's chest. So did Deed.

Silka's teaching had been thorough. Deed could handle any kind of attack, from a headlock to an attempted hip throw, from a choke hold from behind to an overhead club attack. From a gun pointed at him to a bear hug. From a knife attack to a well-thrown haymaker. All moves and their responses were second nature to Deed. The former samurai's fighting techniques were difficult to master, but Deed had been driven to be as good as his teacher and friend.

Possibly, it was because he was the youngest of three brothers. Possibly it was another reason. Regardless, Deed Corrigan was becoming as well-known as Holt, but for different reasons.

"Sun, moon, mountain, river. All divine," he repeated one of Silka's favorite sayings. "Skills . . . and inspiration . . . necessary to develop self, also divine."

He drank from the stream and chewed on a piece of jerky. His thoughts wandered to James Hannah and his likely relationship with Agon Bordner. What would happen? Would Hannah accept Bordner's offer, whatever it was? If Bordner was planning on taking over all of this part of Texas, what would he want Hannah to do? If Bordner was behind the attack on the Bar 3, then he obviously had a gang of men hidden somewhere. Where? Blue didn't know. His thoughts went to his family and he shivered. Deed was an exceptional fighter whose natural instincts and skills had been honed by Silka's teaching. He and Holt had learned much as well, but it was Deed who had become special.

He spoke the answer to what Hannah would be hired to do, as if delivering a sermon. "James Hannah will be hired to kill Deed. Bordner will figure his own men can handle the rest of us."

For a moment, he didn't move. He couldn't. How could this be? Was Agon Bordner such an evil man? He wished Holt was back with them again, but that wasn't going to happen; Holt had made that clear. He had crossed the line from Confederate soldier to bitter guerrilla fighter to outlaw. He had decided it was best that he stay away. Wherever *away* was.

Bina's gentle face came to his mind. Her image was always close. She had been his wife for five years and theirs was love at first sight. A Mescalero Apache educated by missionaries, she was a compassionate woman, as well as a spiritual teacher in her own way. Being with her made him whole. She loved to sit on their porch at dusk and watch the birds flit around the land. A bird feeder had been one of her earliest requests. It was the only request he could recall. In some ways, she reminded him of his late mother. When he was little, he thought his mother could actually talk to the birds and hoped that one day he would be able to do that.

What would Bina say about Agon Bordner? Or James Hannah? She would tell him to wait, but to be ready. Yes, that's what she would say.

Blue shut his eyes and prayed.

His mother had believed in daily meditation, but never insisted that her sons do the same. She felt every person was his or her own master. No person should interfere with another person's search for identity of purpose. Bina said much the same thing.

No answer came from his prayer, except they must be prepared for this unthinkable action. Maybe that was the answer. Deed had told him about the Rangers coming to Wilkon, but it was unrealistic to think they would be able to stop a massive takeover . . . at least, until it was too late. A stray thought entered his mind: have a meeting with the Sanchezes, the family that owned the Lazy S.

Yes, that made good sense. Together, they could plan how to survive any further advance by Bordner.

Overhead, a hawk surveyed the land, moving across bundles of white clouds and dipping toward something unseen. Blue took another swig from the stream and thought again about Bina. Her English was quite good and he knew some Apache. Bina's faith was fascinating, believing that man was connected to all animals, all insects, all plants, all rocks and minerals. A oneness with the world. A giant circle of the spirit. That had been his mother's belief as well. Occasionally, he wondered if she had been an Indian or had such a bloodline. None of the brothers knew anything about their grandparents, only that they had lived in Ohio and died there.

His wife had actually taught him much about the power of the Great Spirit and the directing of its great force, the energy of the universe, to heal and guide. That every being had an identity and a purpose. To live up to this purpose required the power of self-control, which brought true happiness. He had used some of her beliefs in sermons, like "One cannot be taught until one tries to learn" or "Nothing is free; everything has a cost." And the thought he liked best was "Enjoy the world. Do not let the world enjoy you."

She had told him that often more than one spirit occupied a body, and when that happened, the person was torn between doing good and bad and would then be different personalities at different times. Only a special ceremony could drive out the bad spirit. It reminded him of the Bible stories about Jesus forcing demons out of a person.

Of course, Bina also believed if someone stepped on a black bug, it would rain. He chuckled at the thought. It was more like something Holt would say. But it was part of the Apache belief that humans were connected to the circle of all life, all animals, all plants, the sky, the earth, the winds. Not above it or in its center, just another part of the great circle.

Her name meant "musical instrument" in Apache and Blue thought it was a most appropriate name. She told Blue that he should answer to only one authority, the Great Spirit. To Blue, it seemed like Bina had come from some faraway place, and yet most of her thoughts were very practical. Their love was deep, in spite of the difference in race — and the anger it caused among some of both races. They had met on the reservation, a planned Christian gathering, and that had begun a serious courtship.

Most of his friends were aghast at the idea of his being with an Indian; some townspeople couldn't believe he would possibly think of taking a savage into his home. He didn't care; he wanted to be with her — forever.

Even now, there were people in Wilkon who looked at her, at them, with disgust. He managed to forgive their ignorance most of the time. Interestingly enough, the Sanchezes had greeted her warmly. Maybe it was because they, too, felt the sting of racial prejudice.

There was one woman who came up to him after a church service and told him that he was going to hell for living with an Apache woman. Bina had laughed when he related the incident to her and told him that they both should pray for the woman.

"I miss you, Bina," he whispered.

The sorrel snorted and Blue immediately became alert. This was not country in which to assume one was safe. He stood and walked to the horses, lifting his Winchester from its saddle scabbard and cocking it one-handed into readiness by pushing the stock against his upper leg for leverage. Nothing troubling was in sight and the horses were grazing again. Gradually, his thoughts returned to Deed. Dedrick William Corrigan was his full name but everyone called him Deed, except their mother. Holt's birth name was Holton Jefferson Corrigan, their mother's father's name. His own birth name was Bluemont Wade Corrigan, a combination of their father's and their paternal grandfather's names. *Bluemont* had brought more than his share of fistfights in school, but his brothers had always been eager to step in and turn things around.

Uncocking the rifle, he returned it to the scabbard and lifted himself into his saddle. Grabbing the lead-ropes of the sorrel and the packhorse, he eased into a lope. Soon he was into broken country that became rolling plains. Cattle country. If Agon Bordner thought it would be easy taking control of the LC ranch by killing Deed, he was seriously underestimating Silka. And himself. And Bina.

Ahead were six grazing cattle. LC steers. He reined toward the animals and got them moving. This wasn't LC land; it was pasture filed on by the Lazy S and recognized as theirs. Certainly there was no need to cause problems with Felix Sanchez and his family. The Sanchezes had owned the ranch for three generations. Next to the Bar 3, it was the biggest ranch in the region.

The six steers trotted in front of him, eager to get away from his presence. Finally, they curled off into a wide spoon of land that was the beginning of LC pasture and he let them go. The sorrel snorted as if wanting to chase them.

"It's all right, Captain. They're home. So

are you," he said.

Blue Corrigan rode into the LC ranch yard, happy to return. A number of sturdy buildings comprised the ranch. Two large barns held their best horses and three milk cows, as well as serving as the storage area for feed. The ranch yard also featured two corrals, a bunkhouse, and a small cooling house for meat and butter. Farther to the south was a well that provided water all year round and an empty bunkhouse. Outside the barns was a small toolshed. The main house had a separate wing built so that Silka and Deed could live separately from Blue and his family, giving them all their privacy. Another bedroom had been kept for Holt; Deed had insisted on it. The additions gave the house a strange, bulging appearance, but no one seemed to mind.

The ranch was a good one, thanks in large part to their parents' careful selection of the land. Three protected valleys were rich in grass and water. Springs dotted the area, coupled with a healthy stream that cut across two of their main grazing areas. Five thousand head of cattle and a string of mustangs were spread throughout their acres — acres that were owned by them, truly owned with all of the necessary owner- ship files. Their third valley had been bought from another ranch just after the war and it, along with the other two valleys, gave them a fine operation. The herds were shifted from one valley to another as needed. Blunt hills and long benches offered natural fencing to keep the animals from drifting.

The ranch itself lay in one of the valleys with a well-built two-story ranch house featuring a porch and a second-story balcony. Silka had directed the construction of this large house after the war; most of it was built by Blue and Deed. The one-armed rancher surveyed the ranch and took satisfaction in its appearance; they had painted all the buildings a year ago.

Three ranch dogs barked an alert and the stallion pawed the ground and flattened its ears. An Oriental man came to the door of the main house. His hand shielded the sun from his face. In his other hand was a rifle.

"Afternoon, Silka," Blue yelled as he walked his horses toward the house.

Silka's face lit up in recognition and he waved back. A smile cut across his flat face and he shouted, *"Konnichiwa!"*

Returning the Japanese greeting with gusto, Blue swung down and flipped the reins over the hitchrail in front of the wood-planked porch, then tied the lead-ropes to the rack. He left the pack alone except to retrieve a wrapped package.

"Where Deed?" Silka eased onto the porch.

"Stayed at the stage station. Be there another week or so. Needs to stay until they can get someone to replace him," Blue reported. "Got any coffee on?"

"Sure, that we have. You go ahead. Bina be most glad to see you," Silka said. "I want closer look at stallion first."

"Well, he's a handsome one," Blue said, stepping inside and laying his package on the table near the door.

Hurrying from the kitchen, Bina welcomed him with a long embrace. Kissing wasn't something Apaches did, but she took to it enthusiastically on occasion. She was a bright part of the Corrigan family, with an inviting smile and warm eyes. Their house matched her personality. Warm and definitely accented in blue, her favorite color. Even the sofa was blue. A wall cabinet held a collection of small items, also mainly blue. He liked to think her emphasis on blue was because his name was the same as the color.

Over coffee, he shared what had happened at the station and in El Paso. Bina offered no comment about Holt, or James Hannah, or Agon Bordner, but said Jeremy Regan was asleep, as were their two children, Matthew and Mary Jo. All three had spent the morning riding with Silka.

"How is Jeremy doing?" Blue asked, sipping the strong coffee.

"Well, as good as one could expect, I think. He misses his mom and dad something fierce," she said. "But he never grumbles. I think he really likes being with Matthew — and Matthew likes him around. So does Mary Jo."

"That's good. It'll take time."

She looked up at him and smiled. "I've been thinking we should adopt him. If he's willing. Make him a part of . . . us."

"That sounds wonderful, Bina. Knew you would think of somehow helping the boy, so I got you a present in El Paso. Hope you like it." He got up and handed the wrapped brown-paper package to her.

Smiling, she opened the gift and withdrew a straw hat decorated with fake wildflowers and blue ribbons to tie under her chin to hold it place.

She stood and put it on. "Oh, Blue it's beautiful. I love it, Blue. I love you." Her kiss was an invitation.

CHAPTER SIXTEEN

Morning's cooling breezes had disappeared around the Forsyth station. Hermann Beinrigt and Billy Lee Montez had a fresh team waiting for the expected stage coming from El Paso. The horses stood in the corral, ready to be hooked up and came with Billy's usual unneeded advice. Two days ago, Tade Balkins had brought in a stage from there and told them to expect a visit from Willard Epson on the next stage. Tade liked Atlee and the way she had run the station and wanted her to stay in charge.

Deed Corrigan watched the two men. He was glad Olivia was busy helping in the kitchen because he wanted to be alone. Lately, Benjamin had been spending time with him too, usually with the horses. This morning, however, the boy was doing schoolwork as mandated by his mother.

Deed's right hand was weak so he continued to carry his Remington revolver shoved into his pants for left-hand usage. Years ago, Silka had insisted he learn to handle all weapons with either hand, so it wasn't difficult, just slower.

The young gunfighter paused at the barn door and listened to the land. Shadows had lost control and the heat of the day was increasing. But his mind wasn't on the coming day, it was time for him to get back to the ranch. Fall roundup was getting close and this autumn's effort would be more important than ever. The Bar 3, under its new ownership, would bring tension. Hopefully nothing more than that, but it wasn't likely.

The Beinrigts had agreed to stay and help Atlee. Hermann was not yet at full strength, but getting better all the time and he was eager to help. Deed knew he wasn't needed here anymore. Not really. No one said so, but he knew. Of course, he had stayed to be around when the district agent came. With the Beinrigts in place even that wasn't necessary.

He walked past the barn, scuffing his boots against the dry dirt. His spurs tried to sing, but only sounded like tinny clatter. At the gray edge of the stage station yard, a coyote appeared.

"Not today, friend," he said. "The chick-

222

ens are not out yet. Go find a rabbit."

The scrawny animal disappeared.

He couldn't remember feeling so sad since his parents and little sister died. He was being a fool staying here; others may not realize it, but the only reason he remained was to be near Atlee. Just seeing her was like finding a beautiful flower in the middle of winter. He had known other women. Sally Cummins in Wilkon was quite fond of him, but he didn't care that much for her. It was silly to think about Atlee. At all. The best thing for him to do was to ride away.

Ride away. Yes, that's what he must do. He would wait for the arrivals from El Paso. If Willard Epson didn't come, he would leave anyway. It had been early spring since he last had been at the ranch, taking a herd north as the grass was turning green. That was home . . . or was it? Oh, how he would miss Elizabeth, Benjamin, Cooper . . . and Atlee. Had they become home, his real home? He shook his head to dismiss the thought.

Billy's shout brought Deed from his reverie and he wondered if the district agent would be onboard as Tade had said. He hoped Willard Epson would be agreeable, but he still had an uneasy feeling he hadn't shared with anyone. He rubbed his right hand; the injury was healing nicely. Opening and closing his right fist repeatedly forced the end of stiffness.

Out of the corner of his eye, Deed saw Atlee Forsyth standing in the doorway of the station. He figured she was wondering the same thing. Surely, the district manager would recognize her value to the stage-line. Surely. He wanted to go over and kiss her good morning, but knew that was ridiculous to even think. He glanced her way again and she smiled as if reading his mind and he blushed.

The coach banged into the station yard and the team of proud horses strutted to a stop. Billy hurried up and opened the coach door with an enthusiastic greeting, more so than usual. Had he the same feeling about the district agent being onboard?

The first passenger sitting next to the door was, indeed, Willard Epson. He turned to the woman next to him, said something, and bounded out.

As, the stout driver swung down from his seat he yelled to Billy, "Hey, Billy, the El Paso Bank was robbed. They're saying it was the Holt Corrigan gang. Got away with over ten thousand in gold and paper. Posses are combing this part of Texas."

"Ten thousand! That is mucho."

"You betcha. The bank was holding an army payroll, they said," the driver declared. "Not everybody's sayin' it was Holt Corrigan though. Hell, the bank president hisself claims there's no way it was. Ain't that somethin'."

Billy glanced at Deed. The young gunfighter shrugged. He wondered if Holt had held up the bank while Blue was in town. Surely Holt wouldn't do that to his brother if he knew Blue was there.

The shotgun guard followed the driver from the stage and both headed for the station. Halfway there, the driver stopped and turned around. "Say, Mr. Epson, you're going to want to have some of Mrs. Forsyth's eatin'. Best on the line. By far."

Even if he hadn't recognized Epson from Blue's earlier description, Deed would have realized the tall, long-jawed man coming toward him in the rumpled suit and bowler that didn't quite fit his head was the district manager. Epson waved his understanding to the retreating driver, then continued to Deed.

"Mr. Deed Corrigan, I believe." Willard Epson shifted the briefcase to his left hand and extended his right. "I met your brother in El Paso. Believe he was there on some horse-buying business. I trust he gave you our check and our thanks . . . for helping drive off the Comanches." He tugged on his bowler in a nervous movement. "Thanks, too, for stepping in here. That was an awful incident."

He saw Deed extending his left hand and switched the briefcase back to his right. He wanted to ask about Deed's right hand, but decided against it.

"Sorry about the left hand, Mr. Epson, but I sprained it . . . on some harness a few days ago," Deed lied. He didn't want to make it sound like he was vital to the station's continued protection. "Got the money and no thanks needed for my helping here. I wasn't really needed. Mrs. Forsyth runs quite an operation," Deed responded. "I assume you're here to look things over. Best you've got, I'll bet."

"Well, perhaps so, but I started out thinking I needed to have a man in charge," Epson said, his face reddening as he avoided Deed's stare. "Just wouldn't be right, you know."

"No, I don't know." Deed took a step away from Epson.

"Wait, please," Epson said, tugging on his soiled paper shirt collar and keeping his eyes on Billy as the one-eyed Mexican began to unhitch the tired horses. "On the trip all I kept hearing from the passengers was that they were looking forward to Mrs. Forsyth's station and her cooking." He licked his lips and stared at Deed. "So I thought why not? At least I should give her the chance, you know. Nobody's talking about our other stations like that. In fact, I've been thinking about making it a home station. You know, with sleeping quarters for passengers." He tried to smile. "And you'll be here . . . to help."

"Actually, Hermann Beinrigt is taking my place. Olivia, his wife, has been an important addition as well," Deed said. "Hermann really knows his way around horses. Been doing a lot of work." Deed motioned toward the barn. "He's over there now. With the new team."

"Really? Where are they staying?"

Deed explained and hoped he hadn't made a mistake in telling Epson of the change.

"Well, good, I look forward to meeting them," Epson said. He wanted to add that he was relieved that a Corrigan wasn't going to be around the station — it made him uneasy with the reputation of the outlaw Holt Corrigan — but didn't dare express the thought. After all, *this* Deed Corrigan was a known gunfighter.

"Good. Both are helping serve now, I believe," Deed said. "That's very good news about making this a home station. Mrs. Forsyth will be pleased." He grinned. "Guess I won't need that buckboard after all."

"Buckboard? I don't understand."

"Well, if you decided the station needed a man running it," Deed said, "All of us would have been riding out of here within the hour, headed for my ranch."

Epson's jaw dropped and then he began to chuckle. "That's blackmail, Mr. Corrigan."

"No. That would have been justice."

"Good enough. I'd better go see Mrs. Forsyth," Epson said. "I'll be needing a place to sleep until the inbound stage comes tomorrow."

The rest of the day was a blur at the excitement of Epson's announcement. For Deed, it was bittersweet. It was time to leave.

Early the next morning, he was saddling his buckskin gelding when Benjamin walked into the stable.

"Where ya goin', Deed?" he asked with his hands in his pockets and a hard look on his face.

"Mornin', Benjamin. I'll be heading for

my ranch, son," Deed said, knowing this was part of leaving he wasn't going to like.

"You're leavin' . . . us? Well, it figures. Never wanted you here anyway. No way you could replace my pa."

"Wasn't trying to replace your pa. Just wanted to help. Make sure the station stayed up and running. Now Hermann and Olivia will be helping your mother," Deed said, tightening the cinch. "And I've got work to do on my ranch. Roundup's coming."

"I-I thought you liked us. Especially Elizabeth, Ma, and Cooper. Maybe not me because of the way I acted but —" The boy's eyes were reddening.

Deed turned toward him. "I do like you, a lot, Benjamin. You. Your sister. Your mother. Cooper. All of you. But I can't stay."

"Well, like I said, I shoulda known you'd leave."

Deed took a step toward the boy. "Hey, wait a minute, fella. I didn't say I wouldn't be back." He paused and added, "I was going to ask your mother if you could join us for the roundup. You can stay with me at the ranch."

Benjamin looked at Deed suspiciously. "You mean it . . . or are you just saying that?"

"No, I mean it. Really. But your ma will

have to say it's all right."

"Let's go ask her!"

Benjamin leaped forward and, for the first time since Deed arrived, hugged him. Deed caught and enveloped the boy in his arms.

Then stepping back and letting him down with his hands on Benjamin's shoulders, Deed said, "You'll be a good addition to our roundup. You're a smart, hard worker and you know horses."

"You won't be sorry. But I am sorry for the way I've been acting. I wanted to be Ma's man."

"You are and always will be. Nothing will change that. Now let's go talk with your mother before I ride."

They walked together toward the station, chatting easily. Atlee was standing in the doorway as they approached. Fifteen feet behind them came Billy and Hermann, having just fed the horses.

"I was just going to call you all in for breakfast," she said and smiled. "Should have plenty of time to eat before today's stage gets here."

Benjamin jumped onto the porch, barely able to contain his excitement. "Ma, Deed wants me to come to his ranch for the roundup. I can, can't I?"

Atlee tried not to look startled at the

change in Benjamin and covered it with the question, "What about your schoolwork?"

The boy frowned momentarily, then said, "I'll get it done before I go, I promise."

Stepping up beside him, Deed put his arm on Benjamin's shoulder. "I should've said something to you first."

Her eyebrows raised. "Where are you going?"

He tried to smile, but couldn't. "Heading for the ranch. You don't need me here any longer. You got great news from Epson." He glanced toward Billy and Hermann walking toward them.

"I see."

"Ma, can I? Can I? Please!"

Her eyes left Deed's face and focused on her son. "Yes, you can. If you get all your schoolwork done and Mr. Corrigan wants you."

"He'll be a good help, I'm sure," Deed said, avoiding her returned gaze. "Be a good experience for him, too."

"Certainly. What about Elizabeth?" Atlee motioned toward the kitchen. "She'll be heartbroken to hear you're leaving and coming back for Benjamin."

Deed grimaced. He hadn't thought of that.

Crossing her arms, Atlee told her son to

wash his hands and face, then asked Deed if it would be possible that Elizabeth could go and play with Blue's children for the same days that Benjamin was on the roundup with him.

"Oh, that's a great idea!" Deed said. "We've got plenty of room and Blue's kids would like having Elizabeth to play with!" He was aware she had taken a step closer to him and had the feeling she was going to say something else, but didn't.

"It's settled then," she said finally and reached out to touch his arm. "Come and eat before you go. Mr. Epson's already at the table."

"I'm not surprised. He made a smart decision yesterday. Congratulations!"

Atlee smiled, withdrew her hand to push back a stray lock of hair that had escaped from her tight bun. "He told me you were going to take all of us away from here if he didn't give me the job."

"Well, I might've said something like that." Deed rubbed his chin and watched Benjamin hurry past them and into the station.

Atlee smiled. "That is so like you, Deed. Very kind." She looked into his face. "Would you really have done that?"

He could feel redness crawling up his

neck. "Yes. I would have, if you'd have come." He looked back at her. "I'm sorry about not asking you about Benjamin earlier. He saw me saddling up and was upset. It just sorta came to me."

"Of course he was upset. Though he didn't show it, I think he was starting to change his feelings about you. You mean a lot to him. To both children."

"Losing your pa is rough for a whole family, but for a boy it is especially so because he feels he has to become the man of the house. I was lucky. I had two older brothers and Silka to be the men of the house."

Glancing toward the washstand, Deed saw Billy and Hermann. Not looking at her, he said, "I'll wash up and be in. Be good to hit the trail with a full stomach."

Atlee's voice was crisp. "Did you plan on riding out without even saying good-bye?"

"Well, no. No. I wouldn't have done that."

"I would hope not." She touched his arm again. "You know you're an important part of . . . this family."

Billy and Hermann joined them on the porch and exchanged morning pleasantries, mostly about the weather. Neither man was aware Deed planned on leaving and both were upset by the news.

"*Ich bin nicht* zo strong yet," Hermann

Beinrigt declared, waving his arms. "Ve be needing *du. Ja.*"

Billy blurted something that was mostly Spanish; the only word Deed caught was *Comanches.* Without waiting for Deed's response, Atlee spun and went inside.

Quietly, the young gunfighter said, "Now that Mrs. Forsyth has been given the manager's job, I need to get back to the ranch." He cocked his head. "But I'll be back. Benjamin's going to help with our roundup."

Both men thought that was a good idea as the threesome headed for the washstand. A tin basin awaited with a bucket of fresh water, a bar of soap with three bubbles bursting on its surface, and a roller towel. They washed up without talking, then entered the station. All three held their hats in their hands. Benjamin, Elizabeth, and Willard Epson were already at the table. The fireplace was aglow with new wood and stirred ashes. Wonderful breakfast smells rushed to meet them. Even for Atlee, the breakfast was grand. Hotcakes, warm syrup, eggs, bacon, fresh biscuits, and apple-butter jam and hot coffee.

A bit of syrup stuck to his chin, Epson greeted Deed with a waving fork. "Morning, Deed. Better sit down before I eat up all the profits. I can see why everybody's raving about the food here." He stuffed a piece of pancake and egg into his mouth. "You know, even after the railroads are going again in Texas, this would be an excellent spot for a home station."

"Makes sense to me." Deed headed for the table as Billy and Hermann found chairs.

Benjamin wanted Deed to sit next to him. So did Elizabeth. He suggested the boy move over one chair so he could sit between them. Olivia came from the kitchen with a plate stacked with steaming hotcakes and a fresh pot of coffee. From the expression on her face, Deed guessed Atlee had told her that he was leaving. It aggravated him; why should he feel guilty about going to his own ranch? The only reason he had stayed this long was to be near Atlee and that was a silly reason, he told himself. The sooner he left, the better for all of them.

Olivia poured coffee into Deed's cup and leaned close to whisper in his ear, "She *ist* most upset. She cares . . . about you. You know this."

Deed forked two flapjacks, planted them on his plate, and muttered, "No, I don't know that."

Elizabeth leaned toward him and declared, "I helped make the batter for the hotcakes."

"I'll bet they're extra good," Deed said. She beamed.

Quietly, Deed turned and told her he would be leaving for his ranch. Her face broke into sadness and tears festered in the corners of her eyes.

"Now don't cry," Deed whispered. "I'll be coming back. Benjamin's going to help with our roundup . . . and you will come with us, to play with my brother's children. It'll be lots of fun."

He took a sip of coffee and told her about Blue's children, Matthew and Mary Jo, and a visiting child, Jeremy. He didn't explain about Jeremy's reason for being there. Elizabeth's countenance brightened as he told her about the new adventure.

"We could go with you now and help," she said, wide-eyed.

Deed took another sip and told her there was much work to do before the roundup started.

"Isn't there stuff we could do?" she said.

Deed looked up and saw Atlee standing across the table, watching the exchange.

"That's enough, Elizabeth. Mr. Corrigan needs to go," she said.

The rest of the meal was mostly quiet with Billy and Hermann discussing a horse they thought should be taken out of rotation for a few days. Even Benjamin and Elizabeth were silent. Deed excused himself, thanked Atlee and Olivia and left.

He checked the cinch on his saddle, rechecked it, hoping against hope that Atlee might come to say good-bye. Finally, he swung into the saddle and nudged the bay into a smooth lope. He didn't intend to look back, but he did. Atlee was standing in the station's doorway with her hand shielding the sunlight from her face. She saw him glance in her direction and waved. He swallowed, waved back, then spurred his horse into a gallop.

The ride home was the longest and loneliest he could recall. Twice he stopped and almost turned around, but knew he couldn't. Blue and Silka needed him at the ranch; they had been most understanding to let him stay this long at the station. Atlee Forsythe was a widow, a new widow; he had no business thinking about her as he did.

CHAPTER SEVENTEEN

After a week of drunkenness and mental conflict, Holt Corrigan decided to ride for his brothers' ranch. If nothing else, he could go by Samuel Holton for the rest of his life. He told his landlord of his plan to look for work on a ranch up north and the quiet man had advised that jobs were scarce, but he had heard that Agon Bordner was hiring. Thanking him, Holt shook the man's hand and left.

First, though, he must tell his fellow ex-Confederates of his intentions. He owed them that. Purchasing a second horse from the livery, Holt bought supplies and left El Paso. The ride north was dusty, as a dry autumn settled around the land. He rode carefully, keeping away from ridges and places of possible ambush. It wasn't likely any soldiers would be out here, but the way to stay alive was to be careful all the time. At night, he kept his fires to a small hatful with no smoke and put them out as soon as his supper was finished. Once, he observed some tiny blue flames in the fire and knew it meant spirits were close. He assumed they were friendly and told them so.

Studying the barren region, he rode up to the deserted-looking cabin in the belly of a forgotten canyon well north of El Paso. Smoke twisting from the chimney told him his friends were there as planned. The nose of a rifle was evident from the corner of the lone window, then it disappeared.

"Yo, the cabin! Can I come in? Looking for some hot coffee," Holt yelled as he neared, keeping both hands in full view of the cabin's unseen occupants.

Like him, the men inside were considered outlaws. They had missed the window of amnesty by several years and by their own decisions. Now the United States Army and the Texas Rangers sought their capture.

A lanky, bearded silhouette stepped into the doorway with the heavy door creaking its objection to opening.

"Ya alone, Holt?" The silhouette hollered back. A rifle was cradled in his arms.

"Alone as always, Everett."

The silhouette was Everett Reindal, a former lieutenant in the Confederate army under Early's command. He and Holt hadn't met until after the war. Everett looked more haggard than the last time Holt had seen him, over a month ago.

Walking his bay to the cabin's hitchrail, Holt dismounted and flipped the reins around its pole and then led the packhorse to the rail and tied its lead-rope to the crossbar.

"Put yer hosses in the corral out back," Everett said, motioning over his shoulder with his rifle. "That's whar ours be."

"No thanks, Everett. I'll be riding on in a bit."

"Somebody chasin' ya?"

"Not that I know of. I'm heading for my brothers' ranch."

Everett frowned. "What 'bout the El Paso Bank? Thought we was gonna hit thar next. Yeh were supposed to be checkin' it out."

Holt took off his hat and slapped it against his pants and coat to remove some of the trail dust and give him time to form an answer. There was no easy way around it, he was quitting their mad crusade, if that's what it was. When he thought about it, he realized most of them just liked stealing.

"Naw, not me. Some old Confederate friend of mine runs it," he answered and held out his hand. "Did you know Dave Co-pate. He was with me at Sabine Pass."

"Yer kiddin'," Everett Reindal shook Holt's hand, but his eyes sought more information.

"No. I talked to him about three weeks ago. In his bank office."

Everett looked doubtful. "Weren't he 'fraid ya'd rob him?"

"Didn't act like it. He was glad to see me." Holt returned his hat to his head and proceeded to tell that he had decided to return to ranching and get on with his life.

Everett turned toward the other unseen occupants of the cabin. "Y'all hear that? Holt's givin' up the fight."

"War's been over a long time," Holt said.

"Never thought I'd hear ya say that," Everett spat. "It ain't fer us. We're never givin' up. Nossir."

Rushing to the doorway, a grizzled man in torn Rebel pants and a misshapen hat demanded, "How do we know ya ain't got Federals trailin' ya? Go a long way to gettin' amnesty iffen they got us."

"Don't be a fool, Hoffman. You can start over today," Holt blurted. "Nobody knows what we look like. Hell, nobody even knows *your* name. The Federals only know *mine*." He folded his arms. "I came to tell you what I was going to do. You can do anything you want."

The grizzled man put his hand on the heavy gunbelt holding four revolvers. "Maybe we won't let ya go."

From the cabin, another voice called out, "Ya be a fraud, Holt Corrigan. Ya tolt us ya'd never surrender."

A fourth man in a filthy hat with the right side brim pinned to the crown limped to the doorway and waved his arms. "Come on, Holt. This hyar's only the start. France'll be comin' to he'p us real soon."

"France, Leap?" Both Everett and Holt asked at the same time.

"Yessirree. Once France gits in, we'll have the money we need for guns an' cannon . . . an' we kin drive them Yanks all the way to D.C.," the man called Leap proclaimed.

Holt looked at Everett and shook his head. Clearly Leap was insane. Everett knew it, too.

Holt took several steps off the porch and back to his bay; pulling free the lead-rope of the packhorse, he stopped and said, "My brothers need me more than you boys do. They're going up against Agon Bordner and his bunch." He pulled free the reins, stepped into the stirrup, and swung up. "You're always welcome at our table."

"Hate to see ya go, Holt," Everett Reindal said. "Ya know we might end up ridin' for

Bordner. Hear tell he's payin' good money."

Leap continued outside, babbling about seeing French ships.

"If you do, don't come tellin' me about fighting for the South. You'll just be hired guns, doing bad things to good folks."

From the cabin came a loud Rebel yell and "Long live the Confederacy!"

Holt wrapped the lead-rope of his packhorse around his saddle horn and swung his horse away. He waved and kicked his horse into a gallop and the packhorse reluctantly followed. He half expected them to shoot at him. But the only thing he heard was Everett's yell, "Ride careful, Holt Corrigan. Ride careful."

Telling his friends good-bye was the easy part, he knew. A trial, maybe several, would come next. What if he were put in prison? A shiver went through him. He trusted Blue to know what was best. He was through running and pretending to fight a war that didn't exist except in the minds of a few. Besides, he knew Agon Bordner and his gang would be going after the LC ranch. His brothers would need another gun, after that he would surrender.

Holt's mind raced into the past as he rode. Thoughts long kept locked into place came rushing out. He wondered what had happened to the silver medal he had received from Jefferson Davis for the Sabine Pass victory. There had been other battles, too many, but none so dramatic. He remembered the day the news came that Lee had surrendered to Grant. He had gone on a one-man rampage attacking Union camps, firing at anything that moved. It wasn't long before he and a handful of like-minded Rebels were holding up Union payroll wagons. That had evolved into holding up Union banks. All the time, he had told himself that they were fighting for the South. How foolish it all seemed now.

Just as foolish was the thought that the Federal army was going to let him get away with such actions. Foolish —

Nightfall came and he camped in a narrow hollow. Holt rested on a log and pushed sticks into his small fire. Behind him was a tall, crested bank that made up one side of the hollow. Not far away, his horses grazed contentedly. His small coffeepot bubbled with the heat and Holt sliced some bacon into a skillet. He was hungry and put in six slices, before rewrapping the bacon in an oilskin and returning it to his saddlebag. He grabbed a biscuit from another sack.

The bacon spat and gurgled and he took a slice, spearing it with his knife. It was too hot to eat, so he laid the meat on a flat rock and poured himself a cup of coffee. After eating the bacon and drinking down the coffee, he added a few stick to the coals and retreated once more to his saddlebags resting with his other gear. He pulled out the piece of Confederate flag, returned to the fire, and tossed the jagged cloth into the hungry flames. Standing erect, he saluted as the flag remnant turned black and gradually disappeared. Satisfied with his little ceremony ending his private war, he kicked dirt over the dying fire and doused it with the remains of his coffeepot. First, though, he put the grounds into a handkerchief. Wasting coffee grounds was something he had learned not to do.

Out of long habit, he cleaned and reloaded his revolvers and rifle, touching them with the feather from his hat. His mind flitted away, further and further. Was he seeing glimpses of another life? Were his brothers with him in another time? He was afraid of heights and believed that's how he had died in a previous life, falling from some high place or being pushed. There were times during the war when he had the strong feeling that he had been in this battle before, only with different weapons and against a different enemy.

He shook his head. At times there was great sorrow within him, a sadness that seemed to well up from somewhere else. During the war, he had heard that the actions in one life had a direct effect on the next. A person must be reborn endless times until he found the purpose God had for him. If so, what was his purpose?

Once, after a successful battle, he had run into a long-haired, wild-looking preacher who told him that the reason Mary didn't recognize Jesus at the tomb and that the disciples didn't know him on the road was that he didn't look the same because Jesus had been reincarnated. The thought had really stuck, although he never told the story to anyone.

Finally, his thoughts slid to a pretty summer day when he walked with Allison Johnson. They kissed behind the Johnson barn and she promised to wait. He rode out to enlist the next day.

He stretched out on his bedroll and tried to sleep. Maybe he should ride back and rejoin his comrades. He didn't remember going to sleep. Morning sun woke him. His resolve came with its growing warmth. His brothers, and Silka, needed his gun and his savvy.

When he walked to the dead fire, a tiny

flame popped through the dirt, then another and another. He decided that was a sign he was headed in the right direction. Deciding he was hungry, he stoked the fire into full strength and grabbed the skillet and coffeepot.

A jay landed on a nearby branch and began to scold him. He decided the bird wasn't an omen, just hungry. He tossed pieces of a biscuit in the jay's direction. Immediately, it flew down and gobbled them up.

He laughed. "That's all you get, buddy." Then he tossed some more crumbs.

Satisfied, the jay returned to the branch and whistled softly.

"You're welcome."

He finished his breakfast, saddled up, and rode out, singing about goober peas. The jay followed for a few minutes before flying away.

"Well, I thought we were going to be friends," Holt muttered. "You remind me of Allison Johnson." He began to laugh. Spluttery at first, then a long bellow. It was the first time he had been able to even smile about her decision. This was going to be a good day, he decided.

CHAPTER EIGHTEEN

A lone quail fluttered from the thick brush and sought another place to hide. Seconds later, Deed Corrigan cleared the halfmoon hill rimming the southern lip of the Corrigan ranch yard. He reined up the bay and studied the busy scene below. A soft autumn breeze ran through his shoulder-length hair on its way to a row of cottonwood trees. Overhead, the sun was easing into afternoon.

Behind the house he could see the top of the old oak tree that shaded the graves of their father, mother, and sister. How long ago that seemed, almost like it was part of another life. He thought of Holt and what he would say about that, shook his head, and studied the activity. Neither of his parents' faces, nor that of his sister, came to his mind anymore. Only blurred images. Silka had become a father — guiding, teaching, caring. He touched the brass circle at his neck.

In the farthest corral, a cowboy rode a semibroke mustang, a regular fall task to turn all of their horses into good work mounts. He guessed it was Chico. Standing next to the corral was Little Jake, waiting to take the next horse. All their horses would be needed for the fall roundup. The systematic search of the territory for cattle was hard, time-consuming, and involved the co-operation of all the ranches in the area. Or had in the past.

Not far from the corrals, another man was singeing the whiskers off a new rope over a small fire. Most likely it was Harmon. Tied to two trees was another new rope, pulled tight to get out the kinks. He smiled; ropes didn't last long around there, even when they had been waterproofed with beef tallow. Old ropes were cut up into shorter piggin' strings for tying calves' legs to quiet them for branding.

He felt guilty about not being here before. Breaking horses was something he usually was involved in and good at doing. But he shouldn't have had the guilt. His presence had given Atlee Forsyth the strength to go on, and the protection from Indians. It had been important to stay. Still, it hurt to see others hard at work.

Sitting on a bench beside the ranch house was Willy, repairing a saddle. A few feet away were two more saddles. It was a time when all gear must be in top shape; a bridle or cinch snapping at the wrong moment could bring serious injury or worse. At his feet was a long-eared brown dog napping; another was inspecting something just inside the barn door.

Silka was shoeing a roan; he had learned the skill moving across the country and took pride in his work. An anvil and bellows was kept very busy this time of year. Of course, like most ranches, there was a keg of good 'nuffs, or shoes of various sizes ready to put on a horse without heating them. As expected, Silka didn't like them.

The horse wrangler, Harmon Payne, was a well-built cowboy who liked to spout phrases from Sir Walter Scott and Tennyson. The Corrigans knew he had been a teacher in Ohio before coming to Texas. Something had happened there, but no one asked. He was loyal to a fault and tougher than his thin frame would indicate. Willy Court was average-sized, cocky, and always interested in a fight, and he, too, would stand for the ranch. Jacob Jason, or "Little Jake" as most called him, was a short, fiery hand, ready for anything and anyone. Chico was a hardy

Mexican; he knew little English, but knew cattle and horses well. Deed wondered if Blue was planning on hiring any other short-term help for the roundup. He figured the three hands would be kept on during the winter months.

Not far from the southern corral was the chuck wagon they had brought back. It, too, would be needed for the autumnal gathering. All of the area ranches supplied their own. He figured their black cook, Too Tall, was back, too. The short man also did the cooking for the ranch. His real name was Oliver Gistale, but nobody called him that.

Chickens were pecking the ground on the west side of the house, oblivious to the rest of the world. Somewhere a rooster strutted, letting the world know who was in charge. He didn't see Blue or Bina, but saw the children playing on the east side. He nudged the bay into an easy lope and hallooed the ranch as he neared. The dog snapped from its nap, barked, and headed toward Deed. Silka looked up and waved. All three children stopped playing, then came running and laughing toward him, too.

"Uncle Deed! Uncle Deed!" the two Corrigan children clamored together. Jeremy lagged a few steps behind, unsure of who this stranger was in front of them.

Grinning, Deed swung from the saddle, knelt, and spread his arms. The two kids piled into him, talking at the same time. He gathered from their happy chatter that their parents, Blue and Bina, were both in the barn.

Standing a few feet away, Jeremy watched with his hands behind his back.

Deed smiled, patted both Corrigan children, and said, "And you must be Jeremy. I'm Deed."

"Yes, sir."

"I've heard a lot about you, Jeremy," Deed said. "You're a brave young man."

"If you say so, sir."

Deed laughed. "How about calling me Deed?"

"Yes, s— Deed." The boy smiled.

"Come and join our little gang," Deed motioned. Without hesitation this time, Jeremy took a half skip and rushed into them. They all laughed.

From the barn came Blue, joining Silka in his advance to welcome Deed. The children giggled and hurried to return to the game near the house. A hearty handshake from both men made him feel at home again.

"Good that you are home, Deed," Silka said, patting the young gunfighter's shoulders. "No one can break the horses like you do, son."

"Don't know about that, but I'm ready to take my turn."

"Well, we have a blind bucker. Set him aside, hoping you'd give him a go," Silka said. "If you can't set him straight, we'll just let him go. Too dangerous."

Having dealt with a blind bucker before, Deed knew that this was a horse that went crazy with fear whenever it was ridden, bucking into anything. More dangerous to itself than its rider, the horse was likely to injure itself bucking over something or trying to.

Before he could respond, Blue told him that Taol Sanchez, oldest son of their neighbor, had ridden over yesterday to discuss the roundup. The Sanchezes felt the Bar 3 should be invited to the roundup gathering, in spite of the unfortunate circumstances. A two-week target date for the roundup to start had been set.

"How like Ol' Man Sanchez," Deed responded. "Thinks everybody is good if given a chance."

"Well, it's not as simple as that, Deed," Blue said. "But he does believe in the goodness of people. In this case, though, he knows the Bar 3 land is too great to ignore. Likely some of our cattle have drifted over there, too."

"You mean *theirs.*"

Blue grinned. "Guess so."

"What about Ol' Joel? Who's gonna be the wagon boss?"

In previous years, the Bar 3's veteran cowhand had served in the important role as wagon boss, the man in charge of sending riders to cover the land. So a new person would have to be chosen. Blue thought someone from the Lazy S would be the likely replacement.

"What if the foreman of the Bar 3 wants one of his men to run the roundup?"

"We'll deal with that if it comes," Blue answered. "So far, I haven't heard if they even plan to join us."

"Not sure riding with them is a good idea, Blue," Deed said, leading his horse.

"You want the Sanchez boys to do that alone?"

Silka shook his head and they walked toward the barn without talking.

Breaking the silence, Blue asked about things at the station. Deed told them about the division agent approving Atlee as the station manager and that he was considering making it an overnight stop, expanding the station with sleeping quarters for passengers. He explained the German farming couple had agreed to stay on and help, so he felt it was a good time to leave.

Studying his brother for a moment, Blue asked, "How did it go? When you left."

"Went fine," Deed said, glancing at the children now back at their play. "Oh, I invited Benjamin, the Forsyth boy, to join us for the roundup. Be a good experience for him." He paused and added, "Uh, and Elizabeth, his sister, you know, to join your kids for a few days. Hope that's all right."

"Of course it is. And Atlee?"

"Uh, she said it was fine, as long as Benjamin promised to get his schoolwork done first."

Blue smiled. "Good, but that's not what I meant. I'm sure she was sorry to see you leave."

Glancing away, Deed tugged on his hat brim. "Uh, no, I don't think so. Well, I was good help, you know, but she's got it under control now."

Talk continued about the roundup and the idea of branding the newborn calves early, before Agon Bordner could make another move to control the region and rustle any cattle he could find and brand them with his Bar 3. Bordner's takeover of the Bar 3 reminded Silka of the perilous days of feudal Japan where nothing and no one were safe. Blue believed the man would abide by the unwritten rules of the roundup, that ranchers who went out to brand calves before the others were called "sooners" and were frowned upon. Blue didn't want the family breaking those rules. Deed and Silka didn't think that would deter Bordner or his foreman, Dixie Murphy.

Deed stopped and his bay nudged him from behind. "Have you seen any Bar 3 riders around?"

"No. It's been real quiet," Blue answered, pausing alongside his brother. "At least around our range."

"Are you worried about them?" Deed started walking again.

Silka studied the leaves of a maple tree as they passed. Its leaves were beginning to show the first signs of crimson. He smiled and commented on their beauty. Both the Corrigan brothers agreed, but weren't really paying attention.

"What do you want to do?" Blue asked, his voice barely hiding his agitation.

"I'm sorry, Blue. That wasn't right of me." Deed kicked a rock as they continued down the hill. "You think this Agon Bordner is going to be satisfied with the Bar 3 and the two little places?"

Blue took three steps before responding.

"Wish I could say yes, but he does sound like a man who wants to be a king —"

"And we stand in his way . . . us and the Sanchezes," Deed finished the statement.

"That's about it." Blue stared off, as if he could see a rider. "We've been keeping a close eye on our range and our cattle. One or two of us ride a part of it every day."

Blue informed Deed about the herd's condition. Overall it was in good shape in spite of the dry summer. There hadn't been any signs of screw worm, usually identified by cattle twitching and giving off a rancid odor. As usual, they also worried about steers being bitten by rattlesnakes, displaying swollen jaws or low-slung heads. Only one steer had been put down because of such an encounter. Patches of locoweed, a boghole, or alkaline water were all noted and cattle kept from them. Because of the dryness, there was concern about quicksand where there had been a stream. The ground had to be worked until moisture came to the top.

Most of their herd was young and, largely, shorthorn of English lineage. A few mossy-backed longhorns roamed the hills, continuing to make riding among the herd a dangerous proposition. At this time of the year, the Corrigans liked to keep their herd on a higher range, leaving the lower lands for winter. Cattle that had been raised on the prairie had a tendency to stay out of timber, even if the trees gave them respite from winter storms. So the lower lands were the best practical solution.

Blue told the story of Willy getting completely covered in mud while getting a calf out of a bog. The calf's mother thanked him by trying to butt the muddy cowboy after the small animal was successfully removed.

That brought a laugh from all three, then they walked in silence for a while, and Deed asked about Bina. Two dogs ran over, checked them out, then pranced away to more interesting adventures.

"Well, right now she's taking care of the new stallion and some of our best mares. They're in the barn." Blue grinned. "About this time next year, we'll have some fine new colts."

"Don't know anybody who can handle horses any better," Deed said and smiled. "It's good to be home, boys. Seems like forever."

"Well, a lot has happened since spring," Blue said and patted his brother on the back.

"Seems so. Where's that bad horse, Silka?" Deed asked.

"He is over here. There. The paint."

"That's a good-looking animal. Goes crazy, huh?"

"Hai. It is pity we cannot ride such a fine horse," Silka said.

A spotted, black-and-white mustang stood quietly in the corner of the unused corral. It was saddled and bridled. A lead-rope held it close to the corral bar.

"When no one is on him, he is so quiet. *O soroshi* when a man gets on."

Deed recalled *o soroshi* meant "awful" and that it wasn't like Silka to overstate anything.

"Where'd you get him?" Deed asked.

"Just showed up this summer with a bunch of mustangs we rounded up," Blue said.

"Go and ask Bina to join me, will you?"

Slipping through the corral bars, Deed walked up to the paint horse. Its ears laid back on its head and the animal trembled.

"Hey, boy. I'm not going to hurt you. Can't we be friends?" He put his hand on the horse's chest, then worked his hand up to its nose. The horse jerked frantically to get away, but the lead-rope held it close to the corral.

Deed was patient. He guessed somewhere in the animal's life it had been harmed or threatened by a man. No one would, or should, ride such a dangerous horse. But sometimes, it just took a different approach to make it a worthwhile animal. Certainly, the paint was a handsome steed and worth the effort.

Bina slipped through the corral bars and walked over to him. Her eyes were a question.

"Hi, Bina, sorry to greet you like this, but I need your help," Deed said.

"Of course, what would you like me to do?"

"Have you ever been around this horse?" Deed asked, stepping back from the paint.

"No, I have not. It is good-looking horse."

"I think so, too. I am told he goes crazy when he's ridden. I want you to talk with him. Maybe we can calm him down," Deed said, running his hand over the horse's neck. The horse trembled even more and tried to jerk away. "Right now, he's dangerous and not worth keeping."

Bina walked up to the horse and spoke to him, rubbing its ears, nose, and all around its body. Deed didn't recognize any of what she was saying and assumed she was talking in Apache. The horse was calm, but indifferent. She stopped and began talking to the horse in a distinctly different language.

Her words were careful as if she wasn't as sure of herself. He knew some of what she was saying and realized she was talking to the horse in Comanche. The horse's ears went up and it leaned against her to listen. In Comanche, she told the horse not to be afraid, that he was a warrior's horse, and that a real warrior would soon be riding him. This would be an honor. Deed smiled; he didn't catch every word, but enough to realize she was instructing the animal on how it should act.

Silka and Blue watched from outside the corral.

"I think we've just discovered something, boys," Deed called back. "This is an Indian horse. He doesn't like white men. Scared of them."

"Are you sure?" Blue asked.

Deed looked over at Bina. "Well, it looks that way, doesn't it, Bina?"

"He is not Apache horse. He is Comanche horse. A fine one. I know not if he will let you ride him. You are white man. I tell him you great warrior, that it is honor for him."

"But he's a gelding. How can that be? I didn't think Apaches or Comanches cut their horses." Deed stepped next to her and patted the horse. Its ears went back again.

"Apache and Comanche sometimes do

this. Learn from white man. Not all things from white man bad." She smiled and looked at him.

"I know a little Comanche. Not like you, but some."

She smiled. "It is not words. It is smell. You smell like white man. He is afraid of white man." She cocked her head. "I do not quite smell like an Indian either, but enough."

Deed frowned. "What can we do about that?"

"You go live in Comanche lodge for a moon, a month." She smiled.

Deed laughed out loud. "Don't think we've got that long. Anything else I could do?"

She patted the paint horse again, talking to it in the Comanche language. She stepped away and looked at Deed. "You must fool him, Deed Corrigan. I go for some things in house. You wait."

"All right."

She walked through the corral and went to the house. Deed went over to Silka and Blue, standing behind the corral fence, and told them what they were going to do.

"You really think you can make him think you're a Comanche?" Blue asked. "Even if you do, we can't do that with every rider."

"Well, maybe he ends up in my string. If it works."

"Uma no mimi ni nembutsu," Silka blurted. He meant the project was a wasted effort.

"We'll see. I have to try. That's too much animal to go to waste," Deed responded.

"Maybe you should blindfold him," Silka said.

Blue pushed his hat back on his forehead. "Don't know what good that'll do. He already bucks and runs like he can't see."

Silka folded his arms. "It is to keep horse from knowing Deed is not Comanche."

Blue grinned. "Sometimes I think Deed is one, a wild one."

"You're lots of help," Deed chuckled. Returning to the horse, he talked quietly, trying to remember any Comanche phrases that might help and thought the horse might be somewhat more calm than earlier, but it might be his imagination. Horses raised by Indians weren't always changeable to white riders. He remembered a fine horse raised by a woman that went absolutely nuts when a man tried to ride it. Nothing could change it. Around a woman, the horse was sweet and gentle; around a man, the horse was a killer.

Bina returned with a small bowl; two eagle feathers with the ends tied with rawhide strings, dancing in the air; and several long ribbons.

"What's all that?" Deed asked.

"Put your hands in this. It is cold ashes and grease. It cut down on your . . . smell. Maybe fool him into thinking you are Comanche warrior."

"You make it sound like I need a bath. Do I need to put a feather in my hair or something?"

She smiled. "No. This horse will not care. Really. After you rub your hands, act like you are painting it for war, I will show you. Maybe this works. Maybe it does not. He may be loco."

"I know, but I've got to try."

Deed submerged his hands in the gooey mixture of ashes and grease, then held them up. A few ash flakes fluttered away and a string of grease ran down his right hand.

"Streak his face and his chest with . . . paint."

Carefully, Deed smeared lines of grease onto the horse's face and chest and ended it with a handprint on the horse's shoulder. Approving, Bina handed him the two feathers and ribbons and took the bowl.

"Tie one feather onto his mane. Tie the other on his tail. Tie a ribbon to both."

Deed talked to the horse as he tied on the

feathers and ribbons. "All right. I'm going to get on."

"Wait!" Silka yelled. "I have idea. Wait." Silka sprinted away and returned with a coiled rope and a small brass ring. "We do nose-and-leg tie."

"Sure."

"I will help."

Working quickly, Silka loosened the saddle cinch and slid the metal ring into place. He retightened the cinch, adjusting the ring so it was in the middle of the horse's belly. They tied the rope on the bridle, then ran it between the paint's front legs, through the ring, and then tied the taut rope to the horse's right hind ankle.

"If he rears or bucks, he'll pull his hind leg out from under himself. Maybe that will calm him down. He will know it not a good thing to do. You alert and jump," Silka advised.

Deed talked to the horse, reassuring him, and swung into the saddle, but kept his boots out of the stirrups. The paint stood with its ears alert. He nudged the horse forward with his knees, talking reassuringly as he did, mostly in English.

As if suddenly aware of the weight on its back, the paint horse tried to rear. The rope yanked its hind leg forward as the animal raised its head. The horse bounced on its rump and fell over. Deed kicked free and jumped away. He stutter-stepped backward and maintained his balance.

Walking over to the horse, he talked to it as the startled animal stood and shook the saddle, rattling the stirrups like they were playthings.

"Okay, bud. We're going to do this again. There's nothing to be gained by acting up."

From the corral, Silka yelled for him to forget the idea. Deed ignored the advice, grabbed the reins, checked the cinch, and remounted.

The paint horse started to rear again but felt the pressure of the rope pull on his back leg. He crow-hopped sideways and Deed encouraged him to walk. The paint hesitated, then began moving. Another attempt to rear reminded the horse of its limitations. Gradually, its head dropped, indicating it was comfortable with the man on its back. Deed wanted to shout, but knew this was only the beginning. It would take several rides before the paint was ready to be used on the roundup. He wondered if the horse was going to require painting, feathers, and ribbons each time it was ridden. He hoped not.

"What shall we call him, Bina?"

"Call him Warrior."

"Warrior. I like that. Warrior, it is," Deed said and patted the horse's neck. "I'm going to bring him over your way, Silka. Will you please take off the rope."

Reluctantly, Silka removed the rope. The paint horse took a few tentative strides and realized it was free of restraints. The bucking that followed jerked Deed's head back and his hat went flying. The young gunfighter shoved his boots forward and withstood the animal's attempt to throw him.

"Hang on, Deed!" Blue hollered. "If he starts running, jump off. He'll hurt both of you."

Quietly, Bina stood inside the corral, against the fencing, and said, "Deed, he will stop this. He has not been ridden for a long time . . . by any rider. He is full of life. He is not loco."

Silka stared at her, unconvinced.

After three more jumps, the paint horse settled down and began to walk again as if nothing had happened.

Deed caught his breath and yelled, "Open the gate and let's see what happens."

He directed the paint toward the opened gate. The paint horse saw the opening and burst into a gallop and, in three strides, was running all out across the yard. After circling the open space, horse and rider disappeared in a blur over the first ridge. Silka wanted to get a horse and go looking for them, worried about Deed.

Bina told him to wait and Blue tried to act more confident than he felt. His younger brother could ride, really ride, but this was different. A horse like that could hurt its rider and itself, but Bina seemed quietly assured. Maybe his brother really *was* more Comanche than he thought.

Minutes passed.

"I go for Deed. He may be hurt," Silka declared and headed for the barn.

"Wait, Silka. I see him coming. Over there. See?" Blue pointed with his lone arm toward the south. A silhouette was apparent. Deed and the horse were loping easily toward the ranch yard. The eagle feathers and ribbons fluttered in the wind.

Bina laughed. "It is Deed . . . and Warrior."

CHAPTER NINETEEN

Two black, polished surreys pulled into the Bar 3 ranch yard. As if a king were arriving, Agon Bordner got out of the first carriage, said something to the black driver, and headed for the magnificent ranch house. He was more agile than his huge frame would suggest and his bearing would make any Eastern potentate jealous.

He looked upon the region as his kingdom, his right. No one else deserved to own and operate this land. No one. All of Texas would be awed by what he would achieve here. He had decided it was time to make the next move in controlling this territory and fully expected it to happen as planned. Being closer was vital to his strategy; he trusted Rhey Selmon, but no one else. Not even his Bar 3 foreman, Dixie Murphy.

From the other surrey, two cooks and a gray-haired butler emerged, giving orders to each other. Pulling into the ranch yard were two buckboards. One piled with foodstuffs and a second laden with cooking gear, a large bed, a rocking chair, and an oil painting of Bordner, looking like a prince. The fat man would leave the settling into the spacious main house to his staff; he wanted to talk with Selmon and Murphy.

"Good to see you, boss!"

The hearty greeting from Dixie Murphy came from the doorway. The cattleman's lean frame was dwarfed by the huge door. He had fought for the South during the conflict and fled to Mexico with Nathan Bedford Forrest's cavalry, returning when Bordner contacted him through a mutual friend.

"Have you eaten?" Dixie asked.

"Of course not."

"I'll have Terrell fix us some steaks." Dixie motioned toward an unseen kitchen.

"That won't be necessary, Dixie," Bordner responded. "My people know what I want. We've been over the menu several times. They'll handle the meals from now on."

"Uh, sure. How 'bout a whiskey till it's ready."

"That would be fine, if it's good whiskey. Is Rhey here?"

"Inside."

"Good."

The Bar 3 ranch house was big and attractively decorated with oil paintings of Texas scenes and mostly French furniture. Bordner liked the decor, but decided he would expand the kitchen and put in a wine cellar. His bed would be installed in the first bedroom and Dixie would move to another. His favorite rocking chair would be brought into the main room as well. It was the only chair he had found that could hold him. The large oil painting of himself would need to be displayed prominently as well.

Rhey Selmon was sitting in the main room drinking whiskey when Bordner and Dixie entered. As usual, the gunman wore his bearskin coat and twin crossed gunbelts. He made no attempt to stand.

"Glad you're here, Agon. I'm headed for Wilkon this afternoon as ordered."

Selmon was the only Bordner gunman who called him by his first name or dared to do so to his face. Bordner smiled, knowing that Selmon, with two men, was to kill the town marshal, then have Macy Shields take over as the Wilkon lawman. Bank president Willard Hixon would handle the town council. One of Bordner's men, Jephrum Virdin, had become the apparent owner of the Wilkon General Store in the past week, so there was another Bordner man to help with the voting. The previous owner had left town without notice.

Selmon swallowed the rest of his whiskey, slammed the empty glass on a nearby coffee table in front of him, and stood.

"I want it done clean. Just the way I told you. Exactly the way." Bordner accepted a glass and watched Dixie pour brown liquid into it. When the foreman paused, the fat man pushed the glass against the bottle to indicate more whiskey was needed.

"Waid and Peter are going with me. They'll get the lawman," Selmon said, adjusting his fur coat. "Then Macy Shields will arrest them. Citizen's arrest." He chuckled.

"How good are Waid and Peter?" Bordner asked.

"Good enough. Why?"

"Change of plans." Bordner studied the painting on the wall again.

"Oh?"

"You and Macy will kill Waid and Peter after they kill the marshal."

Selmon shook his head. "That's not going to sit well with the boys, Agon."

"So what? I don't want any loose ends." Bordner stared at him until Selmon looked away. "Oh yeah, almost forgot. We don't need to worry about the county law either. Had a nice chat with Sheriff Matthew R. Lucas. In fact, he's coming by for supper."

Licking his lips, Selmon smiled. How like his boss to take care of every detail. Obviously, Sheriff Lucas was now on the take.

Bordner tasted his drink, frowned, and told Dixie, "I'm thinking we should hit the Lazy S and the LC during roundup. Get it done all at once. We can blame it on the Comanches again."

"No, boss," Dixie gulped his own whiskey and continued, "Everybody will be spread out, looking for cattle. Tough to get everybody, or even find all of them." He poured another. "Besides that, I'm not interested in going against Deed Corrigan. You know that."

Selmon nodded. "Neither am I, Agon."

"Is Hannah gonna get rid of Deed Corrigan like you talked?" Dixie growled.

"Yes."

Bordner took three black cigars from his inside coat pocket and handed one each to his key men and bit off the end of one and spit it on the floor.

"When?" Selmon asked, his eyes flashing.

"That's up to him. He hadn't left El Paso when we did. Said he had some business to handle first."

"I'll believe it when I see it," Selmon growled.

Bordner stirred his drink with his finger and ignored the comment. "All right. We'll do this more slowly. I want the Lazy S before roundup, then we'll take over the Corrigan ranch after Deed's dead. Probably after the roundup." He swallowed most of the whiskey. "No mistakes this time."

No mistakes meant no one left alive.

"So you want the Lazy S before the roundup?" Dixie asked. "Could let them Mex boys do their gatherin' and brandin'. Save us the trouble."

"No. I want control of the two biggest ranches now," Bordner snapped. "Besides, I intend to rename the whole thing. Got a new brand already registered." He made a motion that looked like two *M*s pushed together forming a crown. He smiled, "This whole thing'll become the Crown Ranch."

"Give us a couple of days. We'll hit them and the house at the same time," Dixie growled.

"Good," Bordner said, waiting for Dixie to light his smoke, then the foreman's own.

"Check with Simpson. I'm getting hungry."

Selmon wanted to know how James Hannah was going to kill Deed Corrigan and

274

get away from his brother and that damn Jap. It didn't matter to him if Hannah didn't get away. That was okay too.

Bordner looked annoyed; he wasn't used to being questioned, even by Selmon. He drank the glass of whiskey in one gulp, then responded, "I don't know, Rhey. Last I heard Deed was still at that stage station outside of Wilkon. I figure he'll go there. Get Corrigan while he's alone."

"No, he's not at the station. Some of the boys saw him and his one-armed brother talking with Old Man Sanchez two days ago," Rhey Selmon growled.

"Well, I guess that's Hannah's problem." Bordner looked surprised. "But if Hannah fails, I've got another way to get rid of both of them. Legal-like. And then we get rid of Hannah."

Selmon laughed out loud.

Sunday found Blue Corrigan taking his turn in the pulpit of the town's church. He really didn't have the time to prepare because of roundup preparations, but considered it his responsibility. The handmade pews were full as usual. Bina and their three children were in the front row to his left. She was always reluctant; many white people weren't comfortable around her, especially in the church. She told him the Great Spirit was not contained within a building and that he could be worshipped anywhere. He didn't disagree, but felt it was important for their children.

Townspeople were still coming in so he decided to wait before starting. The church door swung open and Agon Bordner entered, nearly blocking out the sunlight. Down the middle of the church he strolled, smiling broadly and greeting everyone as he entered. He glanced at Blue, nodded, and took a seat on the front row to his right. Only one other person sat there — an elderly woman who was hard of hearing. In the back row, several hard-looking men were taking seats and urging others to move.

"Welcome. What a good morning to gather together and worship our Lord," Blue announced. "Let us begin our service with a prayer and then we'll sing Hymn 37, 'A Mighty Fortress Is Our God.' "

The congregation thumbed through their hymnals, a recent gift from the Corrigans and sent all the way from Cincinnati, Ohio.

He stepped away from the homemade pulpit and it swayed slightly. "Please bow your heads. O Lord, hear us this morning as we humbly seek your love. Grant us your forgiveness for our sins and touch us with your grace. Help us to love each other more and to help our community grow strong. We ask this in your holy name, amen."

He lifted his eyes and began to sing.

"A mighty fortress is our God,
a bulwark never failing;
our helper he amid the flood . . .
of mortal ills prevailing.
For still our ancient foe
doth seek to work us woe;
his craft and power are great . . .
and armed with cruel hate,
on earth is not his equal."

The singing was uneven yet joyful. Bordner's voice boomed above the rest of the congregation and Blue tried to ignore its intensity. Few did, however. The rest of the service went without incident. Blue's sermon was short and based on Deed's thoughts — and Bina's.

"As we go about our daily tasks, it is important that we see God's hand everywhere we look. In things we don't really see, but should and savor for their specialness. Like the richness of ripened corn or the glory of contented cattle . . . the beauty of a snowflake or the song of a gentle rain . . . the sweet song of a robin or the haunting call of an owl . . . the breathtaking wonder of dawn itself and the opportunity to serve God another day." He looked at Bina. "The magic of your wife's smile. Or your husband's." He turned toward the silent audience. "Or the beauty of a stag deer in tall grass, the wonder of a harnessed team of horses working in unison . . . the comfort of a fire on a cold evening . . . or the sheer magnificence of a running horse or a happy child . . . and the love of our families for each other. All are gifts from God. All are miracles from him. All should be accepted with thankfulness. Amen. Let us together say the Lord's Prayer. Our Father who art in Heaven, hallowed be thy name —"

After the service, Blue stood at the back of the church and talked with townspeople as they exited the church. The last to leave was Agon Bordner. Bina and the children waited in the front as usual.

He strolled up to Blue and said in a dry voice, "Very good service, Corrigan. You definitely have a gift of the tongue. May I suggest that you take this gift and apply it elsewhere. I will buy your ranch. With cash."

"Our ranch isn't for sale, Bordner. Neither is the Lazy S."

"That's too bad, Corrigan." Bordner put on his rumpled hat and headed for his carriage. Four mounted men waited. A fifth helped him into the vehicle. It wasn't easy.

Adjusting his great weight, Bordner looked back at Blue, slightly out of breath. "I would hate to see anything happen to your fine family."

Blue's granite face broke. "Touch my family, Bordner, and you will die a horrible death."

"My, my. Such words from a man of God." He turned to his driver and ordered him to drive away.

Blue heard his shrill laughter as they left.

CHAPTER TWENTY

Dawn was an hour away, but Deed Corrigan was up and fully dressed, stoking the reluctant fire in the stone fireplace into rebirth. Silka was still sleeping in his room, which was part of the added wing of the ranch house. As far as Deed knew, so were Blue and his family. Their regular hands, Chico, Willy, Little Jake, and Harmon were in the bunkhouse. He figured Too Tall would be coming from there soon to start breakfast.

Coming back to the ranch three days ago held mixed emotions for him as his thoughts were rarely away from Atlee Forsyth. He missed her terribly. But he needed to be here and she didn't have any feelings for him. He kept telling himself that.

He had shared his feelings about Atlee with Silka and the old samurai told him that she needed time and that he should work hard to keep from thinking about her too much. So far he hadn't said anything to

Blue; that would bring an uninvited warning from his older brother. Maybe he should talk with Bina; she was level-headed and compassionate. She would give him a woman's perspective.

The fire was well banked, as usual, last night. Among the ashes were nuggets of embers waiting to be coaxed to life once more. He added larger chunks of wood as soon as the fire decided to respond. Today he planned on readying more horses for the roundup; he liked working the half-wild mustangs because it kept his mind off Atlee. Some would need reshodding as well. Warrior was developing into a fine horse, but one Deed only trusted himself to ride. Roundup was scheduled to start next week.

As was his custom, he said a silent prayer as he worked the fire and watched the golden sparks pop up to greet him. It was a prayer of thanks and a wish for a good day; it was a Japanese prayer Silka had taught him long ago.

Two days ago, he and Blue had met with Felix Sanchez, the patriarch of the Lazy S family, and his oldest son, Taol. It was the Sanchezes' recommendation that Blue take over as wagon boss. They also reported that Dixie Murphy would be participating in the roundup and was looking forward to it. The news had pleased everyone, except Deed. He didn't trust Murphy, or his boss, Agon Bordner, and had said so. Blue and the others were willing to give them a chance. He had no doubt that working with Dixie Murphy and the rest of the new Bar 3 riders would be awkward at best, but Blue insisted that they, at least, try to act civilly.

He cocked his head to try to catch the faint sound over the now crackling wood. It wasn't a coyote or wind. No, someone was in pain. Great pain. He grabbed his Winchester cradled against the doorframe, strapped on his gunbelt, and shoved a second pistol into his belt. Opening the door carefully, he stepped out on the porch. The uneven gray light made it difficult to distinguish a tree from a rider. Then he saw a lone figure.

A man, barely in the saddle, was advancing toward the ranch house. A sombrero bounced on the man's back, held by a stampede string at his neck. The horse was lathered and moving more out of fear than any direction being given. The rider yelped again, an agonizing cry for help, then slumped against the horse's neck.

"Silka! Blue! Willy . . . Harmon! Chico! Little Jake! We've got trouble!" Deed yelled and hurried toward the horse and rider.

The horse stumbled, then came to stop. One rein dragged on the ground. White with sweat, the animal was heaving for breath that wouldn't come fast enough. Even in the grayness, Deed recognized the rider as Paul Sanchez, the youngest Sanchez son.

As Deed approached, he could see Paul's white shirt was soaked in blood. The young Mexican's eyes fluttered open.

"S-Señor Deed . . . our ranch it's . . . been a-ttacked." He struggled to say more, but couldn't.

In their long johns, Willy and Harmon were only a handful of steps behind Deed, both holding six-guns. Chico was fully dressed and so was Little Jake. Silka came dressed and carrying his long samurai sword in one hand and its sheath in the other. Blue came running from the main house, wearing only pants and boots. In his right hand was the Walch 12-shot navy revolver.

"Get him down," Deed said, then told Harmon to go for water and rags.

As they stretched the badly wounded Mexican vaquero on the ground, Bina arrived, also fully dressed and holding a shotgun. Laying the gun beside her, she knelt beside Paul and began pulling part his blood-soaked shirt. Harmon brought a bucket of water with a dipper and towels from the bunkhouse. They were the only cloths he could find. The young Mexican rose on his elbows and drank gratefully from the filled dipper offered by Blue. Too Tall, the short, fat-bellied black cook, came, panting for breath. Quietly, he told Blue that coffee was on. Chico led the worn-out Sanchez horse away, walking it to cool it down before letting the animal have any water.

After a few sips of water, Paul Sanchez sank back to the ground, muttering. In a halting mixture of English and Spanish, Paul explained that their riders had been shot from ambush. An ongoing gunfight had ensued, but he didn't know if all the vaqueros were killed. He remembered seeing their foreman, Cliente, alive and fighting. At the same time, another force of gunmen struck the grand ranch house itself.

"Is it Comanches?" Deed leaned over.

"No, Señor. It is Americanos from the Bar 3. My father t-told me to ride for . . . y-you. T-That you would . . . help us." Paul shut his eyes to absorb the pain enveloping his body.

"Of course, we will," Deed said with clenched teeth and stood. "Willy, Little Jake, saddle our horses. Get everybody ready to ride."

Paul Sanchez reopened his eyes and saw Bina. "T-Thank you, Señora. Y-You are most kind. My family —" He gave a long sigh and was unconscious.

Riding a black-tailed roan, Willy brought up two saddled horses, one was Deed's buckskin. He belched and it filled the morning with thunder. Silka laughed. Chico rode up, leading a third mount. He had turned the Sanchez horse over to Too Tall, who didn't like the idea but accepted the animal with the warning to continue to walk the horse and not to let it drink until it was completely cooled down.

Little Jake rode beside Chico, ready to join in the fight. Deed swung into the saddle, holding his Winchester. Silka took the reins of a stocky bay and mounted, returning his sword to its sheath and pulling his rifle free from its saddle scabbard.

"Bina, leave Paul here. There is nothing more we can do for him that rest and the good Lord can't handle. We'll move him to the house when we return. You need to get back inside, barricade the door and stay there. We don't know if they will come for us, too." He looked around at Blue climbing into the saddle. "No. Blue, stay with your family and make sure you are all safe.

We must ride. Now. It might not be too late."

Bina nodded and stood, grabbing up the shotgun. Blue glanced at her and told Deed that he was not staying behind, but was coming, too.

Too Tall was frightened, holding the Sanchez horse. "But, what if they come here?"

"I don't think they will, but stay alert," Blue said. "If they do, we'll hear their shots and return."

"I no worry. You go. Hurry. Sanchez family good people," Bina declared.

Willy's expression was sour. "But, but, Deed, it sounds like there's thirty guns. You can't —"

"Willy, I know what's there. But we can't leave the fight to our friends. Maybe we can drive them off before it's too late. Or maybe we can end this thing," Deed said and kicked his horse into a gallop. "Stay here if you want."

Red streaks were cutting swaths across the dull sky as they rode for the Lazy S. Harmon wondered what they would do, or could do, against a horde of gunmen. But he knew his employers; Deed was brave, but not foolhardy, and so was his brother. He wasn't sure of the former samurai; Silka might

286

decide a glorious death would be to ride straight into the attackers. He shivered at the thought.

Harmon glanced at Silka who nodded and said something in Japanese. The cowboy admitted to himself that the Oriental was mysterious and hard to figure.

Blue looked over at Deed. "This would be a good time to have Holt with us, wouldn't it?"

"Any time, big brother. Any time."

Harmon was always fascinated by the way Blue rode one-handed, holding the reins and balancing his rifle against the saddle pommel. He made it look easy. Harmon had tried it once and the gun had slid away after only a few strides of his horse.

To avoid giving in to his doubts and fears, in a strong voice Harmon declared, "And this stern joy which warriors feel . . . in foemen worthy of their steel.' "

"I like that, Harmon. What's it from?" Blue asked.

"Sir Walter Scott's *The Lady of the Lake,* canto 5."

Willy raised and lowered his shoulders and Silka declared, "If they still there, we surprise them. Catch in crossfire. Velly good."

This time Harmon nodded. It sounded

good to him.

All rode with their rifles readied over their saddles and waited for Deed's commands. Blue had no problem with Deed taking control. They rode without further words, until sounds of gunfire broke through the early morning.

"Well, that's a damn good sign. The Lazy S boys are still alive and fighting," Deed observed. "Maybe we *can* catch these bastards in a crossfire."

They reined up alongside a gathering of rocks and boulders. It looked like the stones had met long ago and never left. Deed studied the Sanchez ranch yard with his field glasses.

"Can't see how many for sure. Looks like they've got the ranch surrounded," Deed advised, lowering the glasses. "They're spread out around that old stone fence. You know, the one that goes all around the ranch yard."

"Well, we've still got time then," Blue responded.

"Not much. The Sanchezes won't be able to stop a full-out charge."

As they rode closer, he outlined what they were going to do. Blue, Willy, and Chico would head for a ridge west of the ranch house. It was a long hiccup of land, crowded with brush and timber, a good position from which to direct fire at the attackers on that side. Silka would ride with a reluctant Harmon to the north side. Their destination was a group of cottonwoods, twenty yards from the stone fence. Deed and Little Jake would swing to the east side and positions there. After neutralizing the other parts, the south side would then be in a crossfire.

"Start shooting when you get into position," Deed advised and patted the rifle lying across his saddle. "Maybe they'll get smart and give up."

"If they don't?" Harmon asked, shifting the rifle ahead of him.

"Then we're in for a long morning," Deed responded.

"Ame futte ji katamaru," Silka said.

"What's that mean?"

Deed smiled. "It's a Japanese expression. Means rained-on ground hardens. Uh, adversity builds character."

"Oh sure."

"We gonna shoot 'em in the back?" Willy asked, wide-eyed.

"No. We'll give them a chance to surrender. Our first shot will be over their heads," Deed said. "Our second won't. Remember these bastards killed our friends at the Bar 3 and they're trying to do that at the Lazy S." He wasn't at all certain that Silka would give any Bar 3 men such a chance, but kept the thought to himself.

Blue started to say something about killing, but changed his mind and only said, "Keep us safe, Lord."

Nodding, Deed touched the small circle at his neck. Silka did the same and they split into three groups and rode toward the ranch.

A few minutes later, Blue and the others dismounted quietly on the back side of a long ridge west of the Sanchez ranch house. They tied their horses away from where they intended to fire. Spreading out, they crawled into positions behind rocks and earthen mounds. Twenty yards in front of them, silhouettes were shooting at the dark ranch house from behind the stone fence. In places, the rocks had crumbled into heaps. Scattered gunfire occasionally answered from the house. Here and there were dead raiders and a few bodies of vaqueros.

Gunfire opened on the north side.

"That'll be Silka," Blue said. "Guess it's time."

He laid his rife against a boulder and drew his Walch handgun. Ahead of them, Bar 3 gunmen turned toward the sounds of the increased gunfire, uncertain of its meaning.

His first shot clipped the dirt to the right of a gunman with a long scar along his right cheek. He squinted toward the north and yelled, "What the hell? Nobody's supposed to charge till we get the order from Selmon."

Willy belched so loud it made all of the Bar 3 gunmen jump, even the scar-faced leader. Chico and Willy opened fire with their rifles, spitting lead in the direction of the spread-out attackers, completely surprised by the counterattack.

On the far side of the ranch, Deed turned to Little Jake. "We're late. There's no time to hide."

He tied the reins together, looped the connected leathers through his left arm, and pulled both pistols from his belt. Glancing at Jake, he kicked his horse into a run toward the eight Bar 3 gunmen strung out along the east barricade. The tough, short cowhand followed, levering his Winchester into action, and holding his reins with his left hand, wrapped around the rifle.

The east side Bar 3 attackers were concentrating on the surprise firing across the ranch yard. Galloping toward them, Deed's two pistols dropped the first Bar 3 gunman as he spun toward him. Deed's horse slammed into the second man as the young gunfighter fired at the remaining line of attackers.

One wounded gunman, whose hat flew off revealing a bald head, gulped, "Damn! That's Deed Corrigan!"

The taller gunman next to him stared at the two horsemen thundering toward them. "Deed Corrigan? Hell!" He dropped his rifle and raised his hands. Nodding, the bald man lowered his rifle. Deed rode past, shooting at the other Bar 3 gunmen with both hands.

Less than a minute behind Deed and Jake came Silka, swinging his long sword from horseback. Harmon bit his lower lip and followed, his worst fear realized. The samurai had already dispatched the four Bar 3 gunmen on the north and hopped back on his horse to help Deed. The bald gunman raised his rifle to shoot at Deed's back. Silka's sword nearly decapitated the gunman. His rifle fired into the morning sky as he fell dead against the short wall.

From the west side, Blue's clear voice rang out. "Bar 3, you're surrounded. Throw down your guns and put up your hands. Or die behind that stone wall. Your choice. Make it now." So far, he had only wounded two men and hoped that would be the end of it. Chico and Willy had already moved to a new location where they could fire directly into the remaining Bar 3 raiders on the south.

All along the south barricade, some of the Bar 3 men dropped their guns and stood.

Swinging around the crumbling corner of the rock fence, Deed emptied both of his guns into a lanky gunman, standing three feet from the corner on the south side. Beside him, a fat-bellied outlaw hurried a rifle shot at the charging gunfighter. Deed's sweating horse jumped sideways as the bullet burned its neck.

As the fat gunman recocked his Henry, Deed threw both empty guns at him, which he was able to duck, and the man brought his rifle up to fire again. An instant behind the tossed guns, Deed's throwing knife followed. The razor-sharp blade, carried behind his neck, drove into the man's throat. His rifle exploded, its bullet singing into the air. The gunfighter leaped from his horse toward the staggering man, who was pulling at the embedded blade with both hands. Deed picked up the dropped rifle and slammed the butt into the gunman's stomach. As the gunman groaned in pain, Deed slammed his open hand into the man's throat. Then Deed's left hand came thundering against the man's neck and he collapsed.

Behind him, Jake caught a bullet and slumped against his horse.

Around the ranch yard, all was quiet. The shooting was over.

Silka thundered up, brandishing his bloody sword.

"Deed, you 'right?" Silka asked.

"Yeah, but Jake's been hit." He pulled the knife from the dead gunman's throat, wiped it on the man's shirt, and returned the blade to its scabbard behind his back.

They turned to the wounded cowhand, leaving Harmon to handle the remaining gunmen still standing. Jake gritted his teeth and mumbled something while Silka worked at cleaning the wound. Blue and Willy eased across the yard, directing the surrendered Bar 3 attackers. From the house came a brown-and-white dog, trotting among them. From the tree line, Chico appeared, leading six saddled horses. Deed picked up his revolvers and began reloading one.

"*Sí,* is Bar 3 hosses. More in de trees. All without shoes," he declared. In his other hand was a large sack filled with Indian weapons and feathers. He held up the sack. "Here is their leave-behinds to make it look like Comanche. *Sí.*"

"Unshod horses and feathers. That figures," Blue responded, studying the wall for any stragglers. "Makes them appear to be Indians. Willy, go with Chico and bring up the rest of their horses."

"Will do, boss."

On the west side, a disgruntled Rhey Selmon, in his bearskin coat, stood quietly, his guns laying at his feet. He told the man next to him to surrender, that Agon Bordner would take care of them, and ordered the scar-faced man to do the same.

From the long adobe house came Felix Sanchez with a pistol in each hand. His shoulder was bloodied; his silver hair was matted with sweat. A sombrero bounced on his back, attached by a rawhide string.

"Gracias, amigos. Gracias," Felix shouted. "How is my Paul?"

Behind him came two small children, his grandchildren. His oldest son, Taol, stepped into the yard from another door, brandishing a rifle and looking for someone to shoot.

"He's hurt bad," Blue said, "but he's tough. My Bina is with him."

"God is with us."

"Let's hang these bastards by those trees," Deed growled.

Blue looked at him. "No, we're taking them to town. They'll stand trial . . . and then hang."

"What about Dixie Murphy? And what's

his name, the fat man?" Deed growled, reloading his second handgun. "They're behind all this."

"I know. But we're going to need some of his men to testify to that. The sheriff can be the eyewitness, then he'll arrest them." Blue's manner indicated he didn't intend to argue about the matter.

"All right, but I want to be there when he does."

"Sure."

The closest Bar 3 gunman, holding his bleeding arm, looked at Deed. "A-Are you Deed Corrigan?"

"I am. Want to make something of it?" Deed's face was dark.

"Hell no. Dixie told us you were dead. Said that gunslick James Hannah did you in."

Snorting, Deed said, "James Hannah's a friend of mine."

"Should've known Dixie was full of it."

Chapter Twenty-One

"Dixie! We got ambushed!" The scared rider reined up his lathered horse at the Bar 3 ranch yard, jumped down, and ran inside.

Dixie Murphy was talking about cattle with Agon Bordner at a round table. The fat man was devouring a stack of hotcakes, smothered in butter and hot maple syrup, along with six fried eggs. A plate piled with bacon and slices of ham was to his left. They were awaiting word on the successful attack on the Lazy S. The necessary Lazy S loan papers lay on the table between them.

Dixie turned toward the shouting. His hand dropped to the holstered handgun at his waist.

"What the hell's goin' on, Wyman?" the crooked cowman yelled.

"It's the Corrigans. They hit us. Had us surrounded. We never saw them comin'." The scared cowboy swallowed and fought to gain control of his emotions.

"What? That can't be." Dixie looked at Bordner, wiping syrup from his chin. "There couldn't be more than seven or eight of those bastards to begin with." Dixie stood and slammed his fist on the table. The impact turned over the syrup pitcher. Bordner reached over and resettled it, ignoring the spilled stickiness. It was his first reaction to anything so far.

Wyman explained what had happened at the Sanchez ranch, then added, "I thought you said James Hannah was going to take care of Deed Corrigan." He swallowed to find courage. "They were all there, including that Oriental with the big sword."

Shaking his head in disbelief, Wyman continued, "Rhey had us spread all around the Sanchez ranch house. Behind that old stone fence of theirs. We picked off all their riders first. Had 'em where we wanted, holed up." He shook his head again. "Then, all of a sudden . . . the Corrigans were around us, tearing us apart."

"How'd you get away?" Dixie growled, crossing his arms.

"Almost didn't. They got Pete. Me an' him were holdin' all our hosses."

"I didn't tell you *when* Hannah was going to kill Corrigan, dammit, did I!" Dixie yelled and waved his arms.

Looking up, Bordner put a fried egg into his mouth and let the yolk drip down his chin as he spoke. "I assume the objective of eliminating the Sanchezes was not achieved."

Wyman glanced at the furious Dixie, then at Bordner, then away. "I . . . uh, I don't know."

"Did they get Rhey?"

"Don't know. Guess so."

"Did you leave the sacks of Indian weapons behind?" Bordner asked and shoved another egg into his mouth.

"Ah, they was on two of our hosses we was . . . watchin'."

"So, the attack was not only a failure, evidence of it being a staged Comanche attack is now in Deed Corrigan's hands." Bordner gulped coffee and waved at the cook to bring more.

"Ah, guess so."

A gunshot blistered the room and the cook dropped the coffeepot. Wyman stared wide-eyed at his reddening shirt around his shirt pocket. A second bullet hit him just below the nose and the cowboy crashed to the ground. A third went into the top of his head. His leg twitched and then was still.

Stunned, Dixie looked over at Bordner. A smoking revolver was in the big man's hand.

A long-barreled, silver-plated Smith & Wesson, it looked almost like a derringer in his huge fist.

"Now, Dixie," Bordner said calmly, "Take this piece of garbage, put it on his horse, and ride for town. Halfway there, shoot the horse and leave both." He paused to drink the rest of his coffee and looked around, irritated that the cook had disappeared into the kitchen. "It'll look like he and his horse were wounded leaving the ambush and made it that far."

Dixie nodded without speaking, staring at the missing forefinger on his left hand.

"Ride hard for town. You need to be there before they do. Find Sheriff Lucas and tell him the Bar 3 was attacked and outlaws stole thirty head of horses," Bordner said, cutting into the remaining pancakes. "Tell him that the horses had been brought up to the big corral for shoeing for the roundup and they were all unshod."

Dixie nodded again and managed to ask what if the Corrigans came to town with some of his men.

"I would expect that. They may even come here first. That's another reason for you to be gone."

"Stay in town after you tell the sheriff. Tell Macy, ah, the new marshal, too," Bordner said and began buttering the sliced pancakes, then decided they were cold and yelled, "Simpson, bring in some fresh hotcakes. These aren't worth eating." He looked up at Murphy. "Tell Macy that I expect our men to . . . escape."

Late afternoon lay on their shoulders as Deed Corrigan, Felix Sanchez, and Chico rode into Wilkon with nine tied Bar 3 gunmen on their horses. One was Rhey Selmon. A buckboard, driven by Taol, the oldest Sanchez son, held the bodies of the dead gunmen. One was the body of Wyman, found on the way. Another five wounded attackers also rode their horses, flanked by three Sanchez vaqueros. Blue, Willy, Harmon, and Silka, carrying rifles across their saddles, rode alongside.

Up and down both sides of the main street, people stopped to gaze and whisper. County Sheriff Matthew R. Lucas exited his small office next to what passed for a courthouse, an old warehouse converted for the town's greater good. Lucas was a short, stocky man with a no-nonsense manner, not unlike that of a teacher. Not far behind the county lawman came Marshal Macy Shields and Dixie Murphy.

"Afternoon, Mr. Corrigan, what have you

here?" Shields asked.

Deed glanced toward the senior Sanchez and let him speak first.

"We bring the gunmen who try to kill us . . . like they kill our *amigos* at the Bar 3 this spring," Felix Sanchez spoke slowly with his head held high.

Sheriff Lucas smiled. "Glad you weren't hurt, Señor Sanchez." His graying hair told of a strong man who had served the county for twenty years.

"They wound *muy mal* my youngest son, Paul," the gray-haired rancher said. "If not for our Corrigan *amigos,* we will have not made it, I fear."

"Sounds like the same bunch that hit the Bar 3 last night. Mr. Murphy, the foreman of the Bar 3, reported his ranch was attacked last night and thirty horses were stolen," Lucas reported, trying to look stern.

Deed's eyes shot toward the gray-haired county lawman. "What?"

Calmly, the sheriff motioned toward Murphy, standing next to the city marshal on the corner of the boardwalk. "I said Mr. Murphy reported his ranch was attacked last night and thirty of his horses were stolen."

Blue reined up next to Deed, who told him about Dixie Murphy's claim.

"Convenient," Blue declared loudly, staring at Murphy. "So what happened to the outlaws' other horses, the ones they would've been riding?"

Murphy shrugged.

"Bet we can get a few of these boys to say different," Deed said quietly to Blue.

"Not our job, Deed. It's the sheriff's." Blue turned toward the nervous lawman and expressed their concern that Murphy was lying.

"It's pretty obvious this is the same bunch that wiped out the Regan family," Blue said.

"Maybe," came the tight-lipped reply from Lucas. "I'll check into it, but the horse stealing sounds legit to me." He motioned toward the arrested gunmen. "Mr. Murphy said they had put twenty-eight head in the corral. They were to be shod before roundup." He shrugged his shoulders and looked over at Macy Shields who smiled.

"Marshal, all right if I put this bunch in your jail?"

The skinny town lawman folded his arms and smiled again. "Yeah. I'll need to release Jimmy Wedgeberry first. He was in overnight for being drunk and raising cain."

Macy Shields was dressed in his customary white suspenders, or they had been white once, and a faded blue bib shirt. His eyes were tiny and too close together. As usual, he wore a bandana tied over his head like a pirate, instead of a hat. He had figured in several pointless killings in Texas and Kansas. Nothing was ever proved, however.

Blue leaned forward in his saddle. "There are nine bodies in the wagon. We weren't about to bury them on good Lazy S land. Figured they're the county's problem." He straightened his back.

Tugging on the brim of his hat, Deed growled, "Or we can dump them on Bar 3 land. That's where they came from."

Sheriff Lucas frowned and stared at the wagon, unable to meet either brother's gaze. "Oh, all right. Can you drive 'em to the city's cemetery? I'll get some boys to bury 'em."

"Yes, but you'd best get some boys there to dig real quick. Won't be long before the smell'll be something awful," Blue answered. "If you want, I'll say words over them." He motioned toward the wounded gunmen in the wagon. "Better have Doc take a look at them, too."

"You're leaving me with quite a mess."

"Maybe so, but they left the Sanchezes with loyal hands killed. One of their sons is shot up, and our good hand, Jake, wounded," Deed said, nudging his horse forward to stop next to the sheriff. Deed's eyes were hot as he glared at the uncomfortable lawman. "An' I don't buy that crap about stolen horses for one minute, Lucas. And if you do, you're not the man I thought you were."

Blue reined his horse away. "Come on, Deed. Let's get this done. We've got work to do."

Deed nodded, then spun his horse toward the boardwalk where Dixie Murphy and Marshal Shields stood. "Murphy, tell that fat-ass boss of yours that this is not over. The Regans were friends of ours. So are the Sanchezes. We don't forget friends."

Murphy spat a brown stream of tobacco juice into the street and snorted, "Go to hell, Corrigan."

"Deed, *come on,*" Blue yelled. "He isn't worth it."

Deed glanced at his brother as Murphy's hand dropped to his holstered gun. Deed looked back with his own Remington in his fist. No one saw him draw.

"I'm not as nice as my brother," Deed said between clenched teeth. "I don't think everybody is good. Or honest."

Sheriff Lucas waved his arms. "That's enough, Corrigan. Mr. Murphy is a law-abiding citizen in this county. You remember that."

"Sure, Sheriff. Sure. And I'm a buffalo." Deed spun his revolver in his hand, holstered it, and loped away to catch up with Blue and the others. The wagon rolled toward the cemetery at the far end of town.

Nightfall brought a sense of comfort to Wilkon after the day of excitement. The Corrigan brothers, Felix Sanchez, and their men rode out at dusk. Dixie Murphy decided to stay overnight, telling the livery operation to leave his horses outside and saddled in the corral. He would be taking them back to the ranch in the morning and would hire some men to help. The livery corral brimmed with milling horses, serving as the only visible reminder of the day's activity.

A hearing was scheduled for the morning in the justice of the peace's office. Quietly, Murphy met with the two lawmen to make certain they understood what was to happen. The three men stood behind the jail, smoking and talking. After a few minutes, they split up with Murphy heading for the Longhorn saloon; Sheriff Lucas heading for his home on Third Street; and Marshal Shields entering the jail.

Inside the jail, the Bar 3 gunmen were

crowded into five small cells. Rhey Selman gripped the cell bars and said, "Macy, get us out of here. We're not going quietly."

"Shut up, Selman, and listen."

Macy Shields explained what was going to happen . . . that a deputy would be in charge for the night and would be given a jug of whiskey. As he spoke, Shields handed keys and three revolvers to Selmon.

"Keep 'em out of sight," Shields ordered. "This needs to go quiet-like. Your horses are at the livery corral — still saddled. Murphy wants you to take all of them so he's got an alibi. Go back to the Bar 3 but stay out of sight. Go to one of the outer shacks."

"All right. When do we do this?" Selmon asked, keeping one gun and passing on the other weapons.

"My deputy'll be here in an hour." Shields grinned. "Be patient. When he's snoring, you can open the cells."

"What about him?"

"Coldcock him. Don't shoot," Shields said. "And don't run to the corral. Walk. Ride out the same way, real easy-like. Two or three at a time. If you do it right, nobody will know you're gone till morning, when I check in."

"What about the Corrigans?"

"Leave that to Bordner."

Chapter Twenty-Two

At midday, a grim Sheriff Lucas rode up to the LC ranch yard. With him were eight riders, all townsmen, all uneasy about their assignment as members of the sheriff's posse.

From the corral, Deed and Blue met them as they rode into the yard. Silka and Chico came from the barn. It was obvious something was wrong.

"The attackers broke out last night. Coldcocked the deputy. Got a night's lead on us," Lucas stated with little emotion.

With his hands on his hips, Deed snarled, "Been to the Bar 3? There's where they came from, Sheriff."

From the back of the posse came a gruff reply from Dixie Murphy. "I told you they were my horses, Corrigan, but not my men. I intend to get them back. Whether you go or not."

"They're headed toward El Paso," Sheriff

Lucas declared without looking at either man.

"Kinda headed the wrong direction, aren't you?" Deed said.

"Thought you'd want to ride with us," Sheriff Lucas said. "Some of these boys need to . . . get home. We'll go next to the Lazy S and see if they want to help."

Deed was silent and glanced at Silka, who nodded.

"All right. Send the husbands home to their wives," Deed finally said. He turned to Blue and suggested that he, Silka, and the others continue with roundup preparation. He asked Chico if he would go with him, but that he certainly didn't have to do so. The Mexican readily agreed and Blue thought it made sense. Silka thought it would be better if he went along, instead, but Deed told him it was more important for him to stay at the ranch. The former samurai's face was unreadable, but he didn't say anything more.

Soon, Deed and Chico were riding away with Sheriff Lucas and the posse. After picking up the middle son, Thomas Sanchez, and two vaqueros from the Lazy S, five men from the original group left for town and the rest continued on. The outlaws' trail was not hard to follow with so many horses involved. They were definitely more interested in gaining distance than in deceiving pursuit.

Thomas Sanchez took the point at Deed's request and his trail-reading skills were quickly apparent. The day was overcast with the likelihood of an autumn rain coming . . . and soon. After pausing at a feisty creek to water their mounts, the posse continued with little talking among themselves. Deed even refrained from chewing on Dixie Murphy, who was now bringing up the rear. For the first time, Deed realized the crooked cowman had put on a bright red scarf around this neck. Deed was certain he wasn't wearing it earlier, but said nothing.

The afternoon sun was easing toward the horizon and Deed suggested to Thomas Sanchez that they should look for a place to camp for the night. Sheriff Lucas insisted they keep going for another hour or so, that they were cutting into the outlaws' lead. The logic was hard to argue with and Deed and Thomas agreed.

Ahead was a towering mesa with its twin positioned on the other side of the trail. The area was known as Oak Tree Canyon. Through it lay more open country with occasional bursts of scrub pine. On either side of the mesas were heavily forested areas, broken by rock and a sometimes creek. A perfect place for an ambush, Deed thought and drew his Spencer from its saddle scabbard. He leaned forward and patted his buckskin on the neck. Chico noticed Deed readying his rifle and did the same. Deed saw Sheriff Lucas was wearing his lawman's badge; the metal star danced a little, even in the overcast afternoon.

"How come you're wearing a star?" Deed asked. "Kinda gives us away, doesn't it?"

The gray-haired lawman glanced at his shirt and shrugged his shoulders. "Thought it made sense for people to know we're the law. You know, the law is coming."

"Interesting," Deed said. "Most lawmen I know don't wear their badges on the trail. It gives them away. Where we're riding could easily be an ambush."

"It'll be fine, Corrigan. You take care of yourself."

"That's what I am trying to do." Shifting in his saddle, Deed studied the nearing mesas. He yelled to Thomas three horse lengths in front of him, "Thomas, I don't like this. Ride careful."

The young Mexican nodded his agreement and patted the rifle laying across his saddle in front of him.

Halfway up the hillside on the left, a

flicker of light came and disappeared in an instant.

"Thomas, ambush!" Deed yelled and kicked his horse, firing in the direction of the brief flash and wheeling toward the trees to his right.

Rifle fire from a dozen spots exploded from both mesas. Thomas Sanchez went down, then his two vaqueros under the heavy fire. Five bullets sought Deed at once and drove him from his frightened horse. One bullet creased his horse's chest. Another drilled a hole in his hat and one cut across the top of his left ear, barely missing his head. A fourth sliced across his upper left arm, ripping through his shirtsleeve. And a fifth clipped his left thigh. The buckskin ran on. The young gunfighter hit the ground. His carbine went flying into the woods. So did his hat. For a minute, he wasn't cognizant of what was going on. Around him, bullets tore into the posse, except for Sheriff Lucas and Dixie Murphy who were riding safely toward the mesas.

Deed saw Chico get hit in the face and crumble to the ground. One of the two townsmen with the posse flopped next to Deed. He stared at the young gunfighter through frightened eyes, tried to speak, and died.

Blinking away the shock, Deed reached up and touched his left ear; its top was bleeding and hurting. He had come close to being killed. Crawling on his hands and knees, he found his carbine, grabbed it, and moved on reaching a shallow ravine that once had been a creek. Sounds of gunfire gradually lessened as he forced himself to keep moving. He knew the outlaws would soon leave the mesas to see if any posse men remained alive.

He had to find a hiding place before he passed out. He must. His left arm was throbbing and his shirtsleeve was crimson. He was certain he'd also been hit near his left thigh. He didn't think any of the wounds were serious, but he was losing a considerable amount of blood and was growing weak from the shock.

Splatters of a cold rain drummed against the land.

At the end of the ravine sat a fat pool of water — stagnant water. To his right was a long rock shelf, running twenty yards. He forced himself up onto the shelf and crawled along its uneven frame, dragging his carbine with him. Maybe he could lay there and rest. Maybe. Fifteen yards along the way, he came to a crevice that looked like a possible hideaway. He stood, became dizzy, and dropped again to his knees. Patience was the key, Silka would remind him if he were here. Do not panic. Think.

Rain was coming hard now and that would wash away any signs of his movements. Standing slowly again, he saw the crevice opened into a cave that was at least twenty feet long and almost man-high. He slipped inside and slid to the ground. If they found him here, he would die, but he couldn't go any farther. He cocked the Spencer using both hands.

Crawling across the rocky floor was a black spider. Deed watched the tiny creature as it moved up onto his boot.

"Evening, little buddy," he said. "Got some Indian friends that think you're a pretty powerful fellow. Sorry to bother you, but I had to get out of the rain."

The spider crawled up across his boot, down, and wandered toward the back of the cave. Shortly afterward, he fell asleep.

On the trail, outlaws squished across the soaked land, swearing at being wet and making certain none of the downed posse lived, with additional shots to their heads. Wearing a yellow slicker over his bear-fur coat, Rhey Selmon looked up at the sheriff and Dixie Murphy.

"Ya did good, lawman. Agon will be

pleased. Probably a bonus in it for ya," Selmon praised and wiped rain from his face.

Sheriff Lucas looked nauseous and said nothing.

"I don't see Corrigan's body, do you?" Murphy said, shifting in his saddle.

"No. Haven't found it yet. Washita said he hit him in the head. Knocked him off his horse," Selmon said. "I hit him, too. Arm or shoulder. Could've been hit four or five times. Ike was shooting at him, too."

Watching the rain soak the land, Murphy said, "Well, I want to see his body. I want to put a bullet between his eyes, for good measure. The bastard almost ruined things for us." He swung his horse toward the mesa. "Keep looking."

Less than two miles away, Holt Corrigan heard the gunshots before the rain came. He had seen the clouds, quickly gathered wood for a fire, and taken refuge under a cliff before the sky opened up. He knew he wasn't far from the largest ranch in the area, the Bar 3, but still a long way from his brothers' ranch. The intensity of gunfire told him that it wasn't a hunt; it was a gun battle. All that gunfire meant someone was surely dead. As soon as the word *dead* came to his mind, he tried to unthink it. He didn't want to pull death to him by thinking of it. Besides, there was nothing he could do about it, one way or the other. Probably a disagreement over cattle ownership, so he began assembling his gathered wood for a fire and soon got it started. He was surprised to see the fire turn hollow, and he jammed short branches into its middle to eliminate the bad sign. There wasn't anything he could do at the moment, except make certain his guns were cleaned and ready.

CHAPTER TWENTY-THREE

It was dark when Deed Corrigan awoke. The rain had stopped and the night was cold. He woke up shivering. At first, he didn't know where he was, but gradually his mind returned him to the situation. His left arm was stiff, so was his left thigh. His ear burned with pain. Gradually, he determined that neither his leg nor his arm wound held any lead. He was hungry and thirsty. The second desire should be easily handled. Outside the cave were puddles of rainwater collected in the rock shelf's pockets. He forced himself to make certain his Spencer and handgun were dry and ready. It took twice as long as it should.

Cradling his Spencer in his right arm, he half-crawled, half-dragged himself to the first rain puddle and drank it dry. He edged himself along the shelf to the second water and did his best to clean his wounds, even putting his ear into the cool water. He was weak, but he was alive. More than he could say for the rest of the posse, he feared.

Obviously, Sheriff Lucas was involved with Agon Bordner's grand scheme. Probably on the take. How sad, Deed thought. At one time, Matthew R. Lucas had been a good man.

Using his right hand against the rock wall for balance, he stood and tried to put weight on his wounded left leg, but couldn't and almost fell down. The rock shelf itself was wet as he worked slowly toward the lower land. Halfway across, he slipped and fell. The pain in his left leg made him bite his lip to keep from crying out. Slowly, he stood and started again. He figured the outlaws would search the area for him and he wasn't going far without a horse.

There was a definite possibility that his buckskin would be near, unless they had taken it. After the initial fear, the animal would seek him out. Horses liked the comfort of being around people, and the buckskin was a favorite. Likely the animal would return to the trail to graze and wait. The repulsion of blood and dead bodies might change that, however. But Deed had to try and return to the trail. Some of the other posse horses might there as well. And, he reminded himself, so might be a bunch of outlaws.

But it was early. Dawn was least an hour away. Not too many outlaws liked getting up early, especially on a cold, wet morning. Still, he had to be wary of guards left behind to watch for him and any other posse member that made it.

Backtracking through the woods was slow. He couldn't put any weight on his wounded leg and it was bleeding again. A long, crooked branch was serving as a crutch. Deed couldn't remember feeling so weary. He even considered leaving his Spencer, but knew that wouldn't be wise. From the cover of brush, he studied the awful reminders of the ambush. White corpses lay in various poses of death, apparently untouched since the fighting. As expected, three horses were grazing nearby; one with its saddle upside-down. His buckskin was among them.

The smell of woodsmoke reached him before he saw its reason. Two men were crowded around a small, balky fire trying to keep warm. A blackened coffeepot sat on top of a half-burned log. A skillet of bacon slices was sizzling. Both bacon and coffee smelled delicious. On the ground nearby were tin cups and plates. Obviously, the guards were there to watch for Deed's return. Neither were paying attention as he worked his way along the edge of the trail to a position where he could cover both easily.

Dizziness tried to grab him, but he shook his head. Not now. Not now. He saw that his hat still lay within the trees near where he had fallen. Crawling, he managed to get to it and put it on, ignoring the hole through the crown and the fact that the edge rested on his injured ear.

Then, leaning on his crutch, he took a few steps forward.

"Mornin', boys," he said, aiming his carbine at them.

Both men jumped and reached for rifles lying beside them.

"Don't. Unless you want to start the morning . . . dead," Deed growled.

"You must be Deed Corrigan," the long-faced outlaw said. "Looks like our boys cut you up pretty bad."

"Looks can be deceiving," Deed said, shifting his weight to his bad leg, then shifting it back. "You can tell Murphy and Lucas I'll be coming for them."

The taller outlaw with a long chin that held a long-ago scar straightened his back. "Tell them yourself, Corrigan. They'll be along. All of 'em. Real soon."

"You'd better hope not. The two of you

won't see them arrive."

"I gotta move that bacon. It's gonna burn." Leaning over in front of the fire, the taller outlaw took hold of the skillet as if to shift it away from the flames.

Dropping his crutch, Deed realized the significance of the man using his left hand to control the skillet and stepped back and to the right as the outlaw flung the hot grease and bacon at him while reaching for his holstered gun.

Two quick shots from Deed hit the outlaw heart high as two pieces of bacon reached his waist and the grease splattered around his boots. The movement sent a dull ache through his left arm.

"Your turn." Deed swung his recocked Spencer in the direction of the second outlaw. The man took a half step forward, froze, and raised his hands.

After directing him to unbuckle his side-arm and drop a backup gun, Deed told him to take the two rifles and his pistols over to the wooded area and throw them into the forest. While that was being done, Deed picked up a slice of bacon, ate it, then retrieved the dead outlaw's revolver, shoving it into his belt. His gaze rarely left the submissive outlaw; then Deed ordered the man to lay down across the fire from him with his head pointed away and his arms and legs outstretched.

Satisfied the man couldn't or wouldn't do anything quickly, Deed ate another piece of bacon while he searched the dead outlaw for any hidden weapons and found a short-barreled Smith & Wesson Bulldog revolver. He shoved the gun into his back waistband, ate another piece of bacon from the ground, and poured himself a cup of coffee. It was hot and strong, but tasted good. He was weak and couldn't move quickly, and the rest of the gang would not likely be far away. The gunshots might have alerted them, but he couldn't worry about it.

Drawing the outlaw's main gun, he began hobbling toward his buckskin, leaving the crutch where he had discarded it. As he walked past the terrified outlaw, Deed slugged his head with the butt of his Spencer. It didn't make sense to gamble on the man staying in place for long and Deed needed time.

The buckskin's head came up and its ears pricked as Deed neared. Would the animal shy away from him? Deed's strength was draining fast; he wouldn't be able to trail after the horse if it moved away. But the buckskin nickered and rubbed its nose against Deed's chest as he came close.

"Yeah, it's me, boy. We're going to ride out of here, but you have to help me."

Deed took the downed reins, shoved the carbine into its sleeve and led the horse to some boulders that looked like God had been playing dice with them before leaving. There was no way he would be able to mount the horse with his wounded leg. He would get on from the wrong side, and do so from an elevated position. Finding the right rock, he led the horse alongside, then eased his good leg into the stirrup and tried to slide his left leg across the saddle.

The buckskin wanted to move out, but Deed held the reins tightly with his right hand and forced himself to complete mounting. His left leg screamed in pain. At least he was in place and he eased the reins. The buckskin took off with a familiar canter, then into a smooth lope. Deed hoped he would be able to stay conscious long enough to reach their ranch. He had to, to do otherwise was to die.

"Not today. Not going to die today."

The buckskin's ears twisted to catch the words.

"It's all right, boy, I'm just a little weak right now." He forced his left arm toward the pommel and wrapped the reins around his wrist and the pommel to help keep him upright if he passed out.

CHAPTER TWENTY-FOUR

Thirty minutes after Deed rode away, Dixie Murphy, Sheriff Lucas, Rhey Selmon, and the rest of the Bar 3 gunmen rode up to the ambush site, leading the rest of the un-ridden horses. They were surprised to see the lone outlaw drinking coffee by his camp-fire.

"What the hell happened?" Murphy screamed as he reined up next to the man, who stood and wiped off his pants.

"Ah, Deed Corrigan. That's what hap-pened. He jumped us. Got away. About a half hour ago, I reckon," the outlaw said, scratching his boot heel on the ground and rubbing his sore head where Deed had hit him.

"Why didn't you go after him? That's why you boys were here," Murphy demanded.

"I didn't have no gun. Made me throw 'em in the woods. Yonder." He motioned toward the thick grove of trees. "Then he knocked me out. When I came around, I looked, but couldn't find them."

Rhey Selmon cursed and so did Dixie Murphy.

"If he gets away, there's no telling what kind of hell he'll create," Lucas said, shaking his head.

"Won't be too good for you, that's for sure," Selmon grunted and turned toward his men. "You three, grab an extra horse each and go after Corrigan. He's hurt . . . bad. Stop him."

The three men nudged their mounts forward, grabbing the reins of three other saddled horses.

"Push 'em hard and you'll catch him," Murphy declared, waving his arm in the direction of Deed's escape. "Just let 'em go when you switch. They'll head for the Bar 3 after a while." He bit off a chaw from a square of tobacco. "We'll take a roundabout way to the ranch. Don't want anybody tracking us there. Come as soon as he's dead."

Sheriff Lucas watched them gallop away with the extra horses beside them. "What should I do?"

Selmon spun toward him and fired. "Nothing, Sheriff. Nothing at all."

The county lawman's eyes widened, his

hands extended as if to stop the bullets.

"No —"

Selmon fired three more times and Lucas fell facedown from his horse. Mud popped around him; his leg twitched and was still.

"What the hell was that all about?" Murphy screamed. "You just killed the county sheriff."

"Agon's orders."

Selmon turned toward the cattleman and fired again. Murphy grabbed his arm and screamed again. "Damn you, I'll —"

Holding up his left hand, Selmon explained, "Agon thought it would look a little suspicious if you were the only one in the posse not hurt."

"Oh, damn. Couldn't you have just grazed me?"

"I was trying."

"Damn."

Chapter Twenty-Five

Dizzy and weak, Deed Corrigan weaved in the saddle. Ahead was a cluster of cottonwoods. He remembered there should be water, especially after the rain. His horse needed to rest as well.

Over the hill behind him came three riders, whipping their horses in a fierce gallop. They had to be Bar 3 gunmen coming to finish the job. He spurred the buckskin into a run it couldn't keep up long. Ahead was a small ridge. That would have to do. He was too far from the cottonwoods to make it. Nearing the ridge, he slowed his horse and untied the reins from his left hand. He pulled his carbine from its sleeve and tossed it on the ground. Trying to dismount while holding the gun could prove disastrous. The horse threw its head, wanting to run in spite of its weariness.

"Not now, boy. I need you to stop. Whoa." Angling across the hills, Holt Corrigan saw three horsemen chasing after a lone rider, who was wounded. Deed! It was his brother!

Dismounting, Holt drew his rifle and knelt. He raised the gun to his shoulder and began firing. The lead rider grabbed his chest and tumbled from his horse. Holt's next shots missed, but the two remaining gunmen were now aware of his presence. From the ridge in front of them, Deed propped his rifle against a rock, laid his wounded arm across the barrel and shot one-handed. A second rider's face turned red and he fell off the back of his horse. The third rider tried to turn his horse around, but the animal wouldn't obey. Bullets from both Deed and Holt brought him down. The three empty horses ran past Deed as he slowly stood.

Who had helped him? Was it one of the Lazy S vaqueros? He wasn't far from the Sanchez ranch. He watched as the figure remounted and rode toward him, waving.

Holt!

How in the world? Deed wondered but was very happy, whatever the reason. He was weak and went to his knees.

"Hey, Deed, what the hell you doing out here?" Holt asked as he rode up. "Wait a minute. You're hurt. Really hurt." He swung his horse around toward the attackers. "Hold on, Deed. I gotta check on these bastards first, so they won't cause us more problems."

Holt walked his horse next to the closest outlaw and jumped down, holding his rifle in his right hand. The dead gunman's face was a red pumpkin. He yanked free the man's pistols and a knife and threw them in Deed's direction, then went to the second downed gunman. Stepping close, he kicked the prone man in the ribs. Hard. The grunt that followed was what Holt expected.

"When you turn over, peckerhead, you'd better have empty hands," Holt growled. "I'd like an excuse to put a bullet in your head."

"I-I'm hurt. R-Real bad."

"Tell somebody who gives a damn," Holt responded. "You bastards were trying to kill my little brother." He pointed his rifle at the slowly moving man. "I oughta put a bullet in your head just for good measure."

"P-Please . . . mister," the long-faced outlaw said, holding his side. His shirt was mostly crimson.

"Shut up."

"P-Please I was j-just followin' orders."

"Who sent you?"

"Uh, nobody."

Holt fired and the outlaw screamed and grabbed his right knee. "That's one knee gone. Want to try two?" Holt levered a new cartridge into his rifle.

"Oh God, no! No! Dixie Murphy and Rhey Selmon, they sent us."

"That's better. What's going on here?"

The outlaw jabbered about what had happened, the attack and arrest at the Lazy S, the escape from jail, the ambush of the posse, the involvement of the county sheriff. Holt stripped the man of his weapons and tossed them toward his brother, then walked on to the third outlaw. The man was dead; Holt disarmed him, shoving his guns into his waistband and heading for his brother.

"Hey, are you Holt Corrigan?" the long-faced outlaw asked. "I heard you was dead."

Holt smiled. "Heard that, too. I'm Sam Holton."

"Sam H-Holton? Do I know you?"

"No. I don't hang around with scum." Holt hurried to his wounded brother.

"I'm all right. Nothing serious. They caught us in an ambush yesterday."

"I heard." Holt looked up. "Think any more of those bastards will be coming?"

"Don't know. I doubt it. Getting too close to the Lazy S."

"You've got blood in your hair, on your ear."

"Yeah, they nicked my ear. Think a little piece is gone."

Holt examined Deed's ear. "Yeah. But no one will notice if you keep your hair long."

"I guess I was lucky."

"Are you carrying any lead?" Holt asked.

"No. Just been bleeding a lot."

"Your ear looks like somebody bit it."

"Yeah, a bullet."

"Can you ride?" Holt asked, shoving his rifle into its sleeve and pulling his canteen from his saddle and handing to Deed.

"I got here, didn't I?"

Deed took the canteen and drank deeply, holding it with his right hand. His left hand was at his side. He tried to put weight on his left leg but it wouldn't hold him and he fell.

"Careful, little brother. Go slow."

"Yeah, maybe so. Can you get my horse? The buckskin might let you. He's a good one," Deed said.

"Sure. Can you hold mine?"

"Got it."

After slipping the canteen sling over his saddle horn, Holt walked to Deed's grazing horse. The buckskin raised his head and his ears went up as Holt approached.

"Easy, buck. Easy now. I'm Deed's brother. Nothing to get excited about. Right?" Holt held out his opened palm for the horse to sniff, then slid it along the animal's face to take hold of his halter, then the reins. "See, buck. Nothing to it. Going to be fine, you and me. Let's go over here where Deed is."

He led the horse back to Deed. The buckskin shook its head and snorted, smelling Deed's blood.

"You're all right, Buck. It's old blood," Holt helped Deed into the saddle, holding the reins of both horses, then retrieved Deed's Spencer and returned it to the saddle scabbard.

"Tie my hands . . . and my boots," Deed said. "There's piggin' strings in my saddlebags."

Holt looked over at the wounded outlaw, who was laying down, holding his bloody knee. Two of the outlaw horses were grazing nearby; the third was nowhere in sight.

After Holt had laced his brother into place, he jammed the collected outlaw guns, barrel first, into the muddy ground.

"Deed, think I'd better get rid of those rifles on their horses before we go. Don't want to give ol' one knee any ideas," Holt said.

"They might not let you get close."

"We'll see. If they don't, I'll send 'em running."

Mounting, Holt swung his horse toward the quiet horses. The closest bay tensed as he rode up, but didn't move. He eased alongside the animal and yanked the rifle clear and laid it across his saddle in front of him. The second rifle was lifted as easily and Holt pulled away, balancing both guns in front of him.

The wounded outlaw watched him and called out, "You better keep ridin', Corrigan. Bordner's gonna git all of you. You, too, Holton."

Holt's eyes were hot. For an instant, his fingers found the trigger of the top rifle, then he relaxed. "Tell that fat bastard *we'll* be coming after *him*. Tell him to get his fat ass out of here."

The outlaw muttered something the Corrigan brothers didn't understand as they rode away with Holt leading Deed's horse. After a few minutes, Holt threw the two outlaw rifles into the brush.

"Holt, I'm mighty glad to see you," Deed said through clenched teeth. "Blue said he talked with you in El Paso."

"Yeah, he told me to quit fighting a dead war and come home. So, here I am."

Deed smiled. "Blue makes a lot of sense sometimes. Kinda like Ma used to."

"Right."

"You didn't rob the El Paso bank?"

"No. Blue said it was owned by Confederates. So I went to see for myself. Ended up talking with Dave Copate. We fought together at Sabine Pass. Good man," Holt said. "He told me a lot of what Blue said."

"We got word at the Forsyth station that the bank had been robbed."

"Really. Well, it wasn't me."

Deed shook his head. "Yeah, the stage driver said that the bank president claimed it wasn't you. Was real strong about it."

Holt was silent, then changed the subject. "How far to the next . . . friendly ranch?"

"The Lazy S is about three hours from here. Due north."

They rode on, each with his own thoughts, into a wide and broken land. Ahead of them grazing cattle were mere dots on a light brown canvas. Overhead, the sky was a mass of jagged gray clouds, as if a long heavenly fire had turned ashen.

Holt was worried about more Bar 3 riders following them or coming up on them from some unseen draw. They were crossing Bar 3 land; he knew that. Deed was mumbling to himself, barely conscious.

They passed a cluster of stunted cedar, enclosing what had once been a buffalo wallow. Ahead he saw a large open tank holding water. As they approached, Deed woke up, shook his head, and told him to head toward a patch of brittlebush far to the left and to a gathering of trees just beyond. He grimaced that the tank was filled with scum and gestured that good water lay within the trees. Holt nodded and wheeled his horse in that direction, still leading Deed's horse. They passed a snow-white steer skeleton, cleared a fat ridge, entered a shallow wash, and rode into a magnificent meadow, unseen from just a handful of yards away. In front of them was a sparkling pond, fed by two occasional streams and offering solace to a small gathering of cottonwood, pecan, and oak trees. A half-dozen steers drank from its wetness.

"Told ya," Deed muttered.

"Lucky guess," Holt growled. "Want down?"

"No thanks. Better not. Might have trouble getting back on." Deed's face was white with shock.

"All right." Holt dismounted and led both horses to the pond. Several steers moved away as they advanced. All wore Bar 3 brands.

While the animals drank, Holt Corrigan studied their surroundings. It was fine cattle country. Far to their left was a long arroyo that appeared to be filled with cattle. To their right was a patch of sandstone bursting with heavy rock. The sandstone was still heavy with last night's rain. In all directions, the land was empty of riders. At least it would be difficult to surprise them in this flat country. Somewhere a quail whispered an inquiring song. Holt wondered if it was a sign and what kind. He decided it must be a good sign; how could a bird singing be an indication of bad things coming?

After the horses had watered well, they took off again. Holt knew the land, but not like Deed and Blue did. It had been long years since his departure. Deed was asleep in the saddle and Holt let him rest.

A late afternoon sun laid slanting rays across the two Corrigan brothers as they rode closer to the Lazy S. Ahead of them, two antelope were surprised from their grazing and began to run. Deed was apparently asleep, bobbing in the saddle. Holt watched four riders appear in the horizon and advance from a ridge to the northwest.

He knew at once it was Comanches.

Taking a knife from his belt, Holt turned to Deed. "Little brother, wake up. Got four

Indians coming. Wake up." He leaned over and cut free Deed's hands with his knife.

Deed blinked his eyes, trying to regain his senses, then began rubbing his stiff hands.

"Got an idea, Deed. Make like you're crazy in the head. You know, yelling crazy stuff. Wave your arms," Holt told him as the watched the warriors advance.

"You think it's worth it. I can shoot."

"We'll try that next."

Deed began to holler a mixture of Japanese phrases and biblical verses, anything he could recall. *"Nakitsura ni hachi! Ame futte ji katamaru!* There is a lion in the way; a lion is in the streets. *Tonari no shibafu wa noi!* The Lord bless thee and keep thee; the Lord make his face shine upon thee, and be gracious unto thee; the Lord lift up his countenance upon thee, and give thee peace. *Fuku sui bon ni kaerazu!"* He waved his right arm wildly, looking up to the sky.

As they rode closer to the Indians, Holt said the Comanche words for medicine man while he made the signs. He put his fist at his forehead, extended two fingers skyward, then spiraled his fist upward. That was followed with holding up one finger. His left hand held his rifle in front of his saddle.

The Indians made signs of understanding and moved out of their way. After clearing a short ridge, Holt said, "Come on, let's ride before they change their minds."

They galloped hard across the broken plain and gradually brought their horses back to a trot, then a walk.

"Damn, that was wild," Holt said, shaking his head.

"Sure was. I was out of stuff to yell," Deed said and chuckled. "Never can tell about Indians."

"Yeah. Never. You sure must be feeling better to yell like that."

"Didn't have much choice."

They rode silently for another hour when three riders became visible from the northwest. They were largely silhouettes. As they came closer, Deed could make out their sombreros and a stray ray of sun found one of their large-roweled spurs.

"They're friends, Holt. Lazy S vaqueros. Wave at them."

"You're sure."

"Yes."

The Corrigan brothers rode easily forward as the three vaqueros slipped beside them, eager to hear what had happened. Deed's bloody shirt and pants told part of the story. Four brown and lean men with unrelenting dark eyes flashed ready smiles. Each was armed with a rifle and gunbelt; each had an extra cartridge belt across his shoulders. Large-roweled spurs seemed a part of their bodies.

The lead vaquero with steel-gray hair and piercing eyes groaned when told the news about Sanchez's son and the vaqueros with the posse. A cigarette dangled from his lips.

"Are you the one they call *El Punta*?" he asked.

"No, I'm Sam Holton," Holt held out his hand.

Taking it firmly, the man said, "I am Cliente, foreman of the Lazy S."

"Good to know you," Holt said. "I take it you've met my little brother." He smiled. "Guess that gave it away. Sorry. Too many folks trying to catch up with Holt Corrigan these days."

Straightening his back, Cliente said, "I understand. Señor Deed Corrigan is a most honored man in our *ranchero*. He save us. He and his brother, Blue. And Silka, the one with the long knives. You are most welcome . . . Sam Holton."

"Thanks. Agon Bordner behind all this?"

"*Sí,* the fat man and his guns. Many guns. They outnumber us two times. Maybe more," Cliente tossed his dead cigarette. "We are cowmen, not gunmen."

"All of us will have to get smarter and

tougher," Holt drawled.

"*Sí.* Let us ride for our *ranchero,* amigos," Cliente said. "Your brother need rest. We will send out a wagon to bring home the bodies of Thomas Sanchez and our friends who rode with the posse."

Deed bit his lower lip and asked if they would also bring Chico's body back for burying at their ranch. Cliente readily agreed, then said something in Spanish to two of his men. They wheeled their horses and galloped back. Deed guessed Cliente was being careful and didn't want to take a chance on Bar 3 riders coming up on them. A look at Holt told him that his brother was thinking the same thing.

Motioning for the Corrigan brothers to follow, Cliente rolled another cigarette and said, "So now we fight the law as well as the fat man." He snapped a match to flame on his pants, inhaled, and added, "Roundup will be a *buen' ocasión* to attack us, I fear. We will be spread out and worried about our beeves."

Deed nodded, too tired to respond. His wounds were bleeding again, bringing fresh pain. Sleep would be welcomed. Forcing himself to speak, he said, "Not having the roundup would play right into their hands. They'd brand everything that moved."

"*Sí*. It is a tough thing we are in."

"Well, it's a cinch they won't be joining us this year," Holt said, searching his coat pocket for a cigar.

Deed smiled at the use of *us*. It was good to have Holt back. They rode for a few minutes; then Holt turned to his brother, leaned towards him, and just above a whisper, said, "Earlier I told those boys I was Sam Holton. You should know that I am going by that name for now. At least to outsiders. I'll deal with the other later."

"Sure . . . Sam."

As soon as they reached the Lazy S hacienda, Cliente jumped down and went inside; he found Felix Sanchez and told him about Deed and Sam following. Felix met them at the hitchrail in front; reddened eyes told them that the news of his son's death had already reached the family. Cliente was beside him.

"Amigos. It is *bueno* that you make it, Señor Deed," Felix said in a voice thick with sadness.

"Felix, I'm so sorry about Thomas. We rode right into it," Deed said.

"Sheriff Lucas shall die by my hand," the big Mexican rancher said.

Holt leaned forward in his saddle. "You know something? Don't be surprised if

Sheriff what's his name is already dead. With Deed getting away, his value to Bordner isn't much."

Deed looked at him with a question in his eyes. "What about Murphy?"

"Naw. He's too good a cattleman."

Felix Sanchez waved his arms. "*Por favor,* where are my manners? Come in and eat. Señor Deed, you must rest. You come as well, Señor Holton." The Sanchez family swarmed around Deed, insisting that he be treated for his wounds even as Deed insisted he was fine.

"Señor Deed, you have been bleeding *muy mal,*" the gray-haired Maria Sanchez, Felix's wife, declared. "Come now and let us clean your wounds. Find some new clothes."

Sanchez's daughters, Tina and Lea, laughed and took him by the arm. Both were in their late teens and striking young women. Felix nodded agreement and his oldest son, Taol, shouted his support. Holt laughed and patted his brother on the back.

Maria turned to Holt. "You must eat too, Señor Holton. You have saved our Deed." It was obvious they realized he was Deed's older brother, but honored Holt's wish to be called Sam Holton.

"Sounds great."

Felix Sanchez told them that his youngest

son, Paul, had been moved back home and was resting well and Felix's thanks for saving Paul and all at the ranch came again. Deed was so tired he wasn't sure he could stand. They entered the great house, taking in its quiet majesty. Adobe walls held the temperatures well and everywhere the Corrigans looked were paintings, Mexican artifacts, Indian pottery, and handwoven rugs. A large gun rack held a dozen rifles and three shotguns.

Heavy chairs, hand engraved, awaited them around the massive wooden table. Felix and Cliente were already seated and talking. Holt sat down, after washing his face and hands outside. A few minutes later, Deed joined them wearing a new shirt and pants, flared at the bottom. He looked pale, but acted like he was fine. His ear was bandaged and it smelled like his arm and thigh had been dressed as well. He was wearing his gunbelt, but had discarded the outlaw revolvers picked up at their camp.

"You look ready for church services, even Blue would be pleased," Holt said and added, "I'm going to ride with Cliente and his riders back to the ambush. Felix wants the bodies back here as soon as possible. You'll stay here, all right?"

"Uh, sure. Sure."

Felix's daughters brought in steaming plates of tortillas, beef, and beans, with plenty of fresh, hot coffee. After finishing, Deed asked if it would be all right for him to lie down for a few minutes. The two daughters led him to one of the extra bedrooms and he was asleep in minutes.

Chapter Twenty-Six

Rhey Selmon reported to Agon Bordner and was surprised at the oversized boss's reaction — or rather, the lack of it. Savoring a freshly baked apple pie, the huge man stopped eating as his top gunman reported that all of the posse had been killed except Deed Corrigan, but he was wounded and three men had gone after him to finish the job.

In the far corner, a man was playing the violin for Bordner's enjoyment as he ate. He hadn't shared with Selmon or Murphy that two Texas Rangers had made an appearance while they were gone. Bordner had fed them generously and given them a place to sleep, then they had ridden on. He was certain they believed his story about an unknown band of renegades attacking his ranch, stealing horses, and then attacking the Lazy S.

Bordner looked up, apple syrup dripping

down his chin. "What about Lucas?"

"He's dead," Selmon said. "Murphy's wounded. Just skinned his arm. Like you ordered."

"Good. Good." Bordner took another bite of pie, enjoying the combination of crust and fruit. "Fine job on the pie, Simpson," he yelled to the unseen cook.

Outside of the ranch was a burst of noise and Selmon went to see what was happening. He came back, frowning.

"That's Benson. He's shot up some," Selmon said. "Some stranger gunned down the other two."

Bordner licked his fingers and called for more coffee. Without turning toward Selmon, he asked, "What stranger?"

Hitching his gunbelt as if to challenge someone, Selmon said that a stranger who called himself Sam Holton showed up as they were closing in on the wounded Deed Corrigan. He made the difference and they rode off together.

"This stranger was leading Deed's horse. Deed had his hands tied to the pommel and his boots to the stirrups, to keep him steady," Selmon said. "Like I said, he was carrying lead. Don't know how bad though. He's a tough sonuvabitch." He cocked his head to the side. "From what Benson says, this other guy was, too."

"Ever hear of a Sam Holton?"

"No."

"Well, well, that's not a good day's work, Rhey. You didn't kill them," Bordner said and pushed another quarter section of pie into his mouth and followed it with coffee.

Selmon looked at him, worried about what Bordner would do.

Bordner told him to keep the arrested and escaped Bar 3 men there on the ranch, except when on specific assignment. To make it easier for them, he had ordered extra whiskey and a wagonload of prostitutes to be brought in for their enjoyment. He planned to keep three for himself.

Rhey Selmon smiled and left to tell the men.

The fat man was pleased with several outcomes of the last few days. The men who had attacked the Lazy S and survived the Corrigan counterattack were back and no law would be looking for them. So were all of their horses. That brought his force to twenty-two men. Not as many as he wanted, but enough if he used them well, and more were available for hire in El Paso. The Lazy S had lost another three men; he was certain Felix Sanchez had no more than ten men left to operate and protect his ranch.

Murphy was ordered to go to town and report on the posse's demise. He was to say he didn't know if Deed Corrigan was alive or not, only that his body wasn't there when he rode away. He was to tell the town editor that he had been hit on the head and had been unconscious until after the ambush was over. Bordner wanted the town council to select an interim county sheriff until an election could be held and he wanted Macy Shields to hold both jobs, at least for now. It would make the final takeover of the region's cattle lands so much easier. He prided himself on thinking long-term. That was the key. None of his men knew all of his plans. Not Dixie Murphy. Not Rhey Selmon. Not Macy Shields. Not anyone.

He finished the pie with a flourish and lit up a black cigar. The women should arrive anytime this afternoon.

After returning from town, Murphy was to oversee the gathering of cows with calves for fall branding. There would be no co-operation with the Sanchezes or the Corrigans, of course. He had already merged the two small ranches into the Bar 3 and all of the new animals were being marked with his bar crown brand. He loved the look of it. Sheer power he thought. Murphy's men were to stay on their side of the boundary between the Bar 3 and the Lazy S spreads. Bordner wanted it to appear that he was a law-abiding citizen and any trouble that occurred was not his doing.

He didn't like hearing about a gun-savvy stranger helping Deed Corrigan. Things he couldn't control upset him. He planned on having Murphy drive some cattle to the railroad crew working around Houston to provide some immediate cash. Selmon would also be directed to rob the El Paso stage, at least once more. Bordner had kept his men away from robbing the trains; he didn't like the idea of Pinkertons backtracking them . . . to him.

Bordner pulled on his cigar and waved at the violinist to leave. The house was quiet and he liked that. He took the cigar from his mouth, studied it, and called out for Selmon. The gunfighter was in the other room and responded quickly.

"Did you leave all the bodies where they fell?" Bordner asked.

"Yeah."

"Do you think the Sanchezes will send a wagon to bring back the bodies of their men?" Bordner ran his finger along the table.

Selmon rubbed his chin. "Hadn't thought about it. But, yeah, I reckon so."

"Yes. So do I. Here's what I want you to do." Bordner had decided he wanted to hit the Sanchez ranch again, right now when they wouldn't be expecting it.

"Take men with you and wait. Out of sight. When you see the wagon and their men leave the Lazy S, I want to you to hit the ranch again. They won't be expecting it." He returned the cigar to his mouth.

Controlling the county law would make it all go smoothly. Since the owning family was Mexican, he didn't expect much of an outcry from the rest of the community. Except for the Corrigans. They would be dealt with separately.

CHAPTER TWENTY-SEVEN

It was late afternoon and cool. Holt was checking his rifle as Cliente picked three men to go with him and the burial wagon.

Deed woke up suddenly and scrambled from the room. He was light-headed, but knew he was stronger than he felt. His voice was steady, even though he was not. He walked toward the front of the hacienda, using his right hand to balance his movements, touching anything that went in the direction he sought to go.

From the kitchen, Tina Sanchez heard him and came to see to what was happening.

"Wait, Holt! Wait. I think Bordner will use this time to strike here," Deed hollered.

"Señor Corrigan, you must get back in bed," Tina said and took his arm.

"No. I can't. Please, I must stop them." He brushed her hand from his arm and continued toward the doorway. She wasn't sure what to do and hurried after him.

Holt was the first to hear and stop what he was doing, then Cliente did the same, holding up his hand for his men to wait.

"We're outside, Deed. Getting ready to leave," Holt called back.

"Wait. Hear me," Deed opened the door. "They will attack as soon as you leave. It makes too much sense. Felix and his wife are dealing with their sadness . . . and Cliente will have three or four men with him. That leaves only a handful to guard this place. It is perfect for them. If they come, it'll be with twenty guns. Maybe more," Deed said. "How many can you stand?"

Tina Sanchez stopped behind him, admiring his broad shoulders, but used the excuse of steadying him to put her hands around his waist and hold him upright. Both girls were smitten by the Corrigan brothers.

"Eight," Cliente said and grimaced. "They kill half our men before."

"Well, let's give them something to shoot at, first," Deed said, holding onto the porch railing.

"Have you lost more blood than I thought, little brother?" Holt looked at Deed as if he were crazy.

Tina touched Deed's arm; he looked at her, swiveled, and said, "Tina, I'm fine.

Really. *Muchas gracias.*"

She flashed a wide smile, sought his eyes for an instant, and releasing him, stepped away.

Deed explained they could fix five or six dummies and put them in the yard as if they were talking. It would make the Bar 3 gunmen think they could get most of the Lazy S men in one quick attack. Likely, it would put the attackers in an exposed position, or at least bunched together.

"Think it'll work?" Holt asked, laying his rifle against the wagon.

Cliente grinned. "I like it."

"Well, the shadows will help," Deed said. "Even if it doesn't, it'll confuse them."

The Sanchez women, even Maria, eagerly joined the masquerade effort. Flour sacks were filled with straw and tied to become dummy heads. Wooden frames were nailed together to provide the body and hold shirts, pants, and the sacks. A sombrero topped each dummy and a serape was draped across what appeared to be a shoulder.

An hour later, six dummies were placed on the south side of the main ranch yard, grouped together as if they were talking. Even Holt was impressed. In the dusk, they looked almost real. Deed said people would see what they expected to see.

Satisfied, Cliente left with the burial wagon and three outriders, all were Sanchez women disguised as men. Cliente would ride for an hour, then stop and wait. He would turn back when he heard gunfire. In the dusk, sounds of gunfire would travel a long way. There was a risk that Bar 3 men would attack the wagon first, but they decided it wouldn't be worth it to Bordner since the ranch would be forewarned.

Holt stationed all of the vaqueros on the flat roof of the ranchero. They were spread out, covering the complete ranch yard from above, and were to remain out of sight until he gave the signal to fire. Holt and Deed took positions inside the house, each watching a different direction. The oldest son, Taol, settled into watching the north. Felix refused to stay out of the fight and joined his son with his pistols and a band of cartridges over his shoulder.

Now they must wait, letting late afternoon shadows creep across the yard. It would be dark in two hours. For the Corrigan brothers, waiting was easy; Silka had taught both the importance of waiting. It wasn't the opposite of attacking, just a matter of timing the attack. Although Holt was worried about Deed, his wounded brother assured him he was strong enough to help.

Outside, a light breeze whispered through a cluster of junipers near the front door and caught the sleeves of the dummies, making them dance in the fading twilight.

"Maybe it'll look like they're excited," Holt whispered and motioned toward the dummies.

"Yeah. From a distance, it'll probably help. Unless the sleeves really start whipping around," Deed said.

"Wait, I hear something. Down by the fence," Holt said and shifted his rifle into readiness. "Down there." With his right hand, he reached up and touched the cardinal feather in his hatband.

"Yeah, I see them. Must be ten or so right there," Deed said. He propped his Spencer carbine on the back of a second chair in front of him and aimed it out the opened window. The chair was turned away from him and the back made it easier to steady his gun. On the floor beside him was a box with reloading tubes. In his gunbelt, Deed had returned the two outlaw handguns taken earlier.

Felix had told them not to worry about shooting out window glass, but the Corrigan brothers knew the value of glass and thought it best to open the windows where they might be firing. Felix and his son were unseen, watching from another part of the house.

"Looks like they're planning on getting closer. I see a few climbing the fence," Deed said.

Holt looked over at him and grinned; turning a chair around was good luck. He wondered if his brother knew that. Then he saw Deed touch the small, Oriental brass circle hanging around his neck on a rawhide thong. Holt knew what Bushido meant and nodded.

"Yeah, I don't think the bastards in front of our dummies will try that. They'll stay behind the fence," Holt said and wiped the sweat from his forehead. "Figure it's too risky. Your idea is working." He moved next to the window. "But I got a few coming over the fence on this side, too. They're right next to that batch of sagebrush."

"When do you want to welcome them?"

"Let's wait. They closer they get, the bigger the surprise. For them," Holt said.

"Agreed. But not too close. If they get next to the house, our roof shooters won't be able to stop them."

"That's why we're here, little brother."

A long row of orange flame erupted in the semidarkness, all from the Bar 3 rifles along the stone fence in front of the dummies. The roar tore into the silence. Sombreros flew from the dummies and the filled sacks split open. The clothes whirled in different directions and two shirts fell from their wooden frames.

"Now," Holt said and fired.

His first shot caught the closest raider crawling toward the house in the head. Levering his Winchester, he missed the second man but Holt's next shots slammed into him and the man collapsed and didn't move. Above, the roof was alive with vaquero rifle fire at the targets along the fence, well defined by the gray land behind them.

Deed fired at the lead attacker on his side of the ranch yard, balancing the gun barrel on the chair in front of him. The man was slammed backward by the heavy shot and crumbled to the ground. Deed laid his wounded left arm across the top of the gun and levered a new round. Bullets crashed into the window, but stopped as the vaqueros on the roof poured lead into the small groups.

Firing again, Deed saw the attacker spin halfway around. He gave up on the Spencer, yanked free his revolver and moved to the side of the window. The sudden movement made him dizzy for a moment and he leaned against the wall to right his head. His left arm was bleeding again. He wouldn't have the range or impact, but he could shoot quicker with the handgun. Cocking and firing so fast it sounded like a long round of thunder, the young gunfighter dropped two attackers.

From somewhere, a cry went up to retreat, to run, and the attackers inside and outside the fence broke and ran. A gruff voice yelled at them to stand and fight, but the words were ignored.

Holt shoved new cartridges into his rifle and fired at the fleeing shadows. Two men stumbled and fell. From the roof came cries of victory.

Deed heard firing from the front part of the house, followed by Spanish yells of vengeance. His Remington empty, he drew a second handgun from his belt, cocked and fired as a would-be attacker reached the stone fence. Deed knew Blue would have let him go. The man grabbed his side. Bullets from the roof slammed him to the ground.

Almost as soon as it started, the battle was over. Racing across the land came Cliente with the buckboard and riders. They fired at the fleeing men as they grabbed their picketed horses. Holt was glad to see Cliente keep his riders moving toward the ranch, instead of following the escaping Bar 3 men. The attackers might be scared now, but they would soon realize their superior numbers. Holt and Deed watched as the attackers rode away into the night, and Cliente kept coming toward the ranch.

From the northern part of the house came Felix and Taol, both lighting cigarettes.

"Aiee, it was good," Felix declared. "Let us follow and end this."

"No." Holt's word was firm. "They still outnumber you. We could ride into an ambush ourselves."

Felix shook his head. "*Sí,* you are right, Señor Holt. It is that I want this over. I want this fat man and his devils stopped."

"I know. We all do. But we've got to be smart. Bordner is."

From the rooftop, the vaqueros were firing into the bodies strewn about the ranch yard.

Deed hobbled over to them. He was sweating heavily and his left sleeve had a circle of crimson.

"You all right, Deed?" Holt asked, watching his brother. "You're bleeding."

"Yeah. Just a little weak, that's all." He looked down at his sticky shirtsleeve. "Guess I popped it open. No big deal."

"When Cliente gets here, we shall put the dead men in his wagon and dump them on Bar 3 land," Taol said, watching Cliente bring the wagon into the yard.

Cheering went up from the roof and the women riders waved their rifles in triumph.

"Yeah. Take their guns and bullets, though. We may need them," Deed said.

"What if Bordner tries to claim his men were attacked on their own land?" Holt asked, shoving new cartridges into his rifle.

"That would be hard to prove," Deed responded.

"*Sí,* you are right, amigo," Taol said. There was a sadness in his eyes and his shoulders rose and fell.

Deed put his hand on the younger Mexican's shoulder. "In the morning, you and I will ride to town. We'll wire the Rangers and tell them what happened. That should put an end to it. At least for now."

"I'll go with Cliente to bring back . . . the bodies," Holt said, "then, when you come back from town, we can ride to our ranch. Together."

"Sounds good to me," Deed said. "It's been cool. Chico's body should be all right, I guess."

"Unless the coyotes have torn it up." Holt glanced at the Sanchezes talking quietly.

"Maybe one of the Sanchez women could ride to the ranch and tell them you're all right. They'll be worried about the posse. Especially that old samurai."

"Makes good sense. I'm sure they'd be glad to," Deed answered. "I've been thinking to suggest they start stationing a few men on the roof. All the time, night and day."

"Good idea, little brother."

CHAPTER TWENTY-EIGHT

Wilkon was well into its morning routine when Deed Corrigan rode in with Taol Sanchez. The night's rest had strengthened the young gunfighter, but his left arm remained weak and numb and he carried it at his side. His leg was stiff, but definitely healing. He was wearing the same borrowed shirt, having refused the offer of another. If there was time, he would see the doctor; he had promised Holt.

The ride into town had been a quiet one with the two men lost in their thoughts. Deed liked Taol and felt sorry for the tragedies Agon Bordner had brought on his family. He knew, too, that Bordner wouldn't stop with the Lazy S, he would want the Corrigan spread as well.

What they found in town was a surprise. After wiring the Rangers at the telegraph office located within the lumberyard office, they went to the marshal to report what had happened, more of a courtesy than a necessity. The marshal was responsible for town matters only; the county sheriff was in charge of enforcing the law in the county, but Deed now knew Sheriff Lucas was crooked.

Macy Shields greeted them with a sneer and told them that Dixie Murphy had already reported on the posse's fate and he had sent a deputy with a burial team to the ambush site. As usual, he was wearing a bandana tied over his head instead of a hat, as well as once-white suspenders. Murphy, too, had been wounded in the ambush, he said.

"So the bunch that got away swung back and hit you Mexes again. Is that it?" Shields said without standing. He was seated behind the marshal's desk. A cup of coffee rested on the scratched desktop, along with stacks of paper.

Deed bristled. "Yeah, your boss tried again, Shields. But you boys still aren't good enough." He cocked his head. "I'd like it if you referred to my friend as *Mister* Sanchez."

"I don't give a damn what you'd like, Corrigan. I'm the acting county sheriff now, too. Lucas got it in the ambush." Shields reached for his coffee with his left hand as his right dropped to his lap. "Town council just voted. Smart of 'em."

"Let's see . . . Bordner owns the bank . . . and the local law. Anything else?"

Taol stared at Shields through slitted eyes. "We will have justice. It will come."

"Maybe so, Mex. Maybe so," Shields said. "If I was you, I'd see what Agon Bordner wants to give you for your place . . . and ride on while you still can."

"Come on, Taol," Deed said. "We'll deal with real lawmen when they get here."

Shields's right hand moved toward the holstered gun at his waist.

"I wouldn't try that, Shields," Deed said, his gun already in his hand.

The crooked lawman took a deep breath and moved both hands to the desktop. Deed holstered his gun and they turned to leave.

Shields found his courage. "Oh, by the way, I wouldn't try buying anything in the general store, Mex. Lazy S's credit's no good there. Neither's your money. The town only wants Americans around here." He chuckled. "For that matter, neither is yours, Corrigan. We don't like your brother's Injun wife." His eyes widened to match the sneer of his mouth. "Maybe Bordner'll be good enough to pay you for that piece of land you're sitting on, too."

Taol Sanchez's teeth clenched and his hand dropped to his handgun.

Deed took a step in front of him to stop his draw.

"Come on, Taol. Nothing good's going to come from staying here."

"*Sí,* but just one time, I —"

"Anytime you want to die, Mex. Anytime," Shields said and stared at Deed. "Hear you took some lead when the posse went down. I can see your ear's bandaged. That's a real shame, Corrigan."

"How would you know that?" Deed's eyes were cold as he turned back to Shields.

"Murphy said you and he were the only two that made it out."

"Interesting, since he wasn't around when the shooting started. Neither was Lucas. I'd like to have a chat with him about that," Deed growled.

"He done left for the Bar 3."

"Convenient."

They left and Taol suggested they check at the general store. If Shields was right, they would need to make arrangements in another town, probably Amarillo, and that was a two-day trip one way. Taol yanked free the reins and mounted.

"Yes, we should," Deed said as he swung into the saddle, "but likely it's as Shields said. Bordner is trying to tighten the noose around us."

Taol's face tightened. "I think we ride to the Bar 3 and end this."

"It's not going to be that easy," Deed said. "Matter of fact, Bordner would like us to try that."

"*Sí,* but it feels *bueno* to think of it."

As they rode down the street, a store owner in shirtsleeves ran from his drugstore toward them, waving.

"Mr. Corrigan . . . do you know what happened to the posse? My brother is with them," the bald man said, his eyes asking the rest of his question.

Reining up, Deed shook his head. "Taol's brother, two of his men, and I were with the posse. We were ambushed two days out of town. South of here, near Oak Tree Canyon. Evidently Dixie Murphy and I were the only ones to make it." He made no mention of his belief that both Murphy and Lucas were involved in the setting of the ambush. This wasn't the time or the man to share it with.

The man's face wilted.

"I think the marshal is putting together a burial committee to ride out there. The Sanchezes are headed there as well."

"How'd you and Mr. Murphy make it

safe?" the businessman blurted.

"With me, it was God's plan. I was only wounded," Deed said. "With Murphy, it was Agon Bordner's plan." He leaned forward and patted the distraught man on his shoulder.

"I-I don't understand," the man said.

Deed clicked his buckskin into a walk. "You'd better . . . or Bordner will own you, too."

He glanced over at Taol and said, "Let's check out the store."

Nodding to the man, they rode on, reined up at the store with the big sign reading Wilkon General Merchandise, swung down, and went inside.

At the marshal's office, a huge man came from the cell area, holding a broom. Sear Georgian glared at Shields. "Well, so Deed Corrigan is hurt. Maybe I hurt him some more."

"Good idea, Sear, but don't wear a gun," Shields said. "You don't want to give him an excuse to use his."

"I won't need it. I'll break his back. Tear him apart." He placed the broom against the wall and left.

Shields felt a shiver run down his back. Sear Georgian was a monster. He didn't know why Bordner kept him around. It had to be for moments like this. Georgian would beat Deed Corrigan senseless, especially with him being wounded.

Inside the general store, a man neither knew stepped from behind the counter. He was tall with combed-back, curly hair, a nose that looked like a turnip, and a mustache that needed trimming. He wore a crumpled suitcoat and wrinkled tie.

When he spoke, his voice was nasal and thin. "Mr. Sanchez . . . Mr. Corrigan, I believe. Correct? I am Jephrum Virdin, owner of this establishment. It is my duty, my responsibility, to inform both of you that your business is not welcome here." He glanced away at several customers. "I would ask you to leave."

Taol's face turned dark red and he mumbled a curse in Spanish.

"Virdin, this madness will end soon," Deed snarled. "And your fat boss won't make it. When that happens, you'd better not be in Wilkon when I ride in."

"Is that a threat, Mr. Corrigan?"

Deed's smile was hateful. "I don't make threats, Virdin. Just a helpful projection of what life holds for you."

A fury was growing within Deed, a fury that could be reckless and unstoppable, a fury he tried hard to contain most times, a fury that had gotten him into trouble before.

Taol spat that they should leave and Deed suggested he go out to the horses, that he wanted to buy something for the Sanchez women. Taol took a deep breath to release his own anger and left.

"I told you that your business wasn't welcome, Mr. Corrigan," Virdin said, crossing his arms and trying to look intimidating.

"Heard that." Deed walked over to a table displaying big silk scarves, neatly stacked and folded. He picked up three — one, crimson; one, pink; and one, turquoise. Setting them aside, he selected two more — one in pink; the other, green.

Turning to Virdin, Deed asked if he had any dolls. Stunned, the man pointed at a nearby shelf where three dolls were sitting. He examined them and took the middle one with blond hair and dressed in a blue gingham dress with a white apron.

"Get me six sacks, Virdin. Small sacks."

The surprised man went to the counter and returned with the requested brown sacks. Deed took them, placed the doll inside the first and then slid each scarf inside a separate sack. He dropped three gold coins at the man's feet.

"Keep the difference, Virdin."

Turning, he heard scuffling, followed by a fierce curse.

"Hold these for me, Virdin." Deed handed him back the filled sacks, pulled his holstered Remington, and ran to the store doorway. Virdin watched him go, then picked up the coins.

On the boardwalk, Sear Georgian stood laughing and kicking at an unconscious Taol. He was huge, more creature than man with ham-like fists and broad shoulders.

Cocking his gun, Deed growled, "Back away from my friend, mister."

The brute of a man stepped backward and grinned, showing a mouth of broken and missing teeth. His face was heavily pockmarked with earlier acne and his thinning hair was slicked back and long.

"Ah, Deed Corrigan. Ya gonna shoot me? I ain't carryin'." He raised his fists, then kicked Taol in the ribs again. "He 'tacked me, ya know. Jes' defendin' myse'f."

Watching them from ten feet away, an older, stoop-shouldered woman with a blue scarf tied around her head, revealing mostly white curls declared, "He did not, you brute. And you know it, mister. You hit him from the back. I saw it."

Georgian laughed and a string of phlegm wiggled from one nostril, then jumped back.

371

"So what are you gonna do about it, Corri-gan? I'm gonna kick this Mex to death."

Deed knew he had no business fighting anyone, much less a thug like Sear Geor-gian, who was three inches taller and forty pounds heavier. But if he didn't step in, the man was going to beat on Taol until he was broken. Georgian was unarmed, so any use of a gun by Deed would be tantamount to murder, no matter the circumstances. There was nothing left to do but try to stop him. The anger growing within him was actually welcoming the idea.

He looked back into the store, uncocked his gun, and said, "Virdin, take this gun for a few minutes. I won't need it until later. Got something to do."

The storekeeper hurried to the doorway and took the heavy gun, stunned by his desire to help and even more amazed by his own statement, "Be careful. He'll kill you, Mr. Corrigan."

Deed nodded.

"Now yer gonna die, Corrigan," Georgian growled and delivered a roundhouse swing at Deed's head as he turned back.

The old woman screamed her alarm.

Deed's left arm blocked the powerful blow, taking it full force on his wounded arm. It felt like a club had slammed against him. His arm went numb and the wound began to bleed. Georgian followed with a high right that Deed managed to duck and counter with an opened right hand to the big man's Adam's apple.

Georgian grabbed his throat with both hands, gasping for air. If Deed had hit him harder, it would have killed him. Still, the blow gave Deed time to set himself. He realized the man was a brawler used to winning by sheer strength and the fear of his opponent, but he was no fighter. But any one of Georgian's blows would be enough to knock him out. That would mean destruction of his body or death.

Moving in front of the unconscious Taol, Deed balanced himself in a wide stance and drove his right leg into Georgian's midsection like an axe while the bigger man tried to clear his throat of the earlier blow. Deed's wounded left leg buckled and he nearly fell.

Georgian pushed Deed away and rattled him with a thundering right to his head that brought blood to his mouth. Deed countered with a right hook to Georgian's face that popped the skin with a stomach-turning sound, cracking a red line down his cheek. Screaming obscenities, Georgian swung fiercely, but missed.

Moving away from the blow, Deed tripped

on Taol and fell. Grinning, the bloody-faced big man ran at him, but the young gunfighter spun to his right, extending his right arm to balance himself on his hand. Rotating his hips, he drove his aching left leg into the bigger man's stomach. As soon as his boot hit Georgian, Deed jumped to his feet. His spurs jingled as he stood and tried to ignore the pain in his leg and arm, and the roar in his head. Georgian was struggling with the pain in his stomach.

A small crowd had gathered beside the old woman to watch the brawl, but no one made any attempt to stop it.

Deed staggered the bigger man with a vicious back slap of his open right hand to Georgian's face. Georgian launched a wild swing that thundered against Deed's shoulder and made his knees wobble. Seeing his weakened position, Georgian made a vicious grab for Deed's face to gouge out his eyes. As the huge man's hands reached Deed's face, the young gunfighter's left elbow hit Georgian's nose like a sharp axe cutting into a log. Georgian staggered sideways. Deed moved in, missing with his right fist, but connecting with a left to the man's stomach.

Ignoring Deed's blow to his midsection, Georgian rushed and grabbed him, squeezing against his back. Deed gasped, felt an awful pain run down his spine, then bent his knees as best he could and rammed his head upward into Georgian's exposed chin. The big man staggered backwards, releasing Deed. The young gunfighter followed with another open-handed jab to his stomach and Georgian whimpered.

Swinging and missing, Georgian brought up his knee toward Deed's groin, but Deed spun to the side, letting the blow slam into his thigh. It still made him gasp. Deed's anger was total and his rage took over. It was time to end this. If the fight went longer, the man's sheer strength would wear him down.

Rebalancing himself, Deed drove his fist into the man's chest, right at Georgian's heart. He forced his left arm to raise and half-block Georgian's wicked swing. It was losing power; even so, the blow was hard enough to make Deed wince.

Deed managed to back off, then went into a half crouch, ignoring the pain in his leg and arm. Hate was making him fierce and powerful. His left arm swung at his side, too weak to raise again. Georgian's face was a mass of blood and skin and he was definitely moving slower. He lunged at Deed in a desperate attempt to grab him again.

Deed's opened right hand drove into

Georgian's stomach, then quickly thudded against his neck. The big man stumbled and as he fell, Deed grabbed a handful of Georgian's hair and held him as his right elbow smashed into the man's face. Georgian thudded against the boardwalk and didn't move.

Deed weaved and caught himself against the store's support beam. Certain that Georgian wasn't going to move, he turned to Taol, now trying to stand. A cut above Deed's eye was bringing a string of salty blood into it; he wiped it away.

"Can you ride, Taol?"

"*Sí*. Did you kill him?"

"Don't think so, but he won't feel very good for a long while," Deed said. "Let's get out of here."

He helped the young Mexican to his saddle; Taol's grimace indicated cracked ribs. A white-faced Virdin walked from the store, holding the sacks, now carefully folded together and tied with the doll sack on the bottom, and Deed's revolver and ceremoniously handed them to Deed.

"Mr. Corrigan, that was impressive, sir," Jephrum Virdin said. "I didn't think anyone could stop him like that." He took a deep breath and added, "I never did like Sear Georgian."

Heaving for breath, Deed mouthed his thanks, taking the gun first in his right hand. His left arm was stiff, but he managed to take hold of the string holding the sacks together. He looked down at his hands; both were bloody and sore.

Running down the boardwalk came Sheriff Macy Shields. He stutter-stepped as he approached the prone body of Sear Georgian. "What the hell?"

Watching him from his saddle, Deed held his handgun against the pommel. The energy from battle was leaving him fast.

"You're under arrest, Corrigan, for assaulting a citizen of Wilkon," Shields bellowed.

Virdin waved his arms. "No, Macy, that cannot be. I have to live in this town and Sear started it all. He just wasn't good enough to end it." He stared at Shields. "Go and get the doctor. Georgian is badly hurt." He couldn't resist looking at Deed. "Ride away, Mr. Corrigan, and your friend, Mr. Sanchez. You will not be bothered more this day."

"Maybe, but we're not turning our backs on dirtbags like your so-called sheriff here." Deed raised his gun so Shields could see it. "Shields, throw your gun in that horse tank." He shifted the sacks to rest in front of him on the saddle.

Shields glared at him. "I won't do that."

Deed cocked his gun. It felt heavy and he added his left hand to its support, which didn't want to move quickly. "I won't ask again. I'm tired of what Bordner is doing. So killing you is just a start to making it right again."

Shields hesitated, then tossed the gun into the tank. The weapon splashed and sank.

"Now, that hideaway. In your back waistband. Bring it out with two fingers."

Shields grumbled and slowly complied. The second gun, a short-barreled Colt, splashed into the dirty water and sank.

Deed told Taol to pull away and the Mexican nodded and eased his horse away from the hitchrail. As Deed followed, a young woman ran toward him. It was Sally Cummins.

"Oh, Deed, are you all right?" she asked with widened eyes. She was wearing a light brown, fitted dress with a short waistcoat. The color of the cloth matched her hair, pulled back into a bun.

"Yes, Miss Cummins, I'm all right."

"Will you come to see me . . . soon? I miss you, Deed."

"Guess that'll be up to Agon Bordner and his gang." He blinked and saw Atlee Forsyth and wished she was here.

Putting her hand on his leg, she bit her lower lip. "Oh, this whole thing is awful. Just awful. I wish everyone could get along."

"That's a nice wish," Deed said, touched the brim of his hat with his right hand still holding his gun, and pulled his horse away from the hitchrail. "Take care of yourself, Miss Cummins."

CHAPTER TWENTY-NINE

At the Forsyth relay station, the morning El Paso stage rumbled into the yard right on time. Pervious Findel was the driver, a happy, red-haired man known for singing while he drove. Most said he sang well. A former Union artillery captain during the war, Pervious was dependable and always on time, or ahead of it. Just like today.

> "A tear was in her eye . . .
> I said, I've come from Dixie land . . .
> Susanna, don't you break down and cry . . .
> I said, Oh, Susanna . . .
> Now, don't you cry for me . . .
> 'Cause I come from Alabama
> with my banjo on my knee."

He timed the ending of his song as he reined up in the station yard.

Billy Lee Montez and Hermann Beinrigt hurried out with a new team. Helping them was a determined Benjamin.

"All out, folks. Some good eatin's here. Hot coffee too," Pervious hollered as he slammed on the heavy brake. "We'll be rollin' again in fifteen minutes so don't you all dally."

Passengers emerged from both sides of the coach, stretched, and headed for the station. At the doorway, Atlee Forsyth waited to greet them. The last two passengers to emerge were familiar: James Hannah and Rebecca Tuttle.

The bespectacled gunman recognized Billy and Hermann and reintroduced himself. "Good day to you, men. I'm James Hannah. Came through here with Deed Corrigan a while back." He looked at the German farmer, smiled, and said, "Believe you caught a nasty arrow on that trip, sir. Good to see you up and around."

"*Danke.* It *ist gut* to see you, Herr Hannah."

Pushing his glasses back on his nose, Hannah continued, "You remember Miss Tuttle, I'm certain. She's my bride, Mrs. James Hannah."

Rebecca blushed and Hannah grinned.

"Where's Deed? I want to see him," the gunman asked, waving his hand toward the barn.

The German farmer tugged on the bridle of the lead horse and told him about Deed returning to his ranch.

"You folks better get somethin' to eat," Pervious yelled as he climbed down from the driver's box. "Gonna be a long spell before there's more grub. None like this, I reckon."

Hannah nodded. "Thanks. But we're getting off here."

"Thought you folks were going to Kansas."

"Yeah, we are. But I've got some business here first."

From the station doorway, Atlee Forsyth watched as the passengers came toward where she was standing. For an instant, she expected to see Deed Corrigan step out of the stage.

She missed Deed, thought of him often, and felt guilty about it. She should be missing her late husband and she did. But her heart was looking for something to heal the loss he left, and Deed was that answer. She knew it was wrong to feel this way, but she did.

"Oh, Deed —" she caught herself and looked back at Olivia Beinrigt in the main room setting the table. "Stage is here, Olivia."

"*Gut. Ve ist* ready."

The last couple to get out were familiar to Atlee: James Hannah and Rebecca Tuttle. The two of them walked slowly toward the station with the bespectacled gunman doing most of the talking.

At the doorway, Atlee greeted the all the passengers warmly and motioned them into the main room. Then turning to the couple, said, "Well, how good to see you again, Mr. Hannah . . . and you, too . . . Miss —"

"It's Mrs. — Mrs. Hannah," Rebecca said with a wide smile.

Hannah blushed and asked, "Is Deed around?"

It was Atlee's turn to blush. "Oh, I'm sorry. Uh, Mr. Corrigan went back to his ranch some time ago."

Frowning, Hannah asked if the ranch was far. Atlee explained the location, then excused herself to help with the other guests. Hannah joined Rebecca inside the station. She was talking with Olivia.

"Would it be possible to rent a buckboard or a carriage?" Hannah interrupted. "My wife and I need to go into town."

Rebecca looked surprised. "I thought we were going on to Kansas, honey."

"We are, dear. But I need to see Deed Corrigan. It's important."

"Certainly, dear."

Atlee walked over from the table with a coffeepot in her hand. "Mr. Hannah, if you promise to return it soon, I can let you borrow one of our buckboards." She smiled. "Or you can wait here, Mr. Corrigan is expected back sometime this week. He's asked Benjamin to help with their roundup. And my Elizabeth is going along to play with his brother's children."

Hannah took off his glasses and cleaned them with a white handkerchief from his pocket.

"Where would we sleep?" he asked, returning the glasses to his nose.

Atlee said they could sleep on the employees' bed, the one not being used by the Beinrigts.

"That would be excellent. We'll wait."

CHAPTER THIRTY

Blue Corrigan saw the riders clearing the ridge as he walked out of the barn. Late morning sun was trying to warm the day. He knew in one glance it was Deed and Holt, leading a third horse with a blanket-wrapped body strapped over it. Two days ago, Tina Sanchez had ridden over to tell them what was happening. The news was most appreciated; both Blue and Silka were getting worried. Hearing that Holt was with Deed gave Blue a warm feeling that he couldn't quite describe. And seeing them now made him raise his eyes to the sky and thank the Lord.

He yelled at Silka who was shoeing the paint horse called Warrior. The animal had gradually settled into a solid working horse and could outrun any horse on the ranch, except the sorrel stallion, Captain.

Willy and Harmon had gone to inspect one of their line cabins and wouldn't be back until tomorrow afternoon. Little Jake was in the bunkhouse recovering from his gunshot wound.

"Silka, it's Deed!"

The older man hurried the horse to the closest corral and let it loose. "Aiee, we are blessed." He continued to where Blue was standing watching the riders.

"Is that Holt with him?" Silka said, putting a hand to his forehead to block out the autumn sun.

"Yes."

"It is a good truth then. They bring a body," Silka said.

"I'm afraid it's Chico."

"Aiee. I remember."

Blue and Silka waved and Deed and Holt returned the greeting. In minutes, the two brothers reined up alongside Blue and Silka. Happiness was evident even in Silka's usually stoic face. They dismounted and shook hands.

As they walked the horses to the barn, Deed and Holt took turns telling them about what had happened to the posse, to the outlaws chasing a wounded Deed, the second attack on the Lazy S, and the problems in town. Blue and Silka knew most of it already, but not the events in town. They had stayed for the Sanchez family's burial

386

of their son and the two vaqueros.

Deed said, "We brought Chico's body home."

"That was the right thing to do," Blue responded.

Silka studied Deed. "How bad is your ear, son?"

Touching his bandaged ear, Deed said, "Oh, it's all right. I was lucky."

"Looks like it," Blue said and patted Deed's shoulder, then turned to Holt. "Mighty glad you came along when you did Holt. And mighty glad to have you with us."

Holt smiled and touched the feather in his hat. "Took some time for me to get smart."

Deed led his buckskin toward the barn, his limp barely noticeable. The blood that had been on his pant leg and shirtsleeve were barely noticeable. The Sanchez women had done a good job of cleaning them. He was tired, but it felt good to be home.

Holt followed with the other horses. Silka and Blue stayed with them. Holt told them about Deed's fight in town with Sear Georgian as Taol had relayed it to him. Holt knew of the big man and thought it was an amazing fight.

Silka frowned. "You should not have done that. You were hurt. You could have been hurt bad."

"Oh, I think he thought I was wounded worse than I was," Deed said. "Only a couple of flesh wounds. They just bled a lot."

"Evidently he wasn't hurt too much," Holt laughed. "Taol told me that the big son of a bitch was cut down like a tree." He turned to Silka. "You taught him well, old man."

Chico's body was carefully taken from his horse and laid on the ground. After unsaddling and rubbing down the horses, they led them to the water tank, then to stalls where they were grained.

"I think we should bury Chico before we go inside," Deed said.

"Yes," Blue agreed.

Neither Holt nor Silka responded. Deed went to get a shovel and Holt followed. They would bury the cowhand's remains in the family cemetery. Blue went to the house to inform Bina of his brothers' return and made a stop at the bunkhouse to inform Jake. The short cowhand got up and joined them at the grave site. His arm was in a tight sling, prepared by Bina.

After Holt, Deed, and Silka took turns digging, Chico was buried. Jake volunteered to help, but they wouldn't let him. Blue returned before they were finished and told them that Too Tall nearly had dinner ready. At Deed's urging, Blue stood at the head of the grave next to a temporary marker Silka had made. A running iron had burned CHICO into the main piece of the small, nailed-together, wooden cross. No one knew Chico's last name or when he was born or if he had any relatives to contact.

Blue removed his hat and so did the others. Holt picked up a small dirt clod and massaged it in his hand, letting the crumbles fall through his fingers. Touching a new grave was good luck, he told himself. Only Deed noticed.

With his eyes closed, Blue said, "Lord, we give to you this day the soul of our good friend, Chico. You know his full name, but we never did. He was a steady and loyal hand. Keep him close. Amen."

"Amen," the others muttered.

Their walk to the main house was subdued; Jake excused himself and went to the bunkhouse. No one wanted to think beyond the moment. Holt walked with his arm around Blue. Even in the sadness of the day, it was good to be back. He would tell Blue and Silka later that he planned to go by the name Sam Holton. A lot of men changed their names, maybe Chico had. His eyes took in the ranch buildings; it was like seeing them for the first time, and yet, it wasn't. More like seeing them as if they had been part of another life. He smiled. They were.

Finally, Blue started talking about their cattle. It had been an excellent summer and the fall crop of calves was plentiful. He shook his head and declared they would have their hands full finding and branding all of them.

At the porch railing were two pans of fresh water, soap, and new towels. The men took turns washing up as the talk continued about the roundup. Blue thought they should separate the herd for market next spring, putting the steers and older cows in a separate group in one of their valleys.

Deed dried his hands and asked, "Makes sense to me. How soon are we starting?"

"Everything's ready, but we'll be short-handed without Chico. Little Jake shouldn't be in a saddle, but I know he'll try, no matter what we say."

"What am I going to do about the Forsyth kids? I promised Benjamin he could ride with us," Deed asked. "And Elizabeth would stay with Bina and your kids. But it may not be safe. We're likely to get hit by Bordner's men." He shook his head. "What am I saying? It won't be safe for your family to stay here either."

"You think he'll try something now, during the roundup?" Blue said, "I was counting on Benjamin becoming a welcome hand."

"What about me? Am I chopped liver?" Holt asked.

"Of course not," Blue chuckled. "We've needed you for a long time." He cocked his head. "I figured you'd take Chico's string. We'd set aside some gentle ones for Benjamin."

"That sounds better," Holt said.

Deed's concern went unanswered and they headed for the front door, continuing to talk of cattle.

Bina greeted them warmly when they entered. Holt was careful to step into the house with his right foot first, that would bring good luck to everyone within.

"Bina, you know my brother, Holt. It's been a long time though," Blue said.

"Oh, Holt, how good to see you again," she declared. "Blue talks often of you."

Holt smiled. "Now I know why he's done so well, Bina. He has you."

Deed agreed with his statement and slid past the two of them and into the main room where Blue had already gone.

Her smile was broad. "You are most kind."

She said something in Apache that Holt didn't know, but assumed it was a welcome message. Realizing her statement was not understood, she quickly apologized, "Oh, I am sorry. I forget when I am excited. I said our lodge is yours. Of course, it is. This is your parents' home. Forgive me."

"Thank you. It's good to be here." Holt ignored the thought that the ranch was indeed his, or at least his parents'. The statement was caring.

From around the corner, Blue's children and Jeremy came running to their Uncle Deed. He grabbed each one with a big hug.

"Uncle Dee, you hurt," Matthew said, pointing at the dried blood on his clothes.

"Yeah, I uh, I fell down. Kinda clumsy of me."

Mary Jo put her hands on her hips and declared, "Uncle Deed, bad boy. You were fighting. I know." It was like being scolded by his mother.

He laughed and said, "Come and see your Uncle Holt. You probably don't remember him. He's your father's brother and mine."

He introduced them to the bearded stranger. "This is your Uncle Holt. Uncle Holt, this is Matthew . . . and Mary Jo . . . and Jeremy."

Forgetting his plan to go by Sam Holton

for the moment, Holt squatted on his heels and drew the three children close. "My goodness, it is good to see you. Let's see, Matthew, I only heard about you." He smiled and touched Mary Jo's cheek. "And you were only a baby."

Jeremy tried to step away, but Holt took his arm gently and pulled him back. "And you, sir, I'm proud to meet for the first time. Jeremy, I hope we can become good friends."

The boy smiled. "I do, too."

Blue came over and suggested the children go help in the kitchen and let the men talk over some matters. All three children hugged Holt again and ran toward the kitchen.

Holt stood and shook his head. "Man, now that's something to come home to."

"Yes, I'm very lucky."

"Seems to me luck runs in the family," Holt said. "Maybe I can catch some of it."

"You already have." Blue patted him on the back. "Let's go in here while we wait."

The four men walked into a living room warmed by a huge stone fireplace that dominated the room. Right away, Holt was pleased to see the well-banked fire was burning evenly. An occasional blue flame told him spirits were close. He decided they were the spirits of their parents and sister.

A large blue sofa and rolltop desk made up the rest of the room, along with a small table holding a kerosene lamp. Blue headed to the rolltop desk that had belonged to their parents. Above it was a framed photograph of their parents on their wedding day. Next to it was another photograph of the three children with them. In the picture, a twelve-year-old Blue had his arm on the shoulder of four-year-old Deed who was looking at his oldest brother and ten-year-old Holt was looking at the camera and smiling stiffly.

Blue rolled up the front piece where a bottle of Tennessee whiskey and glasses sat. The bottle was nearly full. Holt was surprised there was liquor in the house, but said nothing. He guessed the bottle had been there for years.

"I keep this for Christmas Eve. And for special occasions, like the birth of my children," Blue said. "This is a special occasion."

He poured a finger full of the brown liquid into four glasses.

"Here's to Holt's return," he said, handing out the glasses and holding up his own.

Both Deed and Silka were amazed at Blue producing whiskey, but it did seem like an appropriate time. Silka nodded and held his glass next to Blue's.

"Ame futte ji katamaru," the old samurai declared.

Deed and Blue repeated the acclamation. Holt mumbled something no one understood, but grinned afterwards.

He clinked his glass against the others. "It's great to be home." He swallowed the fiery drink in one gulp and returned the glass to the desk. Blue added his.

"Reckon that's all the whiskey we'll drink. For a long time," he smiled at Silka. "Right, Silka?"

Without any expression, the Japanese warrior added his emptied glass to the desk. "Hai, it is so." Holt wished he could have another, but still felt uncomfortable asking.

"If you don't mind an old Rebel making a suggestion," Holt continued, "I think it's time we attacked that fat bastard. You've been on the defensive long enough."

"That's easy to say," Deed snapped, putting his emptied glass beside Holt's and Silka's. "They've got twice as many guns as the Lazy S and us combined. And they own the county law. Hell, they might even own a Ranger or two, for all we know."

"He's just a man."

"Right, and a fat one, but if we attack the

Bar 3, Bordner'll have the Rangers all over us," Blue said. "I think that's what he wants. An attack from us or the Sanchezes so he can go to the Rangers and have us arrested."

"Blue's right," Deed added.

"I think we get with the Sanchezes and get on with our roundup," Blue said. "If we don't, all the calves around will be wearing Bordner's brand. Then it won't matter."

"How the roundup would go without involving the Bar 3 is a serious consideration," Blue said.

"We can't leave our beef along there," Deed said, referring to the border of their ranch and the Bar 3 land. "Murphy's men'll brand everything that moves."

"Well, riding on their land will mean shooting, you know that," Blue said. "Felix Sanchez is willing to stay on their own land to avoid more bloodshed."

"What if Holt and I take care of the stray cattle on the Bar 3 land? I know I'm not afraid to cross over and I'm pretty sure Holt isn't either," Deed said and added, "But first, I'm going to ride to the Forsyth station and tell Atlee that the kids can't come. It's too dangerous."

Holt said, "You're right, Deed. They will be very disappointed, I'm sure, but now's not the time. And when you come back, I will be with you when you ride onto Bar 3 land."

"Thanks, Holt. That helps, I guess. What about Bina and your family, Blue? Do we dare leave them during the roundup?" Deed responded.

From the other room came the call that dinner was ready.

"We can talk more after we eat," Blue said. "It's not a good idea to keep Too Tall waiting."

They laughed and it eased the tension.

Holt could see the kitchen as they walked to the dining room table. Mismatched chairs surrounded it. The table was set with a bouquet of dried autumn flowers and leaves as a centerpiece.

The kitchen itself was controlled by a cast-iron stove, the same one that had toiled in the house since it was just their parents. Too Tall, the black cook, filled it with his intensity. A large upright pantry contained white ironstone plates, heavy iron tableware, pots, pans, two buckets, a large copper double boiler, and a dozen empty canning jars. On the floor, a large box was filled with sacks of flour, beans, and salt. A large china water basin, a lamp — and their meal of roasted grouse with peas and mashed potatoes — covered most of the small kitchen counter. Blue had shot six grouse yesterday.

At the table, Blue said grace and Too Tall began serving filled plates. Bina followed with hot coffee. Holt sat between Matthew and Mary Jo, with Jeremy next to her. They bombarded him with questions, most of which brought chuckles. The talk stayed happy until after the meal was finished and the children left.

Meanwhile, at the Bar 3, Agon Bordner was furious. He had just learned from Macy Shields that Deed had whipped Sear Georgian in front of witnesses. Before that, Rhey Selmon had informed him that vaqueros were stationed on the roof of the Lazy S ranch house night and day. Attacking them again would be difficult and costly in men.

"What the hell!" Bordner yelled and slammed his fist on the dining room table. "I don't believe it. Deed was shot, Rhey and Dixie told me. Shot several times. Can nobody whip him!"

"Well, boss, he sure looked like it, but he tore up Sear something fierce. Be down for a long time," Shields said.

"Why didn't you arrest him?" Bordner screamed again.

Shields shrugged his shoulders. "He had a gun on me."

"Did Corrigan hold a gun on Sear?"

"No. He gave it to Virdin while they fought," Shields continued. "Leastwise, that's what folks told me. I wasn't there."

"Virdin? What the hell. Why was Virdin there?" Bordner growled and glared at his gunman.

Shields straightened his back. "Corrigan bought some scarves in Virdin's store before the fight."

"I told Virdin to shut Corrigan and Sanchez out."

"He said he told them."

Bordner rubbed his unshaved chin.

"Dammit, boss, he stood up for Corrigan. Virdin did. Told me I couldn't arrest him 'cuz he lived in town. Virdin said that."

"I thought you said Corrigan had a gun on you."

"He did. Virdin gave it to him . . . when the fight was done."

Bordner shook his head. "Damn! Simpson, I'm hungry. Bring me something to eat." He stared at Shields again. "Get out of my sight, Macy. I thought you were better than that." The enormous man waved his gunman and his protests away.

He was also angry with himself. In the past few days, he had been going over his last conversation with James Hannah. The famed gunman had come to his house after considering Bordner's offer and said, "I'll take your money, Bordner."

"I'll take your money."

Bordner had been tossing that phrase around in his head. He replayed the conversation out loud. "Hannah hadn't said he would take the job or that he would kill Deed Corrigan. He had simply stated, 'I'll take your money' and I had been so damn glad Hannah had returned that I hadn't really listened.

"The only thing I asked the son of a bitch was 'when' and he said that he had some other business in the area. I said 'fine.' Then he downed his drink, took the money, and left, and I let it go at that."

He slammed his fist on the table and yelled again for Simpson.

"What a stupid fool," he muttered and forced himself to think of his next move. He prided himself on that ability. Whatever was done was done and the key was to move on. An idea was trying to break through and he must let it. What if they left the Lazy S alone for a while and attacked the LC ranch while the men were working the roundup. What if Rhey Selmon and some of his men slipped into the Corrigan compound. He didn't care what happened to the Indian wife of Blue's; she deserved raping, living like a white person. Same with Blue's children.

Bordner licked his blubbery lips. Yes. Yes. That would break them, pure and simple.

Grinning, he yelled again, "Simpson, I want a steak. Medium rare. And eggs. Over easy."

CHAPTER THIRTY-ONE

Two days later, Deed Corrigan rode to the Forsyth station, leading a saddled bay horse. It was Blue's idea; the older mount was no longer useful for ranch work, yet it was a sturdy animal with years of light service left. Blue suggested he give Chester to Benjamin to ease his disappointment in not coming to the roundup.

He didn't like what he had to do. Even seeing Atlee again was going to be tough. The day was overcast and it matched his thoughts. He was also carrying scarves for Atlee and Olivia and a doll for little Elizabeth. Maria Sanchez and her daughters had been pleased with his earlier gifts, so he hoped the Forsyth women would be as well. Especially Atlee. Still, it wasn't the way he wanted to return.

Benjamin saw him coming and ran from the station to meet him. Elizabeth was only a few steps behind. Cooper bounded next to them, barking joyfully.

"You came back! Is it roundup time?" Benjamin asked as the gunfighter stopped in front of the station.

Deed dismounted slowly, feeling every ache in his body more than he should. "Benjamin, we're going to have to wait on you helping with the roundup. We've got some bad people trying to take our land. It's going to be dangerous. I hate it, but you can't come now. Maybe later when all this is settled."

Benjamin looked like he had been hit in the face. Without saying a word, he spun around and went toward the station.

"Wait, Benjamin, please," Deed called. "This is Chester . . . and he's yours. He would've been in your roundup string. I thought you might like to have him anyway."

The boy stopped and turned around. "He's mine?"

"All yours," Deed responded. "Well, if it's all right with your mother."

"Can I ride him?"

"Hop on. He's a good horse."

Benjamin took the offered lead-rope. The reins were tied and resting over the saddle horn.

"That's your saddle, too."

Stepping forward, Elizabeth asked, "How

about me?"

"Well, it's too dangerous for you, too, at the ranch," Deed said.

She dropped her hands to her sides, lowered her head, and began to sob. Long tears filled her little face.

He went over to her, knelt, and hugged her. "I brought something for you."

She stopped crying. "What is it?"

"I'll get it for you now." He went to his saddlebags and produced three folded sacks. He handed the largest to Elizabeth and her eyes brightened.

Looking up, he saw Atlee standing in the doorway.

"What do you say, Elizabeth," Atlee said.

"Oh, thank you . . . Deed. Thank you very much." She opened the sack and pulled out the doll and her mouth opened wide. "Oh . . . oh, it's beautiful. I love it. Thank you. Thank you." She rushed over to Deed and hugged him. "I'm going to name her Jessica. Jessica Forsyth."

Dancing past her mother, Elizabeth disappeared inside the house, singing a made-up song about Jessica Forsyth.

"Well, good day, Mr. Corrigan," she said. "Is something wrong? We've been hoping you'd come. Every day, I think." She chuckled. "Won't you come in? Olivia just made some cookies and the coffee's hot."

"No thanks, I need to get going. The boys are waiting on me." He took off his hat and stood. "We've got bad problems at the ranch. Agon Bordner and his men are trying to take control of every ranch around. Only two left." He grimaced. "I can't have Benjamin and Elizabeth there right now. It isn't safe. I just can't. I-I'm sorry."

"So am I, but I understand, Deed. I really do," Atlee said. "Please come in for some coffee. You were very nice to come all this way, even if it was bad news." She studied his face. "You've had trouble already, haven't you? What happened to your ear?"

Deed put his hand to his bandaged ear and told her in several sentences about the posse's ambush and his escape, and the attacks on the Lazy S. He didn't mention the fight in town, but did say the county law was now in the hands of a Bordner man.

"Oh that's awful! You're lucky to be alive, Deed."

"I am a lucky man, Mrs. Forsyth."

She frowned. "Atlee, remember? Or have your forgotten all about me?"

"There's no way I could forget you . . . Atlee." He looked into her eyes for a moment, then away. "Oh, I brought a horse for Benjamin. It's one of our older mounts.

Real gentle. Thought it might help . . . some. If that's all right."

"That's very generous of you, Deed."

He cocked his head. "Oh I almost forgot. I brought something for . . . you and Mrs. Beinrigt, too."

He walked to the doorway and handed her the two sacks.

"I thought you'd like the pink one. The green one is for Mrs. Beinrigt."

Biting her lower lip, Atlee opened the top sack and withdrew the silk scarf. "Oh, it's beautiful, Deed. So beautiful. How very thoughtful of you." She folded it and tied it around her neck.

"Glad you like it."

Billy Lee Montez and Hermann Beinrigt came out of the barn just as he walked toward Atlee. They barely noticed Benjamin riding the bay around the yard.

"Señor Deed, you are back!" Billy Lee said.

"Willkommen," Hermann added, in welcome.

Deed wanted to talk with Atlee, that's all he had thought about riding over, but she told him that they could talk later, not to worry about her children, and went inside. He walked over to the two men and they began telling him about the station and how smoothly it was running. Deed thought they were trying hard to convince him; he glanced over his shoulder. The doorway was empty. He felt something sink inside.

He turned back to force himself to listen to them as they explained changes they had made in handling the horses, reshoeing, and feeding. Hermann had introduced a checking system when a team of tired horses came in. Deed nodded, but didn't really hear them. Part of him wished he hadn't returned. It was silly to think of Atlee.

Inside the station, Olivia finally spoke up about Deed. She and Atlee had become good friends. "You must *nicht* let Deed Corrigan get avay, Atlee. Your husband vas *ein gut* man, but he *ist nicht* here. Deed *ist.* You haff mourned long enough," Olivia said, folding her arms. "Deed Corrigan *ist gut* man. He vants you . . . *und* you vant him. *Lasst* him go *nicht,* Atlee."

Outside, Deed was distracted by a sharp call, "Hey, Corrigan!"

He spun around. It was James Hannah. He was cleaning his glasses. Excusing himself, Deed walked over to the bespectacled gunman. Hermann and Billy Lee returned to the barn, still talking to each other about what more they wanted to do.

"Good to see you, James," Deed said,

holding out his hand.

Hannah returned his glasses to his nose and shook Deed's hand enthusiastically.

"What brings you here?" Deed asked.

"You."

"Me?" Deed was wary. Blue told him that he might be working for Agon Bordner.

Hannah cocked his head. "Bordner wants you killed. Paid me five hundred dollars to do it."

Deed shifted his legs to balance himself. If this was going to turn into a gunfight, he must be ready. He glanced down at his gunbelt, then at Hannah "That's a lot of money."

Hannah watched Deed setting himself. "Yeah, it is. But you be easy now. You aren't going to need that gun with me. I thought you boys might be wanting another gun. This Bordner wants the whole region. All of it. But if you don't want my help, I'll ride on with my bride."

He laughed. "I just couldn't see letting that much money go to waste. So I told him that I would take his money." He shook his head. "I didn't say that I'd do anything for it, just that I'd take it. I guess he was too excited to really listen to what I was saying.

"It's going to pay for a nice honeymoon for my bride and a new start in Wichita.

I've got relatives there. So, I thought Mrs. Hannah and I could go to town. What's the name, Wilkon, yeah, that's it," Hannah said flicking away imaginary dust from his vest. "Then I'd be real close if you needed me. We are friends, remember. Oh, and you remember Rebecca Tuttle, don't you?"

Deed frowned. "Yes, she was going to El Paso to marry some farmer."

"Uh, the farmer didn't ever show up and —"

"Well, congratulations, James."

Deed chuckled and Hannah joined in.

Deed told him what had happened at the Lazy S, with the posse, and in town and that Bordner's man was now county sheriff as well as town marshal. Hannah chuckled again when he heard about Deed downing Sear Georgian.

"Damn it, man. No wonder Bordner wants someone to kill you. None of his men are good enough."

"Are you?"

Hannah licked his lips. "Come on, Deed. I'm not interested in that kind of talk. As I said, if you don't want me, we'll catch the next stage to Kansas."

"I'd like your help," Deed said. "A whole lot. Bordner's got twenty guns and a lot of ego."

Hannah pushed on his glasses. "I'll tell Rebecca that we're headed for Wilkon. Mrs. Forsyth said there was a buckboard we could borrow."

"Thank you. I'm glad you're here, James."

They shook hands again and Hannah went into the stage station. As Deed watched him, Atlee came to the doorway.

"Deed, would you mind going with me around back for a minute. I need some . . . help." Her face was creased with a frown. "Olivia likes her scarf. Green is her favorite color."

"That's great. Of course, glad to help."

She stepped off the porch and walked to the corner of the station. "Benjamin and Elizabeth will be fine. They were disappointed, but they'll be fine. I told them there would be other roundups when the danger was gone. Your gifts were very thoughtful . . . and very appreciated."

He followed her around to the back of the station, wondering what she wanted. Maybe it was a load of supplies, but he couldn't remember them ever being placed there before. She stopped at the back of the station and waited.

Pushing back his hat from his forehead, Deed stepped closer, still unsure of what she wanted. He didn't see anything that needed moving.

"It would have been fun having your kids at the ranch. And Benjamin would've been a good addition," he said awkwardly. "I'm so sorry about all this."

"You've been so wonderful. Don't know what we, I, would have done without you Deed."

Deed scuffed his right boot in the ground and watched the dirt turn up around it. "Wasn't much. You'd have been fine without me. You're quite a woman . . . Atlee." He looked up and she was staring into his face, only two feet away.

Reaching out, Atlee touched his arm and held it, then moved closer. "May I ask you something? Promise you won't laugh."

"Of course. You can tell me anything or ask me anything. I probably won't know the answer though." He forced a chuckle.

"I really think I can ask you anything, Deed," she whispered. "It's part of what makes you so special. To me."

Deed tried to think of something to say, but couldn't.

She took a half step closer to him, her hand remaining on his arm. Deed could smell the deliciousness of her. A little like violets, he thought, mixed with the fresh smell of soap. And woman. It was intoxicating.

"Will you wait for me?" she asked, looking into his eyes.

Deed swallowed. "I, uh, I don't understand."

Tears began to roll down her cheeks and he touched her face to remove them without thinking about it.

"I was married to a good man. We had plans together. And Caleb was taken from me."

"I-I know that. I am very sorry but —"

She touched two fingers to his lips to shush him and left them there. "I am in m-mourning . . . and must be," she stammered. "But you came along and turned everything upside down. I know my life should be with you . . . now. I know that." She blinked. "I'm in mourning and need to be. W-Will you wait for me, s-so I can become your wife, if you'll have me?"

Gently, he removed her fingers from his mouth and held her hand. "Atlee, nothing would make me happier than to have you beside me as my wife. I will wait forever if —"

She pushed against him and her mouth found his. They held each other and kissed, and kissed.

"I love you," she whispered.
"I've loved you since I first saw you."
Nothing else mattered.

Chapter Thirty-Two

Riding back to the ranch was a blur for Deed. All he could think of was Atlee's declaration of love for him. Her kisses were imprinted on his mind like fire. Hannah and Rebecca sat beside him on the buckboard seat while his horse was hitched behind. Rebecca did most of the talking. She seemed determined to comment on everything they passed.

Their destination had changed somewhat. Rebecca would stay in town at the Wilkon Hotel while Hannah went to the ranch to help guard it. Deed had shared the concern about Bordner's men attacking when they were gone and Hannah decided that he should stay there. Deed told him that his older brother Holt was with them and that he was going to stay at the ranch as well. Bina and her children were going to be with the roundup; it was safer they thought.

Rebecca didn't like being separated from

her new husband, but gradually understood the seriousness of the situation. After letting her off at the hotel and getting her settled in the best room available, Deed and Hannah headed for the ranch. The town itself was quiet, something expected at roundup time. Hannah told her not to use his name and, if asked, to say her husband was coming in on the next stagecoach.

Clearing the last ridge, Deed pulled up so Hannah could see the entire ranch yard and get an idea of where Bordner's men might attack. He had already told the gunman that he didn't think Bordner knew about his brother returning, and that Holt was going by Sam Holton. Hannah asked a few questions, mostly about available rifles and ammunition. Clucking to the horses, Deed headed for the ranch. As they pulled up, Holt stepped from the house, cradling a Winchester in his arms.

"Well, well, I do believe it's James Hannah," he said cheerfully. "Good to have you with us."

"And to you . . . Sam Holton," Hannah said.

Deed said, "James has agreed to stay at the ranch and give you a hand while we're working the roundup."

"Sounds good to me. Got some fresh coffee on," Holt declared as they shook hands. "Bina . . . that's Blue's wife . . . she left us some good food. We sure won't starve."

"How about guns?"

They walked inside and Holt showed him their collected weapons and the boxes of cartridges.

"Got two barrels of water in the kitchen, too," Holt said. "All the comforts of home."

"Sounds good to me," Hannah said. "When do you expect them?"

"I'm guessing they'll wait a day or two. Keep an eye on who's working the roundup," Deed said and poured coffee for the three of them.

"You don't think they'll get suspicious when they see Blue's wife and children at the roundup?"

Deed nodded. "We hope they don't. Bina's going to be dressed like a man. And the kids are going to stay inside the chuck wagon during the day. They won't like it, but they'll do it."

After drinking his coffee, Deed saddled and rode out on the paint horse, Warrior, heading out to the roundup camp. Hannah settled into reading Henry Wadsworth Longfellow's *Tales of a Wayside Inn* and Holt strolled around the ranch. They would take turns guarding when night came. The ranch dogs trailed Deed to the far edge of the ranch yard before turning back. The thought nettled him about leaving the ranch, but he pushed it away, confident that Holt and Hannah could do serious damage to any attackers. In fact, both men seemed to be looking forward to it.

At the roundup camp, he rode up to a wild symphony of sound of bawling calves and yelling men, mixed with heavy dust, wood smoke, and the smell of burning cowhide. Most of the valley was covered by grazing cattle gathered during the day. Herefords made up most of the herd, but there were longhorns mixed with them.

Short-term fences of brush and logs kept the gathered animals from straying. From dawn to dark, riders worked to bring in the cattle, separating them into one herd of cows with calves and a separate herd of steers and older cows. An occasional bull was in this group as well. Come spring this bunch would be moved to market in Kansas.

A sturdy pole corral had been built to hold calves while the youngsters were branded. Their mothers were allowed to stand around the corral as long as they weren't unruly. New calves were branded to match their mothers; unbranded strays were divided as to ownership. A long rope tied between two cottonwoods held the horses not being ridden at the moment.

Two Sanchez riders were overseeing a smaller herd of unbranded strays. They wouldn't allow these cattle to drift back to the main herd. Any cattle carrying brands other than the Lazy S or LC were eased out of the herd and made to return to their home ranges. As Deed rode up, four riders cleared the woods; each had a roped cow and a calf trailing behind them. He didn't recognize any of the men.

Blue rode toward his brother and waved with his lone hand, still holding the reins. It was his first time serving as the roundup wagon boss and he wanted everything to go well. He directed the combined team of LC and Lazy S riders so there would be no gaps in the ground covered. He had hired six men from town to help with the roundup and they were proving to be good hands. Deed eased the paint toward his brother. In spite of the turbulent time, the roundup was well organized and underway as planned. A lot of that was due to Blue's leadership.

Riding between them, Willy brought a terrified calf toward the branding fire. He was working as one of the cutting riders, or ketch hands. Their job was to separate unbranded calves from their mothers.

Willy yelled, "Got a Lazy S comin' in."

Blue looked at Deed and grinned.

Off to the side, Taol and two men were charged with removing scrotums from the young calves. Each removed bloody sack was tossed into a large pot, usually accompanied by a Mexican cheer. A supper of fried "mountain oysters" would be a traditional celebration when the roundup was over. Another group was also checking beeves that had been separated from the others for disease, sores, or open wounds. Any cow with thin flanks, or a swollen jaw, or a drooping head, was given special treatment. Likely the animal had been bitten by a rattlesnake. At their feet were medicine bottles, cutting tools, and large cans of ointment.

Sweating heavily, Harmon Payne coordinated the branding while other sweaty men worked diligently and fast over a hot fire. Behind them both, Cliente, the Lazy S foreman, was keeping tally in a leather-bound book. A thin cigar extended from his mouth.

Blue told Deed that Silka, Little Jake, and some vaqueros were working the heavy thickets for cows and their calves entrenched in the thick growth encircling the ravines. All riders had stayed on the combined land of the two ranches. Unspoken was the need at some point to cross into Bar 3 land. There were too many strays to ignore, especially Lazy S cattle.

Deed asked where Blue wanted him. Blue suggested he stick around and help with the gathered calves. It was too late to ride out to the heavy brush. Deed had the feeling that Blue was favoring him and told him that his wounds had healed, except for the top of his ear. Blue dismissed his suggestion as the reason and said he was welcome to ride out if he wanted to do so, but they were almost overrun with the calves gathered so far.

The remainder of the afternoon went fast. Several cowboys went to the creek to soak their feet; others began talking horse and boots. A boghole had been discovered to the north and that brought stories of other bogholes and quicksand. Later that night, as they gathered around the campfire and ate, Deed sat quietly with Silka. Blue was eating with Bina and their children, happy to be free of the chuck wagon.

"I'm going to ride back, Silka. If Bordner's men hit the ranch, it'll probably be with a lot of men," Deed declared.

Silka shook his head. "It is long ride there and back. Maybe for nothing. They may not come or it may be only a few. They will think only a woman stays."

"It's our ranch," Deed said. "I heard Cliente talking about sending men back to their ranch tonight. And he's got four vaqueros already standing guard on their roof."

"Tell Blue. I ride with you," Silka said and laid down his plate.

Blue understood and wanted to go with them, but knew he couldn't. His primary responsibility right now was to the roundup. After saddling his buckskin and Silka's favorite bay, they rode out. It was already dark, but they knew the trail well. Holt and Hannah were glad for the interruption; there had been no signs of trouble and both were bored. Holt insisted Deed and Silka sleep and would be awakened if necessary.

The night was uneventful and the two men rode back to the roundup camp early the next morning. They rode in and dismounted as far from the gathered herds as possible. A horse freed of its rider might shake the saddle and scare the cattle. Deed reported that all was well at the ranch and Blue was relieved.

Shortly after breakfast, a mossy-eared longhorn bull broke away from the second herd, angry at the rider working his cows, and charged the camp, looking for something to ram. Yells broke through the camp. Willy was loping his horse to the calf pen when he saw the bull coming at him. He swerved his horse but not enough and the bull slammed into the bay and sent Willy flying. The enraged bull spun around and headed back for Willy, stunned on the ground. Frightened, Willy's horse went running.

Cliente got a rope over the bull's head and Harmon added a second, but the animal snapped them like they were string. Taking his empty dish and cup to the chuck wagon, Deed ran for his Spencer on his horse. Cliente was closer to his rifle and fired into the charging animal. The bull staggered, but kept coming. Deed fired and then Cliente again. Stumbling forward, the bull fell on its horns five feet from the dazed Willy.

"That was too close," Blue said and walked over to the downed cowhand. "Willy, are you all right?"

"Huh?"

Blue helped him to his feet; Harmon rushed over to help. They half-carried, half-dragged him to the campfire. One of the vaqueros brought Willy's bedroll from the chuck wagon and spread it out. Bina came with water and towels.

"Willy, you rest here for a while." Blue

and Harmon laid him down on his blankets.

"I'm fine. Jes' fine." He tried to stand and fell.

"Stay put, Willy," Blue commanded and eased the man to his sleeping blankets.

Cliente reported that Willy's bay only got a long scratch and should be just fine. They decided to have a couple of the men skin the bull; Too Tall would direct the effort.

"Some beef would be good," the Mexican foreman said with a grin. "He was one of ours. So dinner is on us."

The day was long and hard. Deed rode with Silka and two vaqueros and they each went through five horses working in the long draws and heavy brush where the cattle liked to hide. Several cows wearing old H-5 and Roof-M brands were found, along with a handful of Bar 3 animals. All were herded to Bar 3 land. When they couldn't see any longer, they rode in. Blue announced they would move the camp tomorrow, closer to Bar 3 range.

After rubbing down their horses, Silka headed for a nearby stream and placed his lariat in it for the night. He thought it gave the rope stiffness needed to lasso calves. A recovered Willy got to belching loudly around the campfire and one of his especially forceful presentations scared the horses and cattle. It took half an hour to calm the herd and the remuda. Willy apologized, but no one thought it was funny. Several hands thought it would have been better if the bull had knocked him out. Blue suggested he take a walk after eating from now on, away from the camp.

As soon as supper was over, Deed and Silka rode again for the ranch. Both were weary and sore, but felt it was important. Before they left, a full moon rose and showered the land with a silvery light as they rode, giving everything a strange glow.

Gunshots broke into the night as Deed and Silka neared their home. They reined their horses to a stop on the ridge that overlooked the ranch yard. Silhouettes were moving like ants on disturbed dirt.

"Looks like they weren't surprised," Deed said and yanked his Spencer free of its sleeve.

Drawing his Winchester from its sheath, Silka pointed at a small group of men riding away. "Look, they run."

"Let's encourage them to keep running."

"Hai."

They fired almost simultaneously at the fleeing men. Silka levered his Winchester four times and Deed fired once more. They didn't expect to hit anything; it just felt good. The sound of horses galloping away filled the night and then there was silence.

From the house came a loud yell. "Deed. Silka. You missed all the fun. Come on in!"

Deed recognized the voice as his brother's.

A moment later, Hannah added his challenge. "Hey, that was fun. We dusted those boys real good."

"Hey, Deed! We got fresh coffee on," Holt yelled. "I think there were five of them. Think they thought only Bina was here."

Deed and Silka rode toward the house, watching the shadows for any possible movement. Halfway to the house, a body lay sprawled.

Appearing in the doorway, Holt appeared. "I knew it was going to be a good night. See that moon? Full as can be. That's good luck for sure."

CHAPTER THIRTY-THREE

Now that the roundup was over, Deed was going to ride over to the Forsyth station and see Atlee and her children. It was Blue's suggestion and he could hardly wait. His brother had told him to take Hannah to town in the borrowed buckboard, then go on to the station. Both Holt and Silka agreed with the idea.

Hannah had wanted to move to town to be with his bride now anyway, although the Corrigan brothers invited him to bring Rebecca to the ranch. Hannah winked, saying they had important matters to deal with. He was glad that Deed would take him and return the buckboard back to the Forsyth station.

Everything was gradually feeling normal around the ranch. Deed's mind danced with thoughts of Atlee. Everything in him wanted to ride out the Forsyth station and take her in his arms. But he knew the trouble with

Bordner was far from over. It only meant that attacking the two remaining ranches wasn't efficient.

Bordner's men hadn't tried anything since their ill-fated attack on the LC ranch house. The gathering of strayed Lazy S and LC cattle on Bar 3 land had also gone without incident. With nothing from Bordner, Blue thought it meant the fat man was going to settle in as a rancher. Deed and Holt figured something bad was coming. Holt had pointed to a hollow fire last night as a sign of danger coming.

Deed promised to only be gone for the day. Blue decided to ride over to the Sanchez ranch and discuss any concerns they might have. Dropping Hannah off at the hotel in town, Deed turned the buckboard toward Atlee. Tugging on his hat and looking down at himself, Deed cleared the cottonwoods lining the back side of the station yard. His heart beat faster as he drew closer. His saddled buckskin was on a lead-rope behind the wagon. Maybe Atlee had changed her mind. Maybe she had just felt particularly lonely that day. Maybe —

Benjamin saw him and came running with Cooper at his side.

"Is the roundup over? Are the bad guys gone?" the boy asked almost before Deed pulled to a stop.

"Yes to the first. No to the second," Deed grinned. "Thought I'd bring back the buckboard Mr. Hannah borrowed and get a chance to see you. How is everyone?"

"Ma will be very happy you're here," Benjamin chirped. "She talks about you all the time."

Deed dismounted. "How's Chester?"

"Oh, he's great. I rode him this morning," Benjamin said. "He's in the barn right now. I take real good care of him." He glanced toward the barn. "You want to see him?"

"Sure. Later." Deed wrapped the reins around the brake handle and climbed down. He knelt to rub Cooper's ears. "Think I'll go inside and see everyone first."

Benjamin said, "Sure. They're getting ready for the stage." He looked toward the north, placing his hand above his eyes to shield them from the sun. "It's the one from Kansas."

Deed patted the boy on the shoulder and walked to the opened station door. "Anybody around here know when the next stage comes in?"

Surprised whoops followed, then Atlee hurried toward him. An instant before reaching him, she stopped, catching her emotions.

Flustered, she smiled. "W-Well, Mr. Corrigan. H-How good to see you. I-Is your roundup over?"

From behind her came a happy German, then a warm "*Willkommen! Willkommen, Herr Corrigan.* Come in."

"Oh, yes . . . Deed, please," Atlee said, touching her hair.

"Thank you. I-It's good to see you again."

Squealing, Elizabeth came hurrying from the kitchen, holding the doll Deed had given her.

"Deed . . . Deed . . . you're back!"

It made him feel good that she had always called him by his given name, almost from the first.

He leaned over and held out his arms. She half-jumped into them and he hugged and spun her around. Her giggling filled the room. When he put her down again, she showed him her doll and asked him if he remembered her name.

"Let's see. Is it Jessica?" Deed's smile covered his face.

"Oh, you remembered!"

Atlee stepped to them and took his hand. Holding it at her side, they walked to the table where Olivia waited. Both women were wearing their scarves.

"Herr Corrigan, now I can thank you for

429

this beautiful scarf. *Danke*," Olivia said. "I think Hermann *ist* jealous. *Ja*." She chuckled.

"Glad you like it. I hear the stage is coming soon," Deed said, aware that Atlee still held his hand. "Didn't see Hermann or Billy Lee when I came in."

"They must be in *der* barn getting *der* horses ready," Olivia said.

He turned to Atlee, hardly containing himself from hugging her. "Where do you want me to put the buckboard, the one the Hannahs borrowed?"

Atlee's face glowed. "Oh, I suppose around in the back of the barn. I'll show you."

Olivia winked as Deed excused himself and they went outside, still holding hands. As soon as they rounded the barn, Atlee leaned against him, bringing his face to hers with a hand. They kissed.

"Oh, Deed, I miss you so."

Deed touched her face. "Not as much as I miss you, Atlee. You are all I can think about."

Their embrace was interrupted by the thundering advance of the incoming stage. They heard Billy Lee and Hermann telling each other to get the new team.

She laughed. "I guess I've got to go to

work. How long can you stay?"

Deed shrugged his shoulders. "I've got to go back later today. I promised to only be gone for the day. Troubles with Bordner are only going to get worse, I fear. At least we have our brother Holt with us. Blue talked to him in El Paso and he came back."

"Oh, that's wonderful about your brother, but not about you leaving so soon!" She kissed him on the cheek and spun away to go back into the station.

The day went too fast and he reluctantly rode out on his buckskin, waving as he rode. They had had only one other quiet moment together, in the kitchen, but he told himself it would keep him happy for a little while. He wanted to ask her how long she needed to be in mourning, but couldn't bring himself to do so.

The evening went slowly with Deed's mind wrapped around being with Atlee. It was late morning when he saw riders coming as he walked from the barn. Retrieving his carbine propped against the barn wall, Deed stepped outside and into a morning shadow, cocking the gun with practiced ease.

Three riders.

He recognized them: the acting county sheriff, Macy Shields, and the two Rangers

431

who had come to the Forsyth station. This wasn't going to be a social call.

"Aho, the ranch!" The call came from one of the Rangers.

"Morning, men," Deed called out. "What can we do for you? Are you finally getting around to investigating the trouble the Bar 3's been bringing?"

From around the corner came Blue and not far behind him was Silka. Holt stayed in the house.

"What's this all about?" Blue asked as he stepped beside his brother.

"Don't know, Blue. This here's Macy Shields, one of Bordner's men. Bordner set him up as acting sheriff. Acting is probably the right word for him," Deed said, not taking his eyes from Shields. "I met these two Rangers at the Forsyth station when I was helping there. This is Mr. Rice . . . and I think this is Mr. Williams. This is my brother, Blue, and our partner, Silka."

"You have a good memory," Ranger Rice said.

"Thanks. It comes in handy now and then."

Rice leaned forward in his saddle and pushed back his hat with its pushed-up brim. "Boys, this isn't a good day, I'm afraid. You two and your brother, Holt, are

432

accused of robbing the Wilkon bank. We need to take you in for questioning."

The second Ranger looked around. "Is Holt here?"

Deed snorted. "No, he's not. You know that."

Blue said, "I don't know whether to laugh or cry about this silliness, Ranger. When did this supposedly happen?"

"Yesterday," Ranger Williams responded. "And it isn't silly to us. The bank president recognized you, Blue, and said you called your brothers, Holt and Deed, by name. He said you all wore masks." He hesitated. "Having just one arm stood out." The tall Ranger took a deep breath. "He said you were in the bank for a loan before that and were turned down. He guessed you needed the money. About two thousand in gold and certificates were taken."

"Yesterday? I was —"

Blue stepped forward, nudging Deed to the side and stopping him from continuing his statement. "Put the gun down, Deed. So you think we robbed the bank and came back here. Does that make any sense to you? Or am I missing something?"

The shorter Ranger growled. "That's not our problem. We need to search your place for Holt."

"I just told you he's not here," Deed snapped.

"Can't take your word for it. We've got to search." The shorter, stockier lawman with the misshapen hat declared. He brushed his long black trail coat as if that would remove the layers of dust.

"Look away then, but knock on the door before you go in," Blue said. "My wife is putting our children down for a nap."

"Come on, men," Marshal Shields said and eased his horse in the direction of the house.

Blue turned to the Rangers. "Gentlemen, we have no problem with you boys looking through our place. But we must insist that this man stay outside. He's more coyote than lawman and I don't want him in our house. If you weren't here, he wouldn't be allowed to stay on our land."

"Wait a minute, I'm the law in this county," Shields snarled. "It's my job to keep the peace."

"Then keep it by staying on your horse," Deed said, glaring at him.

Williams, the taller Ranger, tugged on his trail coat. "That'll be just fine."

Shields's hand dropped to his holstered handgun.

"You didn't have the guts to try that

before, Shields," Deed's hard voice made even the Rangers wince.

Ranger Williams said, "That's enough, Shields. Ranger Rice and I will conduct the search. You wait here." He swung down. "And don't do anything . . . stupid."

Blue turned to his brother. "Deed, why don't you get our hands out of the bunkhouse so the Rangers can search more easily, all right?" He winked and only Deed caught it. "Tell Bina that the Rangers are going to search the house on the way, will you?"

"Sure." He spun around and headed for the house.

"Rangers, you're welcome to start in our house or the barn, whatever," Blue turned back to the mounted men. "Just leave your horses and we'll see that they're watered."

"I appreciate that, but you know we have to take you in for a hearing," Rice, the shorter, stocky Ranger, dismounted.

"Who's conducting this hearing?" Blue asked.

"It'll be Judge Pence. Oscar Pence. You know, the circuit court judge. He's in town."

"That's interesting timing." Blue held out his hand and took the offered reins of both horses.

The two Rangers walked to the house,

talking quietly to each other. Bina met them at the door and welcomed them inside. Deed was already walking toward the bunkhouse.

Shields started to get down and Blue said, "Stay on your horse, Shields. When we take the horses to water, you can ride over. Wouldn't keep a good horse from that, even when it's being ridden by a crook."

The county lawman glared at him. "You're gonna be sorry, Corrigan. You and your damn brothers. All o' you are going to prison. You should've known you can't beat Agon Bordner. He's gonna be king of this whole region."

Blue laughed and led the Rangers' horses to the water tank. Shields followed without saying anything more. From the bunkhouse, Deed reappeared with Silka, Holt, Willy, Harmon, and Little Jake. None were armed. Holt had slipped out of the back door and gone to the bunkhouse after Deed had told him what was happening.

A few minutes later, the Rangers reappeared.

"Rangers, you're welcome to search the bunkhouse and the barn," Blue said, holding the reins of the drinking horses. Casually, he said, "These are our permanent hands . . . Willy, Sam, Harmon, and Jake.

They'll stay out of your way."

The Rangers nodded and headed for the bunkhouse.

"Sam, Willy, will you saddle us some horses," Blue asked.

Holt smiled and he and Willy hurried toward the barn. The Rangers were coming out of the bunkhouse and headed for the back side of the barn. He was uneasy, but trusted his brother's instinct.

Deed moved over to where Blue was standing with the horses. "What are we going to do?" he whispered.

"We're going in. Clear this thing up," Blue responded.

"This is a setup, Blue. You know that," Deed snapped.

"Of course it is. But I don't see any other way," Blue muttered.

"How about using our guns."

"That's just what Bordner would like — us firing at Texas Rangers doing their duty."

Inside the barn, Willy and Holt began saddling mounts. The animals blew softly as they placed blankets on their backs. Most of the roundup horses had already had their shoes removed and been turned out for the winter. Only those needed for the next few months were in the barn and kept shod.

Holt saw a spider prance across the back

of the stall. Good luck, he decided. Definitely good luck. As he swung the saddle into place, Ranger Williams stepped beside the opened stall.

"Sorry we have to do this," Williams said. "But we have to, you know."

Holt cocked his head and reached for the cinch under the horse's belly. "Yeah, guess so. They didn't do it, you know."

"Don't think so either. Do I know you?"

"Don't know. Where you from?" Holt said. "I came from Kansas."

"Oh. You looked sorta familiar to me."

"Really? Some folks around say I look like I should be one of the Corrigan brothers." He grinned.

Williams smiled. "Not hardly."

From the next stall, Willy yelled, "You know, I had a guy say that about me. Last year it was."

Williams turned toward his partner. "See anything, Rice?"

"No. It's clear."

"All right, let's get moving to town."

The Rangers reappeared from the barn with Holt and Willy leading the saddled horses. "We'll take the two of you to town. Will you go peacefully?"

"Yes. But we're keeping our guns until we get there," Blue said. "I don't trust Bordner or his bunch."

Ranger Williams looked at his fellow lawman. "That'll work for us. No tricks now."

"No tricks. May I tell my wife good-bye?" Blue asked.

"I'll go with you," Ranger Rice declared.

"That won't be necessary," Ranger Williams responded. "He just gave us his word."

Ranger Rice mumbled something under his breath and remounted.

After a brief good-bye, Blue returned to the group carrying several towels and a newspaper. He said the towels were for washing themselves in the morning and the paper, for catching up on their reading. What no one knew was that Blue had a needle and a small circle of thread in his pocket to execute an idea Bina had suggested. He shoved the towels and newspaper into his saddlebags and mounted his horse. Deed noticed his brother had a glove shoved into his back pocket. Also unknown to anyone was a loaded derringer hidden in Blue's boot, again Bina's suggestion.

Coming up next to him, Holt said, "I won't let you guys take this fall."

"I know. Ride for the station. We're going to need Mrs. Forsyth to testify," Blue said quietly. "Same with Felix Sanchez. Tell Silka to bring the money from the drive. All of it.

We're going to end this. One way or the other."

"I'll take care of it."

Blue looked at his brother and nudged his horse into a lope to catch up to Deed. The two brothers rode out with a Ranger on either side of them. At Deed's insistence, Shields rode in front.

A half hour later, Rhey Selmon in his bearskin coat and six riders cleared a ravine and rode up. The man with a long scar across the bottom of his face and the blond gunman with strange eyes and a weak chin rode on either side of him. They were surprised to see guns in the Corrigan brothers' hands. Both Rangers drew their six guns from their double-rowed cartridge belts and demanded to know what the riders wanted.

"Just thought you might want some protection riding to town," Rhey said. "Comanches are still out, you know."

Deed laughed. "So are you bastards."

Waving his gun, Ranger Williams said, "That's not needed. You boys head on back to where you came from. Do it now."

Rhey gave Shields a hard glare. Shields shrugged his shoulders and the gunman reined his horse around and kicked it into a gallop. His men followed without a word.

The scar-faced man turned to look at them, then hurried to catch up.

CHAPTER THIRTY-FOUR

When they reached the jail, Blue and Deed surrendered their gunbelts and stepped into separate cells. Deed made no attempt to mention his throwing knife behind his back; Blue kept the derringer in his boot and the lawmen didn't search them. Ranger Williams promised either he or Rice would stand guard and both Corrigan brothers said they appreciated it.

An hour later, Judge Oscar Pence came to visit. Stoop shouldered and gray bearded, he looked like a man in charge of the world and had the reputation of being hard but fair. His voice carried a definite Missouri twang though and his manner was more woodsman than magistrate. In his cheek was a chaw of tobacco and his hand held a small tin can for spitting tobacco juice. He wore a shoulder holster carrying a long-barreled revolver. Deed guessed he would know how to use it.

"Deed Corrigan and Blue Corrigan. Heard about both of ya. And that brother, Holt, too. Hard men all o' ya. Especially Deed. Heard ya whupped a giant o' a man a few days back. Mostly to protect a Mexican friend. I like that."

Judge Pence paused and looked at Blue. "Hear ya preach some, Blue. That's good. Won't help ya none in my court, but it's good." He spat in the can. "I trust ya know what y'all are in here for. You're accused of robbin' the town bank. Serious stuff."

"We know the charges. They're false," Blue answered. "It's the latest trick by Agon Bordner to get control of all the ranches around here."

"Heard 'bout that, too. This hearin' is all about findin' the truth," Judge Pence declared, his graying eyebrows arching. "Whar's yer brother. He's accused o' this, too."

"Don't know, Judge. They came to the ranch and took us," Blue said and glanced at Deed.

"Heard he's been ridin' outlaw after the war."

Deed finally said, "He's a good man. Fought for the South. Was one of the heroes at Sabine Pass. But he's been blamed for every bank and stage robbery around."

443

"Heard that, too. He'd get a fair trial in my court."

Blue took hold of a cell bar with his one hand. "Judge, I assume a hearing is more informal than a trial. That right?"

"I'll give ya some leeway as long as it makes sense to me, if that's what you're askin'," Judge Pence said. "Are ya representin' yourselves?"

"Yes, we are."

"Kinda risky, ya know." The gray-haired man folded his arms. "Ya be up against Sylvestor Tritt. Been brought in by the bank from El Paso. Slick. Real slick. Been in my court a time or two representin' some real scum."

"How long ago did he get here?" Deed asked, stepping to the front of the cell.

"Don' know. Does it matter?" Judge Pence spat into his can.

"Well, it's a long way to El Paso and we were supposed to have robbed that bank just yesterday," Deed said. "I'd like to know when he got the word to come here."

Judge Pence blinked his eyes. "Hmm. So would I." He straightened his worn cravat. "The hearin' will start tomorrow mornin'. Nine o'clock. Sheriff Shields told me it was goin' to be held at McCollum's restaurant." He chuckled. "Evidently there's a lotta folks

444

who want to sit in." He spat and looked at the accumulating brown juice.

"I'll bet," Blue said. "We'll be ready, Judge."

"Hope so, son. Hope so." He glanced over his shoulder. "Oh, there's a stranger outside. Asked to see you. A Mr. James Hannah. Do you want to see him?"

"Sure. He's an old friend."

"Well, I hear he's a professional shootist."

"Maybe so, but he's our friend and has our backs. Everything around here is owned by Agon Bordner. The sheriff. Bank. General store. We have our doubts about you," Blue said.

Pence's face hardened. "Wal, I ain't owned by nobody nowhere."

"We sure hope so, Judge." Blue smiled.

Judge Pence stomped away, alternating talking to himself and spitting into his can. After the Corrigan brothers had a brief conversation with Hannah, he left. Most of the rest of the night was spent in preparation for the hearing. They didn't sleep much; Blue insisted that his brother join him in prayer. For once, Deed agreed.

Morning found them escorted to McCollum's restaurant by the two Rangers. It was a cold day, blustery and gray. They went first to the outhouse behind the jail so the brothers could relieve themselves. The walk was casual with the two lawmen more interested in the weather than the hearing. Neither noticed that Blue had hidden his good right arm inside his shirt and stuffed his empty left sleeve with towels to appear as if it were his good arm. A left-hand glove, stuffed with pages of the newspaper, had been sewn to his shirtsleeve, giving the appearance of a hand. The fake arm hung at his side.

Rearranged for the trial, the restaurant was already packed with townspeople when Blue and Deed entered, escorted by the two Rangers. Several greeted them with encouragement. More didn't look at them. Eight Bar 3 men had already cornered the best tables near the back of the restaurant where the trial would be held. The front of the restaurant was lined with additional interested people, standing and waiting. At the back near the kitchen, a table had been set aside for Pence to preside. One chair was placed for him; another at the table's edge for witnesses. Two other tables had been arranged a few feet away — one for the prosecution and one for the defense.

Shields was already sitting at the prosecution table, grinning like a cat. Next to him was a narrow-faced man with a carrot nose in a finely tailored black suit. His black eyebrows were thick, nearly becoming one. A matching goatee gave his thin face an evil look. Blue and Deed decided this must be Sylvestor Tritt.

Agon Bordner sat at the table closest to Shields and Tritt. At his table were Dixie Murphy, Willard Hixon, Jephrum Virdin, the scar-faced gunman, and the blond gunman from the ride to town. All were talking and laughing. Deed noticed that Dixie and all the gunmen were armed. They should have expected as much with Shields as the sheriff. Someone was missing. Who? Oh yes, Deed thought to himself, it's that gunman in the bearskin coat, Rhey Selmon. He's too easily recognized to be here, even when the hearing is about us, he guessed.

As Deed and Blue moved to the defendants' table, Murphy snarled, "This is going to be a wonderful day. You Corrigans are going down."

Tritt glanced at them, then back to a paper he was studying.

Ignoring the threat, Deed looked around and saw Atlee enter the restaurant with Silka. He smiled at her and she mouthed, "I love you." Deed felt his heart bounce and returned the silent message. A few minutes later, Felix Sanchez walked in, accompanied by Cliente and Taol. They stood at the front area of the restaurant. Deed was glad to see they were armed with gunbelts. Felix's eyes sought both brothers in a silent affirmation of support.

Ranger Williams walked over to the Sanchez men to tell them they couldn't have weapons in the courtroom. Instead of complying, Felix pointed to the tables of Bar 3 gunmen.

"Take them first."

The Ranger pushed his hat back on his forehead and walked away. He wasn't about to try disarming those tables. Not alone. And not with just Ranger Rice helping. Everyone should have been disarmed when they entered. That was the sheriff's job. He would talk with the judge.

As Deed and Blue sat down at the table reserved for the defendants, Judge Pence entered from the kitchen and took his position behind the first table. In his right hand was a gavel; in his left was the tin can. A chaw was evident in his mouth. He wore a black robe and Deed noticed a slight bulge near his upper left arm. The magistrate was wearing his gun.

After banging the table for attention, Judge Pence made a simple statement that the purpose of a preliminary hearing was to determine whether sufficient evidence existed for the accused to be bound over for actual trial. He declared that the trial would be conducted in such a way as he decided and that he, and only he, would determine if such was needed. For emphasis, he spat a thick brown stream into his tin can.

The blond gunman yelled, "Hang the no-good bastards. He tried to kill our friend, Sear."

Bordner's hearty chuckle punctuated the declaration and he withdrew a black cigar from his coat pocket, bit off the end, and lit it. Smoke declared his sense of control in the room.

Judge Pence slammed down his gavel. "This is my hearing. I will not tolerate any kind of outburst from those in this court-room." He glared at the man who had shouted.

Ranger Williams sidled next to the gray-haired magistrate and told him of armed men in the room. Judge Pence nodded, banged his gavel again, and announced, "I have been informed by a trusted Ranger that several men were allowed into this courtroom carrying guns. I'll have none of that here. Sheriff, you and the Rangers move through the citizenry and take their guns. Put them in the back of the room

449

where they can be obtained when this hearing has ended." He spat into his can. "Do it. Now."

Shields got slowly to his feet and looked at Bordner who nodded approval, then whispered, "Give them your visible weapons."

Rangers Williams and Rice and Sheriff Shields accepted the guns, shoving most of them into their waistbands. The Sanchez men and Silka complied with the command and Shields slunk back to his chair. The Rangers took a position beside the judge.

Looking around the room, Judge Pence said, "All right. Court is in session." He turned to Sylvestor Tritt. "Is the prosecution ready?"

"We are, Your Honor."

"Proceed."

Clearing his throat, Tritt stood, straightening his coat. "The prosecution will show without a doubt that the three Corrigan brothers did rob the bank of Wilkon and abscond with over two thousand dollars of this town's money. I call Willard Hixon as our first witness. He is president of the bank and a respected citizen of this town."

Looking nervous, Hixon rose from the table and took the witness chair.

From the table, Dixie Murphy growled,

"Tear 'em up, Hixon."

After being sworn in by Shields, Tritt asked him to describe the events of yesterday. He told the story of the robbery, almost as if reciting something written for him. The three Corrigan brothers, wearing masks, had entered the bank around four o'clock with guns drawn. He was alone in the bank at that time, except for a single teller. The brothers had taken $2,300 in gold and certificates. He finished, took a deep breath, and was visibly relieved.

"Mr. Hixon, it is my understanding that one of the brothers, Blue, I believe, had sought a loan from you earlier in the day. Is that correct?" Tritt asked.

"Uh, yes, it is. Blue said they were desperate for cash and needed the money to keep the ranch going through the winter," Hixon said and licked his lips. "I couldn't in good conscience give them such a loan. The fine people of Wilkon deserved better."

"Thank you, Mr. Hixon. We appreciate your forthrightness in this unfortunate matter." Tritt glanced at Bordner who smiled. "And we have a witness, the teller who was also working in the bank at that time."

Judge Pence nodded and turned to Blue. "Do you boys wish to question this witness?"

"Yes."

Hixon's look at Bordner was one of near panic.

Blue started to stand and the cuff of his left "arm" caught on the edge of the desk. He looked down and bit his lip, unsure of what to do. Deed leaned over and grabbed a piece of paper on the desk in front of Blue, hitting and clearing his shirtsleeve as he did. Blue resumed with his left "arm" resting against the table.

"Mr. Hixon, you, sir, are a liar and are doing so under oath. That's perjury."

"What?"

The crowd burst into angry yells. Judge Pence pounded his gavel for silence, then reprimanded Blue for his statement.

"Sorry, Your Honor, our parents always taught us to tell the truth. So I don't have much sympathy for liars. But this is a court hearing, so we'll do this piece by piece, witness by witness," Blue said and turned to Hixon. "You said we came to you and needed a loan or we wouldn't get through the winter, is that correct?"

"Well, I —"

"Is that what you said, Hixon?"

"Uh, yes, I —"

"Your Honor, I'd like to call our ranch partner, Nakashima Silka to come forward.

He is bringing with him the money left over from our cattle drive to Kansas this summer," Blue said and looked toward the front part of the restaurant. "If the judge would like to do so, he is welcome to count it. There is $4,012. As anyone in this place would agree, we don't need more money . . . and we certainly didn't ask Hixon, or anyone else, for a loan. You will also note we didn't trust Hixon enough to put the money in his bank."

Brushing against Bordner as he passed, Silka brought the money forward in a large satchel and opened it in front of the judge. Deed thought it looked strange for his friend not to be wearing a sword. Judge Pence studied the contents for a moment and said, "It's not necessary for me to count it. There is obviously a lot of money there. I accept the fact ya had no need to borrow."

From somewhere in the audience, a voice called out, "Go get 'em, Blue!"

Judge Pence stared, but didn't say anything.

"Thank you," Blue said. "Now, Hixon, your first lie is exposed. Let's look at the rest of this fairy tale you told. You said three Corrigan brothers came into your bank at four o'clock yesterday. Is that right?"

"Uh, yes." Hixon's forehead was glistening.

"You said the robbers were masked," Blue continued. "How did you decide it was Deed, Holt, and me?"

Hixon straightened his back. "You called out to your brothers by name, Deed and Holt. And, of course, you were one-armed. Uh, like now."

"I see," Blue looked down at the table. "You're certain you saw me like this? My right arm gone and my left hand all right."

"Absolutely. Come on, Blue. You had a gun in your left hand, pointing it right at me."

"Deed, help me, will you?"

Deed assisted his brother in taking off his shirt to reveal that his right arm was good and not his left. He rebuttoned his shirt, letting his right arm fill out the correct sleeve. The empty left sleeve dangled at his side. Gasps popped throughout the restaurant and Judge Pence put his hand over his mouth to hide a chuckle.

"So, you were wrong again, Hixon. I have no left arm. You have no truth."

"Well, I —"

Sylvestor Tritt jumped up. "Obviously, Your Honor, under the stress of being robbed at gunpoint, anyone could make such a mistake. The defendant was trying to fool the witness with a trick."

Blue looked at Tritt. "Tritt, perhaps you're right. It was an attempt to catch your witness in another lie . . . and it did. We were certain your client was lying and that changes everything, doesn't it."

"I warned ya," Judge Pence said, but with almost a gentleness.

"Your Honor, we have two witnesses to testify about our whereabouts two days ago, when this robbery was supposed to have been committed." Blue looked toward the front of the restaurant. "My brother, Deed, was visiting the Forsyth stage station yesterday. He has helped them during the fall. The station manager is here to so testify," Blue said. "And I was visiting our neighbors, the Sanchezes, to discuss how we might get rid of the awfulness of Agon Bordner and his gunmen. Mr. Felix Sanchez is here, along with his oldest son, Taol, and his foreman, Cliente. I can bring them forward now or later." He paused and added, "I don't know where our brother, Holt, is. For all I know he may be at our ranch. I do know he wasn't with us in the bank two days ago. *Nor were we.*" He glared at Hixon. "And so does Hixon."

A murmur ran through the crowd that

Judge Pence ignored. He pointed at Tritt. "This is a hearing, not a trial. I have no problem with not keeping with procedure. If you agree, Mr. Tritt."

The prosecuting attorney was annoyed. This wasn't how the hearing was supposed to go. Bordner had told him this was going to be easy. Behind him, Dixie Murphy was making comments about shooting the two Corrigan brothers and leaving. He was beginning to think that made sense.

"Your Honor, I would prefer to stay with accepted procedure."

"As ya wish." He glared at Tritt, then at Bordner. "But I must advise ya that I am already inclined to dismiss this hearing for lack of evidence. And to charge yer first witness with perjury." He looked back at Tritt. "Are we clear . . . Tritt?"

"Of course, Your Honor, but I believe you will understand the seriousness of the matter if we are allowed to continue."

"I wasn't finished questioning your witness, Tritt," Blue declared, his fingers poised on the table.

This time Judge Pence chuckled out loud, spit into his can to help regain his composure, and said, "Please continue, Mr. Corrigan."

"Thank you. Before we go any further,

Hixon," Blue said, staring at the nervous banker, "When did you hire slick stuff here?"

Hixon was startled and glanced at Bordner adjusting a gold ring on his pinky finger. His cigar was stuck in the corner of his mouth sending a curl of smoke around his massive head. He didn't appear to be listening.

Shrugging his shoulders, Hixon answered, "Uh, I hired him yesterday."

"The day after the bank was supposedly robbed. That right?"

"Yes, that's right."

Blue's smile didn't reach his eyes. "Tell me then, how that happens. Tritt is from El Paso. That's a long way from here."

Hixon hadn't expected that. The crowd blurted "Ahhh" in unison.

Tritt folded his arms. "If it pleases the court, I was in town on business this week. Other business."

Spinning around, Blue asked, "What other business would that be, Tritt?"

The prosecuting attorney ran his hand along the top of his head. He hated being called Tritt without the respect of *Mr. Tritt* and that the Corrigan brothers were not intimidated by his very presence. His eyelids blinked rapidly.

"My business is confidential and of no concern to this court."

Judge Pence leaned forward. "This court wants to know. It seems a bit contrived for ya to be hyar. Remember, Mr. Tritt, I know yer record and it mostly smells."

From his table, Bordner stood and yelled, "This is ridiculous. I hired Mr. Tritt to work on a railroad opportunity I am considering. He's been staying at my ranch the last week. Satisfied?"

After spitting into his can, Judge Pence snarled, "Sit down, Bordner. I didn't ask ya. But it is interestin' that nobody around here seems to know anything without checking with ya first."

"We're finished with this witness for now, Your Honor, but we reserve the right to call him back," Blue said.

Looking at his notes, Tritt told J. R. Peterson, the teller, to take the stand. A small man in a tight paper collar, he stood, holding his hat, in the middle of the room. He hesitated and said, "No. I'm not. This is stupid. No one tried to rob our bank and Hixon knows it. I'm leaving town." He turned and rushed for the door.

Shields was livid; he jumped up to go after the frightened man.

"Don't try it, Shields," Deed snapped.

"You aren't that good."

For an instant, the sheriff considered going for his gun; Deed wasn't armed.

"What's the matter, Shields? I don't have a gun. This is a perfect chance for you." Deed stood with his arms outstretched.

Shields licked his lips and glanced around. Both Rangers were holding their guns on him. Without saying another word, he returned to the prosecution's table.

Judge Pence reinforced the command and asked Tritt if he had any more evidence to present. Tritt turned to Bordner, shrugged, and said he did not. Blue was asked to present his witnesses and he called Atlee Forsyth and then Felix Sanchez to the stand. Smiling at Deed through her testimony, Atlee declared that Deed was at the station and Felix declared that Blue was at their ranch when the robbery was supposed to have happened. She looked radiant, wearing Deed's pink scarf around her neck and a tailored tweed suitcoat and skirt.

Stunned, Tritt asked that the witnesses' testimony be dismissed because they were not worthy and because they were friends of the Corrigans.

Disgusted, Judge Pence said, "Their testimony is valid. Contrary to Mr. Hixon's."

Blue decided to press further. "Your

Honor, it is clear we did not rob this bank. I want to take advantage of this courtroom situation and present evidence of a much more sinister nature. If it pleases the court."

Pence grinned. "I'm listening."

CHAPTER THIRTY-FIVE

Blue Corrigan pointed at the sulking attorney. "Let's take a good look at all this. Slick here was hired by Agon Bordner and brought to town last week for this hearing only. Bet on it. Bordner owns the bank, hired Hixon, and had him make up this tale about us robbing the bank.

"Bordner also owns the general store and tried to force the Sanchezes and us out by refusing our business. He took ownership of the biggest ranch around here in a shady way," Blue continued. "To continue with Bordner's attempt to own everything around here, I would like to call Mr. James Hannah to the stand." He motioned toward the front of the restaurant.

Bordner growled, "This isn't a hearing. It's a joke." He stood up and brushed the ashes off his suitcoat.

"Sit down. I'll decide that, Mr. Bordner," Judge Pence declared. "I'm sure y'all will have an opportunity to speak your piece."

James Hannah appeared from the crowd at the front of the restaurant and ambled to the witness chair. After being sworn in, he straightened his glasses.

"Mr. Hannah, would you please tell the court of your involvement with Mr. Bordner?"

"Be happy to," Hannah shifted in the chair so he could see the fat man clearly and glared at him. Only Deed seemed to notice he was wearing a shoulder holster under his suitcoat.

"Bordner tried to hire me to kill Deed Corrigan," Hannah testified. "He was afraid of him and none of his men wanted to tangle with Deed. From firsthand knowledge, I can tell you they were smart not to try. The offer was five hundred in gold. I didn't take the job." He folded his arms for emphasis. "They tried attacking his ranch when the men were gone and that didn't work. I was there. This fake robbery was the only way they could figure out how to bring down Deed and his brothers. It isn't going to work either. The fat man underestimated them again."

The courtroom exploded in a fury of voices. Judge Pence banged his gavel and banged it more to try to bring the room to silence.

"Thank you, Mr. Hannah." Blue held up a sheet of paper. "This telegram is from the governor of New Mexico stating that Agon Bordner is wanted for murder and cattle rustling there. So are Bordner's henchmen, Macy Shields, Rhey Selmon, Sear Georgian, and Willard Hixon."

Waving his arms, Bordner shouted, "This is ridiculous! I am not on trial here. I have never met this man before. I am leaving. Come on, Dixie, let's get out of here. I'm hungry."

"Yes, you are, Bordner . . . and you aren't leaving." Deed snapped. "Neither are you, Dixie."

Bordner's mouth opened and his cigar fell on the floor. He couldn't bend over to get the smoke and asked Dixie Murphy to retrieve it for him. Snorting, the cattleman leaned over and retrieved it. Bordner looked at the cigar and threw it back to the floor. Dixie grunted.

Blue turned back to Hixon, sitting at the table. "You are still under oath, Hixon. Did you fake the loan that the Regans were supposed to have signed? Be careful what you say. This nightmare is all over, but you might save yourself from hanging — if you speak the truth."

Hixon looked down at his hands.

"I asked you a question, Hixon. I expect an *honest* answer."

Sitting up straight, Tritt growled. "You don't have to answer that."

"No, you don't. Slick here is right for a change. But if you're smart, you will. Look at me," Blue demanded. "You are involved in a scheme that killed innocent people. In a few minutes, I'm going to bring in a boy who survived the Bar 3 attack and he is going to identify who was involved. Another witness will nail Bordner himself and his men to that terrible crime. You can listen to slick or you can help yourself stay away from a rope."

Across the table, Bordner demanded that Hixon remain silent. Dixie reinforced it with a threat.

Blue laughed. "Isn't it interesting, Hixon. They don't sound so tough anymore, do they?"

In a small voice, Hixon cracked, "Y-Yes, I-I faked the loan. I-I didn't know anybody w-was going to be killed. H-Honest." He looked up and his eyes were welling with tears. "Stay away from me, Shields."

"What about the Merefords and the Hansons?"

"R-Rhey and his bunch killed them. Made it look like Indians did it. Like they did at the Bar 3 and took back the money Bordner paid them for their places."

"Thank you, Hixon. May God have mercy on your soul," Blue said.

Judge Pence banged his gavel. "I rule Blue, Deed, and Holt Corrigan are innocent of robbing the bank. I question that it was ever robbed." He shuffled this robe and drew his long-barreled revolver, cocked, and aimed it at Bordner. "I also order the arrest of Agon Bordner, Rhey Selmon, Sear Georgian, Willard Hixon, and Macy Shields to be held for a hearing on charges of the murders of the Regan family and the families of the Merefords and the Hansons, and deceitful gain of the Bar 3, H-5, and the Roof-M." He looked toward the front of the restaurant. "Rangers, do your duty. I request the Sanchezes to get their guns and help with this task. You are hereby deputized."

Tritt waved his arms. "But . . . but —"

"Shut up, Tritt," Judge Pence shouted. "You're done here."

Felix, Taol, and Cliente went to the pile of guns; Silka followed to get his sword.

As the two Rangers stepped forward with their guns drawn, Bordner pulled a hidden gun from his coat pocket. Murphy and the

Bar 3 men drew their concealed weapons.

"Drop your guns, Rangers, or you die. You, too, Judge," Bordner declared. "And you bastard Corrigans are going to die now. You've caused me too much trouble."

The Rangers dropped their guns and raised their hands.

Instead of complying, Judge Pence fired and clipped Murphy's shoulder. Murphy spun and fired back, blasting splinters from the judge's table as he turned it over and ducked behind the heavy surface. Judge Pence peeked over the table and fired again. Three other men fired at the gray-haired magistrate, missing.

A wild-eyed Tritt ran toward the kitchen but was stopped by the restaurant owner brandishing a shotgun. He held up his hands and began crying.

Bordner turned toward Deed, smiled, and cocked his revolver. "Good-bye, Deed Corrigan."

Deed's hand dropped behind his shirt and drew his throwing knife. The blade hit Bordner in the heart so quickly the fat man didn't react until it struck deep. Bordner's gun went off, slamming a bullet past Deed's head and into the restaurant wall. Bordner groaned and grabbed the knife to withdraw it as his shirt turned crimson. Deed rushed him and slammed his opened right hand down against Bordner's gun-holding wrist and grabbed the gun with his other hand, yanking it upward and free. A thunderous blow across Bordner's face with the gun in his fist followed. The fat man crumpled to the ground, knocking the table and his chair over as he fell.

At the same time, from the witness chair, Hannah pulled free his Smith & Wesson .44 Russian revolver and fired three times, hitting Shields and a tall Bar 3 gunman. He tried to move to the judge's table for protection. Gunshots from the other Bar 3 gunmen hammered Hannah and he collapsed.

Blue withdrew the derringer from his boot, fired, and missed as the wounded Murphy and the rest of the Bar 3 gunmen headed for the door, brandishing their six-guns. The courtroom was wild with fear. Townspeople dropped to the floor, hiding behind chairs. One woman stood and screamed. Three men ran out the restaurant door.

Deed stalked the fleeing gunmen firing Bordner's gun. From the other side of the restaurant Silka, Felix, Taol, and Cliente closed in with their retrieved weapons. Deed and Taol put four bullets into Murphy as the cattleman fired at Felix. The crooked cattleman stumbled to the floor. The blond-haired outlaw with the strange eyes stared at the dead Murphy, then spun toward Deed firing as he turned. Deed emptied his gun into the outlaw. The outlaw's gun fired into the ceiling and dropped from his hand as he fell.

The rest of the Bar 3 gunmen were stunned, except for the scar-faced cowboy. He swung his gun toward Deed. Silka flew in and drove his sword through the man.

Suddenly it was over. Felix Sanchez commanded, "Drop the guns."

Scared by Silka's deadly attack, the gunmen dropped their weapons and raised their hands. With the help of the Sanchezes, the two Rangers led them away to the jail. Blue walked over to the massive body lying on the floor. He felt for a pulse. There was none. He pulled Deed's knife free, wiped the blade on the fat man's suit and pushed it into his belt. Agon Bordner and his dream of the Crown Ranch were dead.

Throughout the room, people began to stand, talk, and leave.

Along the front of the restaurant, Deed saw Atlee and went over to her. She hugged him tightly. "Oh, Deed, I was so scared."

"It's all over now."

"I love you, Deed."

"I love you, Atlee."

From near the doorway, Silka started to go to Deed, then saw their embrace and stopped. He smiled, touched the brass circle worn around his neck and muttered a Japanese blessing of love.

Judge Pence walked from behind the table, returning his gun to his shoulder holster and shook hands with Blue. "Well done. I was hopin' ya'd git the job done. Jason Regan was my cousin. I knew it was dirty work that got their place. Been trying to find a way to bring down that big bastard ever since." He shook his head and explained that the Rangers also suspected Bordner's gang of robbing stagecoaches, using knowledge of money shipments from his bank ownership, but couldn't prove it.

"Wish we'd known that earlier." Blue rubbed the sleeved stub of his left arm.

"Like I said, we didn't have no proof," Judge Pence said. "Say, I'd sure like to see that telegram."

"Sure." Blue stepped to the defendants' table, retrieved the sheet of paper, and handed it to him as he walked to the slumped figure near the judge's table. "I've got to check on James."

Deed and Atlee hurried to Blue, who was holding Hannah's head and talking softly to the badly wounded gunman. Hannah stared at him with glazed eyes.

"Stay with us, James," Blue encouraged. "We'll get a doc in here." He looked up at Deed. "Get some water from the kitchen. And some towels."

"Sure." Deed went to the kitchen with Atlee following.

"I-I'd rather have some w-whiskey," Hannah stammered. "Tell R-Rebecca that I'm sorry we aren't going to get to K-Kansas."

"Don't be silly, James. You'll be up and around in no time."

Breathing heavily, Hannah took hold of Blue's arm. "You think because I've been hanging out with Deed some of his luck has come my way?"

Blue smiled and nodded.

Hannah shut his eyes, then blinked them open. "Just in case, the rest of Bordner's money is in the hotel room. In the dresser. Third drawer. F-For Rebecca."

"Okay. But you can get it yourself when you're up and about."

Returning from the kitchen, Deed had a bucket of water and Atlee was carrying towels.

Deed looked toward the front door and said, "Doc's here."

Dr. Sandor hurried toward Hannah,

looked at all the people milling around, and grabbed the closest two men, saying, "Take him to my office immediately. I will save him."

Wide eyed, Rebecca came running into the restaurant just as the two men were carrying Hannah out. Sobbing, she asked the doctor if he was still alive. Reassured she grabbed her husband's hand and went with him to the doctor's office.

Meanwhile, the gray-haired magistrate walked over holding his tobacco spit can, almost giddy, and declared, "Thar's nothin' on this so-called telegram. It's blank." A grin was working its way onto the corner of his mouth until he saw Hannah being carried out.

"Is yer friend gonna make it?"

"He is a *good* friend and Doc said he's going to make it," Blue said and murmured a blessing. He stood and turned to Judge Pence. "You're right. Holt told us where Bordner came from and we took a chance."

Judge Pence laughed. "How about that thar witness who was going to incriminate Bordner?"

"That would've been Holt."

"Holt? Your brother?"

Blue explained the situation, including Holt going by the name Sam Holton.

"I see," Judge Pence said. "What about the kid?"

Blue answered, "That would've been Jeremy Regan."

"I thought the whole family was killed. The boy's alive?"

"Yes. He lives with us now," Blue said. "We're going to adopt him. Can you make it official?"

"Sure, we kin do it now. I'll write it up. Goin' back to what ya said, could Jeremy have identified any o' them?"

He grinned. "No, I don't think so. I was bluffing."

Pence rubbed his chin. "I'd sure like to see the boy. I remember that he favored his ma."

"He's a fine youngster. We're happy to have him as part of our family."

"Those were some mighty big bluffs ya ran, son," Pence remarked and spit into his can. "Wish I'd have known that earlier," he smiled, repeating Blue's earlier statement.

"Guess so," Blue said. "We didn't see another way. Didn't think you'd let us do it."

Pence nodded. "Wal, I'd a' bin real tempted to let ya do it, but prob'ly not, bein' that bluffin' ain't truly legal."

Looking dazed, Sylvestor Tritt tiptoed

472

from the kitchen, glanced at them, and hurried past.

Pence put out a hand to stop the lawyer. "Tritt, I don' wanna see ya in my court ever again." He spit into his can and stared at the disgraced attorney.

Tritt lowered his head and left. As he cleared the restaurant door, there was a commotion. Into the restaurant with only his right hand raised came Rhey Selmon in his bearskin coat. His shirt was bloody and he could only raise the one arm. His holsters were empty. Behind him with one of Selmon's silver-plated guns pointed at the wounded gunman was Holt Corrigan. The other was shoved into Holt's waistband.

"Where do you want this bear boy? Saw him hiding when I rode in. He wasn't as brave as he thought," Holt said. "Go on. Get in here."

"Oh, hi, *Sam,*" Blue said.

Holt's gaze took in the room and stopped when it came to the massive body of Agon Bordner. "Came in to give my *brothers* a hand. Doesn't look like you needed it."

The emphasis on *brothers* was deliberate. He touched the cardinal feather in his hatband and motioned toward the street. "Saw another hombre in a coat and tie come busting out of the general store and hurry toward the livery. Anybody we should go after?"

Deed cocked his head. "Ah, Sam, that'll be Jephrum Virdin. Bordner hired him to run the store but he's a harmless fool. In a way he helped me."

Both brothers were trying to make Holt realize a judge was present. Holt was too proud of his brothers' finally stopping Agon Bordner's evil to pay attention, or care.

Judge Pence waved his arms. "Take Rhey Selmon over to the jail. That's where the rest of them are. Consider yourself deputized." He looked over at Blue and winked.

Blue realized Pence knew it was Holt.

Holt looked at his brothers. "Deputized?"

"Uh, Sam, this is Circuit Court Judge Oscar Pence," Blue declared, frowning at Holt.

Turning toward the infamous outlaw, Pence said, "I reckon one o' the heroes of Sabine Pass deserves that . . . and more, Holt Corrigan. Ya bin a' helpin' clear up this mess too. As kin to the Regans, I appreciate that more than ya know. So let's resolve this hyar outlaw issue ri't now."

Holt stood without moving. Selmon attempted to step away, but Holt jammed his gun in the gunman's back and he froze, cursing.

"David Copate, he's a banker in El Paso an' a friend o' mine. He tolt me yer name's bin attached to all sorts o' holdups . . . an' he thinks it's wrong. Jes' like this hyar so-called holdup an' the robbery o' his own bank. Ya weren't at neither. I agree with Co-pate." He cocked his head and grinned. "An' thar's no way a court's gonna prove ya did any other holdup, iffen ya did."

He spit into the can and looked at Deed and Blue. "Ya know you all got amnesty at the end o' that awful war, but it takes a while fer that nasty business to end fer some. An' some are too proud to ask."

Glancing at the dead Bordner, Pence folded his arms, being careful with the spit can. "Holt Corrigan, I also heard ya stopped ol' bear boy thar an' two o' Bordner's gun-slicks from hurtin' a lady at Emilio's." Pence smiled and looked back at Holt. "Yeah, good stuff kin git 'round, too, Holt. Emilio's another friend o' mine." He ran his hand through his gray hair. "Ya know, Texas needs good men like ya helpin' it grow, not run-nin' from past mistakes." He unfolded his arms and spit again. "Ya should have am-nesty, too, Holt Corrigan, an' I'm gonna do it. I'll write this up. Holt, ya are now a free man. But it's gonna cost ya."

Holt frowned. Was the judge asking for a

475

bribe? Blue looked at Deed who shrugged.

"I hereby appoint ya actin' county sheriff. Ya will handle that job till the next county election. Deal?"

Holt nodded and couldn't stop grinning. "Deal."

The three brothers looked at each other and broke into wide grins. Blue walked over to Macy Shields's body and pulled the badge from his shirt. He brought it to Pence.

"How about swearing him in right now, Judge?"

"Good idee." Pence spit into the can, took the badge, and walked over to Holt.

"Ah, hold up . . . yer left hand, Holt. That's plenty good nuff. Ya got business with the other."

Lifting his left hand, Holt repeated Pence's oath. "I swear to uphold the laws of the county and of the great state of Texas to the best of my ability, so help me God."

Pence pinned the badge on Holt's shirt and patted him on the shoulder. "Do good, boy."

"I will, sir."

"Got a feelin' that's so."

Deed and Blue cheered, so did Atlee.

Holt smiled and shoved his gun into Rhey Selmon's back. "Come on, bear boy."

The gunman swore and they left with a

grinning Holt pushing him to walk faster.

Smiling, Pence returned to the back of the restaurant and put his arms around Blue's and Deed's shoulders. He patted them both.

"Reckon the court'll have to decide what to do with the Bar 3 and them other two ranches. Come to think on it, thar's also gonna be a bank an' general store fer sale. Hey, an' a town marshal's job to fill. Got any suggestions?"

ABOUT THE AUTHOR

Each of **Cotton Smith**'s novels brings an exciting picture of the human spirit making its way through life-changing trials, driving through physical and emotional barriers, and resurrecting itself from defeat. His stories of the West are praised for historical accuracy, unexpected plot twists, and memorable characters. They are also enjoyed for their insightful descriptions of life of that era — and for their rousing adventure.

In *Dark Trail to Dodge,* the ex-Ranger John Checker seeks a reunion with his long-separated sister, bridging a terrible childhood, and Tyrel Bannon, a Texas farm boy, undergoes a trying initiation into manhood. In *Pray for Texas,* Confederate cavalryman and pistol fighter Rule Cordell struggles to overcome not only losing the war, but the anguish of a tyrannical minister father. In *Behold a Red Horse,* we see the three Kerry brothers deal with the strongest one being blinded. In *Brothers of the Gun,* John Checker must face knowing his half brother is an evil man bent on destroying him by kidnapping their sister's children and taking them into the Indian Nations. And in *Spirit Rider,* we see a young white man challenged by white society after growing up with an Oglala stepfather holy man who talks with sacred stones. And in *Sons of Thunder,* Rule Cordell tries hard to put his days as a pistol fighter behind him but finds he can't when his friends are challenged by a cunning carpetbagger. *The Thirteenth Bullet* and *Winter Kill* both carry this fascinating psychological edge. *True West* agrees, "Although the characters in Cotton Smith's books are for the most part traditional Western men — strong, dynamic, action-driven individuals — their motivations and mannerisms definitely break the mold of traditional western novels. For one thing, they have and show far more emotion than the average man (in or out of a western novel). Characters are placed in realistic, emotionally driven situations, bringing with them souls filled with concern, fear, joy, and desire."

His love of the West came quite naturally and quite early in life, as did his gift for writing. "I rode with them all, you know," Cotton likes to say. "Roy, Gene, Hoppy, I was right there with them. Roy Rogers and Wild Bill Elliott were my favorites. Yeah, I can hold my own on western movie trivia with anyone." From the earliest he can remember, he was wearing chaps, boots, spurs, and strapping on a set of cap guns. "Like the song says, my heroes have always been cowboys."

That love affair turned into a lifelong study of the American West. "Silver screen fascination grew into an appreciation I will never grow tired of. I believe the excitement is in what really happened during this special time in our nation's history. I believe it lives on in each of us, if we simply stop long enough to let it surface. In this time of special trial, that victorious linkage will serve us well. America will win."

Cotton Smith was born in Kansas City, Missouri; some would say a century later than he should have been. He grew up enjoying both adjoining states, Kansas and Missouri, living mostly in Kansas. His ancestors fought in the Civil War, mostly for the South, as regulars and guerrillas. As a young man, he learned to ride horses from a grizzled wrangler he remembers fondly. He also learned how to roll a cigarette then, too! "Looking back on it, he taught me the right ways around a horse — and he taught me some other things too. Like swinging into the saddle with the horse loping. And springing up from the rear, like the movie stars did. Never occurred to me then that I could get hurt. Guess no young person ever does."

Cotton tells it this way: "There is much we can learn from our ancestors, perhaps today more than ever. The men and women who built this country were exceptionally strong people who overcame enormous odds to establish good families, create towns where only wilderness existed, establish businesses, and leave us with much to build upon. They loved the land and that love was returned manyfold."